Bluster's Last Stand

Book Four

of

The Memoirs of H.H. Lomax

by

Preston Lewis

Wild Horse Press
Fort Worth, Texas

By Preston Lewis
Published By Wild Horse Press
An Imprint of Wild Horse Media Group
P.O. Box 331779
Fort Worth, Texas 76163
1-817-344-7036
www.WildHorseMedia.com

1 2 3 4 5 6 7 8 9
ISBN-10: 1-68179-096-3
ISBN-13: 978-1-68179-096-1

In Memory of Frank Roderus,
Great Friend and Great Writer

Introduction

The publication of *Bluster's Last Stand* brings to print the fourth adventure of that vagabond rascal H.H. Lomax, whose adventures were first chronicled in *The Demise of Billy the Kid, The Redemption of Jesse James* and *Mix-Up at the O.K. Corral.* It is hard to believe that it has been two decades since a new Lomax adventure has been published, but *Bluster's Last Stand* is quite sensational and worth the wait as it helps answer some of the lingering questions behind George Armstrong Custer's fateful and fatal decisions at the Battle of the Little Bighorn. As usual with most of his adventures, H.H. Lomax stood at the center of the action, though not by his choice.

But before I explore Lomax's role at the Little Bighorn, I should explain the reason for the delay in a new edition of his Old West memoirs. Readers of the first books in *The Memoirs of H.H. Lomax* series will recall that they were based upon Lomax's handwritten recollections of his frontier experience. Written in pencil in a feeble hand on Big Chief Tablets, the essays totaled some 22,000 pages by my estimation and put Lomax at the center of some of the most legendary events of the Old West. Lomax's compilation was housed in the Southwest Collection at Texas Tech University, where I worked at the time in the communications and marketing office. Fortunately for me, no serious scholar had ever taken an interest in the Lomax papers because of their uncertain provenance. In them, I discovered a gold mine of Old West history and humor.

I found Lomax's papers fascinating, largely because of his offbeat outlook and his unusual perspective on some of the major events and personalities of the American West. Oddly enough, when I was introduced to the Lomax papers, I was researching for *True West* a story I would ultimately title "Bluster's Last Stand" on the Battle of Yellowhouse Canyon, an obscure battle between buffalo hunters and Comanches on the Texas South Plains. As the overconfidence and hubris that led to the Yellowhouse encounter was small compared to that resulting in the Battle of the Little Bighorn, I thought it fitting to appropriate the article name for the title of this book. After all, I had discovered that Lomax believed Custer would have been more correctly named "General Bluster." Lomax's account of the Little Bighorn and how he happened to get there is the most incredible yet in his frontier adventures.

If the Little Bighorn story is so sensational, why did it take more than twenty years before it came to print, you might ask. That is a fair question with a variety of answers. First, the publishing industry changed. Bantam, which published the original three volumes in *The Memoirs of H.H. Lomax,* dramatically cut back its list of books based on historical events of the Old West shortly after the third Lomax volume was published. Subsequently, Bantam reverted the publishing rights to the various authors. Then four years ago Billy Huckaby bought out the venerable Texas publisher Eakin Press and incorporated it into his Wild Horse Media Group. As I had had three books published by Eakin, Huckaby contacted me and we discussed reviving the first three volumes in the Lomax series and researching new ones.

Second, when I started the Lomax series, I worked at Texas Tech University where it was convenient to review and transcribe the papers during lunch hours and other free time at the nearby Southwest Collection building. In 1999 I took a job as director of communications and marketing at Angelo State University in San Angelo, a three-hour drive from Lubbock and the Southwest Collection. The distance and the responsibilities of running the office, producing the university magazine and managing content on the university website cut into my available time for such extracurricular projects. Consequently, I had to set aside the Lomax papers. Though I missed the access to the Southwest Collection, I found solace in doing research at Angelo State's West Texas Collection on other projects.

Then in 2007, Angelo State University became a member of the Texas Tech University System, opening up the possibility of shared access between the Southwest Collection and the West Texas Collection. Subsequently, the Southwest Collection graciously agreed to loan the Lomax papers to the West Texas Collection so I could continue my research and publish the next volume through Wild Horse Press after my retirement from higher education. In addition to the Southwest Collection and the West Texas Collection, I should also thank the Texas Collection at Baylor University for assistance in confirming some of the details of Lomax's account of his time in Waco.

The third delaying factor was a federal lawsuit by some of Lomax's distant relatives in California and Arkansas, Lomax's native state. In the lawsuit his kin claimed they held the rights to his writings and were thus entitled to any resulting revenues from publication. I believe the lawsuit was not so much about the money as it was about stifling Lomax's voice as it was evident some of his distant relatives were embarrassed by his sometimes bawdy adventures and their potential reflection on the family. As Lomax never married to the best of my knowledge and thus never had any legitimate children, the claim of his relatives was ruled meritless, and the lawsuit was ultimately dismissed after five years of legal headaches and expenses.

After the anguish of the lawsuit, it took me a couple years to get in the mood to attack the Lomax papers and the Battle of the Little Bighorn through his eyes. Lomax's journey to the Little Bighorn starts at the Battle of Adobe Walls in the Texas Panhandle, then proceeds to a whorehouse in Waco, Texas, before taking him to the Black Hills in a failed search for gold that ultimately leads him to meet Custer at Fort Abraham Lincoln. Lomax, who grew up in Cane Hill, Arkansas, during the Civil War, claimed to have accompanied Custer on his fateful journey and to have survived the carnage. Similar claims have been made by a handful of Seventh Cavalry soldiers, but Lomax was a civilian forced to accompany the expedition as punishment for transgressions that Lomax best explains in his recollections written decades later. Suffice it to say, Lomax unknowingly got caught up in the era's complicated politics, involving the army, the federal bureaucracy and the presidential election of 1876. As a result, Lomax believed Custer intended to kill him on the expedition against the Sioux.

It is hard to know for sure how much of what Lomax says is true, partially correct or outright false and shaded by poor memory. In researching the personalities and the events leading up to the Battle of the Little Bighorn, I find Lomax's account generally lines up with what is known about both the battle and the personalities involved in the disaster. Regardless of the veracity of Lomax's tale, I find him—despite his many faults—a much more appealing person than George Armstrong Custer. I will leave it for the reader to decide how much of Lomax's story to accept. Whether you believe him or not, you have to agree that he was a good storyteller, and that may be Lomax's ultimate value to Old West history.

Either way, I'm just delighted to once again be along for the ride with H.H. Lomax.

Preston Lewis
San Angelo, Texas
January 2017

Chapter One

My aim was to shoot George Armstrong Custer, not to make him famous. Maybe I shot him and maybe I didn't. I never knew because it was hard to confirm if you hit your target when hundreds of screaming Sioux and Cheyenne warriors were also firing at him—and at me. But the fact is, I held more rancor for Custer on that hot, dusty day in June of 1876 than I did for the Indian braves committed to scalping me. In the end, you might say that both God and the devil saved me from the fate of the other white men on the hill above the Little Bighorn that afternoon.

I didn't care for Custer, general or colonel or lieutenant or whatever his rank was. Fact was, I called him "General Bluster" because there weren't enough mirrors in the world to adequately reflect his opinion of himself. And my low opinion of the man did little to narrow the waistline of his bulging vanity. In fact, he relished telling me how superior he was to me, him being of Yankee descent and attending West Point, while I was a poor Southern boy with a narrow education. I could read, I could write and I could think. Custer could, too, but he liked to read about himself, write about himself and I imagine, if I could have read his mind, that he liked to think about himself as well. Fact was, if you had ordered a thousand sons of bitches from a Chicago mail-order house and only received him, you'd mark your bill paid in full. Much as I despised the man, I had to admit he was a god on horseback, him and his steed becoming one galloping machine. In fact, about the only thing, in my mind at least, that could've made him look even better on horseback was if he rode his mount over a cliff.

Custer was afoot by the time he met his end that Sunday afternoon at the Little Bighorn so he couldn't outrun all the arrows and bullets coming his way, but I have to admit he did a damn good job dancing around them. It was the best jig I ever saw, at least while I was sober, and let me tell you nothing was more sobering that afternoon than watching the swarms of Indians attacking like angry hornets streaming from a never-ending hive. Even though I escaped death that unfortunate day, I could not evade the shadow of George Armstrong Custer for decades afterwards. Every time I would go into a saloon in later years, I would find, thanks to Anheuser-Busch, a painting of General Bluster valiantly fighting off the Indian hordes. It was enough to turn my stomach, but not enough to make me give up drinking. Fact is, I was the last white man to see the boy general alive, and he was nowhere near as calm as the painting portrayed. The way he was jumping around, the Injuns had as much trouble hitting him as I did.

Of course, I was hopping around, too, that afternoon, ducking every projectile fired my way. Most came from the Indians because they outnumbered us so, but some came from the soldiers, who by the end were shooting blindly and desperately at anything that moved. Custer himself even fired a few shots at me, I'm certain, because he had promised to kill me for embarrassing his beloved Seventh Cavalry. It turns out he's the one that humiliated the Seventh Cavalry with his ill-advised attack on what some said was the largest gathering ever of Indian warriors on the northern Plains. I couldn't confirm that assertion because on that terrible afternoon I was counting my bullets instead of Indians. I needed my last bullet to blow my own brains out so the Sioux and Cheyenne couldn't torture me at the end. I had seen how they left the bodies of those who trespassed on their sacred lands, and it wasn't with a grave, headstone and flowers. What was especially galling was that the cavalry might never have gotten into that mess had Custer taken my advice and never split up his troops to begin with. He didn't listen. The fact of the matter was, he was trying to minimize the number of witnesses around when he shot me. In the end, I came out better than all the rest and made it back to Fort Abraham Lincoln in one scared and scarred piece, unlike the soldiers whose body parts were scattered all over that ridge by sundown that day.

It was Custer's fault to begin with that I was even on the northern Plains. The previous fall I had been prospecting for some of the gold he had reported to the newspapers after his 1874 expedition into the Black Hills. Gold nuggets the size of whiskey kegs, just there for the taking, the newspapers reported. Being naïve about the ways of the press, I figured you could trust newspapermen and what they printed, but that was before I ever met a reporter. After I had encountered a few, I put them in the same class as politicians, about the only group lower on the ladder of human accomplishment being lawyers, of course. I never found much gold unless you count the gold in Custer's scalp, but few other men did either and at least I came out alive.

My journey to the Little Bighorn began, oddly enough, almost two years earlier to the day while I was buffalo hunting in the Texas Panhandle. Actually, I was doing more buffalo skinning than hunting as my aim was not the best with a Sharps rifle, and I wasted more ammunition than my partners thought economical. It didn't matter that I'd first shot buffalo with none other than Buffalo Bill Cody himself, and it didn't help that Cody had nicknamed me "Leadeye Lomax" because I wasted so much ammunition. That nickname left me with a reputation that relegated me to the dirty, bloody, tedious work of skinning buffalo and staking out the hides. I'd hired on with an outfit in Dodge City, Kansas, in the spring of 1874 and had ridden south into the Texas Panhandle, where millions of buffalo still roamed. The problem was, bands of Comanche and Kiowa warriors still wandered through the region as well, upset that we were taking food from their mouths and clothes from their back by slaughtering buffalo.

On the way to Texas I got to be good friends with William Barclay Masterson. He was one of the thousands of "Bills" that rode through the west, but he took up the moniker "Bat" to avoid confusion with all the others like Buffalo Bill, Wild Bill, Curly Bill, and, among the buffalo hunters, Six-shooter Bill, Buckskin Bill, and One-Armed Bill. I suppose any of those nicknames, save maybe One-Armed Bill, might have been better than Leadeye Lomax, but I have to admit I never met another Leadeye in all my travels and travails out west.

As we encountered buffalo in Texas, we shot and skinned them, then hauled them to the new trading post at Adobe Walls. The outpost catered to the hide trade by providing powder, lead and provisions at Dodge City prices and by buying and freighting hides back to Kansas. Our work was hot and dreary as the buffalo seemed inexhaustible. I figured I could skin buffalo for decades and never make a dent in the herds, though skinning wasn't exactly a noble profession to write about to the folks back home in Cane Hill, Arkansas.

The days began to run together on me so that one day was indistinguishable from the next. Until we got to Adobe Walls, the only day that stood out from the rest was the scorching afternoon when I had just squatted down to start skinning another carcass. I glimpsed Bat out of the corner of my eye, and I'll be damned if he hadn't pulled his six-shooter and fired at me before I knew why.

"What the hell?" I screamed, jumping to my feet and slapping at my pistol to defend myself. I intended to teach him not to mess with Leadeye.

"Easy, Lomax," Bat said before I could draw my pistol.

"What do you mean easy? It wasn't me that tried to shoot you. Yet!"

He slid his still smoking pistol back in his holster. "Look at your feet. I just saved you from a miserable death."

"The only thing that saved me from a rotten death was your poor aim, Bat!"

He laughed. "I'm not the one they call Leadeye. Check your feet."

Glancing quickly down, I about jumped over the buffalo carcass when I spotted the dead rattlesnake at my boots, still writhing and turning belly up to the sky. The four-foot snake had been within striking distance of where I squatted. "I never heard him rattle."

"Odd thing," Bat said. "He was twitching his tail, but I didn't hear him buzz."

"Maybe we're going deaf from shooting these buffalo rifles all the time," I offered.

"That would explain me not hearing him, but you haven't fired many Sharps recently, have you, Leadeye? Your skinning knife don't make that much noise." Bat laughed, then stepped to the dead serpent and toed it with his boot. "Way you were squatted, he could've bit you on the neck. We would've never gotten you to a Dodge City doctor in time to save you."

"Damned good shot, Bat," I said after examining his kill. "You knocked his head off."

Bat nodded. "But look at his tail end."

The snake had the typical markings of a diamondback, but his rattle was missing.

"That's why we didn't hear him," Bat said.

"He must've lost his rattle," I answered.

"Could be," Bat replied, "but I've heard stories that Comanche sometimes pin rattlesnakes down and cut off their rattles so they'll strike buffalo hunters without warning."

I shuddered. "Who'd want to touch something that's the incarnation of Satan himself?"

"Who'd want to eat liver?" Bat countered. "Not me, but I hear Comanches do it after a buffalo kill. On top of that, they eat it raw."

Both Bat and I trembled at the idea, then returned to our filthy work.

That was my nearest brush with death as a buffalo hunter until a couple weeks later near the end of June when we pulled into Adobe Walls with four wagons loaded with buffalo hides. Adobe Walls was a scab of a trading post just north of the Canadian River in the northeast corner of the Texas Panhandle. I was told the place had first been an adobe trading post before the War Between the States. By the time of the war, nothing but the walls remained, giving the site its name. From what I understood, Kit Carson had held off some 3,000 Indians in an 1864 battle there. Now, Carson hadn't held them off single-handedly because he was reinforced by some 250 Yankee soldiers, but the Indians gave them fits before leaving.

We approached the new outpost from the north, easing our wagons down the Canadian escarpment that opened up into a broad river plain. A few buildings were lined up north to south in a row, with the Myers & Leonard store the northernmost structure. The store with its picket and chinked walls looked bigger than it was because of the huge fenced yard behind the building proper where they stockpiled newly purchased hides. A small blacksmith shop stood south of Myers & Leonard's and next to Jim Hanrahan's saloon. Further south was the Rath & Company store with a smaller enclosed hide yard behind it.

Early on a Saturday morning after we arrived at Adobe Walls, Bat and I were bedded down in the Myers & Leonard corral near our hides when the earth rumbled with hoof beats and the air filled with the screams and gunshots of Comanche and Kiowa. The red devils sprang out of the earth and attacked us for trespassing on their lands and slaughtering their buffalo. Now buffalo hunting was dangerous to be sure, but the buffalo didn't shoot bullets and arrows at you. Our sleep-muddled brains cleared real fast when we realized our visitors were intent on slaughtering and skinning us.

"Damn," said Bat as he scrambled for his rifle and cover. He fired as he ran toward the back entrance to the Myers & Leonard store.

Grabbing my carbine and gun belt, I chased him inside, uncertain I would live to see sundown. I caught my breath and shook my head, unsure where to shoot as hordes of Indians circled our place, firing through the thin picket-and-chinked walls.

"Leadeye," yelled Bat, "just shoot. There's so many, you don't have to aim to hit one."

Not only that, the attackers rode so near the building that pistols served us better than rifles in the beginning. Fortunately, the Myers

& Leonard store was so well stocked with arms and ammunition that we could've given the Indians gifts of powder and lead until Christmas. On top of that, the Indians didn't realize they had tangled with Leadeye Lomax. The first few hours of the attack were the scariest as the Indians would run right up to the buildings and shoot in the windows, doors or, in the case of the Myers & Leonard store, through the picket slits in the flimsy wall. But gradually, we drove them back from the buildings by noon of the first day.

We used long guns to hold off the attackers for the next three days before the Comanche and Kiowa grew bored with their fruitless assaults. Once they retreated out of range, their withdrawal allowed other hunters to join us. Fewer than thirty of us held off the attackers the first three days. After that, our numbers grew to a hundred as other hunters, fearful of being caught on the prairie by raiding Indians, joined us for mutual protection.

The Indians remained around Adobe Walls for a week or more, always keeping us on edge while we prayed for the cavalry to arrive, especially after we sent two couriers to Dodge City with word of our plight. Two weeks or so after the battle and seven to ten days after the last courier had departed, we argued among ourselves over what to do next. Some wanted to stay until we were rescued while others wanted to retreat to Dodge City. Since the last Indians I had seen had been traveling to the northeast, I wasn't interested in moving toward Kansas for fear the Indians might ambush us.

"We could wait and rot here forever before the army comes our way," Bat said. "As for me, I'm for heading back to Dodge."

"I'm staying here or heading to Fort Griffin," I declared.

"Dodge is closer than Griffin," Masterson countered.

"That's the direction the Comanches headed, north by northeast."

Bat shook his head. "They'll likely circle around and ambush anyone headed to Griffin."

"I may not know where they are now," I said, "but I know where they were when they left, and I ain't heading that way."

He looked at me like he was arguing with an empty feed sack. "Leadeye, you think worse than you shoot. It's probably best we go opposite directions because a hundred of us can't carry enough bullets to feed your reputation for wasting ammunition."

"I ain't heading back to Kansas, not with Comanche on the loose."

Bat grinned. "Sounds like our partnership is breaking up."

"No matter because I'm not returning to Kansas."

Shaking his head, Bat laughed. "You're scared to go back to Kansas, aren't you?"

I shrugged.

"It's Hickok, isn't it?" he asked. "You're afraid you might run into Wild Bill again."

"We didn't depart on good terms."

"Aw, hell," said Bat, "last I heard he was performing on stage back east. Seems he enjoys the glow of the footlights more than Kansas. What did you do to him, anyway?"

"Nothing that needs repeating."

"That bad, was it? What I heard was you got drunk and dumped a spittoon of tobacco juice on his head. Hickok's a fussy one about his hair."

I shrugged. "Just rumors."

"Rumors can get a man killed," Bat said.

"So can Comanche. If you're heading to Kansas, Bat, I'm not going with you."

Bat nodded. "Every man's got to chew his own tobacco. Of course, he shouldn't dump it on Wild Bill's hair."

"Just rumors," I reminded him.

He laughed like he knew better, then slapped me on the shoulder. "I guess our partnership is dissolved. I'll settle up with you before I head out in the morning."

Sure enough the next day, Masterson paid me what he thought I was due, but not nearly as much as I thought I'd earned. It came to about thirty-nine dollars.

"I figure I'm owed more," I protested.

"You're the slowest skinner I've ever worked with," Bat countered.

"But I do the job right."

"Maybe so, but you're the only hide man I know who has to stop whatever he's doing just to break wind. That slows you down, Leadeye."

"Just marking my territory."

He slapped my pay in my hand and laughed. "It's been good working with you. Maybe our trails will cross again on down the line. If you head to Fort Griffin, I wouldn't linger long. There's not a meaner town in Texas."

"There's a fort and soldiers at Griffin and right now that's enough protection for me."

"There aren't many soldiers between here and there," Bat reminded me. "What then?"

"After Griffin I may follow the Brazos to Waco. I drove cattle through there once. It seemed about as civilized as any place can be in Texas, and it's far from the Comanches.

"Then, good luck to you, Leadeye. If you take up buffalo hunting again let me know so I can invest in a lead mine and die a wealthy man from all the bullets you'll waste."

Later that morning, Bat and a couple dozen other hunters rode away from Adobe Walls to the northeast. I headed southeast. Everyone thought I was crazy and destined for a scalping when I left on my own. They were almost right because my departure from Adobe Walls was the first step toward my rendezvous with General Bluster and a place called the Little Bighorn.

Chapter Two

Texas was a big state. You could ride all day and not see anything worth seeing. Most of Texas was a hundred miles from civilization, fifty miles from water, and six inches from hell. Fortunately, I didn't see any Comanche, any Kiowa or, thank God, any Texans. Perhaps more fortunately, no Indians saw me. I rode ten days and almost 300 miles before I reached Fort Griffin, and I still had some 200 miles to Waco.

As I neared Griffin, I saw atop a long plateau an American flag which marked the military post. At the base of the plateau, the town of the same name had attached itself to the fort like a tick to a hound. Fort Griffin had a rancid smell about it, but I was never certain whether it stemmed from the stacks of buffalo hides festering beneath the hot July sun or from the Texans themselves, who bathed only on special occasions and then only when they had enough water. Problem was, the only thing Texans had less of than water was brains, maybe because they were always bashing each other's skulls in fistfights or shooting holes in them in gunfights. Texans were as touchy as a hair trigger, so you had to watch what you said around them so as not to insult their intelligence. As they had virtually no intellect to begin with, it was risking a fight just to greet one with a well-intentioned howdy. They could wring the hell out of hello quicker than any breed of citizen I ever met. So, I kept my mouth shut and my eyes open as I rode down the main street of the town.

I maybe should've gone up the road to the fort and reported to the commander about the trouble at Adobe Walls, but I wasn't far enough removed from the War Between the States to forget that men in blue uniforms had killed two of my brothers. Too, the cavalry failed to rescue us buffalo hunters when we needed them at Adobe Walls, so I wasn't keen on doing the army any favors. Instead I rode down the street to the Bee Hive, a saloon that featured everything I needed save for a hot bath and shave, though that could come later.

Dismounting outside the saloon, I tied my bay gelding and strode inside like I wasn't going to take any nonsense from any Texan, short or tall, drunk or sober, awake or asleep. As I surveyed my surroundings, I realized there was enough ignorance in that room to support two colleges plus an insane asylum in Griffin. The smoke was thick as a river fog and reeked of coal oil, cigarettes, tobacco juice and, worst of all, Texans. Even without a hot bath for the last six months, I smelled like a bouquet of flowers beside these guys and their gals for hire. I elbowed my way to the bar, where a runt of a bartender looked up at me with bloodshot eyes and a runny nose. He was so short he couldn't reach my side of the bar to clean the mess from a past patron.

"You're not from around here," the barkeep said.

I couldn't tell if he was making a statement or asking a question. "What they say about everything being bigger in Texas must not be true by the looks of you."

"I'm from Rhode Island," he replied.

"Long way from home."

"Had to run away. Law was after me."

"Yeah, what for?"

"I knifed three fellows to death."

No taller than he was he must of stabbed them in the knee and they bled to death because he couldn't have reached their guts, much less their hearts. "Give me a whiskey, and I want one Texas size not Rhode Island size."

"Coming right up, stranger," he announced as he kicked an empty wooden crate to the backbar stood on it and grabbed a bottle. He took a jigger from a pyramid of glasses, then hopped off the crate, kicked it opposite me and climbed atop it so he could fill my glass.

I grabbed his hand before he started pouring. "How much for the bottle?"

He studied the amber bottle, shook it, then looked up at me. "It's about half full. I can let you have it for a buck fifty."

"I'll take it."

"How about some smoking or chewing tobacco to go along with it?" he offered.

I shook my head. "Don't smoke, don't chew. I spend my money on more enjoyable pleasures like whiskey."

"And women?"

"I partake from time to time, but figure I need a bath and shave first," I answered as I fished a couple greenbacks from my pocket and offered them to the bartender.

"You can save your bath money here because Griffin gals aren't as particular about cleanliness as those ladies in the fancy city parlors." He snatched my greenbacks and held them up to the light, evaluating their authenticity, before giving me my change.

Shaking my head, I pushed the jigger aside, grabbed the whiskey bottle, uncorked it and took a healthy swig. It wasn't the best whiskey I had ever tasted, but it was far from the worst. I yanked the bottle from my lips and grinned at the bartender. "I'm set on a bath and a good room with a feather mattress."

"If you change your mind, let me know. Ask for Shorty. That's what people call me."

"I would've never guessed, Shorty."

"Now let me give you a bit of advice. Hotels are expensive here and proprietors double you up in bed. You never know what kind of bedmate you might have, other than it's a male. You can find as good a bed in some of the cribs down by the creek. Just pay the soiled dove for the night and you can get a decent bed, a bounce on the bedsprings and a good night's rest."

"Thanks, Shorty. I may just do that. Where can I get a bath?"

"Down the street there's Schulz's. He does barbering and his wife does laundry. You can get a shave and a bath while she washes your clothes. On a hot day like this, you can have clean clothes by the time you leave."

"Obliged."

He nodded. "I didn't catch your name, stranger."

"Lomax," I replied.

Shorty's eyes narrowed. He studied me like he would a wanted poster. "You wouldn't be Leadeye Lomax, would you?"

"That's my brother," I replied, figuring to save myself some trouble.

"It true he dumped a chamber pot full of droppings and juice on Wild Bill Hickok's head?"

"I wasn't there," I lied, "but it sounds like something old Leadeye might do."

"Damn," Shorty whistled, "your brother is either the bravest or the stupidest man around to do that to Wild Bill."

"A little of both," I said as I retreated from the bar. I was tempted to buck the tiger or play a little poker to increase my pocket cash, but it was so smoky in the saloon I figured I couldn't see the pasteboards well enough to know if I was being cheated.

Leaving the saloon, I untied my gelding and walked him to a livery stable, paying a dollar to have him fed and groomed, Next I took my carbine, draped my saddlebags over my shoulder and walked toward Schulz's. I spotted a weather-grayed wooden building with fires burning under a couple black pots behind the place and ambled that direction until I could read the front door's faded black lettering that identified the shack as a barber shop and laundry, though it was hard to be certain since there was no window to look through for confirmation. I opened the door and entered, finding a lean, bespectacled fellow sitting in the barber chair reading the latest edition of the *Fort Griffin Echo*. He nodded until I took a swig of whiskey.

He frowned. "Momma don't allow no whiskey drinking in our place."

"It's for medicinal purposes," I assured him.

"Well, do your doctoring outside, and we'll both be safer."

I corked my bottle and nodded. "Whatever Momma says. I'm told I can get a bath and haircut while my clothes are washed. That true?"

"As long as Momma doesn't see your bottle."

I shoved the bottle under the flap of my saddlebag.

"I'm Charlie Schulz. Bath, shave, haircut and laundry will cost you four dollars."

"I'm good for it."

"I'm sure you are, but Momma's not a trusting woman. You'll need to pay up front."

I reached into my pants pocket and pulled out my wad of money, then peeled off four greenbacks for him.

Schulz smiled and arose, dropping the newspaper in the chair and taking my money. He moved to a door leading to a back room and whistled. "Momma," he called, "we've got a customer who wants the works." He motioned for me to join him so I left my belongings beside the door and entered the back room. As I went in, he pointed to a tin bathtub and a changing screen. "Take off your clothes back there while Momma and I tote hot water for your bath."

I did as I was told for fear Momma would slap me up across the head. Even though I knew her only by reputation, Momma sounded mean enough to whip her husband while he was washing her dishes. I hung my hat, gun belt and knife scabbard on a nail, then extracted my money from my pocket, lifted my pistol and wedged the greenbacks between it and my holster. As I started unbuttoning my shirt, I heard Schulz and Momma enter the room and dump pails of water into the tub.

"Just toss your clothes on the floor for me, sweetie," said Momma.

I removed my shirt and draped it over the top of the screen, then my bandanna, pants, long johns and socks. I stood there naked as Adam on day one and waited for them to fill the tub. After several trips I earned Momma's blessing.

"Okay, sweetie, the tub's ready. Are you?" she asked. "And don't be bashful because Momma's seen enough cowboys in their altogether not to be embarrassed in the least."

As I slipped from behind the screen, I wasn't worried about her being embarrassed. I eyed Momma. Believe me, God had blessed her because her cup runneth over. She wasn't fat as much as she was too short for her weight. She inspected me up and down. "Is that all there is?"

I glanced down at my waist, then shrugged. It was all I had brought with me.

"Your dirty clothes, sweetie. Is that all of your dirty clothes?" She stamped her foot.

I nodded. "I don't have a big wardrobe."

Momma laughed as she grabbed my clothes and departed. "I guess bigness doesn't run in your family."

Bigness certainly ran in her clan, though. Her hips looked like a mountain avalanche as she waddled away, but I held my tongue, as she was carrying the only clothes I owned. As I settled into the tub, the hot water brought a sweat to my brow. It was almost too hot to be comfortable, but with weeks and layers of trail dust and buffalo grit on me, I clenched my teeth and enjoyed the scalding of a real bath. I took a bar of lye soap from an adjacent table and went to work scrubbing away the grime. I washed my hair and scoured my face and whiskers until I was clean enough to attend church, provided Momma returned with my clothes.

Schulz came in occasionally to extract a pail of bathwater and replace it with more hot water. After I had bathed to my satisfaction, though likely not to Momma's, I leaned back in the tub, rested my arms on the sides and just relaxed. As much dirt as I had washed away, I figured it would assay out to about thirty pounds per bucket of water. When Schulz returned with a fresh bucket of hot water, he dumped it between my legs, then pulled his folded copy of the *Fort Griffin Echo* from under his arm. "It'll be another hour before Momma finishes with your clothes. Here's something for you to read. I've got a customer up front for a haircut. When he's done, I'll come back and give you a scalping, unless you want to sit in the barber chair up front in your altogether."

Now I understood why he had no window out front. Since I'd never had a naked haircut, I figured it would be better just staying where I was so Momma couldn't make fun of me again. "The tub is good enough."

"That's most men's preference, though occasionally we get one who likes it in the chair, clothes or not."

"You could offer them a towel," I said.

"Towels are extra," he replied.

I took the newspaper from him.

Schulz left me alone with the newspaper and I began to read local news, which meant very little to me until I got to the telegraph reports and saw a brief *Galveston News* dispatch dated July 13, 1874. The two paragraphs talked about a train of forty wagons being attacked near Skeleton Creek in Indian Territory and then mentioned that eleven of the warriors killed in the assault had recently attacked the settlement at Adobe Walls. That was the first indication I had that Bat Masterson had made it to safety in Kansas.

Another of the *Echo's* reprinted dispatches included one dated July 15, 1874, from the *Army and Navy Gazette* about the Army's Black Hills Expedition under the command of General Custer. I didn't know the son of a bitch at that time so my dislike of him came only from knowing that he had fought at Gettysburg where I had lost a brother to Yankee bullets. I wasn't interested in Custer or the Black Hills Expedition, but I had time to kill and little else I could do unless I wanted to cause a stir in Fort Griffin by running down the street naked.

The article indicated that the U.S. Army expedition had left on July 2 from Fort Abraham Lincoln in Dakota Territory with orders to explore the previously uncharted Black Hills and return by August 30. Some 1,100 soldiers including the Seventh Cavalry and two companies of infantry plus sixty Indian scouts, four Gatling guns, a heavy train of supplies and President Grant's son accompanied Custer. Reported the *Army and Navy Gazette*:

> The country being entirely unknown, the exploration of itself must be full of interest, as clearing up the only mysterious spot of any great size left in the map of the United States. When we add that the reports of friendly Indians represent this remote oasis as very rich in minerals, as well as in the essentials of savage life, it is not surprising that a strong expedition should be needed to explore its vastnesses. It is the last home of the Sioux, and possibly they

> may fight to defend it from intrusion. If so, while regretting their hard fate, we can, nevertheless, see that the expedition will, in all probability, walk through them without serious damage.

Even before I had met Custer, I found myself despising him all the more because of how the paper described him.

> To General Custer, the luckiest of all lucky leaders, whose prudent and successful conduct of the Yellowstone expedition, some time since, brought him so many honors, has the conduct of the present exploration been entrusted. The choice could hardly have fallen on a better man. We have called General Custer a lucky man, and such he has proved since the time he first excited public attention, during the war, by his long curls, picturesque dress, and dashing style of fighting. Closely examined, his luck will be found to consist largely in that mixture of daring and prudence that is sure to make its mark in any pursuit of life. Custer is lucky, chiefly because he is always ready.

After reading that about Custer, I was ready to throw up, but I didn't want to ruin my bathwater. Just about the time I turned to the *Echo's* fourth and last page, Schulz returned with his comb, scissors, razor and stool, which he placed behind me and then sat on.

"Now, sit up straight so I can start to work. This may take a while with all that growth. How long's it been since you've had a trim?"

"Six or seven, maybe eight months," I replied.

"I ought to scalp you and sell it as a buffalo hide as much fur as you've accumulated."

"Some Indians have tried that," I said, "but their squaws are now widows."

"Then I'll just stick to giving you a haircut as I wouldn't want to make Momma a widow, as she's quite a looker."

"Yes, I can confirm she's a looker."

It took Schulz close to an hour to cut through all the weeds and make me look like a civilized person. By the time he was done, my hair would fit under my hat without spilling out and my beard was gone with all the trail dust. I felt about as clean and good as any man can without having any clothes to wear. That problem was solved when Momma returned with my duds all washed, ironed and folded.

"Need any help drying off or putting your clothes on?" she offered.

"None at all. Been dressing myself for years now without lookers to help."

She handed me a towel, then stood there waiting for me to stand up from the dirty water. I waited her out until she finally left the room. After Momma exited, I got out of the tub, dried off, dressed myself, then put my cash back in my pants pocket and strapped on my holster and knife. It felt good to be bathed and wearing clean clothes.

"You were right, Schulz," I said as I bent over to pick up my carbine and saddlebags. "Your wife is quite a looker."

My comment pleased him.

"One more thing, mister."

"What's that?"

Schulz retrieved a bottle of tonic water from a shelf and doused his hand with the liquid. After he returned the bottle, he rubbed his hands together, then massaged my cheeks and neck with the liquid fragrance.

I left the barbershop smelling better than a New Orleans whorehouse. After a bite of supper I figured the aroma would help me find a nice place to spend the night. Following up on Shorty's advice, I wasn't thinking about a hotel but rather a nice woman with a soft bed and a willingness to share it. Hell, she didn't even have to be the prettiest thing as long as she wasn't as wide as Momma Schulz. After all, I wanted to have a fair claim to half or more of the bed and no fears of being smothered if my hired companion accidentally—or intentionally—rolled over on me.

Chapter Three

Down by the creek I had plenty of choices for lodging as business was apparently slow. The ladies were all smiles and invitations. There were plump ones, wee ones, tall ones and short ones with hair that was dark as pitch or light as straw. There was even a redhead, but I didn't give her a second glance as I had always found redheads to be crazy. While the ladies wanted me to check out their goods, I intended to check out their beds first to see whose was the widest and whose had the cleanest sheets, since I was newly bathed and smelling good.

After inspecting five different cribs with brassy proprietors, I feared I would have to lower my standards until I came to the skinniest little thing I'd ever seen. Barely casting a shadow, she was brown-haired and doe-eyed with a shy smile that made me think she was in the wrong profession. As I inspected her, she grabbed her skirt and curtseyed.

"Good evening, sir. Would you care to dabble?"

Well, I'd never heard it put that way. "Maybe," I said, "but I'd like to check things first."

She started unbuttoning her blouse.

"No, not that," I told her. "I want to see your bed, make sure it's solid with a feather mattress and clean sheets."

"It's a bed sturdy enough for a bucking horse," she said as she re-buttoned her blouse. "The sheets were changed yesterday. You'll be the second gentleman to use them."

I stepped past her toward the plank walls of her small crib and poked my head inside the door. The single room was cramped with an iron bedstead and what appeared to be a feather mattress as well as a trunk, small table and chair, tiny stove and a mirror on the wall at the foot of the bed. Opposite the door was a glassless window framed by some flour-sack curtains. The place was manageable for a tiny woman like her but a bit of a squeeze for an average size guy like me. The place looked much like the others I had inspected before it, but her tiny size appealed to me as I would have more room on the feather mattress for a good night's sleep.

I dropped my saddlebags inside the door and propped my carbine up against the plank wall. "How much for the whole night?"

"Five dollars," she answered.

"Why, that's more than a haircut, shave, bath and laundry!"

"I'll guarantee you'll leave satisfied," she answered.

"I'm more interested in sleeping than dabbling."

"I've heard of your kind, just never thought I'd meet one."

"No, I like dabbling, just that I've been sleeping on the hard ground for months. Tonight I want a soft bed for change before I ride on."

We bargained and I brought her down to three dollars for the night. For that price, she agreed to dabble before I went to sleep and again before I got up the next morning for breakfast. We shook hands on our arrangement.

"Payment in advance," she said.

I fished out my roll of cash and pulled out three greenbacks. She took the money, then held it up toward the setting sun to inspect it before sliding it inside her blouse. I feared the money might slide all the way out as she had not been endowed with a great bosom.

"My name's Minerva," she said. "What's yours?"

"Anyone ever call you Skinny Minnie?" I joked.

"One fellow did," she replied. "I didn't like it and cut off his danglers."

Damn, I thought. "You wouldn't happen to be from Rhode Island, would you?"

"Nope, Texas born and bred. Now what's your name?"

"Lomax, H.H. Lomax."

Minerva stepped back and examined me. "You wouldn't happen to be the Lomax that poured coal oil on Wild Bill Hickok's hair and set it on fire, would you?"

"No," I replied. "It was another Lomax."

She relaxed. Smiling, she grabbed my hand and pulled me inside, closing the door. I remained on edge fearing I might slip and call her Skinny Minnie. She stood on her tiptoes and kissed me on the lips. Up close, she smelled as good as me after my dousing with tonic water.

Minerva helped me get comfortable, then she sprinkled water on the sheets to cool them down and we crawled into bed. She had a pleasing way of working the stiffness out of a man's muscles, and I don't remember ever getting a deeper, more satisfying night of sleep. I slept well past sunrise and might have slept all day had I not felt her fingers working the stiffness out of my muscles again. By the time I was wide awake, I was completely satisfied.

"I bet that was better than any hotel you ever stayed in," Minerva whispered.

I wrapped my arms around her and kissed her on the cheek. "I would have to agree, but I guess my time here is done."

"You could stay another night, get a little more rest, maybe dabble a time or two more."

"I've got to ride on." I got up and took another good look at her in the altogether. Her ribs poked out as much as her bosom, but she wore an innocent look that made it hard for me to believe she was a soiled dove, much less one that could cut the jinglebobs off a fellow. I pulled her chamber pot out from under the bed and relieved myself before I gathered my clothes.

"A gentleman empties the chamber pot before he leaves," she said.

I nodded. "I'll do it," I said as I shoved my hand in my pocket and extracted my money so I could do a quick count to make sure she hadn't slipped a few bills out while I slept. It was all there, but my attempt at stealth failed.

"You don't trust me, do you?" she said.

"Not that at all. Just checking to see how much money I had left before I left town."

"Where you headed?"

"Waco," I said as I buttoned up my shirt and tucked it in my pants.

"I got a sister in Waco."

"Oh, yeah, what does she do?"

"The same thing I do."

"That a fact? Why don't you two work together?"

"We used to," Minerva answered shyly, "but we had a falling out."

"Over what?"

"Me cutting the danglers off a gentleman. She didn't appreciate me doing that in her high class house."

I grinned. "I'd have to say I would be on her side."

"I guess so," Minerva said. "It hurts business when you get a reputation like that. Sorta like that Lomax fellow that done Wild Bill wrong. With his reputation, who'd want to have anything to do with him?"

"Not me," I said as I sat on the edge of her bed and tugged my boots on. When I was done with that, I took her chamber pot out by the creek, dumped it out and rinsed it. Returning to her crib, I slid the pot under her bed and picked up my saddlebags and carbine.

"I best be moving on," I announced.

Minerva laughed. "If you make it to Waco, look up my sister. Medusa is her name."

"She have a last name?"

"She only uses her first name and that's an alias just like Minerva so we don't embarrass our folks by our work, them being more religious than my sister and me. Anyway, everyone in Waco will know where to find Medusa."

"Thanks," I answered. "I'll try to look her up."

Exiting Minerva's crib, I walked back to town, grabbed me some overpriced bacon and eggs at an unnamed eatery, then retrieved my horse and tack and started the 200-mile journey to Waco. Like I said, Texas was a big state. I guess God decided the nation needed a large insane asylum, and Texas was well stocked with lunatics to begin with.

My luck continued as I made it from Fort Griffin to Waco without running into any more Indians and only a handful of Texans. Generally, I could smell Texans a mile in advance and would ride off the trail and let them pass before resuming my journey to the town on the Brazos River. Texans liked to brag about everything being big in Texas, but I crossed piddling rivers, passed piddling trees and spit over the piddling things they called mountains. Like I said, all the nuts in Texas didn't hang from trees, just the ones that got caught.

Compared to west Texas, Waco was the Garden of Eden. Even if fall was approaching, Waco had real grass instead of clump grass and trees that would actually support a horse thief's lynching, unlike the country I had escaped after Adobe Walls. I hadn't seen so much green vegetation since I took up buffalo hunting. The only problem was, I hadn't much green left in my pocket. After leaving Fort Griffin, I'd spent more than half my remaining money, and I was carrying fewer than ten dollars on me. On the positive side, I had made it from Adobe Walls to Waco with all the hair on my scalp, save for that I had paid Schulz to trim.

I'd been through Waco several years earlier when I was trailing the first herd of longhorns north to the railhead in Abilene, Kansas, on what became the Chisholm Trail. Waco back then was a rough and tumble cattle crossing sometimes called "Six-Shooter Junction."

By the time I returned in August of 1874, Waco relied less on the cattle trade than it had before and more on the revived cotton business. Too, the fine citizens of Waco had formed a company to build a suspension bridge over the Brazos River and a few years after the war opened the first dry crossing of the Brazos in Texas. The bridge and the arrival of the Waco and Northwestern Railroad had made the city the commercial hub of central Texas with a population of more than 5,000.

The bridge, the railroad and "the Reservation," as I would soon learn, brought a lot of riff-raff like me and college professors to town. Some of the locals had come to calling Waco "the Athens of Texas" because of the preponderance of colleges. The citizens of Waco didn't look any smarter than Texans I had encountered elsewhere, and they certainly didn't smell any better, but they did have a slew of schools—Waco University, Leland Seminary, Waco Academy, Sacred Heart Academy, Waco Female College, Waco Select School and even Paul Quinn College for the education of Negroes. It was said the president of Waco University had baptized Sam Houston himself before the War Between the States. When the preacher raised the hero of San Jacinto from the creek waters, he informed the new convert that his sins had been washed away. "Pity the fish downstream," Houston replied.

Not being much of one for formal learning, I had always believed the best thing that ever happened to my education was the burning by the Yankees of the college up the road from our place in Cane Hill, Arkansas. My momma had wanted me to get some schooling, but I never was attuned to sitting in a chair all day, listening to someone drone on about something I had no interest in and then being expected to remember what I had just not heard.

Of course, Momma had wanted me to go to church more and I had been a disappointment to her there as well. However, I could've made up for it in Waco, which seemed to have more churches than people, causing some to call the Brazos burg "the city with a soul." There was the First Methodist, First Baptist, First Presbyterian, Cumberland Presbyterian, St. Paul's Episcopal, Catholic Church and others. On top of that, the fine people of Waco had a fancy four-story brick jail, promoted as the best in Texas. The way I figured it, Waco shouldn't need a jail with so many churches and pious folks around.

For all its growth, the streets of Waco were still dirt with most of the activity centered on the town square, just a couple blocks from the suspension bridge. The wooden buildings that surrounded the square on my first trip through Waco had been largely replaced by brick structures that looked prosperous and imposing, including three banks and a merchant that advertised furniture, rugs and coffins on his plate glass windows. People milled about the square, including men in overalls, women carrying parasols, cattlemen discussing the weather, cotton buyers evaluating the fall crop, boys making deliveries and farmers selling produce, eggs and butter. There were just as many animals, including horses, cattle, dogs, sheep, caged chickens, even pigs and, worst of all, lawyers, the most vicious form of life ever to walk on earth. I passed a couple saloons and a saddler and, if I'd had enough money, I could've bought confections, butchered meat, a pocket watch, laudanum and remedies to cure every malady known to man.

I steered my gelding toward the suspension bridge and would've crossed to the other side, except I didn't want to pay the toll that the bridge company exacted on every man, woman, child, animal or conveyance that wanted to cross the river without getting wet. I didn't figure that was the way the local citizenry should treat a new arrival, but I didn't feel up to arguing about it. I just pulled my mount off the road and stared at a just arrived train unloading at the station on the east side of the river. As I had no acquaintances in town and just the phony name of Minerva's sister, I waited for a hack to bring a newly arrived passenger across the bridge so I could follow the carriage and ask the driver where I might find Medusa. I prayed she wasn't as touchy or as handy with a knife as Skinny Minnie.

Eventually, a hack pulled away from the station and crossed the bridge. I studied the driver as he passed with a couple drummers holding their carpetbags of samples in their laps. I turned my gelding in behind them and followed the carriage past the square to a cheap boarding house where the driver collected his fare and turned his passengers loose. Then he eyed me like I eyed him. He was a scrawny fellow with brown hair, brown eyes and brown teeth.

"I need some help," I said, nudging my horse beside his seat.

"Don't look like it to me, you having your own mode of transportation," he said, then shook the reins and started his carriage back toward the suspension bridge.

"I'm looking for a woman named Medusa. You ever heard of her?"

"You talking about the mythic Greek ogre or the Texas harlot?"

"It must be the Texas harlot as I don't know Greek anything."

"You'll find her on the Reservation," he replied.

I shook my head. "I'm looking for a harlot, not a squaw."

"Fellow, it'll cost you two bits to find out more."

Not feeling he could be trusted even if I paid him, I tipped my hat to him. "Good day, sir."

Laughing, he took the buggy whip and popped the flanks of his matched grays. "You must not be as randy—or as smart—as most fellows off the prairie looking for the Reservation."

If I'd been afoot, I'd grabbed a horse apple and thrown at him, but I let him pass and headed back to the square. I tied my horse and loitered about until I saw a comely middle-aged woman with rouged cheeks and flaming red hair marching down the street in a dress that was too ostentatious to be worn by a typical woman in a town with so many churches. She made her way to a doctor's office across the square as cocky as if she'd never been broke to a halter, even if she had been rode a thousand times.

I watched the activity all about the square as I waited on her to finish her business. Forty-five minutes later she appeared again and marched back the way she had come toward the north side of the square. I unhitched my horse, mounted and followed at a respectable distance until she crossed a wooden bridge over a small creek that fed into the Brazos.

I nudged my horse to pick up the pace and caught up with her a half block past the bridge. As I drew even with her, I removed my hat and nodded at her. "Pardon me, ma'am, I'm looking for the Reservation. Can you help me?"

She batted her eyes at me, then touched her top lip with the tip of her tongue, exposing a gold-capped front tooth. "Depends on what kind of help you need."

"I'm looking for a woman they call Medusa."

Instantly her demeanor turned sour as stale vinegar. "You a friend of hers?"

"Don't even know her. Was just given her name to look up if I was ever in Waco."

"I'll give you some information and a piece of advice at no charge."

"That's a better deal than the hack driver gave me."

She stopped walking and pointed to the next block and a couple dozen houses. "That's the Reservation and the house with the red shutters, that's the one Medusa runs."

"Obliged," I said.

"Now, for the free advice, stranger. Watch out for Medusa. She hates men and she'll gut you, if you ever cross her."

I guess I'd've preferred a gutting to her sister's style of surgery, but it worried me that the two siblings had a great fondness for knives.

"Thank you, ma'am," I said, replacing my hat. Taking a deep breath, I nudged my mount toward Medusa's place.

"God rest your soul," I heard the harlot call after me.

Chapter Four

The house with the red shutters—actually more of a rich scarlet like the women inside—peeked from behind a wrought iron fence and well-trimmed shrubs. Shaded by a giant pecan tree, the two-story, gray clapboard house featured a narrow, covered front porch bordering a weed-free bed of flowers, their once bright colors subdued by the heat of late summer. The house appeared to be the biggest and best-maintained in the Reservation. By the time I stopped in front of Medusa's place, the sun was about an hour from disappearing behind the western horizon. I figured business would soon be picking up, especially when it turned dark and the fine, pious gentlemen of Waco tugged the brims of their hats down over their faces to protect their reputations, then headed for an evening stroll and a roll in the hay. As a stranger in town, I had no reputation to protect and no qualms about approaching a brothel. It was one way to make acquaintances, at least until your money dried up.

I dismounted outside the gate and looked for a hitching post. Finding none, I tied my bay to the wrought iron fence, straightened my hat and unlatched the gate, which swung easily open on well-oiled hinges. I marched up the walk and onto the porch, taking in the tall, open windows with lace curtains that quivered in the slight breeze that wafted through the house. At the door, I brushed off what trail dust I could and grabbed the door knocker, banging it five times to announce my arrival.

From inside, I heard a woman's voice call out. "Mr. Eaton, please attend to the door. It sounds as if we have a gentleman caller."

I removed my hat, holding it over my chest as the door swung open and revealed a black man finely dressed in a black cutaway coat and trousers, white shirt, starched collar and bow tie. He smiled until his gaze traversed me from head to toe. Then his grin soured.

"This is no gentleman, Miss Medusa, and doesn't appear to ever have been one."

Maybe not, but I didn't appear to have been a former slave, either.

"Looks like a cowhand at best, and a broke one at worst."

Though I couldn't see Medusa, I could hear her. "Send him away then. We don't do charity cases. Point him to Big Red's place. Sounds like he's more suited to a rowdy house than our place."

"Good, sir," Mr. Eaton said, "we cater to a higher class clientele. Might I suggest you visit another house?" He pointed down the street. "Big Red serves the cowhand crowd. We only serve cattlemen and other men of means."

"Is Big Red the one with the gold-capped tooth?" I asked.

Mr. Eaton nodded.

"She ain't my type."

"Good day, sir," Mr. Eaton said as he began to close the door.

I planted my boot inside to keep him from shutting it.

"Good, sir, we will have to call the authorities if you don't remove yourself from the premises."

"Minerva sent me." Before I could say more, I heard Miss Medusa gasp.

Instantly, she was at the door, pushing Mr. Eaton aside and yanking the door open.

"You've seen Minerva?" she cried.

I nodded.

"Please come in," she said, then glanced outside. "Is that your horse tied to the fence?"

"Yes, ma'am."

"My visitors don't leave their mounts out front. There's a carriage house and a stable in the back."

I turned to tend my mount, but she grabbed my arm. "No, no. I'll ask Mr. Eaton to take your horse around back for you." She smiled at him. "Would you mind?"

"No, Miss Medusa. I'll tend to it at this moment."

As Medusa pulled me inside, Eaton stepped past me, closed the door and scurried off.

Medusa was a finely proportioned woman with more flesh on her bones than her sister. She had the same brown hair, though it was adorned with ribbons that framed her face and green eyes that looked excitedly at me. Her dress was fashionable, though I didn't pay as much attention to it as I did her hips, which swayed seductively as she led me across the parlor.

Fine looking as she was, her parlor was even more elegantly apportioned, with thick carpets, plush chairs and sofas, cut-glass gas lamps, three bookshelves filled with leather-bound volumes, and a corner table, where two fiddles rested atop a lace doily. A carved staircase led upstairs to the girls' rooms, I assumed, and a doorway opened onto a smaller room where I could see a small bar and back-bar well supplied with fine wines and liquors.

Medusa steered me to a chair and sat me down, then pulled another chair opposite me. Leaning forward and taking my hands in hers, she smiled. "Tell me about Minerva. Where is she and how is she doing?"

"She's working in Fort Griffin," I started.

"A house of her own?"

"A small one," I answered, shading the truth. "Nothing like this one."

"She got any girls working for her?"

I shrugged. "I don't know. I didn't look past her as she was quite becoming."

Medusa seemed pleased, so I thought I would try to endear myself to her even more.

"Minerva sends all her love. She said she missed you, hoping she could work with you again one day, but was afraid her reputation would damage your business."

Medusa grimaced. "Her temper's more suited to a rougher clientele than the gentlemen I serve."

"It true what she did after some fellow called her Skinny Minnie?"

Medusa frowned. "The incident has been largely exaggerated, often times by her."

I whistled in relief. "So she didn't cut off the fellow's jinglebobs!"

"No," Medusa said, "she left one of them."

I gulped. From what I knew about Minerva and what Big Red had warned me about Medusa, I didn't feel safe in her parlor, even if it was bigger, more elegant and, hopefully, more civilized than Minerva's crib. On top of that, she was still holding my hands, well within stabbing range, should I say something that offended her. When she finally released her grip, I breathed easier.

"I suppose you came here for another dip in the waters," Medusa said. "The girls should be down when it grows dark."

"No, ma'am," I replied. "I just came here to pass along the words of your loving sister and tell you how much she missed you. Besides that, I'm broke and need to find a job to earn some money."

"What kind of work do you do?"

"Whatever I come across. I've cowboyed, hunted buffalo, hauled freight, scouted, chopped wood, laid railroad track and anything else I could to earn a buck."

"You good with a gun?"

"I'm no pistoleer, but I can hold my own against most," I answered.

"Ever do inside work, like in a saloon or a store or a bank?"

"I did a little banking once for a short while," I said, not admitting that it was only about five minutes when I accompanied Jesse James and his gang of their first bank robbery.

"A teller then."

I shrugged. "You might say."

"Banking experience, huh? I like that. You ever tended bar? I don't mean in a saloon, but a small bar in an intimate place like this."

"Nope, I generally prefer to drink whiskey rather than to sell it to others."

Medusa leaned toward me. "Banking experience. I like that," she said.

"Briefly," I reminded her.

"Can handle a gun. I like that. Can you learn to pour and mix liquor?"

"Pouring it's never been a problem. I guess I can mix it, though I generally stick with rye or bourbon."

"You object to putting ice in a drink?"

Medusa was coming up with more questions than I had answers. "I never had enough ice around to keep milk from souring or beef from spoiling, much less waste it in whiskey. Besides, it just dilutes the whiskey. And the kick, I might add!"

"Many of our gentlemen visitors have educated thirsts and even drink wines, so a rudimentary knowledge of mixology is helpful. Do you mind doing other work, even if it's considered woman's work?"

I was okay until she mentioned woman's work. "I ain't a cook and bottle washer, if that's what you mean. Never kept house in my life and don't intend to."

Medusa reached for my hands again. I presented them to her for fear she might draw a knife from somewhere and carve me up if I declined her offer. Her fingers were soft and reassuring.

"I'll give you a dollar fifty a day to work for me, seven days a week. You'll serve and mix drinks for our visitors, throw out any rowdies that might threaten the girls and do any chores, save cooking, cleaning and washing dishes."

"No washing clothes, either."

"We send our sheets and clothes to the laundry, mister. What did you say your name was?"

"Lomax," I said.

She yanked her hands away as if I was diseased with the small pox, then screeched, "Are you the Lomax that tarred and feathered Wild Bill Hickok's hair?"

"No, that must've been my brother. I'm H.H. Lomax."

Medusa reached for my gun hand, took it in hers and patted it with her other hand. "I guess all families have a black sheep somewhere."

"It seems that way," I nodded. At least my black sheep hadn't cut off one of Wild Bill's danglers.

"If you're agreeable, Mr. Lomax, I'll hire you on to help out Mr. Eaton during visiting hours and you can help me out with my banking during daylight hours."

"Are you my boss or Mr. Eaton?" I asked, uncertain I could work under the thumb of an ignorant darkie just a few years removed from slavery. "I'm the boss, but you'll find Mr. Eaton to be most knowledgeable in the matters of this house and of the higher cultures."

I didn't figure Mr. Eaton was that smart, but I realized I'd be dumber than him to turn down a chance to work through the winter in a warm house rather than sleeping on the cold ground shooting buffalo or chasing cattle.

"Room and board's included," Medusa said. "You'll bunk with Mr. Eaton in the back room off the kitchen. Is that a problem for you?"

"Nope," I said. "After the war, I'd herded cattle and bunked with a couple darkies. I found them to be like most other folks, some filled with goodness, some filled with meanness."

"Then it's agreed?"

I nodded. "It's a deal. You shall call me Miss Medusa and I shall call you Mr. Lomax. I prefer formalities in my place. Your pay will start tomorrow because I'll not have you working here dressed like a prairie ruffian. Tomorrow I shall have Mr. Eaton escort you to a haberdashery to buy clothes more attuned to our clientele, not as formal as Mr. Eaton's attire, but definitely an improvement on the rags you are wearing. It'll come out of your pay, of course."

With the business details out of the way, Medusa informed Mr. Eaton upon his return that I would be assisting him in his whorehouse endeavors, though she said it a little more delicately. She formally introduced us and Mr. Eaton escorted me past the small room with the bar, through the kitchen and into the back room, where two bunks sat on opposite sides of the room with a table and two chairs between them. One bed had his trunk at the foot. Along the back wall between the two beds was a waist-high bookshelf holding three layers of books. He pointed to the empty bed. "Make yourself at home, Mr. Lomax."

"It's H.H. Lomax. You can call me Lomax or H.H. or even Henry if you like it better."

"I'm Earl Eaton, but you must call me Mr. Eaton and I will only address you as Mr. Lomax. Miss Medusa runs a formal house." He offered me his hand. I shook it.

"Where you from, Mr. Lomax?"

"Everywhere now, but Arkansas originally."

"Yes, Arkansas, the twenty-fifth state admitted to the union."

I was embarrassed to admit that I didn't know that, so I changed the subject. "Where you from, Mr. Eaton?"

"Can't say for certain," he said. "Those weren't details common to a slave child's existence. Don't even know my age or my birthday."

Those were about the only things Mr. Eaton didn't know, however. As I got to know him, I realized Earl Eaton was about the smartest man I'd ever been around with a strong mix of both book learning and common sense.

"Do you read, Mr. Eaton?"

"Certainly do, Mr. Lomax. Miss Medusa encourages me to do so. In fact, every time I read a book through, she lets me add it to my shelf here." He pointed to all the books.

As I studied the shelf, I realized it was a dozen wooden crates stacked three high and four abreast. There were a hundred or more books there with names I had never heard of on the spines. I don't know that I had ever read that many pages in a single book, much less that many books in my lifetime.

"I'd like to stay and visit, Mr. Lomax, but it's getting close to our busy time when the ladies come down from upstairs and the gentlemen begin to arrive. Your horse is in the stable, but I didn't unsaddle him, figuring you wouldn't be long with us. You may want to care for him and bring your belongings inside. Exit and enter through the back door in the kitchen."

"Will do, Earl."

"No, no, Mr. Lomax, it's Mr. Eaton as long as we work for Miss Medusa. Get unpacked shortly as Miss Medusa wouldn't want you to be seen by the gentlemen callers. You'll find some cold chicken on the table as well as some bread and boiled potatoes for your supper. Eat what you like then retire to our room, if you please." He departed, leaving me to my new quarters.

After Eaton left, I stepped outside, unsaddled and groomed my horse and carried my saddlebags and carbine into the back room. I retreated to the kitchen, grabbed a plate and filled it with the cold grub, then poured me a glass of water to take back into my room. After I finished my supper, I stripped down to my long johns and pulled a chair from the table and set it by the open window over the bookshelf and enjoyed the cool evening breeze.

Gradually, I heard the sounds of women gathering in the parlor and later of men arriving to enjoy their charms. Their interactions were quiet and courtly, all giggles and whispers rather than the guffaws and shouts I was more accustomed to from similar interactions in saloons.

After an hour, someone started playing the fiddle, not the popular tunes I would've recognized, but rather a softer melodic tune with soothing, drawn out notes. Once it was dark outside, I never lit a gas lamp and simply crawled into bed, relishing the softness so different from the hard ground I had slept on every night between Fort Griffin and Waco. The soft fiddle music serenaded me to sleep. It was a deep restful night, though not as satisfying as my evening with Minerva back in Fort Griffin. Even so, I could be proud that I had encountered both the sisters Minerva and Medusa and had survived with my jinglebobs intact and with an easy job to boot, or so I thought.

Chapter Five

Over the next eight months, I earned an education, not just in running a whorehouse but also in rooming with Earl Eaton, who was reading a book every minute he wasn't doing a chore for Miss Medusa or taking care of all the girls' needs. I awoke my regular time my first morning in Miss Medusa's place but everyone else was still asleep. A brothel is more of a night than a day business, not discounting all the daytime chores that still had to be done—beds changed, laundry delivered, meals cooked, ashtrays emptied, liquor restocked, slop jars dumped, cash counted, sundries purchased and floors swept.

About midmorning when Eaton began to stir, I raised up from my bed. "Morning, Mr. Eaton," I said.

He twisted around, shaking his head and rubbing, his eyes. "And to you as well, Mr. Lomax."

I still felt funny being called Mr. Lomax, that being a moniker more fitting to my father.

"You sleep well?" he asked.

Nodding, I said, "Yes, sir, the fiddle music soothed me to sleep."

"Wasn't no fiddle you heard, Mr. Lomax. It was a violin part of the time and a viola the rest of the time."

"One and the same to me," I said.

"That's why you are not a cultured man, Mr. Lomax. There's a great difference between the two. The viola is slightly bigger than the violin and offers a deeper, more resonant sound. The violin is smaller, producing higher ranges of string music than the viola."

"Well, if you know so much, why weren't you playing them last night, Mr. Eaton?"

"I was," he said as he rolled out of bed, yawning and stretching.

I didn't believe him, suspecting he had a good face and a deceitful heart. Either that, or he was putting on airs like a lot of black folks during Reconstruction, as the Yankees called the years following the

War Between the States.

"Maybe if you learned to play the cello we could make some chamber music, Mr. Lomax. Miss Medusa would like that."

"About the only chamber music I can make is on the chamber pot," I answered.

Eaton smiled. "You are not a cultured man, Mr. Lomax. Miss Medusa prefers her employees without rough edges."

"I thought she hired me for my gun and banking experience," I answered. "Did you know I've done some banking with Jesse James?"

Mr. Eaton laughed and slapped his knee. "That's a good one, Mr. Lomax. A little levity is good for the soul. If you've done some shooting with Mr. James, that's even better."

I might not have been as sharp as a briar, but I was getting the idea that Miss Medusa was wanting me for my gun-toting as much as my banking experience.

"Don't you shoot, Mr. Eaton?"

"No, sir, I don't."

"Shooting's a lot easier to learn than playing a fiddle."

"You mean violin or viola."

I shrugged. "I'm getting the feeling, Miss Medusa's expecting trouble. Am I right?"

"Miss Medusa just believes in being on the safe side. There's a madam down the street named Big Red that's not being very sociable to Miss Medusa."

"She got a gold-capped tooth?"

Eaton nodded. "That's her. She thinks she's flashy, but she's really more trashy and uncultured than Miss Medusa. Big Red's trying to steal business away from our house, even hired a ruffian to prowl outside our place and to discourage gentlemen from partaking of the culture we offer."

"It's good to be wanted," I replied, getting up and stretching. "Do I need to start patrolling outside the fence?"

"Not this early in the day, Mr. Lomax. First thing, though, we need to get you some clothes more befitting an employee of Miss Medusa's. You look too rough for her tastes."

The way I figured it, I was a fiddle and Miss Medusa had viola tastes. But she was paying me. "Then let's get started, Mr. Eaton."

He nodded. "We've got errands to run on the square. Once we get back and the girls come downstairs, I'll introduce you to them all."

I dressed as normal until I reached for my gun belt and knife scabbard. "Just leave them here, Mr. Lomax. They're a little showy for Miss Medusa's tastes. She prefers subtlety."

"I prefer—," I started, but Eaton cut me off.

"It doesn't matter what you prefer, Mr. Lomax, unless you are one of her paying gentlemen."

"Okay, Earl," I answered.

"Mr. Eaton," he corrected.

"I know. I was just showing my rough streak."

Eaton chuckled. After we dressed, we grabbed a couple cold biscuits from the kitchen and headed down Third Street the six blocks to the square. Eaton started me off at a barbershop for a bath, haircut and shave, then took me to a haberdashery to buy me some more cultured clothes, then to a hat shop for a couple derbies and finally to a gunshop.

Every store we stopped in the clerks handled Earl Eaton with more respect than seemed usual for Texas. Fact was, they treated this black man better than they did me, even though I was the customer. When we were done, I had me two derbies, two pairs of striped pants, two broadcloth long coats, two shirts whiter than any I'd ever owned before, a box of shirt collars, two string ties, a pair of suspenders, six pairs of socks, a new pair of store-bought shoes rather than boots and, most importantly, three sets of long johns. With my new duds, I figured I could out strut any peacock within a hundred miles of Waco and perhaps in all of Texas.

At the gunshop, Eaton explained that Miss Medusa wanted me armed discreetly, so I selected a .38-caliber, centerfire five-shot Colt revolver with a three-and-a-half-inch barrel. Rather than a belt to hold it, Eaton pointed to a shoulder harness I should wear under my coat like a gambler. I'd never worn a gun under my arm, but Eaton insisted that was what Miss Medusa would expect. He also insisted on purchasing a Remington rifle cane, a single-shot contraption with an ivory dog head that you unscrewed to load and pulled to cock. A button on the cane shaft served as the trigger.

"Carrying a cane'll make you look like a real gentleman," Eaton said.

"That's what I've always aspired to be, Mr. Eaton."

Eaton added a carton of ammunition for both weapons and concluded our business in the gunshop. As with all our previous purchases, Eaton charged them to Miss Medusa's account and ordered them to be delivered that afternoon, except for the cane. He wanted me to take it back to the place with me so people would know I was becoming a man of distinction, even if I did work at a brothel. I felt like a new man, carrying a fancy cane with a carved head, even if the thing was unloaded.

As we walked back toward Medusa's place, my curiosity got the best of me.

"Those merchants treated you well."

"For a black man, you mean?"

I grimaced. "Yeah, you could put it that way."

"It's all due to Miss Medusa. She told folks she would not do business with any store that didn't give me the respect I was entitled as an educated man."

"That's big of her."

"She takes care of her people, she does, Mr. Lomax. You can depend on that."

"That's good to know."

"On top of that," Eaton continued, "she knows enough dirt on everyone of those businesses to ruin their lives, if she were to tell their wives or their pastors."

"So much for a heart of gold," I said.

"Gold's a metal, Mr. Lomax. Remember that. Too, she don't wear gold on her teeth to show off, like some madams in the business."

We enjoyed the cloudless, clear day walking back to Medusa's place. As we approached the wooden bridge over the creek, a big tough walked toward us from the Reservation. Eaton stiffened and went silent, the conversation dropping like a ton of lead.

I studied the fellow, who stood six or seven inches taller than me with menacing eyes that glared at us over a shaggy mustache. He wore a vest over a stained blue shirt and pants that needed cleaning. Most obvious of all, were the twin revolvers riding menacingly on his hips. I could tell by his stare that he meant trouble.

"He's the gunman that works for Big Red," Eaton whispered.

"Calls himself Bull Bonner."

Seems his name was short a letter. By the look of him he probably should have called himself Bully. It was obvious that Bonner was much less cultured than me. I now understood why Miss Medusa wanted to buy me a new outfit. I wouldn't be interested in lingering in a brothel, no matter the girls, with a tramp like that hanging around. As he reached the bridge, Bonner decided the path he wanted was the one we took. Eaton stepped in front of me and eased to the rail. I wished that my cane was loaded.

Bonner edged toward us. "Don't step in front of a white man, boy," Bonner shouted at Eaton. "Get around behind him."

"No, thank you, sir," Eaton said politely. I knew he must be scared, but he didn't show it.

"You heard me, boy! Do it or I'll give you a beating right here on the bridge."

Bonner looked at me. "You gonna let him steal courtesies from you that rightfully belong to a white man? Or, are you a friend of his?"

I stopped and studied Bonner, figuring that if I could have him assayed for ignorance, I'd've hit the mother lode.

"I never saw this gentleman a day in my life—"

Eaton's eyes widened in fear before I could finish my sentence.

"—until yesterday, but we've become pals since then."

Eaton relaxed, but my words splashed like coal oil on Bonner's flaming stupidity.

Bonner lifted his fist and pointed his trigger finger at my nose. "You know he's a no good ni—"

"There's no difference between you and him, save one," I said.

"What's that?"

"His skin may be black, but his heart isn't, unlike yours."

I think my abstract reasoning confused Bull Bonner because he stood there silent a moment as his trigger finger wilted and his fist fell to his side. "Was that an insult?" he wanted to know.

Eaton grabbed my arm. "Come on, Mr. Lomax, let's get back to Miss Medusa's."

"Was that an insult?"

"No, sir, that was not an insult, merely an observation," I replied, deciding I might as well fight ignorance right now rather than later.

"An insult would be that you are a son of a bitch. See the difference?"

Bonner's face reddened, and he swelled up like a bullfrog with gas. "Them's fighting words." He stepped within reach of me, spread his legs and dropped his hands down toward the grips of his twin revolvers.

Unarmed and with an unloaded cane, I shrugged. "I'm not carrying a gun."

He laughed. "I ain't stupid. You're carrying one of them cane guns that you can fire by pressing a button on the handle."

I squeezed my right hand around the cane's heavy carved handle and considered my options. "You ain't as stupid as you look," I offered.

It took him a moment to consider the insult, then he grumbled. "Don't lift that cane toward me or I'll shoot you."

"Fair enough," I said, then held the cane straight up and offered it to him. He took it, uncertain of my intentions. As his fingers tightened around the head of the cane, I reached for the bottom and grabbed it. Then I pulled the cane from his grip and rested the head on the wooden planks of the bridge. "By holding the business end of my cane, I can't shoot you with it, can I?"

"Why no," he said.

"But I can definitely do this!" I yanked the cane back and swung the head as hard as I could for his groin. The ivory head thudded into his crotch so hard I could hear his jinglebobs rattling around in his dirty pants. Bonner screamed and dropped to his knees, clutching his trousers rather than his revolvers.

Then just as Bonner looked at me with eyes that asked why, I yanked the cane from between his legs, drew it back as far as I could and then swung it in an arc for his chin. It clunked against him with such force that Bonner's eyes rolled upward and he collapsed at my feet, out cold.

Eaton looked at me with newfound respect.

"I can't play the violin or viola," I announced, "but I do play the cane quite well."

"I never saw a caning like that," Eaton responded.

"From now on," I said, "we'll call him Steer Bonner instead of Bull."

Eaton laughed as Bonner began to stir.

While he was still groggy, I leaned over and pulled each revolver from his holster and tossed them into the creek. "Are you ready to go on home, Mr. Eaton?"

"Absolutely, Mr. Lomax!"

We marched away, glancing over our shoulders occasionally to see if Bonner had recovered or if things were still bouncing around in his head. He was still writhing on the bridge when we reached the gate at Miss Medusa's.

Miss Medusa greeted us as we walked in the door. "Good day, gentlemen. Did you get Mr. Lomax fixed up? I can see he's got a haircut and a shave."

"Yes, ma'am," Eaton replied. "Not only did I fix him up, he fixed Mr. Bull Bonner, he did indeed!"

She looked from Eaton to me. "He insulted Mr. Eaton. I left him lying back there on the bridge."

"Dead?"

"No, ma'am," I replied, "just wishing he was."

Eaton grinned and explained the incident to Miss Medusa, who eyed me from head to toe.

"I wasn't sure I'd hired enough man for the job, but I guess I was wrong," she said. "Bonner works for Big Red, who's been causing me trouble for a month and a half."

"What started it?"

"One of her girls came to work for me."

"Seems like that would be fairly routine in your business, girls moving around."

"True, Mr. Lomax, but this was her daughter. She wanted a new start."

"At what?"

"Culture, a little book learning," Medusa replied. "Her mother is rather crude."

"And a crook," added Eaton.

"That's correct, Mr. Lomax. Men have been known to go in her place with a wallet and leave without one or get drugged so they don't know what happened."

"What makes you think Little Red won't do the same thing here?" I asked.

"Unlike her mother, she has a conscience and don't ever call her

Little Red," Medusa said, then turned to her servant. "Mr. Eaton, when will Mr. Lomax's purchases be delivered?"

"By three o'clock," he replied.

"Good. We'll have time to get a few chores done and introduce Mr. Lomax to the girls."

I did what Miss Medusa instructed, though some of it seemed more like woman's work than a respectable occupation, but I liked the idea of having a mattress for bed and a roof over my head for winter.

As the women began to come downstairs, I learned they all had names as odd as Medusa. First strode in big-busted Hestia with soft blue eyes, brown hair and thick lips. She would certainly appeal to men who liked climbing mountains on a feather mattress. For those that preferred a prairie landscape there was flat-chested Demeter, who had a shy, understated beauty about her with golden hair, hazel eyes and a button nose. Next I was introduced to Aphrodite, who was the plainest looking of the girls with no feature that really stood out other than her commonness. Artemis was the tallest of the six girls and the most muscular with black hair, dark eyes and thin lips. Selene was a mulatto with the biggest, softest eyes I'd ever seen on a woman. Finally, I met Hemera, who was striking, but shy with dark auburn hair. I took her to be Little Red.

After introductions, the girls went to the parlor with Miss Medusa where they chatted about books she had given them to read. While they were discussing literature with Miss Medusa, I got Earl Eaton alone in the kitchen.

"Why do the girls have such strange names? I've never heard such before."

Eaton shook his head. "You don't read much, do you?"

"Newspapers when I can get one free."

"You won't find culture in newspapers, Mr. Lomax."

"I'm not looking for culture, but for news."

"Are you familiar with mythology?"

"What?"

"Mythology, you know, the Greek and Roman gods?"

"You mean there's more than one?"

Eaton laughed. "The girls don't work under their real names and Miss Medusa prefers to give them names from mythology, names that sound more civilized than the appellations used in common houses."

"Appalachians? Apple what?" I wanted to know.

"An appellation is a title or a nickname," Eaton answered.

"Well, why didn't you say so to begin with?"

"I did, Mr. Lomax, I did!"

I was beginning to think a cultured man was one who used bigger words any time a smaller one worked just as well. Not only was Mr. Eaton more cultured than me, I was beginning to think he was smarter, at least in things that didn't matter, like mythology. I figured when it came to the only thing that mattered in the rowdy west—survival—I was a cultivated genius as Steer Bonner could attest.

Eaton continued. "Miss Hestia is named for the virgin goddess of home and chastity. Demeter is the goddess of farming, planting and harvesting."

"The goddess of flatlands," I offered, recalling Demeter's rather sparse bosom.

"Miss Medusa has a subtle sense of humor, Mr. Lomax, and it's obvious you have a discerning mind when it is properly educated. Miss Aphrodite is named for the goddess of desire, and pleasure, Miss Medusa believing such a name might help her draw a larger clientele than her looks would on their own. Miss Artemis represents the virgin goddess of the hunt while Miss Selene represents the goddess of the moon. Miss Hemera is named for the goddess of day."

Eaton could've been telling a tale so crazy it would've made a stuffed bird laugh, but the last time I'd honed up on mythology was never so I couldn't challenge him on any foolishness. "Just one question, Mr. Eaton. Is Miss Hemera L-R?"

"L-R?"

"You know, the two words Miss Medusa told me not to say, Little Red."

"Yes, sir, she is, but you better not let Miss Medusa hear you say that."

"I've got another question, Mr. Eaton."

"That being, Mr. Lomax?"

"What's Medusa the goddess of or Minerva? I'm assuming she gave her sister her stage name as well."

Eaton chuckled. "Stage name, that's appropriate. The law in town calls the ladies 'actresses.'"

"I bet they give great performances, but what about Medusa and Minerva?"

"Minerva was the goddess of wisdom," Eaton said.

I was relieved she wasn't the goddess of cutlery.

Eaton continued, "Minerva was a Roman goddess rather than a Greek goddess."

"Like a Methodist god rather than a Baptist god, would you say?"

"You could look at it that way," he answered. "Now as for Medusa she was a monster with a hideous face, poisonous snakes for hair and a gaze that could turn people to stone."

Now in her profession, I could see the advantage of being able to harden some parts of gentlemen visitors, but I shuddered to think of a woman having snakes for hair, especially after my close encounter with Bat Masterson's rattlesnake. "Not the goddess of nice," I replied.

Eaton nodded, "No, but it gets a message across to the cultured, at least, not to challenge Miss Medusa in her business. Now we best find something constructive to do."

I figured I'd already done plenty, having put Steer Bonner in his place, but Eaton had other ideas and ordered me to sweep the kitchen floor, which I did. My purchases arrived mid-afternoon, as promised. The clothes were fancier than any I'd ever worn, so much so that Mr. Eaton had to help dress me and show me how to knot my tie. Then he assisted me as I shoved my arms in my shoulder harness and adjusted it for my new pistol. After I had loaded my pistol, Eaton helped me on with my coat.

When he was done dressing me, Eaton stepped back, put his hands on his hips and admired me. "You clean up well for an uncultured man, Mr. Lomax. You no longer look like you ran through the poorhouse to get dressed!"

Earl Eaton's insults were amusing me now because he didn't mean anything by them, just his way of expressing himself. He offered me my cane, which I accepted without loading it. I didn't like the idea of walking around with a loaded cane. When he took me out and paraded me in front of Miss Medusa and all the girls, they offered dainty applause. Little Red even whistled.

"Now, now, Miss Hemera," chided Miss Medusa. "A lady doesn't whistle. It's unbecoming."

"Yes, ma'am," Hemera said shyly.

"Gentlemen, if you will resume your chores," Miss Medusa said, "the ladies and I will continue our discussion on literature."

"Yes, ma'am," Eaton and I said in unison.

As we stepped out of the parlor, Eaton pointed toward the broom in the kitchen. "Why don't you sweep the leaves off the front porch before any callers arrive?"

"Sure thing," I answered, exchanging my cane for the broom and walking out the front door. As I began to sweep up the leaves in my fancy clothes, I realized I was doing woman's work after all. What had I gotten myself into?

Chapter Six

Even if I'd gone to college like my momma wanted, I wouldn't have gotten as strong an education as I did working and rooming with Earl Eaton over the ensuing weeks. He had more smarts than a library full of professors and the common sense that the higher educated class never had, like how to hammer a nail or come in out of the rain. So, I learned about mythology and American history when I wasn't working and about human nature and the finer things in life, such as wine, when I was. For instance, I learned there were two types of wine—red and white—and more types of whiskey than I could count or taste in a lifetime, though I vowed to try. Grapes just didn't stack up to corn, barley or rye when it came to making a drink a man could enjoy.

When we had guests, I worked the bar just off the parlor for Miss Medusa, who insisted on providing undiluted drinks to her clients, unlike other bar proprietors I later worked for who would put almost anything in a drink to dilute it and increase profits. Of course, whenever patrons bought drinks for the girls, I served them watered down glasses as Miss Medusa insisted that the girls always be sober enough to serve the gentlemen and to protect themselves in case a client turned rowdy. Miss Medusa served a subdued clientele of clerks, merchants, drummers, proprietors and cattlemen who had outgrown their rowdy days. Miss Medusa also demanded that the girls treat the gentlemen with respect, no matter their looks or their manliness, what the madam called their virility.

Perhaps the most important lesson I learned was that Steer Bonner was out to get me. Three or four times a night as long as gentlemen were under Miss Medusa's roof, I would slip outside and check the premises, looking for Bonner and other signs of ignorance. Occasionally, I spotted his hulking form in the shadows. I would either pull my pistol from under my armpit or take my unloaded cane and thump it against the fence or the side of the house, reminding him of our first meeting and how an unloaded cane can cause more pain than a loaded one.

One night about six weeks after I started working for Miss Medusa, I went out back and spied Bonner crouching down behind the big tree in the front yard. I pulled my gun and got as close to him as I could before the rustling sound of leaves beneath my shoes caught his ear. He shot up and turned around.

"I've got my gun pointed at your heart and my cane in reserve, Steer," I said.

"It's Bull," he corrected.

"Not if the memory of our first meeting is correct. You quit skulking around Miss Medusa's or I'll re-introduce you to my cane. It can hurt you, loaded or not."

"You owe me, Lomax," he countered. "Before we met I had a matched pair of—"

"Jinglebobs, was it?"

"—pistols," he said. "Nickel-plated revolvers and you threw them in the creek. I ain't been able to afford replacements since. I'll either get the money from you or waylay one of your madam's rich customers one night after the gentleman heads back home to the missus."

"Get back to your place, Steer."

"It's Bull, dammit! Big Red wants her daughter back. Only thing that's kept me from burning Medusa's place to the ground is knowing her daughter is there."

"She goes by Miss Hemera now," I said.

"Herrera, why'd she get a Mexican name?"

"It's He-MER-a, not Herrera."

"Huh?"

"Hemera, the goddess of daylight! Don't you know anything?" I asked. It was obvious Bonner had been born ignorant and lost ground every day since. "You best skedaddle, Steer, before my trigger finger or my cane hand starts twitching." I waved my gun. "Now go on."

Bonner slipped from behind the tree and toward the gate in the wrought iron fence, just as two gentlemen approached from the direction of the square. Bonner lifted the latch and pushed the gate open. As he stepped past the gate, he turned to the two approaching men. "Look how this place treats customers," he said. "If you want to be cared for like gentlemen, then you need to visit Big Red's at the end of the street."

"No, thank you," said the first one.

"We're on business, not pleasure," said the second.

As Bonner stomped away, I slid the gun back into my shoulder harness. "Welcome to Miss Medusa's, gentlemen. Six ladies named for the goddesses of old, just waiting to worship at your altar."

"It's business, not pleasure," the second one repeated.

"At Miss Medusa's, they're one and the same," I said as I held the gate for them. After they passed, I shut the gate and followed them up to the porch.

"We need to see Medusa. This is her place, isn't it?" asked the first.

"We've business with her," said the second.

"This is Miss Medusa's. Most callers have business with her girls. I don't believe Miss Medusa is taking new callers."

"She will us," said the first. "My name is Douglas Wolfe."

At least he wasn't a coyote, I thought.

"And I'm Brian Dreban. We're telegraphers."

"Not familiar with that religion," I replied.

"No, no," said Wolfe, "that's our trade."

"We work the telegraph key for the Waco and Northwestern Railroad, a tap line that connects Waco with the Houston and Texas Central Railway and the rest of these United States, all thirty-seven of them," said Dreban.

"We sling Morse!" Wolfe said.

"Pound brass!" Dreban added.

"Fling lightning!" Wolfe interjected.

"Punch poles! Slam 'grams!" Dreban continued

"Okay, fellows, I get it. You send telegrams. You're pretty proud of your occupation."

"Beats punching cattle or shooting buffalo or robbing banks," Wolfe said.

I felt like I had to defend my current profession, if not my previous ones. "Not as good as working in a whorehouse."

"It's better," Dreban said, "because it's the future."

I was beginning to wonder if these guys even knew what a woman was or if they were too busy slinging Morse, pounding brass, flinging lightning, punching poles or slamming 'grams to care about the finer things in life. They probably didn't know there were red and white wines.

As we stepped inside to the light of the parlor, I got a good look at them. Both were about my height but a little younger. Wolfe was sandy-haired, clean shaven and bright-eyed, especially when he talked about telegraphy. Equally enthusiastic about his profession, Dreban sported a thick head of black hair, a well trimmed goatee and a perfect nose that looked like it had never been in a fight. They each wore white shirts with a garter on their right arms, black pants, black suspenders, conductor's hats and shoes that showed they spent more time polishing them than chasing after women named for goddesses. They had the confident stance of men with a respectable degree of formal education.

When I closed the door behind us, I introduced myself. "I'm H.H. Lomax," I said and extended my hand. The two men reciprocated, I grabbed Dreban's first and shook it vigorously.

"Not so hard," he said. "That's the hand that presses the telegraph key."

I nodded, then shook Wolfe's hand as limply as an old lady. "That's the way we prefer a handclasp," Wolfe said. "It saves our fingers for the future."

I waved my hand toward the parlor where Miss Medusa arose from her seat and glided over to greet her new customers.

Both men took off their caps.

"Greetings, gentlemen. I'm Miss Medusa and allow me to introduce you to four of our ladies. Two are already upstairs entertaining, though I might say their gentlemen consorts are nowhere as handsome as you."

"That's okay," said Wolfe, "we came—"

Before he could finish, Medusa pointed to the available quartet and introduced them and their wares. "This is Miss Artemis, who is most robust should you be interested in a vigorous experience," Medusa began, each girl standing up and curtsying with a smile as she was announced. "Should you be looking for gold, you'll find none purer than in the hair and heart of Miss Demeter. Remember what they say, second-hand gold is as good as new. Miss Selene possesses charms that are as exotic as her home of New Orleans. And finally, you will not find a bigger heart or other attributes anywhere than with Miss Hestia."

Wolfe and Dreban stood there, gap-jawed and wide-eyed like their fingers might find something more enjoyable to play with than a telegraph key.

"Thank you, ma'am," said Wolfe, who reached into his pocket and pulled out a yellow envelope. "We have a telegram for you."

"Collect," Dreban added.

"How much?" Medusa asked.

"Fifty cents," Wolfe answered.

"Just a moment, gentlemen." Medusa retreated into the kitchen and returned with a dollar bill, which she offered to Wolfe. "Keep the change for bringing this after hours."

Wolfe exchanged the envelope for the greenback. It was the only moment in my time working at the brothel that I ever saw a man depart with more money than he arrived with.

Medusa ripped open the envelope and read the message. Worry crawled across her expression, her eyes narrowing and her lips tightening into a grimace.

"Shall we wait a moment, ma'am?" Dreban asked.

A slight nod was the only answer she gave before retreating from the parlor upstairs to her room. She returned shortly with a handful of cash, then counted out $250 to Wolfe.

"Please," she said, "wire that to Fort Worth." She then gave him another five dollars. "This should more than cover the cost of the response. Save the balance for any collect wires again so you can bring them to me immediately."

The girls inched toward Medusa, their eyes clouded with concern and uncertainty. "What's the matter?" Demeter asked softly.

"It's Minerva," Medusa said, "she's moved to Fort Worth."

It struck me odd that a move to Fort Worth could create such a calamity. Though I'd never been to Fort Worth, it had to be an improvement over Fort Griffin if for no other reason than the Fort Worth folks likely took more baths.

Then Miss Medusa spoke softly. "Minerva has been accused of stabbing a fellow. She needs money for a lawyer, especially if he dies." Medusa paused and looked at me.

If the fellow called her Skinny Minnie, I suspect he wished he was dead, especially if she went after her usual target.

"Mr. Lomax, would you please accompany these gentlemen back to their office. I would hate for anything to happen to them, especially when they are carrying the money that my sister desperately needs."

"Yes, ma'am," I answered, then turned to Wolfe and Dreban. "Whenever you're ready."

They nodded to Medusa and her girls. When they turned around, I feared they might trip over their tongues from the scenery, which was a lot more fleshy around my place of business than the telegraph office where they fondled an electric key connected to a copper wire. As we stepped outside, the men replaced their caps and I tucked my cane under my arm as I closed the door behind me.

"You don't really need to accompany us," said Dreban.

"Yeah," said Wolfe, "whenever we carry money for the company, whether it's handling cash for customers or taking deposits to the bank, we always travel in pairs for extra security."

"Are you armed?" I asked as we started toward the square.

"Well, no," said Dreban.

"Company policy only allows payroll guards and railroad detectives to go armed. We don't want our passengers to think railroad travel is unsafe," Wolfe said.

"You just want them to believe their money is unsafe. Miss Medusa's policy may be wiser than your railroad's."

"Policy is policy," Dreban said. "You can't run a big company without knowing what the rules are."

"Nor who the fools are," I suggested.

Both telegraphers laughed.

"You said your name was Lomax, didn't you?" Dreban asked.

"Yeah."

"You any kin to the Lomax that stuck thirty pieces of Adams New York Chewing gum in Wild Bill Hickok's hair while he slept? Took him a week to remove all the gum and he was half bald when he did. You that Lomax?"

"Nope, must be another Lomax."

"I didn't figure you'd know him," Wolfe said.

"Didn't say I don't know him. Just denied sticking chewing gum in his hair."

"You know him?" Dreban asked in disbelief.

"Know him? I taught him how to draw and keep from shooting himself in the foot."

"No," said Wolfe. "You're funning us."

"I don't fun about Wild Bill, and he don't fun about me, at least not where I can find out about it."

"If you know him so well," Dreban asked, "how come you aren't mentioned in any of his dime novels?"

"Let's just say you shouldn't believe everything you read. Besides that, Wild Bill and I didn't part on such good terms."

As we reached the square, I could tell Dreban and Wolfe thought I was crazier than a drunk preacher at a temperance meeting. But I didn't believe in telling lies to make myself look bigger or more important. I only lied when I had to get my tail out of a crack. At the square we turned east on Bridge Street and headed for the suspension bridge. As I had never crossed the bridge before, I was looking forward to the experience of getting on the other side of the Brazos without getting my feet wet. However, that was before I met the toll collector.

Stepping to the toll booth, Dreban and Wolfe flashed passes that allowed them to cross. When I stepped up, the toll collector eyed me. "That'll be a nickel."

"I'm just guarding these men with the railroad. They're unarmed and carrying a substantial amount of money," I informed the squinty-eyed fellow who looked jaundiced in the yellow glow of the coal oil lamp that lit his tiny fiefdom.

"If your friends are carrying so much money, perhaps they can afford to pay your way," the toll collector pointed out.

Dreban and Wolfe stared in amusement as I argued. Two men on horseback rode up.

"Step aside," the toll keeper demanded, "so I can let paying customers pass. That'll be a dime for rider and horse." Each rider edged his mount to the booth, leaned over and paid the little fellow a dime, then resumed his crossing.

"Okay," I said, offering to make peace. "A nickel round trip, right?"

"No," the uppity little jackass replied. "A nickel each way."

"I'm just escorting them to the train station. That's all. It's over and back. Don't need to stay, don't care to stay, just got to make sure they get there safely. You wouldn't want it on your conscience if these two railroad men got waylaid between here and the station, would you? If they got robbed of all their money, now would you?"

The little squirt spit out the window, just missing my arm.

"Fellow, I don't care what happens to the two as they ain't causing me any trouble. You got three options. Pay the toll, swim the river or sprout wings and fly."

A line of folks afoot, on horseback and in wagons was forming behind me.

Wolfe and Dreban just stood there laughing, when I finally reached in my pocket and pulled out a quarter. I slapped it down in front of the collector. "There's a quarter."

"Now you can pass."

"What about my change? I gave you a quarter."

"I don't have any change for a coin that big."

"What? I just saw you take two dimes. That's all the change I need."

The jackass laughed. "All the change I need is for you to move along."

The folks behind me growled. "Get moving, fellow. You're holding up the line," screamed one matron. For her sake, I hoped when she met her maker that there wasn't a line at St. Peter's gate or she might be sent to a warmer climate after an outburst like that.

I moved on, even though I was twenty cents poorer than I should've been. Wolfe and Dreban kept laughing.

"You're a tough hombre, Lomax, paying five times the rate to cross the bridge," Dreban informed me.

"No wonder you and Wild Bill left on such bad terms," Wolfe added.

I thought about showing them what I could do with an unloaded cane, but passed on the idea as they had done nothing more than rile me a little. "If I had a pass like you do, this never would've happened."

Wolfe nodded. "If you worked for the railroad instead of a whorehouse, you might have a pass."

"I hope Miss Medusa doesn't let you keep her books or hers might be the first brothel ever to go broke," Dreban continued.

"Yeah, Lomax, if you ever decide to start robbing banks, remember the object is to leave the bank with more money than you went in with," Wolfe noted.

Both fellows laughed so hard I thought they would fall down before we reached the railroad station and climbed the steps up to the platform. I escorted them as far as their office, dreading my return trip across the bridge.

"My work is done, getting you fellows safely here with Miss Medusa's money," I said. "Time to head home."

Dreban laughed, reached into his pocket and extracted his hand. "Here's a nickel so you can get back without getting wet."

I took the coin. "Thanks, gentlemen, and good night. I hope never to have to cross the suspension bridge again." I turned and walked away, thinking I'd never see the two of them again, much less the east side of the Brazos River. But I was wrong. Without Douglas Wolfe and Brian Dreban, I would never have met that bastard George Armstrong Custer.

Chapter Seven

In the days that followed my first meeting with Douglas Wolfe, Brian Dreban and the toll collector, I went about my duties of fixing drinks for Miss Medusa's gentlemen customers, guarding the place from Steer Bonner's bad intentions and cleaning up the place as necessary—though it galled me to be doing woman's work. At least I didn't have to cook or wash dishes, though I did have to help tote the bedding to the laundry. The thing I learned most about running a brothel was that laundry bills could break you, at least if you ran a respectable place.

The more I worked for her, the more Miss Medusa began to trust me, especially when she saw that I could tend bar without drinking any wine or whiskey behind her back. Though I had no taste for wine, the whiskey posed a temptation, but I managed never to take a nip. It was the right thing to do, especially if I wanted a roof over my head and a soft bed for the rest of me come winter. My pay began to come in, minus the cost of the clothes and arms she had bought me. As I didn't have many expenses or wants beyond what Miss Medusa was providing me, I was saving more money than I ever had in my life. After a couple months, Miss Medusa trusted me enough to make her regular weekly deposits at the bank on the square. With Big Red talking revenge and Steer Bonner always lurking down the street, Miss Medusa felt safer with me making the bank deposits, especially when she had large sums of money, which was almost every week. It seems the fine, pious men of Waco were dropping their dollars in more than just church collection plates.

While Steer Bonner was a hovering menace, he seemed more intent on steering our potential customers to Big Red's place than on attacking me or the house. Miss Medusa, though, feared Big Red might order him to hurt one of the girls or burn the place down. As I explained to Miss Medusa, as long as Miss Hemera worked for us, Bonner wouldn't do anything that might harm her. On those occasions when Miss Hemera left the house, she was instructed to let me know so I could be especially watchful for trouble. I spent a lot of time walking around our place or watching the men that frequented Big Red's down the street.

One late afternoon as the autumn chill was beginning to set in, I happened to notice a smallish fellow leaving Big Red's and heading down the street toward me. What caught my eye was he was carrying a fishing pole. As he neared, I thought I recognized him. I clenched my jaw. It was the little toll taker that had cheated me out of twenty cents, I was certain. He was walking as carefree as any son of a bitch that had just had the starch wrung out of his pecker. I fought the urge to yank my revolver and plug the thief right there, but thought such action might diminish Miss Medusa's trust in me.

I slipped quickly in the door and spotted Little Red starting up the stairs. "Miss Hemera," I said, "could you step outside with me for a moment?"

"Why, Mr. Lomax?" she asked. "If it's my mother, I don't want to talk to her."

"No, no," I said. "Hurry before he passes. There's someone I want to see if you know."

Nodding, Miss Hemera stepped with me out on the front porch.

"See that fellow with the fishing pole? Do you know him?"

"Yeah," she said. "I don't want him to see me." Hemera jumped back inside the door.

I followed her into the parlor, where Miss Medusa was visiting with Aphrodite and Demeter. "Tell me."

"His name's Nathan Quirt," Hemera began.

Miss Medusa turned quickly around, her eyes narrowing. "He's not bothering you again is he, honey?"

"No, ma'am. Mr. Lomax just wanted to know who he was."

"He's a skunk is who he is," Medusa said. "He's mean to girls, slaps them around."

Hemera nodded. "He's why I left momma's. She said I had to entertain him. I didn't care for his meanness."

Medusa nodded. "Some say he pays for his habit either by swindling the bridge company or overcharging folks, rigs and livestock crossing the bridge."

I could confirm the overcharging rumor. "What about the fishing pole?"

"He works different shifts," Hemera started. "When he works days, he'll take his cane pole and tell his wife he's going fishing before supper."

"A wife?" I asked.

"And seven kids," Medusa interjected. "Five boys and two girls."

"All hellions," said Hemera, "probably because he beats them like he does the girls he pays for. I couldn't take it, the bruises, the humiliation. What hurt most of all, Momma was more interested in his business than in me." As Hemera began to cry, Aphrodite and Demeter gathered around, hugging her.

Medusa stepped to her and kissed her auburn hair, speaking softly. "You don't have to worry about that now, honey. Miss Medusa will protect you."

"As will Mr. Lomax," I said, feeling odd calling myself mister.

Hemera slipped from the grasp of the girls and Medusa and came over to give me a hug. "Thank you," she said.

I apologized, too. "I didn't know or I would've never asked you to identify him. Since he was coming out of your momma's place, I just thought—"

"I know," she said. "I know."

By the time she released me, Earl Eaton and the other girls had entered the parlor to see what the commotion was all about.

"Hemera spotted Nathan Quirt," Medusa explained.

Hestia, Artemis and Selene gasped and shook their heads. They, too, gathered around Hemera and offered their support.

"Thank you," she said, "but I'm fine with Miss Medusa and Mr. Lomax to protect me."

Eaton stepped to the back table and picked up his violin, as I now knew to call it. He grabbed the bow and began to saw out a lively rendition of "Camptown Races."

"That's not violin music, that's fiddle music," I said. The girls laughed as did Eaton while he danced around the parlor with his violin.

Medusa said, "Mr. Eaton can entertain us and Mr. Lomax can protect us. With them around, all I have to worry about is Minerva and her legal problems."

And, she didn't have to worry about me. Just as I had never sampled her liquor over the two months I'd worked for Medusa, neither had I tried out the wares of any of her girls. It's not that I found them ugly. Fact was, they were pretty, both in body and in spirit. It was just that I had come to view them more as sisters than harlots. I'm certain Miss Medusa came to trust me more because I didn't try to take advantage of the girls. We were laughing and enjoying Mr. Eaton's fiddle-playing when a knock on the door stopped the merriment. A gentleman was calling so everyone had to stop dancing and play their roles. Maybe the girls were indeed actresses, if that's what the law wanted to call them, because they handled their parts in life with gentility and class, as long as their gentlemen reciprocated.

That evening things returned to normal as much as they could in a bawdy house, especially when the madam was worried sick about her sister's legal troubles in Fort Worth. Try as she could, Medusa could get no information about Minerva. When she learned one client a couple evenings later was from Fort Worth, she offered him fifty dollars if he would check the jail, courthouse and newspapers in Fort Worth for word on Minerva. The fellow agreed to help out and took her money. Medusa never heard back from him. She sent money by post to a Fort Worth newspaper for a mail subscription. When the sporadic issues of the paper began arriving, she read them assiduously in search of information but nothing came of that either. Fact was, Minerva might have changed her actress name to something else, a common practice of women who moved from town to town in her profession. I even volunteered to go to Fort Worth and search for Minerva. After all, unlike her client who spawned the telegram, I had not only met Minerva, but also survived that encounter in one piece with all my danglers intact. I even promised Medusa that she would get a return on whatever she invested in me for the Fort Worth journey.

"You're too valuable here, Mr. Lomax. I fear losing you more than not finding my sister, as she may be a lost soul. You, at least, are salvageable."

I was flattered, I thought, but the mystery of Minerva hung like a shroud over the place. That night after all the gentlemen had returned to their loving homes, and I had locked the house up, I went into my room where Eaton was lying on his bed reading another book.

"I'm worried about, Miss Medusa," he said. "She hasn't been herself since we got that telegram from Fort Worth."

"I don't see much difference in her," I said, as I undressed and climbed into bed.

"You haven't known her as long as I have. Minerva's problems have been weighing her down. I've been praying about it."

I sat up in bed and stared at Eaton, not quite sure how to take the idea of an educated black man praying in a brothel. "I always thought you was too smart to have to pray."

"No man's that smart. I study a lot of books, including the Good Book." He held up the book he was reading. I saw Holy Bible printed in gold across the front of it.

"I'll be damned," I said. "A Bible in a whorehouse."

"That's not a cultured thing to say, Mr. Lomax. Besides, we've all sinned and fallen short."

By my way of thinking, I'd probably fallen farther than any man since the Garden of Eden had been fenced off with barbed wire and posted with no trespassing signs. For some of the awful things I'd done, like listening to a Republican give a stump speech, I figured the devil himself had already placed a brand on my hips and claimed me for one of his herd. Problem was, it was always easier to do wrong than to stay right, or righteous, for that matter. I didn't feel particularly righteous working in a whorehouse as I know my momma and my sisters would've been ashamed. Even so, I never felt better about myself, helping and even protecting these girls who might not have been dealt a winning hand in life.

"Even Miss Medusa and most of the girls read the Bible, Mr. Lomax. It don't matter where you start out in life, but rather where you end up. That's how I read the Good Book."

"My momma used to read the Bible to us kids back in Cane Hill, Arkansas, but I ain't read much of the Bible or any other book since, Mr. Eaton."

"It'd do you some good, Mr. Lomax, it'd do you some good. The Bible can save you from yourself and from death."

"I won't argue with you, Mr. Eaton, but right now you're saving me from sleep. Good night."

He didn't say another thing, but I watched him out of the corner of my eye as he put his Bible down and got up out of bed. He went to his trunk and opened it up, pulling out a quilt. He brought it over to my bed and laid it over my feet. "My bones tell me it's gonna turn cold, that we're gonna have our first freeze shortly. You might need a little extra cover, if you don't mind using a black man's quilt."

"No, sir, Mr. Eaton I don't mind at all. Thank you."

He retreated to his bed, picked up his Bible and resumed reading.

I was still awake when he blew out the lamp. I wished I could've gone to sleep right off, but Eaton's words kept bothering me. Even when I did go to sleep, I was as restless as a herd of longhorns with thunderstorms on the horizon. Religious talk always made me nervous.

Eaton's blanket came in handy come morning because a norther did blow in. We put wood in the fireplace and in the stoves on both floors and gradually warmed the house. Throughout the day Miss

Medusa kept going to the windows, watching the sky and commenting that the weather was bound to get better and clear off. Despite her expectation, the day grew grayer and colder. That afternoon about a half-hour before closing time on the square, she came to me with the money pouch she took to the bank whenever she was ready to make a deposit.

"Mr. Lomax, I'm sorry to ask this of you so late in the day, but could you run this to the bank and deposit it in my account? I kept thinking the weather would clear and I would do it myself. I don't like to leave this much money around with all the fires going. You never know when the house might burn down. I'd hate to lose the money with everything else in a house fire when I could keep it safe in the bank's vault."

I didn't mind going to the bank, even in the cold. Maybe the chill would even out the warmer climes that seemed my destiny after my bedtime theological conversation with Eaton. "The walk'd do me good." I took the pouch from her and retreated to my room to get my derby and cane.

As I returned and passed her, Medusa stopped me. "Don't you have a heavy coat?"

I shrugged. "This dress coat is all I got."

"Well, we'll need to get you a winter coat soon. I can't have you out in the cold and risk catching sickness."

"I'll manage," I said, reaching for the door knob.

"Hold it," called Eaton. "Take this." He held up the quilt he had let me borrow the night before. Even in the gray light of a somber day, I could see it much better than the night before. It was old and worn threadbare, so much so that the batting stuck out in places.

Medusa lifted her hand to her mouth in surprise, then shook her head. "You're letting him take your mother's quilt?" she asked. "Are you sure?"

"Yes, ma'am, I'm sure."

Medusa kept shaking her head. "You take good care of that quilt, Mr. Lomax. It's the only thing Mr. Eaton has to remember his mother by. She was a slave when she made it. It's what she wrapped him in when she escaped Tennessee and made it to freedom in Ohio."

I took the quilt from him, doubled it over and wrapped it around my shoulders. "Thank you, Mr. Eaton." I was touched. I didn't have a thing of my mother's and didn't know what else to say. "I best be going so I make it to the bank before it closes."

The door rattled as I stepped outside, and the wind slapped me in the face. I was glad to have the heirloom as the low clouds spit occasional slivers of sleet at me. I lifted the quilt over my derby and marched to Third Street, crossed the creek bridge and approached the square. The streets were virtually deserted and some stores had closed early as the weather had worsened. From the north side of the square, I looked across to the south where I saw Brian Dreban and Douglas Wolfe, striding down the walk like they were headed toward the bank as well. I called out to them but my shout died in the brisk wind.

Just as I was about to call out again, I saw a hulking figure jump out of a narrow passage between a mercantile store and the bank. The assailant pointed two revolvers at the telegraphers. The two telegraphers raised their hands, then followed the motion of his gun toward the alleyway from which he had emerged. Once Wolfe and Dreban backed into the shadows between buildings, the masked man moved in behind them. I bolted toward them.

I ran as fast as I could, the noise of my footfall blown away in the wind gusts. I slowed when I reached the walk and eased toward the alleyway, ever careful not to drop Eaton's quilt.

"Give me the money," growled the robber, who seemed to tower over Wolfe and Dreban, their escape blocked by a fence at the opposite end of the alley. Their assailant stood with his legs spread almost as wide as the narrow passage. "Boys, I ain't a patient man. I know you're carrying money, now give it to me," he said. "You two only travel together when you're carrying money or visiting Medusa's whorehouse."

I caught my breath when I realized I was slipping up behind Steer Bonner. I should've shot him, but didn't want the expense of a lawyer to clear my good name. Besides I had my cane with me. I let the quilt slip down to my shoulders, then eased toward my ignorant and evidently deaf friend who did not hear my heavy breath as I drew within striking distance. I slid my hand down the barrel of cane until I could grab it by the muzzle.

"This is the railroad's money," Wolfe explained. "You steal it and the railroad detectives will come after you and send you to prison."

Bonner laughed. "The railroad's got so much money they'll never miss it."

"We can identify you. You're the one we saw at Medusa's place," Dreban replied.

"You won't identify me if you're dead."

I don't know if Wolfe and Dreban saw me or not, but they stood there like they were either bulletproof or not afraid to meet their maker on a cold, gray day in Waco.

"You can get shot now or drop the money and live a few seconds longer." Bonner waved his gun at Dreban. "You better drop your money bag."

Dreban nodded. That's when I think he saw me. He tossed his money bag on the ground in front of Bonner.

As Bonner holstered his right-hand pistol, I twisted slightly toward my right so I could draw back my arm and get plenty of leverage with my swing. When Bonner bent over to pick up the money, I swung my cane with the force of a tornado so that the head plowed into his crotch.

Bonner screamed.

I re-cocked my cane and swung it again, just to make sure both of his danglers received an education on the fine art of being a gentleman. Bonner must've understood my lesson because he didn't ask a single question, just collapsing on his face instead and groaning at the unfairness of life that some men were born to great wealth and others to poverty, that some men could stroll away from this alley in great health and others couldn't take a single step without their jinglebobs telegraphing pain and nausea throughout their bodies. Yep, life was unfair like that.

"Damn," said Dreban, "I almost feel sorry for the guy."

Wolfe nudged him. "Let's get the money and get to the bank."

"Thanks, Lomax," said Dreban as he and Wolfe nudged Bonner over so they could retrieve the railroad money bag.

Bonner moaned, somewhere between life and death, likely preferring the latter for the time being.

"Get his revolvers, too," I instructed. "He's apt to be a might sore when he comes to."

Both telegraphers jumped over him as I backed out of the narrow passage. When I reached the walk, they joined me. Both gave me one of Bonner's guns. I stuck them in my trousers, then pointed toward the bank. "We better hurry before it closes."

The three of us scurried down the walk, reaching the bank with five minutes to spare. The bank clerks didn't look pleased to see us so near closing time on a cold windy day when they knew it would take a spell to count and confirm our deposits.

As we waited on the tellers, Dreban looked at me and the quilt. "You always carry your bedding with you?"

"I didn't have a heavy coat handy."

Wolfe shook his head. "I thought the pay would be more in your line of work."

"Not always," I answered, "but there are other advantages that make up for lesser wages. I can name you six benefits right now, Aphrodite, Demeter—"

"We get it," Dreban said, his words dripping with jealousy.

"Named after Greek goddesses, is that right?" Wolfe interjected.

"That's what they tell me. Though I've never been to Greece, I have seen six Waco goddess in the altogether. I tell you, I've never seen a telegraph key that could compare, but I'm not as intelligent as you boys. Perhaps I'm wrong."

My teller finished first. Medusa's deposit was almost seven hundred and ninety dollars, all cash. The railroad and telegraph deposits were several thousand dollars more than would've gone on the railroad account had I not happened along. Not only that, Wolfe and Dreban saved on funeral expenses, thanks to me. Way I figured it, Double Steer Bonner was still back in the alley tallying up the cost to him.

"We're more obliged than we can ever repay," Wolfe said.

"Anything we can do for you?" Dreban said.

"We could take you to supper, buy you a meal," Wolfe offered.

"That's when business picks up at Miss Medusa's."

"How about lunch? We can offer you lunch instead. Surely you don't have customers at lunch time," Dreban said.

"That's a possibility," I said with a kicker, "assuming the girls don't mind. They like a little frisky play in the afternoon to get them warmed up for business later."

"Really?" Dreban said. "All of them?"

"No, boys, just one at a time."

"Damn," Wolfe said. "Why don't we come to your place for lunch?"

"There's just not enough to go around for all three of us," I replied.

"Apparently not," said Dreban, "when one of us is filling his plate and passing empty bowls to the rest of us."

"How about lunch day after tomorrow? Surely, this weather will have broken by then."

They looked at each other, then nodded.

"Sounds good," Wolfe said.

Dreban said, "We'll bring a buggy by to pick you up."

"Sounds good," I said.

"One more thing," Wolfe added. "Leave your cane at Miss Medusa's."

"It's not loaded."

"Doesn't matter. It makes us nervous anyway."

We walked out of the bank together, then parted to our separate ways. It was the start of a friendship that led me to the Little Bighorn.

Chapter Eight

Scurrying through the cold, I returned to Miss Medusa's place, stopping atop the creek bridge to dump two more of Steer Bonner's revolvers in the waters. The pistols landed with a splat, the sound reminding me of my caning Bonner in the groin and instilling in him a greater appreciation of the Eighth Commandment that thou shall not steal. If I had to keep giving Bonner religious lessons, I was going to fill the creek with all his weapons I discarded there. Back at the house, I returned with thanks Eaton's quilt no worse for the adventure, then gave Medusa the receipt on the deposit and explained how I had saved the telegraphers. She seemed delighted that I was able to put Bonner in his place, which was apparently on his knees clutching his cap-and-ball pistol. I asked if I could take off for lunch with Wolfe and Dreban in two days. She said sure, that I probably needed a break, and cautioned me to be discreet about my departures so Bonner wouldn't notice my absence and come calling. I informed her that Bonner would be walking gingerly for a spell, and the girls ought to be able to outrun him if he approached. She just laughed.

With weather bad the next two nights, business was slow with only one gentleman visitor that night and three the next. The first night the girls sat around the parlor near the fireplace, talking about their childhoods, reading books that Medusa suggested or visiting with me. They were all fine girls, each with a heartbreaking story about a hard family life, a love lost, a drunken father or a streak of meanness in a lover.

"You ever have a girlfriend?" Selene asked me.

I nodded. "LouAnne Burke back in Cane Hill, Arkansas." I shrugged, letting her know I couldn't really talk about it. She reached over and patted my hand softly as if she knew the pain of love lost. Thinking of LouAnne, I wondered what she might be doing some nine years after I had abandoned home—and her—in the wake of the War Between the States. It wasn't that I wanted to leave her, but in the aftermath of the hard feelings brought on by the war, some of the fine folks in Washington County were trying to kill me. I feared she might get hurt so I left home without her and never wrote to explain. LouAnne was the most decent female I was ever around, save for my momma and sisters. I should've written her, but I never knew what to say. I squirmed in my chair, uncomfortable with the memories that kept flooding back and misting my eyes. Selene just sat there, silently patting my hand.

My sadness seemed to infect the rest of the girls until Earl Eaton walked in, looked around and shook his head. "My, my, if this isn't a pitiful group," he said, picking up one of his stringed instruments. "We need to liven things up with a little fiddle music."

"Violin music, Mr. Eaton," I corrected.

Eaton shook his head. "No, sir, Mr. Lomax. Tonight, it's a fiddle because we need some spirited music to bring a few smiles. I've seen happier funerals." With the magic of the bow and his fingers, Eaton began to saw out some catchy popular tunes by American songwriters rather than those somber songs by European composers with names I could never spell nor pronounce.

After an hour of Eaton's magic, we were mostly smiles and laughter. We talked and joked, well after our only gentleman caller left that evening, retreating into the howling cold. As we were breaking up to go to bed, Medusa grabbed me by the arm.

"Tomorrow, Mr. Lomax, I want you to go back to the square and buy a heavy coat. This one's on me."

"Thank you, ma'am. That's generous of you."

"And one other thing, Mr. Lomax. I'll have a letter you can mail at the post office. Would you do that?"

"Certainly."

"I wrote a friend in the business that's supposed to be working in Fort Worth now, asking her to check on Minerva, see if she can find out anything." Medusa's worry over Minerva had grown, especially since she couldn't find out anything.

"If you don't mind, Miss Medusa, after I take care of our business, I'd like to cross the river and see Mr. Wolfe and Mr. Dreban. I'll tell them to pick me up out back by the stable where it's less likely Steer Bonner will observe."

She laughed.

"What's so funny?"

"You calling him Steer instead of Bull."

Come the next morning, I left the place with two nickels, my derby, my cane and the letter, which I mailed before walking over to the haberdashery where Miss Medusa kept an account. I selected a functional coat that would get me through a Texas winter, rather than the heavier ones the clerk recommended. The heavy coats were good, but started at four dollars, and I figured a two-dollar coat would keep me plenty warm without running up Medusa's account.

Putting on my new coat, I emerged back into the cold world. I pulled my derby tight against the stiff wind and crossed the square, aiming toward Bridge Street. I hoped Nathan Quirt was off for the day, but I had two nickels in my pocket, my revolver in my shoulder harness and, most threatening of all, my unloaded cane.

Reaching the toll booth, I saw Quirt standing behind the window with a scowl on his face and larceny in his heart. I spat. "What's the cheapest way I can get across?" I asked, tapping the head of my cane against the toll booth in case Quirt had heard of my run-ins with Steer Bonner.

"You can swim," Quirt said.

"Last time I crossed, you didn't give me change on a quarter. Seems like that's twenty cents or four trips across the bridge."

"Don't remember that," Quirt said.

He was lying. I knew it, he knew it and God must've known as well. "What's the cheapest way to get across?"

"Read the sign."

"I can't read," I lied.

"I'll tell you once and that's it."

"Shoot."

"Folks afoot cost a nickel unless you are a proven citizen of McLennan County, then the cost is half price."

"I'm a citizen."

"You can't prove it by me."

"I've been here going on four months."

"You need to have lived here a year."

"What are your other prices?"

"Why do you need to know?"

"To see if I want to live here a year."

Quirt loosed a breath of exasperation. "Animal and rider, ten cents."

"What if you're riding an elephant? Is it still ten cents?"

"What the hell kind of question is that?"

"I need to know in case I decide to join the circus."

"Loose horses, mules or jackasses, as in your case, are a nickel each. I'll give you the jackass price."

"What about loose elephants?"

"Loose cattle, sheep, hogs or goats are three pennies each."

"What about camels?"

He ignored my questions and kept reciting the fare chart. "Wagons, carts, carriages and other vehicles drawn by three or more animals are twenty cents per wheel and five cents per animal. Wagons, carts, carriages or other vehicles drawn by two or fewer animals are ten cents per wheel and five cents per animal."

"Would a zebra go at the horse rate or the cattle rate since he's not a horse?"

Quirt ignored me again. He was either stupid or had never been to a circus.

"Wood wagons are two-fifty per round trip while public carriages and ice wagons are a quarter per round trip. Finally, editors, carriers, reporters, pastors, marshals and policemen cross at no charge when they are on duty and Waco pastors are never charged anytime."

"Good, day," I said. "I'll be passing for free as I'm a Waco pastor."

"Got to have lived here for a year and work at an established church. If you're a pastor, maybe you can walk on water, save us both a lot of trouble. In fact, I think I'll ask the board of directors if we can create a new rate for folks like you, the son-of-a-bitch rate at a dollar a crossing."

I stuck my hand in my pocket, pulled out a nickel and plopped down my toll in front of Nathan Quirt.

"Get moving," he ordered.

So, I departed, wondering if there was any place around that might rent me an elephant.

The train depot was just a short walk from the suspension bridge so I made it quickly and went inside to enjoy the warmth of a potbellied stove well tended. I moved to the telegraph office, opened the door and saw three people in line at the counter. Dreban was at the telegraph key, clattering away.

Wolfe was helping his customers. Looking up, he saw me. "No time to visit, Lomax."

"Is lunch tomorrow still on?"

He nodded. "We'll pick you up at eleven-thirty."

"Meet me out back by the carriage house."

He nodded again and helped his customers. I stepped back into the depot, enjoying the heat before I emerged into the cold and started for home. The toll taker on the east side of the bridge treated me like he appreciated my business.

"Good day, sir. Toll is a nickel." He smiled.

"You're not related to the fellow on the other end, are you?"

"Goodness, no, and I make sure never to get crosswise with him as he has a knack for retribution."

I gave the toll taker my fare and moved across the bridge, scowling at Quirt as I passed his booth. Arriving back at Medusa's house, I found all was well.

The next day Wolfe and Dreban showed up in their buggy behind Miss Medusa's where I waited for them. The cold weather had blown through so the ride was pleasant. I expected they would take me to an eatery around the square or someplace comparable. Instead they took me the poor side of town and the back of a run-down place where a lean-to had been added.

"This family know you're coming to lunch?" I asked.

"It's an eatery," said Dreban.

"It's obvious you don't get out much," Wolfe said.

Dreban picked up a magazine as we got out of the buggy. Wolfe pointed to the lean-to.

"Nope," I said. "I'll follow you!"

Dreban and Wolfe laughed as they walked to the door, opened it and entered. Two tables, one with three chairs and one with four, were crammed in the tiny room, which opened into the kitchen at the back of the house. A makeshift opening covered with wax paper for glass provided a crude window that augmented the light seeping through the gaps in the plank roof.

"Damn, fellows," I said, "I didn't expect you to spend so much on my lunch, just for saving your lives."

Dreban laughed and pointed to the table with three chairs. "I told Doug this might not be the best place to start you out."

I sat down in a wobbly chair. "Furniture's not the best," I observed.

"We didn't come here to eat the furniture," Wolfe reminded me.

A Mexican woman came out the door from the kitchen. *"Buenas dias!"* she said.

"We'll have the special," Dreban said.

The Mexican woman nodded, spun around and marched back into the kitchen.

I looked at Dreban and Wolfe, then shrugged. "Don't I have a choice?"

"Sure you have a choice," Wolfe said. "The special or nothing."

"She only cooks one meal a day," Dreban clarified.

I wasn't sure what I had gotten into with the telegraphers, but I certainly wasn't going to eat a seven-course meal. "I wonder if Lady Astor's ever eaten here. Think you boys could send her a telegram when you return? I bet she'd like to bring all her society matrons here to eat."

"Quit bitching until you taste the food," Dreban said.

Wolfe plopped his magazine on the table and pushed it toward me. "You seen the latest *Scientific American*?"

"Can't say that I have." I couldn't believe I was sitting in a hovel, waiting for a meal I had no idea what it would be and discussing a magazine I'd never even heard of.

"We try to keep up with developments in telegraphy and railroading," Dreban said. "Bet you didn't know they were beginning to build an underground railroad in New York City."

I shrugged and pushed the journal back to Wolfe.

He flipped open the periodical. "Right here on page 307, the story on 'The Underground Railway, New York City.'"

Now I was confused as a blue-nosed mule on his wedding night. That magazine wasn't any 300-plus pages. "Let me see that magazine." I took it from Wolfe and started flipping and counting pages, starting with the cover showing the Myers Rotary Engine. "There's sixteen pages here, counting the front cover. If there were more than 300 pages, it'd be a book."

"Look at the upper corner of page five as you would call it," Dreban said.

I did as he instructed. Sure enough it was numbered 307.

"It's called serial numbering," Wolfe said. "Every time they start a new volume, they start with page one and continue consecutive numbering in subsequent issues. It's how they number scientific and scholarly journals."

"I don't read many scientific and scholarly journals," I said.

"You ought to as it would make you a smarter man," Dreban said.

I glanced at my surroundings. "I'm smart enough to know not to take the man that saved my life to a dump like this to eat."

Dreban shook his head. "Lomax, I feared you'd not appreciate the finer qualities of this eatery."

"Look at this," Wolfe said, pointing to a line drawing of a big structure in his magazine.

"It's a building, so what?"

"That," said Wolfe, "is the new train station for New York City. Grand Central Depot is what they call it. Listen to this: 'The Grand

Central Depot building is an immense structure, the largest of the kind in this country. Its length is 690 feet, breadth 240 feet, height from railway grade to center of the glass roof, 109 feet 7 inches. This depot, together with the adjoining car sheds, engine houses, freight depots, and coal yards covers an area, in round numbers, of 830,900 square feet, or a little over nineteen acres.'"

"Can you imagine that, Lomax?" asked Dreban.

Actually, I hadn't and wouldn't have had to, if Wolfe had left the magazine at his office. Fortunately, the Mexican woman returned with a wooden tray that she put down between us on the table, then unloaded three bowls of poison, three cups of coffee, a platter of tortillas and three spoons.

"Help yourself," Dreban said as Wolfe closed his magazine and plopped it on the table.

I picked up a spoon, but hesitated to take a bite as I inspected the dark brown offerings. It was either a thick stew or a thin chili. "What do you call it?"

"The special," Wolfe answered, grabbing a spoon, then attacking the bowl like he was invincible. Apparently he was because the evil-looking concoction had no effect on him.

Dreban dug in as well, taking a tortilla and proving his invincibility, too.

Finally, when I saw they were still conscious after a few bites, I took my spoonful. I don't know what it was, but it was damn tasty, packing a little bit of a punch with a spicy pepper of some kind that left my tongue simmering. "It's not bad," I admitted.

"What you're really saying is it's damn good," Dreban responded.

"It's a good change from whorehouse fare," I replied.

"We can have all the refills we want, and it'll cost us all of forty-five cents when we walk out of here," Wolfe informed me.

I ate another bowl full and three tortillas. While we talked, four men came in dressed like lawyers, bankers or swindlers, those professions all being roughly one and the same. Unlike them, Dreban and Wolfe had tried a little bit of everything, but they loved telegraphy the most.

"The telegraph is the future," Dreban said. "Imagine a day when every home has a telegraph and you can dash out a message to your folks in another state."

I shrugged. "If that happens, there'll probably be so many damned telegraph wires that they or the birds sitting on them will block out the sun. We'll be walking around in the dark, running into each other and buildings if they are as big as that Grand Central Depot."

"Lomax," said Dreban, "your only problem is you are mired in the past. You can't see the future and the conveniences it will bring."

"This is the industrial age, the threshold of the future," Wolfe added.

I was more interested in their pasts than the future and asked about their backgrounds. Wolfe was born and raised in the sleepy town of San Diego, California. When it was time to leave home, Wolfe couldn't follow Horace Greely's advice to go west without drowning in the Pacific Ocean so he turned east to find his future in Texas.

"Couldn't you have settled in a better place than Texas?" I asked.

He shrugged. "I wanted to start a ranch."

I'd worked cattle so Wolfe was finally getting to a subject that I could talk about as I had herded cattle to Abilene, Kansas, a few years back.

"How big was your herd?"

"Two," he said.

"Hundred or thousand?"

"Just two, both heifers."

"Damn, you weren't planning on expanding your herd any, now were you?"

"I didn't make a good cattleman," he admitted.

As for Dreban, he was born in Texas and had worked cattle and picked cotton, but didn't care for the outside work and started some college after deciding he'd rather work indoors.

They were curious about me, so I explained growing up in Arkansas, surviving the bushwhacking of the War Between the States, riding with Jesse James awhile, working with Buffalo Bill Cody and Wild Bill Hickok for a spell, and punching cattle while trying to help Charles McCoy establish Abilene as the first major cowtown railhead. They doubted most of what I said, but we had a good time visiting and decided we'd have lunch weekly.

And we did. The routine was pretty much the same each week. They'd take me to those dumps to eat. The food was always good, even if we didn't know what it was. It was toward the end of the year as we were approaching 1875 when they took me to this hovel where this Chinaman fixed us a substantial meal, though the only thing I recognized was rice.

While we were eating, Dreban pulled a copy of *Harper's Weekly* from his pocket. "I don't know how I missed this other than it got buried in my stack of reading, but it's a September issue about General Custer's Black Hills Expedition."

"It was in the newspapers," I said.

"We read more journals than newspapers," Wolfe said.

"Anyway, listen to this," Dreban said, then began to read from the article. "On the thirty-first of July gold was discovered along the banks of a creek on which the expedition was encamped, the best pan yielding from five to ten cents' worth of gold, equivalent to fifty dollars a day to the man, if the yield should prove as good as promised."

"So what," I said. "My pa heard about gold like that back in forty-nine. He returned to Arkansas broke with nothing but the clothes on his back, a tintype of Momma and a flag that had flown over Sutter's Mill. He showed me how to pan gold, but convinced me it was nothing but wet, cold and dirty work most of the time. And panning's easy compared to hard rock mining which is nothing but back-breaking work with more dangers than you can count."

Wolfe and Dreban nodded and began to smile at each other. It was like they'd been struck by a gold-plated thought. I'd seen men good and bad fall under the spell of gold, but never men as smart as Dreban and Wolfe.

"There's bound to be some journal articles we can hone up on before spring," Wolfe said.

Dreban nodded. "Prospecting, geology, mining technology and more so there's plenty for us to read."

"We could become partners, Lomax," added Wolfe. "With our smarts and your practical savvy, we're bound to succeed."

"A little luck and no Indians might be better," I said. "Isn't the Black Hills Sioux land?"

"The government'll work things out, if it is," Wolfe said.

"Or the army," Dreban added.

I shrugged. "I thought the telegraph was the future."

"It still is," Dreban replied, "but gold is the present."

Chapter Nine

My journey toward the Little Bighorn accelerated as winter wound down and spring approached. I kept my weekly lunch with Douglas Wolfe and Brian Dreban. They seemed to grow more and more enthused about prospecting for gold in the Dakotas, especially if I went with them. As for me, I'd never been around men with more book-learning, men who read—and understood—periodicals like *Scientific American* and *Harper's Weekly*. The *Police Gazette* was more my reading style, but I figured if I hung around them enough, some of their smarts might rub off on me.

Occasionally, I'd cross the river to see my likely prospecting partners at the railroad depot. Each time, I viewed the journey as an opportunity to annoy Nathan Quirt, the toll taker who was always there, his fishing pole propped up against the outside of his tollbooth until quitting time. Once I borrowed Mr. Eaton's Bible and stepped up to the toll window, where Quirt rolled his eyes at the sight of me. I lifted the Bible and held it across my chest where Quirt could not help but see I was carrying the Good Book.

"That'll be a nickel," he scowled.

"I'm a man of the cloth," I said, shaking Mr. Eaton's Bible at him.

"Dammit, either pay your toll or jump off the bridge and swim."

"I minister at the church of fallen virgins," I said. "You may have passed it on your way to the cathedral of Big Red's." I pointed to his fishing pole leaning against the side of the tollbooth. "I am a fisher of men, but I understand you are a fisher of women at Big Red's."

"Pay up and move on. You're no more Godly than me," Quirt protested.

I opened my Bible and made up an appropriate verse for my fellow man. "From the Book of Abominations, Chapter 11, Verse 23. "In the eyes of Gawd Almighty, the tax collector is lowest of all men, save one, the toll collector. For it is he, the toll collector, that is lower than a snake's belly, and he the toll collector that will be smittened in due time."

"Dammit, move along, you bastard," Quirt instructed.

"It's Reverend Lomax," I corrected him.

"Get moving," he repeated.

I stepped away from the booth, hoping I'd distracted him enough that he would forget the toll. He didn't.

"Stop," he commanded. "Give me my nickel." He pointed a small pocket pistol at me.

Fearing the Good Book was not protection enough to save me from the lead of his iniquity, I rendered unto Caesar his due by paying my nickel and moving on, accompanied by the music of Quirt's profanity.

On another trip I stepped up to the toll collector and identified myself. "I'm H.H. Lomax, Waco reporter and editor."

"Dammit, Lomax," Quirt said, "pay your nickel and go on."

"I'm working on a story for the *Waco Advocate*—"

"No such paper," he interrupted.

"—about a certain toll taker overcharging travelers. Not only is he pocketing the overcharges, but he's also swindling the bridge company from what I hear."

Quirt's doughy cheeks flushed red, like I had hit too close to the truth.

"Some people say that's why this unnamed toll collector has plenty of money to spend at Big Red's. Would you know anything about it, Mr. Quirt?"

Again, Quirt pulled his pocket revolver and pointed it at me. "Pay your toll, you bastard, and move along," he shouted. "Now I understand why Bull Bonner wants to kill you."

"No, you really don't," I replied, plopping my nickel down in front of Quirt, "and you never will until you encounter my cane. I'd be glad to introduce you."

"You best watch it, Lomax. The day's coming when Bull Bonner will get you, and I may just help him do it."

"Sounds like a front page story for the *Waco Advocate*."

"More like the *Waco Jackass* in your case!"

I could tell I was riling Nathan Quirt every visit, so I made certain to keep an eye out for him on his afternoon visits to Big Red's. He would stroll along the street until he saw me watching him and then stomp the rest of the way to the only brothel that would put up with him in the Reservation. As for Big Red's guard, I still saw Bonner prowling about Miss Medusa's place from time to time, just waiting for an opportunity to waylay me, but I was alert and smart enough to never get backed into a corner when he was around.

One early spring afternoon after lunch with Dreban and Wolfe, I returned to the house to find all the girls and Earl Eaton trying to comfort a sobbing Medusa in her parlor. I feared Bonner had threatened Medusa or the girls while I was eating at another hole-in-the-wall.

"What is it?"

"Minerva," answered Aphrodite.

By all the commotion, I feared the worst. Either Minerva had been killed or convicted and sentenced to die for murder. Apparently, the $250 Medusa had wired Minerva had not been enough to hire a lawyer crooked enough to help Minerva walk away from the gallows.

"She dead or sentenced to hang?"

"Worse," said Hestia.

Hemera lifted her hand and offered me a letter. "Read this."

I grabbed the letter, glancing quickly at the return address. The missive came from Fort Worth and the sender had a familiar name. As I pulled the letter from the envelope, I realized that the name was the same that I had mailed a letter to several weeks before when Miss Medusa was seeking details about her sister's legal problems. Medusa's friend had finally answered.

After I read the letter, I understood why it had taken so long for a response. The stabbing had never happened to begin with! Minerva, who was fine and prospering in Fort Worth's red-light district, had swindled her sister, concocting a false story that Medusa couldn't help but fall for and send money. Bottom line was, sometimes you get and sometimes you get got. It hurts most when it's by your own kin.

"She lied to me," Medusa sobbed, "and took my money. I'd do anything for her, save letting her work in my place again, and yet she does this to me."

"It's okay," Artemus said. "She'll pay you back. She's your sister."

"Then why didn't she just say she needed some money, rather than lying about it?" Medusa cried. "I'd've loaned it to her. All I've done is worry about her since I got word."

"Maybe she didn't want to pay it back," Demeter offered.

Medusa sobbed even louder, and Demeter realized she had not been helpful. One thing I'd learned about dealing with women over the years was that you couldn't stop their tears, no matter what you said. Just as every rain cloud eventually peters out, so do a woman's tears. It's just a matter of whether you have to listen to her thunder and dodge her lightening in the process.

Mr. Eaton slipped over to his violin, picked it and a bow up, then looked at me, questioning whether or not he should play to help the storm pass a little faster. I shrugged. I didn't know whether it would make things better or worse. Eaton thought better of it and meekly put the fiddle back on the table. There's not much a man can do to counter a woman's tears other than wade through them in a minor crisis or swim to safety in a major catastrophe. In my experience the secret to dealing with women, whether they were church-going types or the brothel-dwelling variety, was to distinguish between what was a major issue and what was not. The only problem was, even God didn't have an answer to that one. His befuddlement was likely the reason He didn't produce any other creatures after finishing with Eve.

Eaton and I just stood there, as useless as two rowboats in the middle of the desert while Miss Medusa's girls tried to ease her pain, which was probably made of equal parts disappointment in her lying sister and anger in losing $250 in the process. Blood is thicker than water, I had always heard, but I wasn't so certain it was thicker than money.

The bawling might have gone on forever had someone not rapped the clapper on the door. Eaton and I looked at each other. "I'll get it," I offered. Eaton nodded his approval.

"I've got to calm down," Miss Medusa said at the knock. She took a proffered fan from one of the girls, spread it out and waved it in front of her flushed face. "I can't let my problem dampen the ardor of a gentlemen visitor, even if he is early."

I stepped to the door, thankful to whoever was outside for staunching the tears. I didn't think anything could make matters worse. Then I opened the door. I was wrong. There stood Big Red, Hemera's mother, looking as charming as ever, which meant she was about as sociable as a grizzly bear with a sore tooth.

"I need to see Miss Medusa," she said breathlessly.

At the sound of her mother's voice, Hemera spun around, her face clouded with a mixture of fear and curiosity.

Big Red took a step to enter the parlor, but I barred her way.

"Just a moment," I said. "I'm not sure Miss Medusa is taking visitors." I glanced into the parlor where she was getting up from her chair and shaking her head. I nodded and looked back at Big Red.

"Miss Medusa is not available."

"Could I come back and see her another time? It's very important," Big Red answered, like she was scared of something rather than threatening her more cultured rival for the hearts, minds and other parts of her male visitors.

I glanced at Medusa, still wiping tears from her eyes and whimpering as she fought to control her emotions so her rival madam would not realize her anguish.

She flashed five fingers to me. "Come back then," she mouthed.

Turning to Big Red, I nodded. "Return this afternoon about five o'clock."

She raised her gloved hand to her mouth and shook her head. "Oh, no, I can't come back then. It might be too dangerous."

Hemera stepped behind me. "Momma, what's the matter?"

"I don't have time to talk," Big Red answered, "not where I can be seen standing here. Can I come by in the morning, say eight o'clock?"

I glanced at Medusa. She nodded.

"Yes," I answered. "Miss Medusa will see you in the morning at eight o'clock."

Big Red spun around and stepped off the front porch as I closed the front door.

"Bye, Momma," said Hemera.

"Bye, sugar," she said as she scurried away.

The instant the door shut, Miss Medusa strode to my side. "What was that about?"

I shrugged. "I don't know. She seemed worried."

"Terrified," Hemera interjected.

"I'll meet with her in the morning, Mr. Lomax, but I want you with me at all times when she's around, maybe even check her for weapons. I don't trust her. You may want to keep extra watch around the place this afternoon and tonight."

"Be glad to," I answered.

Medusa turned to Hemera. "Do you want to sit in the meeting with me? I don't know what it's about, but she is your mother. You have any ideas?"

Little Red shrugged. "Nothing except she seemed terrified."

I figured the lesson for the day was you don't judge folks by their relatives. I liked and respected Medusa and Hemera, though I couldn't say the same thing about Minerva and Big Red. By the same token, I'm not sure I always measured up to the brothers and sisters I had grown up with in Cane Hill, Arkansas.

For the rest of the afternoon, the question on everyone's mind was what did Big Red want? Fortunately, business was brisk that evening so the gentlemen kept the girls occupied. Starting at five o'clock, I slipped outside to look around. I checked the stable, circled the house and spotted Nathan Quirt strolling down the street toward Big Red's at his accustomed time after getting off work. As usual, he carried his fishing pole and a cocky attitude that might have worn well on a man who deserved it, but not on him. As far as I could see, he had nothing to be proud of, having a reputation for swindling common folk and beating women. When he saw me watching him, he stiffened up and offered me an obscene gesture.

I lifted my cane in acknowledgement, hoping one day I could introduce him more intimately to my walking stick. In fact, I decided it might be worth loading my cane one day with a bullet in case I ever needed to make a point to him. Though he was not as big as Steer Bonner, Quirt wasn't as dumb either. He was much more devious than Bonner. When Quirt disappeared in Big Red's I slipped back into the parlor. I made the rounds every thirty to forty-five minutes until three o'clock in the morning after all the customers had left.

I retreated to my room and caught about four hours sleep and then was up about a half hour before Big Red was to arrive, eating a quick breakfast with Eaton and then greeting Miss Medusa when she came into the kitchen. Hemera joined us a few minutes before eight.

"Any new thoughts on your mother's intent?" Medusa asked Hemera.

Little Red just shrugged. "I was as surprised as you. First time she's called me sugar in years. That's what she called me as a girl."

Precisely at eight o'clock, we heard the sound of the clapper. I jumped up from the kitchen table and went to the front door while Medusa and Hemera moved to a parlor sofa.

I opened the door. "Good morning, ma'am."

"May I come in now?"

"Certainly," I said as I stepped aside.

She scurried in like she was afraid of being seen going into a whorehouse, or at least another madam's whorehouse.

I pointed to the parlor. "Please, go in." I followed her and directed her to a chair opposite Medusa and Hemera.

"Hi, Momma," Hemera said.

Big Red smiled. "Good morning, sugar."

"Do you want me to search her?" I asked Medusa.

She turned to Big Red. "Does he need to search you for weapons, a Derringer, knife or hat pin, something like that?"

Arising from her chair, she lifted her arms. "I didn't come to insult or attack you."

Medusa nodded. "Then be seated, but know that Mr. Lomax is here to protect us, if you start anything. You have been unkind to me since Hemera started working here."

Big Red reclaimed her seat. "I didn't care to lose her, but my stubborn streak got the best of me. That's why I'm here. I need help."

Medusa cleared her throat. "Help? You need my help?"

"I let some of the visitors treat the girls badly, didn't even stop them from hurting my own daughter. One of them has turned real mean. I've already had two girls quit and another one threaten to pull out."

"Is Nathan Quirt the problem?" I asked, anger rising in me.

"Yes," said Big Red. "He's the instigator. The other one is Bull Bonner. I hired him to protect the girls and look after things and now he's taking advantage of the girls, expecting free rides whenever he wants." She snickered for a moment, then looked at me. "Only time he's civil is after an encounter with Mr. Lomax. Seems after that he doesn't want to do much in bed except moan, lust being the last thing on his mind."

"I'm glad to be of service, ma'am," I answered.

Miss Medusa frowned. "Why are you coming to us instead of the law?"

"Bull has friends with the law. I don't think' he's scared of anybody but Mr. Lomax."

"Me and my cane," I added, giving acknowledgement where it was due.

Then Big Red looked at Hemera, the pain evident in her gaze. "My daughter was right. I should've cut off Nathan Quirt a long time ago. Everything's gone downhill since Hemera left. Quirt and Bonner are making our lives miserable."

Hemera began to whimper, her eyes misting over. Then Big Red started crying. Hemera stood up and dashed to her mother, throwing her arms around her. They hugged and mumbled their regrets to each other. When Big Red arrived, I had expected fireworks, not waterworks. If Miss Medusa started to crying, too, I'd need to run to the train depot and have Wolfe or Dreban send a telegram downstream that the Brazos would be flooding by sundown. Fortunately for all of those communities downriver, Miss Medusa controlled her tears.

She looked from the tearful mother and daughter to me. "What are we going to do, Mr. Lomax?"

I didn't relish getting in the middle of other people's troubles, especially women's difficulties, because I never seemed to come out ahead. On the other hand, this may have been my dilemma as well, seeing as what good friends I'd made of both Nathan Quirt and Steer Bonner through my own natural charm—and the striking flamboyance of my cane, of course. Probably the safest thing for me to do was send a telegram to Fort Worth and see if Skinny Minnie might be willing to bring her charm and knife to Waco for a rendezvous with Quirt, but I wasn't certain how Miss Medusa felt about her swindling little sister. Too, I might not have that much time based upon Bonner's intent to kill me.

"Would you care to share your thoughts, Mr. Lomax?" Medusa was growing impatient.

I held up my hand, palm toward her. "Give me a few moments to think. We don't want to start a war as it'll be bad for business. If we do, the law could come in and shut us all down. We shouldn't be seen as being involved in their troubles."

"Okay," Medusa replied, "but what can we do?"

I turned to Big Red. "Let me ask you a few questions."

She broke from her daughter's hug and turned to me, wiping tears from her eyes with a dainty handkerchief, then nodding. "Okay."

"All your rooms where your girls see gentlemen are on the first floor, are they not?"

"Yes, Mr. Lomax."

"Is there a room Quirt generally uses when he buys a woman?"

She shrugged. "It varies with the girl."

"You said you've lost a few girls, right?"

"Yes."

"So, you have some empty rooms, do you not?"

"Two," she said.

I nodded. "Are they rooms with windows?"

"Yes, sir."

"Good! And the windows can be opened, can they not?"

"Of course. I do regular upkeep on the house."

"Here's what I want you to do," I said. "First, start seeing Mr. Quirt in the same room, regardless of what girl he sees. Call it the Quirt Room, if you like, but it must have a window."

"I'll use one in the southwest corner. It has a window on two sides. Would that work?"

"Perfect," I said. "Now, how long until it'll be warm enough to keep the windows open when he visits."

"A week or so," she answered. "It just depends on the weather, of course."

"Good. Let me know when you start leaving them open. The only other thing I'll need is directions to Nathan Quirt's house."

"What have you got in mind?" Medusa asked.

"I'm planning on doing a little fishing when the weather turns right."

Chapter Ten

If my plan worked, Nathan Quirt would get his comeuppance, and I would never have to lay a finger on the toll collector. Granted, my scheme might not be as satisfying as bringing Minerva back to Waco to handle the unfortunate situation, but it would do. As I waited to implement my scheme, I had my weekly lunch with Douglas Wolfe and Brian Dreban, who kept imploring me to go with them to the Dakotas and search for gold.

"We could make a fortune," Dreban said.

I still wasn't sure about leaving a comfortable brothel job with a roof over my head for backbreaking pick-and-shovel work that didn't promise anything certain beyond rheumatism in my later years. "There's no guarantees in mining," I replied. "I need to think about it."

"You're missing the adventure of it. You'll have something to tell your grandchildren when you're old and bored living in the mansion your tons of gold built," said Wolfe.

"I can't believe you fellows would throw away the future, leave the comfort of a warm telegraph office and the security of a railroad job to stomp across dangerous Sioux country in search of a few pieces of gold. What happened to the telegraph being the future?"

"With enough gold, our future can start today. With the telegraph it'll take a while," Dreban answered.

"Believe me, gold don't make you rich," I said.

"How would you know? You've never been rich!" Dreban said emphatically.

"Back during the war," I began. "I was the richest kid in Arkansas with more gold than I figure any Ozarks boy ever had."

Wolfe shook his head. "Now you're bluffing us, another one of your tall tales."

"It's a fact," I countered. "I found and hid four bags of gold after a Union ambush on a Confederate paymaster. Three bags were stolen from me and the fourth just up and disappeared and all I got out of it was enough gold to buy a tombstone for my brothers and to help out a few needy neighbors. If anything, I learned you've got more problems rich than you do poor."

"Lomax," said Dreban, "you're like the wind. A lot of gusts but no substance behind it. You're always telling us you taught Buffalo Bill to hunt buffalo or Jesse James to rob banks or Wild Bill to shoot."

"You brought up Hickok, not me. I don't ever want to run into the reprobate again."

"And now," said Wolfe, "you expect us to believe you were rich during the war? There wasn't enough gold in the entire Confederacy to fill up four sacks, certainly not in Arkansas."

"Why do you fellows want to go partners with a fellow you don't trust?"

Dreban laughed. "It's not that we don't trust you, it's that we just don't believe all your stories. Besides, you'll keep us entertained while we're prospecting."

"Just think about it because we need to make a decision in the next month so we can head up north after the spring thaw and make our way into the Black Hills," Wolfe said.

"If that's the case, you need to start out soon because it'll take several weeks to ride that far north," I explained to the man who dreamed of becoming a cattle baron with but two heifers.

Dreban shook his head. "You're behind the times, Lomax. We'll take the train and make the distance in a few short days."

"Yeah, Lomax," added Wolfe, "this is the nineteenth century, the industrial age."

"I can't afford fare for me and my horse up to the Dakotas."

"We'll take care of that for you," Dreban said, "if you'll just go in with us."

I told the telegraphers I'd think about it as we finished our meal and headed back to our places. They dropped me off at Medusa's and returned to work.

As soon as I walked in the back door, Medusa and Eaton approached me with news.

"Big Red came by during lunch," Eaton said.

Miss Medusa nodded. "She said the temperature's right starting today, and Quirt should be by this afternoon. He'll be entertained in the room on the southwest corner."

"I need to know the location of his home," I answered. "Did she leave directions?"

"She took me to the place," Eaton said.

"I'll need you to show me."

"Don't have to," Eaton explained. "It's on the northeast corner of Franklin at Sixth Street. It's the only house on the whole block. It'll be easy to find."

"I don't know where Franklin is."

"It's the next through street south of the square," Medusa said. "Even you can find it, Mr. Lomax."

I laughed. "I never claimed to be a scout or a guide, Miss Medusa. About all I've ever found was trouble."

Medusa smiled. "You've sheltered us from trouble since you arrived."

"Maybe so," I said, "but I fear that'll change if my plan doesn't work."

"And just what is your plan?" she asked.

"It's bad luck to tell," I replied. "All I need is someone to get a message to Big Red."

"I can do that," Eaton volunteered.

"No, Mr. Eaton. I don't want a chance encounter of you with Steer Bonner. Maybe Hemera, could she go?"

Miss Medusa shrugged. "I don't see why not."

"Good. I need her to tell her mother that whatever girl takes Quirt into the back room should leave his pants and coat on a chair within six feet of one of the windows, preferably one that isn't likely to be seen while her visitor is occupied."

Medusa just shook her head. "I don't know what you've got up your sleeve, Mr. Lomax, but I'm glad I won't be in Quirt's pants."

"He won't be in them either by the time I'm done."

We all laughed, then Medusa went upstairs to send Hemera on her mission to momma's.

"Mr. Eaton," I said, "would you mind saddling my horse for me. I want to change out of this whorehouse suit into the clothes I came to town in so I won't be recognized."

"I'm glad to assist anyone that looks out for the girls in this house or any other."

"Thank you, Mr. Eaton. We'll all have a delightful evening, save Nathan Quirt."

With that I retreated to my room, carefully removed my shoulder harness and pistol and then my whorehouse suit, leaving each piece neatly folded on the bed. I'd never handled my clothes that way in the past, usually just tossing them aside on the floor or the nearest chair, but something about living with Mr. Eaton and the fancy ladies had softened me up. I wasn't sure I liked it, but I didn't necessarily dislike it. Standing there in my union suit, I bent down and dug out my riding clothes and dressed in duds more akin to myself than the fancy brothel clothes. It felt manly to pull on my boots, then strap my gun belt around my waist. I pulled my Colt from its holster, enjoying the feel of a real revolver rather than that peashooter I carried under my coat.

I was aiming at the doorway when Eaton walked back in. He yanked his hands up in the air. "Whoa, boss!" he cried. "I didn't do nothing!" Then he dropped his hands and laughed.

Grinning myself, I slid the pistol back in my holster. "I's just getting the feel of my Colt in case I needed it."

"You think you'll need it?" he asked.

"Not if things go how I plan them."

"Well, good luck, Mr. Lomax. The girls and I will say a prayer for you."

"That's kind of you all. If things go bad, will you play your violin at my funeral?"

"No, sir," he said to my surprise. "I'll play the fiddle at your funeral."

I grinned. "I'd like that. Play some sprightly tunes, ones that'll make me want to get out of my coffin and dance!"

Eaton nodded. "I don't suppose you're taking your cane, are you?"

"Not this time. I don't want anyone to connect me with Miss Medusa's. Thanks to Steer Bonner and his bellowing, a lot of people know me only by my reputation and my cane."

"Especially, Mr. Bonner. He knows you quite well by that cane."

"Yep," I laughed. "They're good friends."

"Your horse is saddled."

"Thank you, Mr. Eaton. Just make sure Hemera gets the message to Big Red as I'm gonna leave the rest of the afternoon, ride over to Quirt's house and make sure I can find it as I may be in a hurry when I need to go there. Then I'll spend some time around the square waiting for Quirt to get off work and watching Big Red's place from across the creek to see if Bonner's lurking anywhere. Don't want him interfering with my plans."

I grabbed my slouch hat and tugged it down over my forehead, figuring I was ready to go. Then a thought hit me. If something went wrong, Mr. Eaton might have to defend the place and the girls. I pointed to my five-shot pistol. "You may want to keep that handy in case Bonner or Quirt cause any trouble here."

"Not so sure about that, Mr. Lomax. People don't take kindly when a black man shoots a white one, though they don't seem to mind the other way around."

"You're smarter than any white man I ever met, Mr. Eaton."

"Smarts don't save you from a mob, Mr. Lomax, but I want you to know you're the most decent man I ever met, way you look out for all these girls and don't try to bed them."

"My momma taught me right."

"Mine, too," Eaton said. "Now, good luck."

I nodded and marched out of our room, through the kitchen and out the back door. My horse was saddled beside the stable. It had been weeks since I'd ridden him and he looked well-fed and ready for some exercise.

I mounted and headed toward the square. I rode slowly with my head down, hoping no one would recognize me. Certainly few of the good women folk of the righteous city of Waco would know me or care, but I saw a lot of respectable men, two dozen or more, who would. They were bankers, lawyers, a judge, merchants, one deputy sheriff, a train conductor, the owner of the laundry Miss Medusa used for her sheets, a mortician and others, who wanted a little more entertainment than looking at stereoscopes of European street scenes while sitting in the parlor with their wives or betrotheds. Fortunately, none of them paid me no mind.

I rode over to Franklin, then turned west and followed the dirt street until it intersected with Sixth Street. Sure enough, on the near corner sat a single, clapboard house, shining from a recent coat of whitewash. A brick walk led from the street to the front steps where the door was framed by two windows with thick curtains. It wasn't a fancy house, but it wasn't a shack either. The only thing disconcerting about the place was the hand-painted sign in front that read: NO VISITORS.

Apparently, Nathan Quirt wasn't a sociable type. So it wasn't just me he wouldn't be inviting to any afternoon teas or Sunday dinners following church. I rode past the house, then turned around and rode back by, always staring at the window. I could have sworn I saw the curtain pulled back and a single eye staring back at me as I passed the second time. Maybe I was imagining things, but it made my skin crawl. Perhaps this was all a trap. Could Big Red have arranged all of this in cahoots with Nathan Quirt and Steer Bonner? Were they planning to waylay me and settle some scores? Or, was I just over-thinking this the way Confederate veterans refought every battle they'd lost in the late war as if that would've made an actual difference. I patted the revolver at my side for reassurance. I hadn't been this scared at the fight at Adobe Walls nine months earlier. There I knew what I was facing—all the Comanche and Kiowa warriors in Texas—while here I didn't know what lay ahead, if anything.

I started back to the square and spent the rest of the afternoon keeping any eye on the suspension bridge and riding down to the creek where I could survey Big Red's place. Occasionally, I saw Steer Bonner walking around the house, but he seemed so lackadaisical about it that I didn't worry about him slipping up on me when I put my plan into action. I made the ride between the square and creek a half dozen or so times and by late afternoon traffic and activity began to lessen around the square. Right on schedule at five o'clock, I saw Nathan Quirt's replacement enter the toll booth on the Waco side of the bridge. Quirt came outside, grabbed his fishing pole and started walking toward the square. I rode toward the creek, then turned my horse east along the bank toward the Brazos until I was opposite the back of Big Red's place. I waited and watched.

From downstream I saw Quirt approach the creek bridge, walking along as if he didn't have a care in the world. He was whistling like a fellow that was about to dip his pole in the waters. I snickered at my plan. Quirt stiffened his gait as he neared Miss Medusa's place, then relaxed again when he was safely past. Reaching Big Red's, he followed his regular procedure, opening the gate, walking to the side of the place where he propped his cane fishing pole against the wall, then retreated to the front porch where he disappeared inside to torment what girls still worked for Big Red.

I spent about ten minutes letting my horse nibble on the spring grass that was beginning to turn green along the banks of the creek, then let him water in the creek. When I figured Quirt had had enough time to enter the back room with one of Big Red's fancy ladies, I nudged my horse into the creek and he strode easily through the water that was two feet deep. Then I rode slowly toward my destination, stopping at a pecan tree about twenty yards from Big Red's, dismounting and tying my horse to the tree. Then I ambled cautiously toward the place, but I spotted Bonner circling the house on one of his sporadic inspections so I angled back toward the creek, certain Bonner hadn't seen me or paid me no mind, if he had. I was glad he had made a round as it would likely be thirty or forty-five minutes before he made another, plenty of time for me to accomplish my goal.

After Bonner disappeared around the front of the house, I resumed my journey to the back gate, trying to move nonchalantly so I wouldn't draw any undue attention from passersby. I reached the gate and pulled it open, its dry hinges screeching like a cat with its tail under a wagon wheel. I passed through the gate and angled toward the front corner of the house, bending over as I passed the open windows along the south and east sides of the place. At the front corner of the house, I grabbed Quirt's cane pole and started for the back window, where I heard Quirt mumbling and then the slap of his hand against female flesh. I could hear one of the girls moaning, not from pleasure but from fear and pain.

I held my breath as I stepped up to the open window and peeked inside. Quirt was sitting on the edge of the bed in his long johns with one of the girls across his knees. He was slapping her bare bottom with his hand. I grimaced at the sound of every smack on the poor girl's naked flesh. The head of the bed was against the opposite wall from the window where I watched. Once he finished beating her bottom and began bedding her, he'd be looking toward the wall rather than the window where I waited. I gazed across the room and smiled. Just as I had requested, the girl had seen to it that his clothes were on a chair about midway between the side window where I stood and the back window. His coat was hung over the back of the chair while his pants were laid across the chair seat, no more than six feet away. It was perfect. If only Quirt would fall in bed with this soiled dove and start plucking her feathers, I could start fishing.

Nervously, I looked along the side of the house and behind me to make sure no one was coming. I figured I might be spotted from afar, it still being daylight, but as long as nobody snuck up on me or yelled at me to check on what I was doing, I would be okay. Then, after the girl begged him to stop, he threw her on the mattress. She grabbed a pillow to put under her head, but he grabbed it and stuffed it under her waist. He began to root around in the bed, like a hog looking for an acorn, which was fitting as he snorted and grunted like a hog enjoying slop.

His noise would make my job easier. When he was fully wallowing in the slop, I unwound the fishing line from around the cane pole, checked the fishhook, then slid the pole in the window and began to toss the line and hook toward the chair. It took six or seven times before I snagged Quirt's pants, hooking onto one of the buttonholes at his fly, which seemed appropriate considering his ongoing activity. The pants made a thunk on the floor when I yanked them off the chair and pulled them toward the window, as proud as if I'd hooked a ten-pound catfish. I dragged the pants to the window and lifted them up high enough to grab them with my free hand and jerk them outside. I felt the pockets and cursed that they were empty. I was hoping to find his pocketbook, but only extracted a dirty handkerchief. The pants would do for my plan, but it would be better if I managed to get his pocketbook, which was evidently in his coat pocket. I silently cursed my poor fisherman's luck and tossed my line in again, hopping to snag his coat. Unfortunately, his coat wasn't taking the bait. I'd never liked fishing as a kid because I didn't have the patience for it. If fish didn't bite within a minute of my hook hitting the water, I was ready to do something else. I kept tossing my hook toward the coat and missing. I spent maybe five minutes trying and failing until my hook finally snagged something. I yanked it and the chair toppled over.

The clatter seemed loud enough to wake up the dead.

I froze.

"What was that?" cried Quirt.

"Whatever it was," answered his bed mate, "don't stop. I need you to finish."

"Okay," Quirt said as he kept plowing away.

I let out a gentle sigh. Thank goodness this gal could think on her feet, so to speak. I began to tug on the pole. Fortunately, the hook had slipped from the chair back and snagged his coat. I tugged on it and gradually pulled the coat from beneath the overturned chair and inched the garment to the window where I dragged it over the windowsill. I fondled the coat and smiled when my fingers felt his pocketbook inside a coat pocket. My plan was working!

I inched away from the window, thinking I would return Quirt's fishing pole, trot over to my horse and take his coat and pants home to his wife. The way I figured it, she would make his life a living hell once she knew where I had found his pants.

I backed quietly away from the window, as proud of myself as a bumblebee with two stingers. Then I smelled this god awful odor. I stopped and immediately felt something hard shoved into my back. Without looking around, I realized the muzzle of a revolver was pressed in my ribs.

"What's it you're doing, friend?"

I swallowed hard. It was Steer Bonner, and he didn't sound very sociable. I figured he'd be even less so once he recognized me. You might say I'd gotten caught in my own fishing line.

I gulped and waited!

Chapter Eleven

"Turn around, friend," growled Steer Bonner, "and don't make any sudden moves or I'll blow a hole in you big enough to drive an ore wagon through."

I dropped the coat and was about to drop the cane pole, but Bonner got a little impatient.

"Turn around, dammit!"

I lowered my head so the brim of my slouch hat screened my face and eyes from him. I held onto the fishing pole and twisted slowly around. "I's just trying out my cane pole. Felt like I snagged a pretty good sized one."

"All you caught, friend, was a boatload of trouble," Bonner informed me.

I planted my feet, wishing I'd dropped my cane pole so I could go for my revolver.

Bonner backed away and twisted his head down like he was trying to see who was under my hat. "Raise your head, friend, or I'll go ahead and finish our business right now."

I lifted my chin a tad.

"Higher," Bonner ordered.

Then I raised my head until I could see his collar, but not enough that he could see my full face.

"I'm growing impatient, friend."

Slowly, I raised my head and watched his smirk wash away in a flood of anger.

"Lomax, you dirty coward," he sneered, "trying to rob Big Red's guests."

"I reckon we're no longer friends, Steer."

"It's Bull, you son of a bitch." Then he smiled as wide as Texas. "And you don't have your cane with you!"

"Thank you, no," I said.

He looked dumbfounded. "Why are you thanking me because you're about to die?"

"Thanks for giving me an idea."

"What's that?" he smirked.

With that, I grabbed the fishing pole midway up with both hands and swung it for my regular target. Bonner's sneer turned to horror. Before he could cock his pistol, I rammed the fishing pole into his cap-and-ball pistol. Bull's eye!

Bonner screamed like he'd been hit in the danglers, collapsing to his knees. I drew back the fishing pole and clubbed him on the side of the head. His eyes asked why, then rolled up behind his eyelids like they were seeking the answer. He fell flat on his nose.

I grabbed one pistol from his hand, then yanked a second from his twin holsters. Tossing the fishing pole aside, I scooped up Quirt's pants and coat and ran for the back gate.

"Wait," screamed Nathan Quirt from the side window. "Bull, are you okay?"

Not waiting for Bull to answer, I bolted through the gate and headed back toward my horse. I didn't care if Quirt recognized me or not because Bonner would certainly tell him when he awoke from the latest lightning strike to his jinglebobs.

"Wait, thief!" Quirt cried again. I glanced over my shoulder as I ran toward my horse and saw him at the back window. "My clothes, my money," he yelled. "Help! Help!"

Reaching my horse, I quickly untied him and led him to the creek where I tossed Bonner's latest two revolvers into the water. I draped the trousers in front of the saddle horn, then checked the pockets in the coat, extracting the pocketbook, which I tucked in my pants. I draped the coat over the trousers. Mounting my bay, I turned him upstream on the way to the square. Once I was out of sight of Big Red's place, I opened the pocketbook and found a couple business cards and almost $250 in cash. I had no use for the calling cards, but that much money would pay for nearly 5,000 tolls to cross the suspension bridge, if my arithmetic was correct. I now considered that I had recovered the twenty cents Quirt owed me with interest to boot.

Tucking the money in my pocket, I rode past the square toward Franklin Street, planning to implement the second part of my plan. The square was quiet, most folks having gone home for the day, except for a few shops just closing up. Nobody seemed to notice I was carrying another man's trousers and coat in front of my saddle. I figured delivering Quirt's clothes to his wife and explaining that I'd found them outside a whorehouse window would create more havoc than the crooked toll collector could manage. I looked back over my shoulder to make sure that Quirt wasn't running down the street in his union suit trying to catch me. He wasn't. Then I turned onto Franklin Street and headed west into the sunset and toward Quirt's home.

There being no hitching post outside his house, likely to discourage visitors, I dismounted and tied my horse to a hitching rail on the opposite corner. Removing the trousers and coat from my saddle, I strolled across the intersection. Ignoring the NO VISITORS sign, I marched down the brick walk and up the two steps to the front door. I knocked firmly and waited. No answer. I knocked again.

"Go away," came a woman's quivering voice. She seemed scared.

"I need to speak to the woman of the house, Mrs. Quirt."

"I don't speak to folks," she called out.

"I've got something to give you."

She didn't answer.

"I won't hurt you."

"Leave whatever it is on the porch and go away, please."

"I can't do that. It's your husband's stuff."

I watched the doorknob turn, then saw the door crack open a fraction.

"What is it?"

"I found these clothes outside a whorehouse window. From the calling cards inside I think they belong to your husband. Would he be Nathan Quirt? Would these be his trousers?"

The door opened enough for me to see her cheek, her eye and part of her nose. Instantly, I felt sorry that I had drawn Mrs. Quirt into my plan. She had a black eye and a bruised face.

"Ma," I heard a boy scold. "Pa told you not to see strangers with your face all beat up."

"Hush, boy!" she said, opening the door enough to stick her arm out.

I could see more of her face, and she had been violated hard. I grimaced at her bruised features. I draped his clothes over her outstretched arm. "Here you go, Ma'am," I said. "I didn't mean to cause you no trouble."

"I don't look presentable," she said. "I took a fall yesterday and got banged up pretty bad. Don't tell anyone you've seen me like this, please."

"No, ma'am, I won't."

She started to shut the door.

"Just a minute, ma'am," I said. "There's something else." I shoved my hand in my pocket and pulled out Quirt's money. I extended my hand toward hers. "Here, take this. It's some money I found today. Hide it from your husband and use it to see a doctor or buy yourself a pretty or get away from your husband."

"I didn't say nothing bad about my husband," she said as she shyly took the money.

"That's a true statement, but just take care of yourself so that you don't take another bad fall." I tipped my hat. "Good day, ma'am. I hope you get better soon."

"Thank you," she said as she closed the door.

I lingered on the step a moment, regretting I had drawn her into my wrong-headed plan. She had been beaten too much to ever threaten him for visiting a whorehouse. At best, Quirt might slap his wife, if he found out I had seen her. At worst, he might beat her again. Now I had even more reason to get even with Quirt. I didn't know his wife, but she deserved better than this. I just prayed my visit didn't complicate her existence.

As I walked away, I thought I glimpsed Mrs. Quirt through the parted curtains. I walked back to my horse, untied him, climbed aboard and rode back to Miss Medusa's place, where I tended and stabled my horse before I walked inside.

All the women were waiting for me along with Eaton. They'd watched my fishing expedition from a second floor window and congratulated me on hauling in Quirt's clothes and escaping from Bull Bonner.

"What did you do with his clothes?" Miss Demeter asked.

"I delivered them to his wife, figuring she'd make his life hell for running around on her. I was wrong. From the looks of her, he's made her life a living hell instead. We're all probably in more danger now from Bonner and Quirt."

"What should we do?" Miss Medusa asked.

"I don't know yet. Let's get through the night. I'll think of something," I answered, starting for my room, several of the girls patting me on the shoulder as I passed.

"Thank you for trying," said Miss Hemera. "I know mother is grateful."

Retreating to my room to change into my whorehouse suit, I felt lower than a lawyer's ethics. I'd let everyone down. As I pulled off my clothes, Eaton entered.

"You okay, Mr. Lomax?"

"I failed the girls," I said, "and I failed her."

"Her? Who you talking about?"

"Quirt's wife. You should've seen the bruises and the fear on her face. She was too scared and ashamed to be seen by a stranger, wouldn't open the door more than a crack."

"Like I said before, Mr. Lomax, you're a decent man, one with a conscience."

I felt more like a failure. Perhaps I should've just shot Quirt and Bonner, but I'd never fancied dying with a hood over my head and a rope around my neck, even if it meant I'd get free room and board for a spell in Waco's jail, Texas's finest.

"You'll figure something out, Mr. Lomax. You've got ingenuity, yes, you do!"

I was dressing in my fancy clothes when Miss Medusa rapped on the wall. "Gentlemen coming."

Eaton arose and went to answer the door. I finished putting on my pants and shirt, then strapped on my shoulder harness and pistol before knotting my tie, slipping into my coat and sliding on my shoes. I strolled through the parlor and headed to the bar to serve liquor to the two clients, who had just arrived with lust on their mind. They took a couple whiskies to build up their courage before heading upstairs with the Selene and Hestia. As I sat in a corner chair, the unoccupied girls clumped around me to boost my spirits. Demeter, Aphrodite, Artemis and Hemera each offered to take me upstairs and lift my spirits, but that conscience Mr. Eaton had identified in me stopped me from availing myself of their generous offer. I respected each of those girls and didn't want to risk hurting any of their feelings by choosing one over the other.

"Thank you, but no. It wouldn't be right."

"Right has nothing to do with it," said Miss Artemis.

The girls laughed, as did I. Other gentlemen arrived and things got busy for a while. An hour or so before midnight, a tall, strapping fellow with a thick mustache entered the place without knocking, a violation of Miss Medusa's rules. His manner and the revolver that bulged beneath the side of his coat frightened Miss Medusa. Closing the door behind him, he studied everyone in the parlor. Miss Medusa stood up from her chair and tried to walk confidently to this stranger, but I could tell she was nervous.

"Welcome, sir," she said, "but we don't allow guns in this house. They just lead to trouble."

"These all your employees?" he asked, ignoring her comment

about guns.

"Three are upstairs. If you're interested in selecting one, you'll need to leave your gun outside."

Disregarding her rules again, the stranger strode into the middle of the parlor and pointed a finger at my nose.

"I want him!"

Miss Medusa coughed. "I don't run that kind of place."

I felt my throat tighten. I unbuttoned my coat so I could get to my gun quicker.

The stranger unbuttoned his coat as well and pulled back the lapel to reveal a badge pinned to his shirt. "I'm deputy city marshal Clyde Tompkins. I'm here to see a man named H.H. Lomax about a robbery this afternoon."

"Why, marshal," said Miss Medusa, "I just don't know what you're talking about. Mr. Lomax was here all afternoon, hasn't been out since breakfast. Everyone here'll vouch for that."

I appreciated the way Medusa was providing me an alibi.

Tompkins shrugged. "Other folks saw him about town. I need to visit with him."

"Sure," I said. "I'll talk with Marshal Tompkins, but we'll visit in my room so he won't scare away any other gentlemen that might grace our humble home with their business."

"I'm on business, just a different kind," Tompkins said.

"Follow me," I said. I heard the trod of his boots on the floor behind me as we walked into the back room. I sat on Eaton's bed and gestured for him to take a seat on mine. He came inside and turned to close the door.

"You can leave it open," I said. "We have no secrets here."

He nodded, then moved toward my bed where he noticed my cane. He looked over at me, shaking his head and grinning. "Is this the cane that keeps encountering Bull Bonner?"

I nodded. "They've been known to make their acquaintance."

"Like earlier this evening?"

"No, sir. My cane wasn't involved earlier today with Bull Bonner."

Tompkins took a seat on my bed and tugged on the end of his mustache. "So you're sticking to the same alibi as the girls, that you never left the place after breakfast."

"They said it. Not me. "

The deputy marshal shook his head. "Way I hear it, you and your cane assaulted Bonner, then stole clothing and money from Nathan

Quirt."

I leaned forward and shook my head. "That's not true, Marshal. I didn't touch Bonner with my cane this time. It was a fishing pole."

"So, you're admitting you beat Bonner and stole Quirt's clothes and money."

"No, sir, not at all. Quirt was abusing one of the ladies at Big Red's. I used his fishing pole to hook his clothes and drag them out the window. Bonner slipped up and got the drop on me, but he was so busy telling me what he was going to do to me that he forgot to do it. Me and the fishing pole convinced him that he needed to fall to his knees in prayer. Last I saw of him, he was thrashing about on the ground like a holy roller. I would say it was a religious experience for Steer Bonner and self-defense for me."

Tompkins shook his head and laughed. "Steer? Having a religious experience? There's no bigger tough in town than Bull Bonner. I don't have any sympathy for him, but what about the clothes and money you stole?"

"I didn't steal them, Marshal."

"How's that? You just admitted you fished them out of Big Red's. You're contradicting yourself."

I shrugged. "No contradiction. I just borrowed his clothes."

"Borrowed his clothes? What about his money?"

"Soon as I left Bonner praying at the cathedral of perpetual pain, I rode straight to Quirt's house. I gave the clothes to Mrs. Quirt and all the money from his pocketbook, close to $250. I didn't see much of her, maybe half her face through the crack in the door, but I could tell she'd been beaten like some of the girls at Big Red's. I felt sorry for her and told her to take the money, see a doctor or buy herself a pretty, just not to let her husband know. The money was as much hers as his. It looked like all he ever gave her was a hard time."

Tompkins shook his head. "I don't know whether to take your word or not. I don't know that I've ever heard a more convoluted story."

I stood up and shrugged. "I can't make you believe my story, even if it's true. You can check it out with Quirt's wife, but do it while he's at work. He might rough her up even more. By the look of her, I think she'd be a lot safer and happier as a widow woman than his wife."

The marshal eyed me hard. "I'll check it out. If your story doesn't add up, I'll be back to arrest you."

"Don't leave Waco until I come back to see you."

I nodded. "I don't plan on going anywhere yet, but I'm thinking about prospecting some in the Black Hills."

"One other thing, Lomax," Tompkins said. "Are you the same fellow that threw acid in Wild Bill Hickok's hair?"

I shrugged, exasperated at all the Hickok rumors that my denials would never stop. "That's the story."

"If he's such a fearsome lawman and shooter, why didn't he plug you?"

Sighing, I walked to my bed and picked up my cane, waving it in the marshal's face. "He was afraid of my cue stick. Remember, you can't play pool without first racking up the balls."

Tompkins laughed and shook his head. "I'll see you tomorrow after I visit with the Quirt woman. You might want to tell the girls here that they don't need to lie for you."

"Why not?" I asked. "They lie for every other guy in town."

The marshal snickered and exited my room. I followed him through the parlor to the front door. He left without a word to the girls, whose eyes were filled with questions. As soon as he had closed the door, the girls scurried to me.

"What did you tell him?" Miss Medusa asked.

"Pretty much the truth. He'll be back tomorrow to either arrest or congratulate me."

"He didn't believe us when we said you were here all day?" Medusa asked.

"I told him otherwise, that ya'll were covering for me."

"But why risk it?" Hemera asked.

"Maybe for once in my life, what's right needs to win out. I don't want you girls hurt, I don't want the girls at Big Red's hurt anymore. I don't even want Quirt's wife hurt again."

I saw tears in Hemera's eyes as she and the others hugged me.

"Thank you, Mr. Lomax," Medusa said, "but we don't want you hurt either."

Time dragged by that night after Tompkins left and the next morning, too. Miss Medusa, Eaton and the girls were worried not only about my fate, but also if I were jailed what it meant for their safety. When Tompkins returned mid-afternoon and walked in again without knocking, everyone gathered in the parlor. The marshal seemed uncomfortable standing there surrounded by so many willing women.

"Afternoon, Marshal," I said, "welcome back to Miss Medusa's."

He nodded. "Mind if we visit back in your room?"

"Follow me," I said.

"Pardon me, ladies," Tompkins said, tipping his hat and trailing me back into my room. When he entered, he shut the door."

"No need," I said. "I won't cause any trouble."

"Yeah, there's a need."

I feared I was in trouble. Maybe telling the truth wasn't the best approach after all.

"Your story checked out," the marshal said, the venom building in his words. "I've never seen a woman so beat up as Quirt's wife. She was scared to see me, scared her husband would find out I'd visited, scared to file charges, scared for her life."

I grimaced. I'd seen only part of her face. Tompkins had seen it all.

"It made me sick to my stomach how she's been battered," he continued. "The frustrating part is that I'm the law, and I can't do anything unless she's willing to file charges. She's too scared to do that."

I nodded, then smiled. "I'm not the law, but I intend to do something about it, even if I don't know just what."

"Count me in, Lomax, count me in," answered the marshal.

Chapter Twelve

The next day I lunched with Douglas Wolfe and Brian Dreban at another of those weird eateries where you could dine on a tasty meal for a reasonable price, even if you didn't know exactly what you were eating. In fact, it was probably better that we didn't know what we were consuming. It's one thing to be alone on the prairie and eating whatever you have to, but quite another to be in town dining on whatever someone else dug up and decided was edible—for someone else.

I still hadn't figured out how I was going to settle my score with Bonner and Quirt, but I knew my time was running out. When I was done with them, I realized I would need to depart Waco, leave fast and head as far away as I could get without running into an ocean. As we ate, Dreban and Wolfe blathered on about the latest issue of *Scientific American* and wanted to know if I'd read anything interesting lately.

"As a matter of fact I have," I said. "I read the label on a patent medicine bottle and discovered it would cure worm fever, rheumatism, piles, crossed eyes, female maladies and flat feet as well as strip paint from wood."

"You remember the name of this medicinal elixir?" Dreban asked.

"Yeah," I replied. "Gullibility Tonic."

"Never heard of it," Dreban said.

"I doubt you've read about it in *Scientific American*," I answered. "In fact, I think you need a dose of Gullibility Tonic right now."

Wolfe snickered at his partner.

Dreban grimaced, then smiled when he caught on. Both of them shook their heads.

"Well, boys, or should I say partners," I announced, "I've decided to accompany you prospectors to the Black Hills."

"Great, assuming this isn't another dose of your Gullibility Tonic," Wolfe said.

"Yeah," echoed Dreban. "If you're serious, we may well be rich by this time next year."

"Maybe, maybe not," I said. "How soon will it take for you to quit your jobs and arrange transportation?"

"A week or so," Wolfe answered.

"Then I want it set for a week from tomorrow. When I leave town, I'll be in a hurry."

Dreban cocked his head and eyed me closely. "You're not planning on robbing a bank to grubstake our outfit, are you?"

"What kind of partner do you think I'd be robbing a bank without cutting my partners in on the rewards—and the risks?" I answered.

"We just don't want any trouble," Wolfe said.

"I can't guarantee that, but I will guarantee I won't rob any banks," I replied.

Dreban looked skeptically at me. "We've heard some rumors you robbed a fellow from a competing whorehouse. Any truth in that?"

"Boys, I can't deny it, but it ain't exactly what I imagine you've heard either. The law's already talked to me about it. It wasn't exactly right what I did, and it wasn't exactly wrong what I did. Let's just say I helped a family transfer money from one pocket to another."

"For an un-read fellow, you sure talk in circles," Dreban informed me.

"For well-read fellows, you two aren't that good at figuring things out, now are you? I just want you to be ready to leave town when I say. I'll have to attend to a few matters before I escape—I mean leave town."

"You're making us nervous, Lomax," Wolfe said.

"Gentlemen, we are now partners. What's there to be nervous about other than how we will spend all our money, once we get rich? By the way, I may need some help on the last night before we leave Waco."

"They way it sounds," Dreban responded, "we may need a barrel of Gullibility Tonic before we can get away from Waco."

"It might come in handy," I answered.

We finished our meal and started back to the Reservation and Medusa's place, them driving me in their rig. We discussed arrangements for our departure and agreed we'd have our regular luncheon the next week and leave after that. What I didn't tell them was what I planned to do to Bonner and Quirt before I left town. The main reason was because I didn't know what I would do to them. The other reason was they wouldn't participate in my scheme, if they knew. They let me out in back of Medusa's place.

"We'll get our affairs in order and pack up for Dakota Territory," Wolfe said.

"I'm gonna work on a truth tonic to counter your gullibility elixir," Dreban added.

I grinned. "See you then."

"Don't do anything that'll get you in trouble," Wolfe offered as their rig rattled away.

I had to admit that Wolfe's parting words were good advice. I wondered if I could arrange for someone else to do my dirty work, so they'd get in trouble instead of me. I walked past the stable, down the dirt path to the back door of the brothel. I entered and nodded to Earl Eaton, who was washing dishes from the lunch meal.

"You're sure thinking hard about something from the furrows in your brow," Eaton said as I walked by. "It's bound to be more mischief."

I shrugged. "Not mischief, just revenge."

"For the Quirt lady?"

"Yes, sir, Mr. Eaton. I never saw such fear in a woman's eyes. I don't know her, don't know that I would even like her if I did, but she shouldn't have to cower like a whipped dog."

"How you gonna do it without getting in trouble with the law, Mr. Lomax?"

"Not sure I can, Mr. Eaton, so I'll be leaving the next day."

"Have you told Miss Medusa?"

"Not yet."

"She won't be pleased, losing you and then having no one to protect this place from Bull Bonner. It's a shame he and Quirt couldn't just turn against each other."

"That's it. All that book reading's done you some good." I clapped my hands.

"What are you talking about?"

"Turning them against each other, that's what I'm going to do. Only thing is they just won't know it."

Eaton yanked his hands from the dishpan, dried them off and scratched his head. "You're talking in riddles that don't make any sense."

"Doesn't matter as long as it makes sense to me. And, with a little help, I can pull it off."

Miss Medusa walked into the kitchen. "Pull what off?"

I turned around and nodded. "Good afternoon, Miss Medusa. I'm planning my departure from Waco, a week from tomorrow."

Her hand flew to her mouth. "Why? What'll we do about Bonner?"

"I'm planning on fixing him when I take care of Nathan Quirt."

"You're not planning on killing them, are you? You're not that kind of man." She paused. "Are you?"

Shaking my head, I laughed. "I'm not going to kill them, though they may kill each other or wish they were dead by the time I'm done."

"That's what they deserve, but I don't want to lose you as a result," she said. "On top of that, the girls won't be happy you leaving, them being fond of your ways."

I was genuinely touched as I cared for them as well. "I'm going into partnership with the two telegraphers. We're going to the Black Hills to prospect for gold and make a fortune."

"This is a lot easier work than prospecting."

I pointed to my roommate. "Mr. Eaton does the real work here. I won't be missed."

Miss Medusa walked over to me and grabbed my hands, squeezing them tightly. "Yes, you will. The girls have grown to appreciate you."

"You're a decent man, Mr. Lomax, a man with a conscience," Eaton added.

I thanked them both for their kind words, then said, "For my plan to work, I'll need some help from you all as well as Big Red, her girls and the deputy marshal."

"This can't be good if you need that much help, including the law," Miss Medusa said.

I just grinned. I'd never come up with a more convoluted plan in my life, nor one I was more anxious to implement. "We'll just have to wait and see, but don't share this conversation."

"One exception," Miss Medusa said. "I've got to tell the girls you'll be leaving. They each might want to treat you for a night before you depart, give you a little going-away present."

"That's tempting," I said, "but I look on them more like sisters than bed partners."

Medusa smiled. "That's why they're fond of you."

"What I plan to do for them is make sure that Steer Bonner doesn't bother them once I'm gone. I'm gonna need some supplies, but I've got to figure out exactly what."

"Whatever you need, Mr. Lomax, you just let us know," she replied.

"Thank you. Now, I'm gonna go to my room and start thinking. First on that list is an unopened bottle of your best whiskey."

Medusa shook her head. "You're not going to start drinking on us now, are you?"

"No, ma'am. I won't even uncork it until next week!"

"My aren't you a mysterious one," Medusa said, "but I'll go get it for you now."

I went in my room, Medusa went to the bar and Eaton went back to the dishes. I tossed my derby aside, pulled off my shoes and reclined on my bed to think. How was I going to pull this off? How was I going to turn those two bastards against each other? I couldn't make them hate each other as much as they both hated me. Then it hit me! I didn't have to make them despise each other. I just had to make them hate me even more! That wouldn't be hard to do, especially as vengeful as Quirt was and as stupid as Bonner was.

Medusa knocked on the door, walked in and handed me an unopened bottle of whiskey.

Taking the bottle from her, I grinned with the satisfaction of knowing my plan was taking shape. "Thank you. I'll share this with my new drinking buddy."

"One of the telegraphers?"

"Nope," I said smugly. "Steer Bonner."

She shook her head. "I don't want to hear any more about Bull Bonner drinking any of my best whiskey."

"You gotta trust me," I said.

"Oh, I trust you. It's Bonner I don't trust." She turned and walked toward the door.

"I'll make you a list of supplies I need from the hardware store tomorrow."

Medusa kept on walking. "Mr. Lomax, I hope this complicated scheme works and you don't go to jail or the gallows."

"That's a good idea, Miss Medusa."

"What jail or the gallows?"

"No, rope," I said. "I'll add it to the list."

"Mr. Lomax," she said over her shoulder, "I fear you have gone crazy!"

"If I might trouble you for a pencil and piece of paper, I will not make any more comments that will contribute to your doubts about my sanity."

She shook her head, laughing as she exited the room. She returned moments later and tossed me a pad of paper and a pencil. "I can't wait to see your list tomorrow. Will we be seeing you before then?"

"Yes, ma'am. I want to be out front when Nathan Quirt visits Big Red's this afternoon."

"Good," she replied. "While you're outside, I'll inform the girls of your impending departure. Be prepared for their reaction."

I nodded. "Fair enough. Now leave me be so I can make my list."

I spent the rest of the afternoon making plans and listing my needs. I already had the bottle of whiskey. Next I needed the location for the showdown, a place where it would be dark without the prospect of someone walking by or seeing the fight if they did. The only place I could think of was that long alleyway on the square where Bull Bonner had tried to rob Wolfe and Dreban.

Gradually, it came to me. I would need an augur; a three-quarter-inch double spur augur bit; a cotton lariat in the shortest length, likely thirty-five feet; a woven cane market basket; a large men's kerchief or bandanna; and one sock, preferably dirty. I couldn't help but laugh to myself as I reviewed the list. I rested on the bed until late afternoon, then got up and put my shoes on, plopped my derby on my head and grabbed my cane. I marched out through the kitchen and parlor, then opened the front door and stepped outside. It was a perfect spring day, one of the few things that could ever be perfect about Texas. I enjoyed the outdoors awaiting Quirt to come marching down the street on his way to Big Red's.

After a half hour, I saw him crossing the creek bridge and then turning down the street toward his destination. I moved out by Medusa's wrought iron fence and waited. Quirt stiffened when he saw me. He was just as arrogant and mean as ever. I saw his hand slide to his side where he kept his pocket pistol. I raised my cane and cocked the handle, even though the walking stick was unloaded. Quirt moved his hand away from his revolver, then I realized he was no longer carrying his cane fishing pole. He scowled as he drew opposite me.

"Where's your fishing pole, Quirt?"

"Bastard!" he said.

I lowered my cane. "Maybe so, but at least I don't beat women."

"She had it coming." He spat toward me.

I laughed. "You have it coming, too."

He glared at me and walked on.

"This time," I called after him, "keep up with your coat and pants. You'll have less explaining to do."

He never looked back at me.

I watched him disappear inside Big Red's and then saw Steer Bonner emerge. He walked out into the street headed my direction. I wasn't sure he saw me, so I stepped out into the street and twirled my cane. Bonner stopped dead in his tracks, stared a moment, then turned around and retreated back into Big Red's. I don't think he was as scared of me as much as he was the walking cane. I waited a minute, then returned to Miss Medusa's. The moment I open the door and walked into the entry way, all six girls gathered around me.

"Is it true you're leaving us?" Hestia wanted to know.

I nodded and shrugged.

"But why?" Artemis demanded.

"I'm going prospecting for gold in the Black Hills with my telegrapher friends."

Hestia put her hands beneath her abundant bosom and lifted. "Here are some hills you can explore."

"It wouldn't feel right," I answered.

"Maybe not," Hestia responded, "but it would feel good."

Demeter jumped in. "I can't believe you are leaving us for those two ugly guys. Apparently, all they punch is telegraph keys."

"I'm just going with them. I'm not leaving you for them."

Hemera seemed the most distraught. "You're the only thing that stands between Bull Bonner and us. Momma says he's even meaner when he drinks, which is pretty much all the time these days."

"I'm not leaving until I fix Bonner's wagon so he won't be able to run over you girls."

Selene grabbed me and kissed me on the cheek. Then all the others did the same and started talking about how much they had enjoyed my stay and how much they would miss me. With all the attention and good words, I felt like the corpse at a funeral. But even funerals have to end, and that one did quicker than I would have liked with a knock on the door.

"Ladies," said Miss Medusa, "it's time to get to work. Don't let your disappointment in losing Lomax show to the gentlemen you'll be entertaining. We have a reputation to maintain."

Fortunately, the night was busy with more visitors than normal. We had to turn some away at the door as they didn't meet Miss Medusa's standards. Hemera said that some of them were former clients at her mother's place. It seemed that Bonner and Quirt were driving business away as well as girls.

It was three o'clock or later the next morning before the final gentleman left to find his permanent bed. Everyone retired, exhausted from the evening's work. An hour after dawn, I got up with Eaton and waited in the kitchen for Medusa, who came in about mid-morning, yawning and shaking her head.

"We're going to have to get Big Red back in business soon so we don't get her inferior clients pestering us," she announced. "I overlooked a couple last night that lacked the proper refinement for a quality house like this and turned away a few more. If we had let in some of those fellows as dirty as they were, our laundry bill would double."

"I'm here to help," I told Medusa.

"What, are you gonna start doing our laundry?" she laughed.

"No, I'm gonna help Big Red get back her lost business," I said. "Here's my list."

Medusa snatched it from my hand. "Damn," she said. "You are gonna hang them, what with a lariat on here, are you not?"

"No, I'm not."

"Then do you care to explain?"

"No, I don't. Can you get the stuff for me?"

Medusa read the list aloud. "One augur, one three-quarter-inch double spur augur bit, a cotton lariat in the shortest available length plus a woven cane market basket, a large men's kerchief or bandanna and a dirty sock." She looked at me like I was crazy. "I've never seen such a confounding list."

"If you're worried, I can just drop it all and leave you girls on your own."

Eaton shook his head and spoke up. "You wouldn't leave the girls on their own."

"Maybe not," I shrugged, "but are you gonna purchase my list, Miss Medusa?"

"Yes, I'll send Mr. Eaton to the store right after lunch."

"Good, then I'll need to see Big Red tomorrow or the next day, after you've bought my goods. Don't I remember you saying she sometimes used knockout drinks on clients?"

"I did and she does," Medusa answered.

"Good. She'll have to use some on Nathan Quirt my last night in town."

"We should be able to arrange that."

"Then I'm going to need someone to visit Deputy Tompkins as I'll need him to help out."

"I'm not so sure this is the type of thing I would invite the law in on, Mr. Lomax," Medusa said.

"He's mad like me about the wife beating. He'll help as long as Quirt gets his due."

"In the end, we all get what we deserve," Medusa said. "It's just that we never know for certain when the end is near. I hope it ain't near in your case–or ours."

Medusa was turning philosophical on me, but I guess that's a madam's prerogative after spending hours of her life with men who were more interested in carnal discussions than in philosophical debates. Shaking her head, Medusa looked at me. "I'll send Mr. Eaton to the hardware store and wherever else necessary to get everything you need. I'll also have him invite the deputy marshal for a visit. I'll get Big Red over here as soon as Hemera rises this morning."

"No, no," I said. "Don't have her come over until tomorrow morning. I need to give her the basket you're buying me."

Medusa shrugged. "I fear this is going to be a scary ride."

"The less you know, the fewer problems you'll have if anything goes wrong or if you have to testify against me," I replied. "And I'll want my final wages before I go."

"I may even include a bonus if this works out for you and us."

"If this works out, I doubt I'll linger long enough to collect my bonus. If it doesn't work out, you can use my bonus to cover my legal fees or my funeral expenses. But first, purchase my list of goods and get the deputy to come by this afternoon."

After lunch, Medusa sent Eaton to buy my needs. On the way back, he stopped by the marshal's office and visited with Tompkins, telling the deputy marshal that I needed to see him. After Eaton returned, he and I retreated into our room and I double-checked the purchases. Everything was there, except the dirty sock. He had purchased a new pair. I held them up. "These aren't dirty socks and I just needed one."

Eaton closed his hands into fists and planted them on his hips. "You know of any place that sells a single dirty sock?"

He had a point.

Shaking his head and lifting his balled fists from his hips, he unfolded his fingers and snatched the new pair of socks from my hand. "Those are for me," he said. "I'll give you the ones I'm wearing."

He sat down on the bed, removed his shoes and switched socks, tossing me both of the old ones once he was done. They weren't as dirty as I would have liked, but they would do. "Thank you, Mr. Eaton."

Eaton bowed. "At your service. Will you tell me what you have in mind?"

"No, sir. It's my secret."

He just shook his head and left to prepare for another night. An hour or so later, the deputy showed up and Eaton escorted him to our room where I could tell him his role in my plan.

"All I need you to do about midnight a week from today is to stay in your office so you can come to the square when I send for you. You know where that alleyway is between the mercantile and the bank, the one fenced off at the end?"

Tompkins nodded. "The place you encountered Bonner robbing the railroad men."

I nodded. "Made a religious man out of him as he was on his knees when I left, praying I suppose. When I send for you next week, I'll need you to come and arrest Bonner and Quirt."

"What for?"

"Fighting, disturbing the peace, attempted murder or whatever you say. You're the lawman."

"Tell me more."

"You don't need to know."

Tompkins nodded. "Fair enough, as long as Quirt's punished."

"I suspect he will be. Just remember midnight next Thursday.

After the deputy marshal left, I went about my business as usual and confirmed with Medusa that Hemera had contacted her mother for our appointment the next morning. She had, so I packed the cane basket Eaton had purchased for me with my spare whorehouse suit, shirt and tie.

About mid-morning the next day, Big Red barged into my room. "Miss Medusa says you need to see me."

"I've got something for you," I said, offering her the basket with my spare clothes plus one of my derbies.

"What's this for?"

"Next Thursday, when Nathan Quirt shows up, make it special for him, two girls or something, then doctor his drink so you can knock him out for several hours. When he's out, dress him in my clothes in the basket. Once it's dark, me and some friends will be around to pick him up out the back window. Don't let your girls in on anything until next Thursday right before Quirt shows up." After Big Red agreed to my instructions, I sent her back to her place.

Then it was just a matter of waiting until the next week when I had to convince my prospecting partners to join in the fun.

Chapter Thirteen

"You want us to do what?" Brian Dreban cried out.

I rolled my eyes and looked at the handful of other customers dining with us in this hovel on the west side of town. The diners stared at our table until I picked up my cane and cocked it. Each man went back to minding his own business. "Now, keep it down, boys," I whispered. "I don't want the whole town knowing about this. As many churches as there are around Waco, someone's sure to think it's a sin."

"Or a crime," said Wolfe. "I don't know."

"You aren't too worried about breaking the law, Douglas, are you," I asked.

"Sure I am," he shot back.

I knew I had him. "I've read enough newspapers to know that by treaty the Black Hills belong to the Sioux. Maybe it's not in *Scientific American* or *Harper's* but that's what the newspapers say. If we go prospecting in the Black Hills, it's trespassing and breaking the law. What's the difference in breaking a law in Texas and one in Dakota Territory?"

"Sounds like there's just too many chances for your plan to go wrong," Dreban added.

"And for us to spend our time in jail rather than prospecting for gold," Wolfe concluded.

"Fellows, I thought we were partners. I guess I can stay here working in a whorehouse and you two can keep banging on a telegraph key."

"We can't return to our jobs," Wolfe said.

"Problem is, we quit our jobs yesterday. Our boss was furious about it," said Dreban.

"He won't rehire us, not after we bought our tickets at discount," Wolfe added.

"Well, partners," I said. "I guess we're all in this together, whether we like it or not. And to show you that I want our partnership to last, I'll buy lunch today."

"It's about time," Dreban said. "You've stuck us with the cost every time until now."

"Hey, partners, I'm the one that saved you from getting robbed of railroad money. That would've cost you a lot more than buying me a cheap meal every week since." I winced when I learned the meal would cost us a quarter apiece, the most expensive lunch we had consumed since we had started the weekly habit.

They carried me back to Medusa's place in their buggy, then waited for me to bring out my saddle, tack, bedroll and carbine from the stable. Then I led my horse out and tied him to the back of their buggy. "Now you're sure he'll be on the same train with us?" I asked.

"Yeah, just not in the same car," Dreban said.

"Funny, Brian. Return tomorrow at noon. You can take your lunch with me and the girls, though it'll be more like their breakfast. Then we'll just wait around until dark to handle our business."

"Your business," Wolfe reminded me.

"I can arrange for something for you two to do tomorrow afternoon while we wait, but bring a couple issues of *Scientific American* in case you're not up to it. When you get here, tie your rig up out back and enter the back door. After lunch, you boys can have some dessert."

"We'll see you then," Dreban said, rattling the reins as the buggy rolled away.

"So long, partners," I called.

"Thanks for reminding us," Wolfe cried back.

I dreaded the afternoon as the girls all knew this would be my last night at their place. Too, it was a Wednesday night so business would not be as brisk as other nights and there would be plenty of time for reminiscing about the months I had spent working for Miss Medusa. We visited the afternoon away and continued our talk into the evening and night, between gentlemen callers, of course. I confirmed with Miss Medusa that Wolfe and Dreban would be welcome at the lunch table the next day as I would need their help with my scheme.

When Miss Medusa advised the girls that the two telegraphers would be assisting me and joining us for lunch, then staying the afternoon, they promised to look their best, in case Wolfe and Dreban wanted a little thank you for helping out. We all retired after midnight and woke up the next day refreshed, though skittish. As I dressed in my whorehouse suit, I wondered what would happen if my plan failed. Eaton arose with me and went to the butcher to buy a ham, which he baked for lunch. He also cooked turnips and biscuits for our meal.

Right at noon, Wolfe and Dreban arrived, tying their rig outside and knocking on the back door. Miss Medusa welcomed them inside. They doffed their hats and gave their thanks for her hospitality, asking her why she'd ever hired a troublemaker like me in the first place.

Miss Medusa offered them seats at the table, and they sat down while Eaton put food in front of them. Medusa and I joined the telegraphers. When Eaton sat down, Miss Medusa passed the platter of sliced ham to her visitors. They helped themselves, then added turnips and biscuits to their plates. We ate and visited, then Eaton offered Dreban and Wolfe apples.

"Care for some dessert?" Eaton offered. "These are pretty good for this time of the year and a little cinnamon on top makes them quite flavorful."

Dreban looked at me. "Are apples what you had in mind yesterday when you said we might be having some dessert?"

"Not exactly," I replied.

Miss Medusa patted a napkin to her lips. "The girls will be down shortly, gentlemen, so there may be some other options, if the apples don't sate your appetites."

As wide-eyed as puppies spotting their first cat, Wolfe and Dreban ate their apples so quickly I was afraid they would eat the core and stem as well. When they were done, Miss Medusa suggested we retire to the parlor. That apparently was the cue for the girls to come down. Barely had we gotten seated than we heard the creaking of the stairs as the girls descended like sinful angels. They had all done their hair, painted their faces and sprinkled on perfume by the pint.

"Are these your friends?" asked Demeter.

I nodded. "This is Douglas Wolfe and Brian Dreban."

Both jumped up from their chairs.

"Ladies," said Dreban.

"Our pleasure," Wolfe said.

One by one I introduced them as they paraded by, each pausing in front of their guests and curtseying to give the boys a flash of their cleavage, save for Demeter, who was blessed with a flatlands build. "Demeter, Hemera, Artemis, Hestia, Selene and Aphrodite," I announced.

"We have heard so many wonderful things about you two," said Selene.

"That you were going to help Mr. Lomax with our tormentor," said Hestia.

"The pleasure is all ours," Dreban said.

"Not yet, it isn't," answered Aphrodite.

"Yeah, that's for later," Artemis said, "after we dine."

"We have certain appetites," Hemera said, licking her lips.

I could tell Dreban's and Wolfe's lips had gone dry from watching this exhibition.

"Of course, we are mad at you two as well," said Artemis.

"For taking Mr. Lomax away from us," Selene interjected.

"We are all going to miss him," Hemera said.

"He's quite the best we've ever had," Demeter went on.

"He's strong and powerful, like a locomotive, Mr. Wolfe and Mr. Dreban. He just keeps charging ahead."

I snickered to myself. These girls were building me up to be quite the gentleman and I appreciated that, making me look like a voracious stud in front of my male friends.

"We don't call him, Hoss, for nothing," added Aphrodite.

"Only problem we've had since he hired on was who would get to spend the night with him," Hestia said.

Miss Medusa entered into the fray. "Yes, I had to work out a schedule each week for Mr. Lomax to spend time with the girls. I give him Wednesday night off because my goodness, even an animal like him needs a little rest."

I could barely keep from laughing out loud, especially when both Dreban and Wolfe looked at me with newfound respect. "What can I say?" I asked them. "Some of us just have a way with the ladies."

"We'll be back," Artemis whispered as they moved into the kitchen for their meal, giggling the entire way.

"Gentlemen," Miss Medusa announced. "When they return, you can have your choice, if you like."

"Oh, we like," Wolfe said.

"I agree," Dreban offered.

I figured they'd have tripped on their tongues if they had stood up. They kept glancing from the kitchen to me and back, shaking their heads in awe.

"How'd you manage, Lomax?" asked Wolfe.

"Six nights a week!" reiterated Dreban.

I shrugged. "It just comes naturally to us thoroughbreds because we know how to pace ourselves." I arose from my chair and nodded at Dreban and Wolfe. "I've got some more packing to finish up so I will leave you with Miss Medusa. I am assuming you will have other things to think about this afternoon without me having to keep you company."

"We do, Lomax," said Dreban.

I turned to Miss Medusa. "I need them with clear heads tonight so don't let them drink any liquor, not even any of that wine."

Miss Medusa smiled. "Absolutely!"

I left the telegraphers in the care of Miss Medusa and retreated through the kitchen, silently mouthing my thank yous to the girls for making me sound like a stallion between the sheets. They giggled at the joke as they worked on their meal.

In the back room, I laid out the clothes I would leave Waco in. They were the same ones I had arrived in. I checked my pistol and holster and pulled the skinning knife from the scabbard on my belt. As I planned to use it that evening, I retreated to the kitchen and asked Eaton for the whetstone he used to sharpen the butcher knives. He pointed to a drawer where I retrieved it, then returned to my room and spent an hour honing the blade until it was sharp enough to split a gnat's eyelash. When I was satisfied it was well honed for the night's needs, I gathered up my few remaining belongings—comb, razor, hand mirror, extra pair of socks, an empty flask, a few coins and the wad of bills I had saved working for Miss Medusa.

After he finished the dishes, Eaton came in and patted me on the shoulder. "Can't believe you'll be leaving us tonight. You've been a good boarder, Mr. Lomax."

I grabbed his hand and shook it warmly. "I've gotten more book-learning rooming with you than I can remember in any of my schooling, sparse as it was. How'd you get so smart?"

Eaton smiled. "Momma wanted me to be an educated man, the first in our family, so she made sure I learned to read. Somehow, she always made certain I had books to read. I don't know how she afforded them, but she did and I always had plenty to read. Said as long as I was reading I didn't have to do chores, so I did a lot of reading, starting with the Bible."

"Not much room for the Bible in a place like this, Mr. Eaton."

He smiled. "There's room for the Bible everywhere, especially a place like this. These girls aren't bad, just don't have a lot of options, sort of like a black man don't have a lot of opportunities to make something of himself."

"I never thought of it like that."

"You're a lot like me, Mr. Lomax."

"How can that be, Mr. Eaton? I don't read books much and I certainly don't know how to play the violin."

"We're trying to do the best for ourselves that we can with what we've got to work with."

He was right. I threw my arms around him and hugged him. "I'm gonna miss you."

"I never had a white man for a roommate before," he said. "I kinda liked it."

"What do you mean *kinda* liked it?"

"You snore, Mr. Lomax. Sometimes sounds like a thunderhead moving in."

I released him and shrugged. "Not much I can do about that."

We visited until late afternoon when it was time for Nathan Quirt to pass on the way to Big Red's for his afternoon rendezvous with her girls. After I ended the conversation with Mr. Eaton, I grabbed my cane, unloaded as usual, and picked up the unopened bottle of whiskey I had received from Miss Medusa. I headed out of the room, through the kitchen and into the parlor. There I found Wolfe and Dreban laid back in two of the parlor chairs. The two telegraphers wore satisfied looks on their faces, as if they had spent all afternoon banging out telegrams or something else. They didn't even have the energy to nod their acknowledgement when I passed. They just smiled weakly.

I opened the parlor door and stepped outside to wait. Finally, Nathan Quirt appeared down the street, acknowledging me with an obscene gesture as he passed. I tipped my derby at him. "Good day, Mr. Quirt," He spat and kicked dirt toward me. I just smiled and watched him all the way to Big Red's. I waited fifteen minutes, then followed his trail, my cane in one hand, the whiskey bottle in the other. Reaching Big Red's door, I rapped on it with my cane. As planned, Big Red sent Bull Bonner to answer.

As Bonner opened the door, he scowled. I waved my cane and shook my head at him. "We've had our differences," I told him, "but I'm here to put an end to them once and for all because tonight I intend to whip your ass."

Bonner swelled up like a bullfrog, and I could see the rage simmering in his eyes. "You can't whip me without your cane."

"I won't bring my cane tonight because I plan to whip you with my bare hands."

Bonner scoffed. "Isn't a man alive in Texas that can whip me in a fistfight."

"I can and I will," I taunted him as I lifted the bottle to eye level. "Just to make sure you won't turn yellow, I brought you some liquid courage, a bottle of the best liquor I could find."

Bonner laughed. "I'll beat you to a pulp."

"You're scared and you know it." I placed the bottle down on the porch, then backed away from the door.

Bonner came outside, staring at me suspiciously. "I wouldn't drink your liquor. You probably poisoned it."

"Uncork it then and I'll take a swig."

Bonner feinted like he was bending down to pick up the bottle, then stood straight up, making certain I didn't plan on whacking him with my cane. When I remained motionless, he uncorked the bottle, left it on the porch, then backed away. I edged up to the bottle, grabbed it by the neck and took a healthy swig, then put it back down on the porch. I swallowed hard so he would know I hadn't tricked him.

"Now you believe me?"

Warily, he picked up the bottle and corked it. "Maybe."

"You better drink every drop, Bonner, because you're gonna need all the courage you can muster to face me."

"When?" Bonner asked.

"Eleven o'clock tonight."

"Where?"

"In the alleyway where you tried to rob those two telegraph operators. I'll be at the end backed up against the wall, waiting for you. Don't bring any guns or they'll wind up in the creek again. Don't bring any other weapons, just the two of us fighting with our fists."

"No cane, right?"

I nodded. "This is the last time you'll see me carrying a cane."

"I'll be there," Bonner growled.

"Enjoy the liquor," I said. "It'll be the next-to-last thing I ever give you."

He looked at me, puzzled. "What else you planning on giving me?"

"The beating of your life," I turned and walked away, striding confidently down the road back to Medusa's place.

As soon as I walked inside, Medusa and her girls gathered around me. "So far, so good," I announced. "The trap has been set. Once it's good and dark, I'll return to Big Red's to make a pickup and then wait on Bonner to show up."

Medusa shook her head. "I don't know about this. You sure you know what you're doing?"

"Sure," I answered, praying I was right.

Dreban, Wolfe and Eaton stood behind the ladies in the parlor. I nodded to them. "Gentlemen, what time does our train leave in the morning?"

"Eight-fifteen," Wolf declared.

"Well, I've got to finish packing. You fellows can either join me or wait out here with the ladies."

Eaton accompanied me back to our room, but Wolfe and Dreban opted to stay and charm the ladies. When I reached my bed, I saw that Eaton had added my coat to the pile of belongings on the bed. Additionally, he had placed a carpet bag beside them. I pointed at the bag.

"Miss Medusa wanted you to have it, saying you needed to look like a gentlemen when you got on the train."

"My baggage will look better than my outfit," I said as I took off my derby and tossed my cane on the bed. I began to take off my whorehouse suit, starting with the jacket and the shoulder harness with pistol. Then I removed my tie, shirt and pants. As I dropped my clothes on the bed, Eaton began to fold them and pack them in my new bag.

"You don't need to do that, Mr. Eaton."

He smiled. "I know. I just want to send you away proper. By the way, call me Earl."

"That would suit me fine, Earl."

After I finished undressing, I put on my regular clothes. The pants were a little tight as I had put on some weight, but I managed. I pulled on my boots and then strapped my holster with the knife scabbard around my waist. I paced back and forth in the room, working the stiffness out of my pants and letting the gun belt settle down to its natural location, then stuffed the dirty socks and new bandanna in my pocket.

Eaton kept on packing, finally putting my pocket revolver and shoulder harness in the carpetbag. He also picked up the carton of bullets we had purchased for the gun and tucked it inside the bag. Then he pointed to the cane. "You want to carry it or strap it to the bag?"

Shaking my head, I picked up the cane and offered it to him. "I want you to have it, Earl. Something to remember me by."

He smiled. "I'll take it as long as it's unloaded."

I laughed. "I never loaded it a single time. Didn't need to, though Steer Bonner might have wished he'd been shot instead of clobbered with it."

Now Eaton laughed and grabbed the cane from me. "Now I'll

look a gentleman."

"You look more distinguished with a cane than I ever did, Earl." I studied my bulging carpetbag. "Don't know why I packed my whorehouse suit and peashooter. You want them?"

"No, sir," he answered. "I'll take the cane out of a man's hand, but not the clothes off his back. You may need the gun more in the Black Hills than I will in Waco." He latched the carpetbag for me.

I squatted down and pulled the lariat, augur and bit from under the bed. I tossed the rope on top of the carpetbag and fitted the bit into the augur.

"This confounds me, your need for the drill and bit," Eaton offered.

I just smiled. The less he knew about my plans, the less trouble he would have if something went wrong. I picked up the carpetbag and lariat. "I'll be right back, Earl." I slipped through the kitchen and out back to the wagon that Dreban and Wolfe had rented for the night. I dropped my load inside, watching the sky and figuring I had half an hour or so to kill before it was dark enough to continue with my plan. I returned to my room, grabbed my work hat from the chair by my bed and shook Eaton's hand a final time. "I'll miss you, Earl. You've been a good friend."

"Thank you, sir. It's been nice having another fellow around the place, someone I could talk to other than the girls."

With that, I walked out of the room I had shared with Eaton for the past seven months and went to the parlor to say my goodbyes. I shook Medusa's hand, but she grabbed and hugged me. "Thanks for taking me on and giving me a warm roof over my head for the winter. I hope all works out between you and your sister. If I run into Minerva again, I'll give her your love."

Medusa grimaced. "You might also tell her to send back my $250."

I shrugged. "It's ironic. If I hadn't met Minerva, I would never have met you and the girls. Odd how things work out in life."

Then one by one, I said goodbye to the girls Hestia, Demeter, Aphrodite, Artemis, Selene and Hemera. Their mythological names, which struck me as so odd when I first met them, seemed strangely appropriate as I prepared to leave them. Maybe they were goddesses in their own way. I wished each the best and received in return a sincere kiss from them all.

"Can we write you?" Medusa asked.

"Sure," I said. "Send it general delivery to Bismarck, Dakota Territory. Don't expect me to answer your letters, though. I'm not much good on writing."

I turned to Dreban and Wolfe. "Are you gentlemen ready to referee a fight?"

They both nodded.

I pulled the brim of my hat down low on my forehead so the girls wouldn't see that my eyes were misting as I walked away.

"Goodbye, Mr. Lomax," called Hemera. "Thank you for everything."

Chapter Fourteen

We knew what we had to do, so we said nothing as we exited Medusa's place for the last time and climbed in the wagon. With Wolfe at the reins, we drove toward the creek, then along its banks until we pulled up behind Big Red's place. I left Wolfe and Dreban in the wagon as I moved toward the southwest corner of the brothel to the windows where I had fished for Quirt's pants and coat.

Reaching the open widow facing the creek, I peeked inside and was pleased to see two of Big Red's girls seated on either side of Nathan Quirt. He was a true gentleman, completely passed out from the knockout drugs they had spiced his drink with. And, he was well dressed in my spare whorehouse suit. "Psssst," I whispered so Steer Bonner, who I hoped was suckling on his the gift bottle of whiskey, wouldn't hear.

The girls smiled and arose, struggling to drag Quirt toward me. One of them shook her head, stepped out of the room, returning shortly with Big Red, who helped muscle Quirt my way. They pushed him head first out the window and I grabbed his arms, then tugged on him. He snagged on something until the girls lifted his legs, then he slid free and I yanked him outside. Releasing my grip as his waist cleared the windowsill, I heard his head clunk on the ground. Quirt moaned, then fell silent.

"Thank you," whispered Big Red. "We appreciate this. Bull's been drinking and mumbling about whipping you in a fistfight."

I smiled. I knew Bonner couldn't resist the liquor. Next I grabbed Quirt by the arms and dragged him toward the back fence. I had only gotten half way when Dreban joined me. We picked Quirt up and carried him to the wagon where we tossed him in back, none too gently atop my augur and lariat. After Dreban and I climbed aboard, Wolfe turned the team around and we drove back past Medusa's where she and Hemera stood on the porch waving. Then we headed toward the creek bridge, crossing it and aiming for the square, where we drove around the block three times, just checking for anything unusual. Confident no one was working late in any of the buildings, we finally drove around to the back of the mercantile where the plank fence blocked the alleyway between the store and the neighboring bank.

Wolfe parked right in front of the fence, secured the wagon brake, then jumped onto the street. He lifted the leg of one of the team, acting like the horse had thrown a shoe or picked up a rock, should anyone come by. Dreban stayed in the wagon looking around for any approaching riders or pedestrians. When everything looked clear, I leaned over, shoved Quirt off my augur, grabbed it, and jumped from the wagon to attack the fence. As quickly as I could, I drilled two holes waist high in the wood about two feet apart. Fortunately, no one passed and I was able to drill two more holes armpit high right over them. When I was done, I tossed the augur back in the wagon and it landed on Quirt's head.

"Ooops," I said. Quirt just moaned, which made me remember the dirty socks in my pants pocket. I climbed in the back of the wagon and stuffed one of the socks in his mouth. Funny thing, Quirt didn't protest a bit. And with the dirty sock in his mouth, he wouldn't protest very loudly if he changed his mind later.

Then I grabbed the lariat and pulled my skinning knife from my scabbard. I cut the rope into four pieces of equal length, then tied two around his wrists and took the other two to the fence, where I slid one in the lower set of holes and the other in the upper set of holes. With that, I ordered Wolfe to lean against the fence and hide the holes as best he could while Dreban and I drove the wagon around to the front of the buildings. We parked by the entry to the blind alley between the mercantile and the bank building, sitting there several minutes and inspecting the square to make sure no one was watching. When we were confident we were alone, we jumped down from the wagon, went around to the back, dropped the tailgate, grabbed Quirt's feet and pulled him to the back of the wagon. We glanced around a final time to see if any witnesses might be approaching. Confident we were as alone as we could be at this time of night, we yanked him out of the wagon and carried him to the end of the blind alley where we leaned him against the back fence.

I grabbed the loose rope at waist level, pulled it across his belly and shoved the end out of the second hole I had drilled. "Tie this rope tight," I called to Wolfe on the other side of the fence. Shortly, Quirt gasped and fell forward as Wolfe pulled the rope snug around his waist and knotted it. Dreban caught Quirt by the shoulders and shoved his back against the fence while I threaded the upper rope under one armpit, across his chest, under the other armpit and through the next hole in the fence. Wolfe tightened and tied the rope without instruction this time. With a little help from the ropes, Quirt stood firm against the back fence, though his head drooped a little. He let out a sickly groan. I pulled the other dirty sock from my pants pocket and stuffed it in his mouth, then took the large bandanna Medusa had bought me and wrapped it bandit style around his mouth and nose. His head still drooped but I figured I'd just have to accept that since I might strangle him if I put a rope around his neck. Like his head, his arms hung limp with the lariat bracelets I had tied to his wrists. I tossed the ends of the rope over the fence. "Tug on those," I told Wolfe.

"You want me to tie them?" he shot back.

"No, just pull on them slowly"

Wolfe obliged. As he pulled on the ropes, Quirt's arms came to life, like those of a marionette.

"That'll do," I said to Wolfe, then turned to Dreban. "Think that'll fool Bonner?"

"Maybe," Dreban answered. "It's dark enough that the ropes aren't obvious, but they're not invisible either. Depends on how much he's had to drink."

"I gave him a full bottle, less a swig to prove it wasn't poison. Imagine him thinking I would poison him. What's the world coming to when there's no trust between enemies?"

Dreban laughed. "Lomax, I'm glad you're on my side."

"That's what partners are for." I was tempted to punch Quirt in the gut or sock him in the eye so he could walk around with a bruise like his wife, but that might be considered assault and I didn't want the law after me. As best I could tell, there was no law against saving a man from a whorehouse where he had been drugged or against stuffing a pair of dirty socks in his mouth to keep him from swallowing his tongue or tying him to a fence. I doubted Quirt would have appreciated my efforts, but he wasn't saying much then.

"Okay," I said. "Let's leave him alone. I suspect he'll have a visitor shortly, who'll want to take out his frustrations on me."

Dreban shook his head as we walked back toward the wagon. "How do you come up with such schemes, Lomax?"

"I don't waste time reading *Scientific American*," I answered. "Gives me more time to think. Besides that, I saw a marionette show when I was a kid. Scared the hell out of me, little wooden figures dancing with strings on their limbs. Maybe I hadn't had as much book-learning as you and Douglas, but that doesn't mean I haven't picked up a few things by now."

"Maybe in a month or so you'll be picking up gold nuggets in the Black Hills."

"Perhaps," I shrugged, "but we're not done here." At the wagon, I ordered Dreban to stay on the walk and watch for Bonner. "If you see him coming, make sure he's not armed then tell him I'm waiting at the end of the alley to whip his ass. If he's sober, whistle once. Twice if he's been drinking and three times if he's drunk."

"Can do."

I shut the wagon tailgate, then climbed into the seat and drove the rig around back where I joined Wolfe, taking the two wrist ropes from him. He then climbed into the wagon and picked up the reins. "Remember, once Bonner starts down the alley, go fetch the deputy marshal. He said he'd be waiting in his office."

"Sure thing, Lomax. You think this will work out the way you planned it?"

"Probably not."

"What are you gonna do if it doesn't?"

"I don't know. Shoot Quirt and Bonner, I guess."

"I didn't sign on for murder," Wolfe protested.

"Then you better pray it works."

"Giddyup," Wolfe said as he shook the reins and drove away.

I felt foolish standing there, holding the ropes against the fence and waiting, waiting for a fellow that might not show, hoping he'd be drunk enough to fall for my ruse in the dark. Working in my favor was my cunning and Bonner's ignorance. The way I figured it, Bonner had sawdust for brains. Besides that, I suspected the ache in his danglers from our three previous encounters would leave him burning to settle the score.

As I waited a couple riders rode past, barely giving me notice after I started singing and swaying on my feet like I had had too much to drink. Maybe a quarter of an hour after Wolfe drove the wagon away, I heard Dreban almost shouting at the front of the alley.

"He's waiting for you, Bonner. You remember the deal, no guns? Just fists, right?"

"Damn right, I remembers," he slurred.

"He's at the end of the alley, waiting for you."

"Did that son-of-a-bitch leave his cane behind?"

"Yep," Dreban answered.

"And he didn't bring a fishing pole either, did he?"

"No, sir. No fishing tonight. He's unarmed and waiting to whip you with his fists."

Bonner growled. "Now he'll pay."

"Then go get him," Dreban said. He whistled once, twice, three times.

I smiled. As Bonner stomped down the alley, I yanked on both wrist ropes, hoping that his arms looked like a man preparing to box.

"I didn't believe you'd show up," I taunted as I played the ropes, manipulating Quirt's limp arms. "Fact is, I didn't think you had the jinglebobs necessary to face me."

He plodded toward the fence. I wiggled the ropes.

"I'm gonna kill you, you bastard," Bonner grumbled.

I heard Quirt moan, like he was beginning to regain his senses. Timing was good. Then he began to move his arms, fighting against the ropes on his wrist. Not quite sure what was happening, he tugged against the ropes and began to kick the fence with a shoe.

"Come on," I taunted Bonner. "You hit first, then I can claim self-defense."

Quirt began to fight against the ropes on his wrists, his attempts at screams muffled by the socks in his mouth.

"Hit me, dammit," I cried. "You scared?"

"Hell no," he answered, then charged toward Quirt and the fence. The fence shuddered when he slammed into Quirt, who gasped in a muffled panic.

"Come on, hit me," I screamed.

Bonner shrieked, then I heard the muted sound of his fist plowing into Quirt's stomach. Quirt struggled against the ropes binding him to the fence and fought me as I worked to manipulate the ropes on his wrists.

"You hit like a girl," I shouted.

"Oh, yeah!" He answered with a flurry of body punches. Quirt's screams were muted by the socks in his mouth. I wondered if he was as terrified as his wife had been when he beat her.

"Is that all you got?" I yelled at Bonner, infuriating him even more.

"No, you bastard. I'm just beginning."

His next punches seemed to be hard ones to Quirt's head, as the impact bounced the back of his skull against the wooden fence five or six times. The blows must have knocked Quirt unconscious as his arms went limp against the ropes in my hands.

"I'm still standing, Bonner. You can't even knock me down."

He answered with a shrill scream. "I can, too, dammit. See if you can still stand after I kick you in the balls."

The wall shuddered as Bonner kicked the fence.

"You missed," I cried.

The wall bounced again. Quirt moaned.

"I didn't that time," Bonner yelled.

"But I'm still standing," I answered.

I heard the whap of his boot against Quirt again.

"That's three times for the three times you caned me," Bonner cried. "Here's one more for good measure." He kicked again.

"I'm still standing," I cried. "You fell to your knees each time I popped your danglers."

Bonner raged against Quirt, pummeling him with his fists in the gut and head. I knew Quirt had passed out and there was no sense in hanging onto the ropes tied to his wrists. I let go and then began to untie the ropes around his waist and chest. I managed to get the rope around his waist unknotted and jerked it through the hole. The way Bonner was beating Quirt, I wasn't sure he would survive. I wanted Quirt beaten, not dead. When I got to the upper rope, I fumbled to untie it, Wolfe having tightened the knot harder than I was expecting.

"You bastard," Bonner kept yelling, as he continued to pummel Quirt.

After what seemed like forever, I unknotted the rope and yanked it free of Quirt's chest. I heard him crumple on the other side of the fence. Bonner just laughed, then kept on kicking Quirt while he was on the ground. I never knew a man to get a worse beating than the one Quirt took that night, but then I never knew a man who deserved one more for the way he treated his wife and the soiled doves he frequented.

I was relieved when I heard a voice at the far end of the alleyway. "Hold on, fellow, what's going on here?"

It was Deputy Marshal Clyde Tompkins.

"Huh," cried Bonner.

"Raise your hands, fellow."

"I'm unarmed," Bonner declared.

"Don't matter," Tompkins replied. "Raise them."

Bonner seemed to hesitate, until I heard the click of Tompkins' revolver.

"Now what's going on?" Tompkins continued.

"This fellow attacked me," Bonner lied. "It's that Lomax fellow that works at Medusa's. He tried to waylay me, but I got the best of him."

I heard the sound of others coming down the alley.

"Need help, Marshal?" asked Dreban.

"Yeah," Tompkins said, check on the fellow on the ground.

"He needs a doctor," Dreban cried.

"You're going to jail, fellow. What's your name?"

"Bull Bonner," he replied. "I was attacked."

"Stand still," Tompkins ordered.

I held my breath, then saw the glow of a small flame through one of the holes in the fence. Tompkins had struck a match to light Bonner's face.

"Doesn't look like there's a scratch on you," Tompkins said, then apparently lowered the match over Quirt. "Damn, you beat hell out of this guy. You're going to jail."

Bonner protested. "He challenged me to a fight, threatened to kill me."

"Who?" Tompkins asked.

"Lomax, the one that works at Medusa's place."

"Remove his mask," Tompkins ordered Dreban as the match flickered out. Tompkins struck another match then held it over the still form at his feet. "Doesn't look like any Lomax to me," Tompkins continued. "It may be that bridge toll taker, Nathan Quirt I believe is his name."

"No," cried Bonner. "It can't be. We're pals."

"It could be and it is and I doubt you're pals anymore," Tompkins answered. "Now move along, we're going to jail."

"You need to send for a doctor," Dreban said.

Tompkins snickered. "I will, once I get Bonner locked up. May go ask his wife, first, if she thinks he needs a doctor. Now move along."

"I didn't do it," Bonner lied as he marched out of the alleyway with his hands up and Tompkins' gun in his back.

I heard Dreban and Wolfe whispering and I looked through one of the holes to see them squatted over Quirt.

"He's still breathing," Dreban said as he and Wolfe untied the ropes from his wrists.

"Catch, Lomax," whispered Wolfe as he threw his rope over the fence.

Dreban did likewise. "We'll come around to get you."

"Yeah," said Wolfe, "I want to get out of here before someone finds us here and thinks we did it."

I heard them trotting away and moments later their wagon came around the corner, moving a little too fast for my comfort. When they reined up beside me, I tossed all the ropes in the back and hopped in the wagon bed as we headed for the suspension bridge. When Dreban stopped the wagon at the toll booth, I jumped over the side, glad to pay the fare for horse, wagon and passengers. The toll collector looked half asleep and didn't even count my coins.

"Who'll spell you in the morning?" I asked.

"Nathan Quirt," he answered.

"Don't count on it," I said. "I hear he's not feeling too good."

I climbed back in the wagon. As we crossed the bridge, I threw the lengths of lariat and the augur over the side of the bridge and into the Brazos. When we reached the east bank of the river, we all laughed.

"Damn, Lomax, you pulled it off," said Dreban.

"Hope I don't ever get on your bad side," Wolfe added.

Dreban nodded. "I guess all that pampering at Medusa's gave you time to think up such a convoluted scheme."

"The girls did more than pampering," I lied.

"That's what I heard," said Wolfe.

We spent the night sleeping in the back of the wagon near the train depot, then woke up early and unloaded our baggage on the platform. I had my carpetbag, but each of them had a carpetbag and a heavy trunk. Wolfe's seemed particularly heavy.

As I helped him unload it, I shook my head. "You sure you haven't already found the mother lode?" I asked.

"Reading material," he answered.

He was toting his *Scientific Americans* around with him. While Wolfe took care of our baggage, Dreban and I returned the wagon to the livery stable, where we picked up our three horses and tack as well as my bedroll and carbine. Back at the depot, we put our horses in the stock pen for loading onto the train and sat on platform benches waiting for the train crew to build up steam and start us on our journey to the Black Hills and the gold that was certain to be our future. Hell, in a few months, we might be rich enough to buy our own railroad, not to mention a mansion, some racehorses and our choice of women, respectable or otherwise. I'd always heard money couldn't buy happiness and my experience with some Confederate gold back in Arkansas during the war pretty much confirmed that, but I decided it could secure me any type of misery that I wanted. We watched as the depot hands loaded our horses into the stock car, then stood up at the call of the conductor to board. I carried my bedroll, my carbine and the satisfaction that Nathan Quirt wouldn't be beating his wife any longer, and Bull Bonner wouldn't be bothering the girls at Medusa's or Big Red's for a long while.

We stepped onto the train and found two bench seats facing each other. I put my bed roll and carbine down on one seat and sat down beside them. Dreban and Wolfe sat opposite me, grins working their way across their mouths.

"I can't believe we're going prospecting for gold," Wolfe said.

"Hard work," I said.

Dreban nodded. "That's what I understand. It leads me to a question for you, Lomax."

"Shoot," I said.

"Why'd you give it up?" Dreban asked. "You know, all that pampering at Medusa's."

"To become partners with you fellows," I answered. "I don't figure I'll ever get another shot at finding gold. With my reputation, I can find pampering anywhere."

The train lurched forward and I began the next leg of my journey toward Dakota Territory, the Black Hills and the Little Bighorn.

Chapter Fifteen

We spent the next few days on different trains. We made good time, even if we were traveling in the wrong direction. Wolfe and Dreban didn't take us the shortest route to the Dakota Territory, but the cheapest, planning to save as much of our money as they could to grubstake our mining operation once we arrived up north. Leaving Waco, we headed south to Bremond, then connected with the Houston and Texas Central Railroad, which carried us to Indian Territory where we picked up the Missouri, Kansas and Texas Railroad, taking us to Vinita, Indian Territory. There we switched to the Atlantic and Pacific Railroad, which got us to St. Louis, then transferred to the Chicago and St. Louis line, which carried us to Illinois and Chicago. There we picked up the Northern Pacific Railroad to Minneapolis where we got on the Great Northern line to Bismarck, which happened to be the end of the line.

By the time we arrived in Bismarck, I had decided the country might have a thousand railroads but not a single one would take you where you wanted to go and not a single one was laid out on a route as the crow flies. I suppose that's why so many men got rich on railroads. Even so, who was I to question two guys who were always reading *Scientific American* and *Harper's Weekly*? Who was I to question two guys who always had their eyes if not their hands on the future? Of course the future didn't look too promising at Bismarck, which Dreban had convinced me was the best jumping off place for an expedition to the Black Hills. Even if the Black Hills were 205 miles west of the railroad terminus, it was still seventy-five miles closer than the Cheyenne route. The Sioux City / Yankton and Fort Pierre routes were even farther. The Bismarck route also offered better water, grazing and wood than its competitors. At least that was what Dreban and Wolfe had read. I wasn't so much concerned about finding water, grazing or firewood as I was scared of running into Indians. Water, grass and firewood had never tried to scalp me. I didn't like the idea of running into Sioux or Cheyenne, who considered the Black Hills sacred. The way I figured it, I might just become another vagabond slaughtered by the noble red man, but Dreban and Wolfe were risking becoming the smartest men ever scalped by Indians. Frankly, I'd about had enough of Indians at Adobe Walls, but Dreban and Wolfe, discounted my fears as we stepped off the train onto the platform in Bismarck.

"You worry too much," Dreban said.

"Do you know how many thousands of acres there are in Dakota Territory?" Wolfe quizzed me.

I shrugged. "I just read newspapers, not fancy magazines, so I don't know anything."

"Hundreds of thousands of acres," Wolfe continued, answering his own question. "The chance of us sharing the same acre with hostile aborigines during our expedition is small."

I took off my hat and scratched my head. "I'm not worried about aboriginals, just Indians. You know how many bullets there are in Dakota Territory?" I asked Wolfe.

Now he shrugged. "Hundreds of thousands, I'd guess."

I nodded. "And it only takes one to kill a fellow. Same with Indians."

When it came to Indians, Wolfe and Dreban were as useless as a tenderfoot at branding time. For all their scientific knowledge, they couldn't counter my argument so they did what scientists always do when confronted with opposition, they changed the subject.

"What do you think of Bismarck?" Dreban asked.

I plopped my hat back on my head, stomped my boots on the wooden platform as the other passengers got off the train because the tracks ended a few hundred yards from the depot. Like most frontier communities, Bismarck was a rough looking town of 200 buildings, mostly log and roughhewn, with a few shingled roofs but mostly puncheon or earthen tops. A smattering of tents and shanties sheltered men and women who had bet on their version of the future and lost. Of course the future had reached Bismarck in the way of the telegraph office, which shared space with the modest Great Northern Depot. From the looks of it, the railroad company had run out of money when it reached Bismarck or had decided this was not only the end of the line but also the end of the world. "Worse than I was expecting," I finally answered. "It looks dead to me."

"What did you expect from a town barely three years old?" Dreban asked. "Besides, if we'd been here a few weeks back in time for the Fourth of July, I'd bet it was hopping."

"From what I've read," Wolfe said, "the townsite was staked out in 1872 and a year later was named Bismarck in honor of Prince Baron Otto Eduard Leopold Von Bismarck-Schoenhausen."

"Otto who?" I wanted to know.

"Prince Baron Otto Eduard Leopold Von Bismarck-Schoenhausen," he repeated. "You know, Germany's Iron Chancellor."

"No, I don't know. Why'd they name it for some foreigner?"

Dreban jumped in. "There's a lot of Germans immigrating here. The railroad's board of directors thought naming the town for the chancellor might draw enough interest from him to invest in the line so they could extend the railroad."

I could see the end of the line from where I stood. "Looks like they'd've been just as good naming the place for me no farther than the chancellor's investment got them."

"Hell, Lomax, when we find gold, we'll each have a town named for us in the territory," Wolfe added.

"Maybe," I agreed, "but we've got to find the gold first and avoid the Indians second." Based on my luck, I figured I'd find Indians before I ever found any gold, but maybe my luck would change with Dreban and Wolfe.

As we waited on the platform for them to unload our belongings from the baggage car and then our horses from the livestock car, a sprout of a boy walked up holding a newspaper.

"Care for a *Bismarck Weekly Tribune*, gentlemen?" he asked. "Only ten cents for all the territorial news and the best routes to the Black Hills."

Figuring I couldn't grow any more ignorant than I already was from reading newspapers in the past, I shoved my hand in my pocket and pulled out a dime. "I'll take a paper," I said.

"Certainly, mister." The boy grabbed my coin, stuck it between his teeth and bit it to confirm it wasn't a slug.

"Don't trust me, do you, son?"

"Can't be too careful, mister, not with the type of fellows that pass through here on the way to the gold fields or with some of the soldiers at Fort Abraham Lincoln across the river. They can't all be trusted."

"You wouldn't deal in periodicals, would you, lad?" Wolfe asked.

The boy scratched his head.

"You know, like *Harper's Weekly* or *Scientific American*," Dreban explained.

"You might find *Harper's* at Stimpson's General News Agent. I'm not sure about *Scientifical* or whatever you called that other one as it don't sound like the type of thing folks around here would read," the boy said. "Stimpson sells books, stationery and all the latest newspapers, though none is as good as the *Weekly Tribune*. Stimpson's also carries notions, fruits of all kind, confectionery and even paper collars."

"Civilization has indeed reached Bismarck," Wolfe said.

"What you gentlemen really need is a subscription to the *Weekly Tribune*," the boy continued. "It's two dollars a year or a dollar-seventy-five for six months. If you subscribe, you'll get a free chromograph of General George Armstrong Custer, the famous boy general of the Civil War now stationed at Fort Abraham Lincoln."

"Who'd want a likeness of that Yankee general?" I asked. My question must have struck the paperboy like a ton of raw liver because it took him a moment to answer. The kid didn't realize that not all of us, particularly those of Southern descent, were impressed with the boy general. Even if he did lean Democrat in his politics, he was still a Yankee. Consequently, I didn't like him, and I hadn't even had the pleasure of meeting the bastard yet.

"A lot of people think highly of him as he pretty much won the War of the Rebellion, he did," the kid began. "He's with the Seventh Cavalry across the river now. People see him from time to time when he's in town or when he comes to the depot to catch the train to go to Washington. I've seen him several times. Some think he's the best thing to ever happen to Bismarck because he's the one that found gold in the Black Hills."

"Thanks, kid," I said. "I'll see if my friends are interested, but the last thing I need is a likeness of a Yankee general. Now run along."

The kid scampered away.

"Either of you interested in a chromograph of General Custer?"

"No," said Wolfe. "All we're interested in is his gold."

We killed time on the platform until they retrieved our baggage, then more time while we waited for them to unload our mounts. That took another thirty minutes as the depot hands were in no rush to unload anything since the train wasn't going any farther west, thanks to the stinginess of Germany's Baron von Bismarck. When our horses and tack were finally unloaded, we saddled up and made arrangements for the depot to hold Wolfe's and Dreban's trunks until we could find a hotel. Leaving the station, we rode toward the main street. Bismarck certainly hadn't prospered from the gold in the Black Hills. It was a sorry looking town from afar and from up close.

Riding through Bismarck was like courting an ugly girl. It was better than being alone, but you didn't really care to be seen by others. Best I could tell, Bismarck only had one church and no jail that I could spot, forcing me to conclude that fewer sinners called Bismarck home than Waco with all its churches and fine jail.

As we rode onto Main Street, I thumbed through my *Tribune* until I found all the advertisements on page seven. "Looks like we've got two choices for hotels," I told my partners. "There's the Capitol Hotel, claiming to be the only first class hotel in town. Another possibility might be the Miner's Hotel at the corner of Main and Fifth, boasting the best accommodations for the least money."

"I like the sound of the Miner's Hotel," Dreban answered, "because mining's how we'll make our fortune."

"Works for me," Wolfe echoed. "More money we save on room, the more we can invest in our equipment and supplies. You have a preference, Lomax?"

"Not in hotels," I replied. "But you boys better heel yourselves well before we go out into Sioux country. You may need pistols and rifles more than picks, shovels and gold pans."

"Lomax," said Dreban, "you fret more than a duck in the desert."

"Fellows," I shrugged, "you don't chase grasshoppers when the hogs are eating the corn. And you can't find gold—much less spend it—when you don't have a scalp." I folded the newspaper for emphasis and continued my ride down the street, wondering if I had done right by joining these two tenderfeet on this prospecting expedition. I figured book-learning could get you out of a library and make you a success in some Yankeeville in the northeast, but I wasn't sure it did much good on the frontier. I'd never seen an Indian reading a book, though I had heard tell of some in Texas stealing books for lining their leather shields to deflect bullets. Pretty clever of them, even if they hadn't read *Scientific American*!

As we rode, people scurried everywhere, as if they too expected to find all the gold in the Black Hills, even if they were mistaken. Our expectations, however, were better grounded in reality. After all, two-thirds of our partnership read *Scientific American* and the other third had a smidgeon of common sense! We spotted the two hotels on Main Street and decided our choice of the Miner's Hotel had been wise as Ostland's Livery and Feed Stable stood on the opposite corner of the street. We could put up our horses there until we got outfitted and started toward the Black Hills and all the riches that awaited us.

We tied our horses outside the hotel and marched inside where the desk clerk greeted us.

"What do you want?" he growled like he was eating fire and spitting smoke.

"All the gold in the Black Hills is what we want," I said, "but we'll settle for a room!"

"You and everybody else in Dakota Territory," he answered. "Business is killing me with all the mopping and laundry to do."

"Tired arms are better than an empty stomach, Sunshine," I reminded him.

"Not when you got to cook your own meal," he said.

I'd met rattlesnakes that were friendlier than this cuss. He had a rip in his britches that went from mad to bitter and back again. I was tempted to pull my revolver and put him out of his misery, but Dreban interrupted.

"Do you have a room available?"

"One," he said. "Ten dollars a night."

Wolfe whistled. "That's a little steep."

I nodded. Our grubstake wouldn't buy much equipment and supplies if we stayed long at the Miner's Hotel.

"Any way we can get it cheaper?" Dreban asked.

"I'll halve the cost if you take it without sheets," he said.

"It's got a bed in it right?" I insisted on knowing.

He shook his head. "This is a hotel. What did you expect, jackass?"

"Well, Sunshine, you're a desk clerk and I expected a few manners."

"Hell, jackass, as ugly as you are, you ought to be grateful I'm even offering you a bed 'cause a lesser man'd be scared to let you room here for fear you'd drive off business."

Right then and there, I decided the first thing I was going to do when I got rich was buy the Miner's Hotel in Bismarck, Dakota Territory, and fire Sunshine's ass.

With a cooler head, Wolfe pulled me from the desk and stepped in my place, him and Dreban making arrangement for us to share a room without sheets. That was the only bargain Dreban and Wolfe could arrange as the clerk would have nothing to do in retrieving their trunks from the railroad depot. We were assigned a room and went down the hall in search of our quarters. Not only did the room lack sheets, it also lacked a lamp, a chair, a mirror, a dresser, a wash basin, a bedstead and even a candle. Besides the double mattress on the floor and one pillow atop it, a slop jar was the only other amenity this room offered.

"It beats sleeping on the ground," Wolfe said.

Dreban clucked his tongue. "We won't all fit on it."

"We'll sleep crossways on the mattress."

Dreban nodded. "That's pretty smart, Lomax."

"Common sense don't come from reading *Scientific American*," I answered.

My partners smiled. "That's why we brought you along, Lomax."

We agreed to spend two nights at the hotel so we could leave the morning of the third day. After inspecting our room and mattress, we went to Ostland's to stable our horses. Dreban and Wolfe made arrangements with a stable hand to pick up their trunks from the depot and store them at the livery stable. We made inquiries about buying a wagon for our expedition, but the proprietor told us wagons were hard to find and pricey. He recommended we go with mules instead. Not only that, he just happened to have three mules he could sell us. My belongings would fit on my horse, but my partners had their trunks and more possessions than me because I had never stayed long enough anywhere to accumulate much more than the necessities and an occasional bottle of liquor when I needed a good drunk to clear my head. By the time Dreban and Wolfe had quit bartering with the stable's proprietor, they had agreed to exchange the trunks and their extra clothes for one of the mules and for free stabling of our mounts for the next three days. When they couldn't convince the stable owner of the value of their back issues of *Scientific American*, they decided they would pack them into the Black Hills for reading and kindling if necessary. I figured the magazines would come in handy for outhouse business. With one mule already to our string, we purchased the other two and the rigging necessary for them to tote our supplies, our equipment and the *Scientific Americans* to the Black Hills.

After that was done, we grabbed the belongings we wanted at the hotel and found us a place to eat supper. We were too soon in town for Dreban and Wolfe to find the out-of-the-way eateries, so we had our supper at a restaurant on Main Street. Then we explored the side streets, working some of the stiffness out of our legs from all that time we had spent in cramped seats on the train cars. We discovered a store that sold mining supplies, but as dusk was approaching and the store was only minutes from closing we agreed to return the next morning to secure the equipment we needed to find our fortunes.

Back at the hotel, we drew straws for the pillow. Wolfe won. Dreban and I shook our heads in disgust, then forced Wolf to sleep in the middle of the mattress between us. We literally crawled into bed that night and the next. We slept as best we could, but a damn tomcat found his way into our room and marched back and forth at our feet, rubbing his fur against our socks. I kicked at him once and he screeched, drawing grumbles from Dreban and Wolfe. I should've shot the cat, as he would ultimately do great damage to my reputation in Bismarck, but without a lamp or a candle I feared I'd miss him and hit something else, like one of the rats I heard scampering across the floor. I guess I could put up with the tomcat if he kept the rats from attacking us.

Morning came cool and we regretted not having any sheets or blankets to fight the early chill. Here it was the end of July and we needed cover against the cool breeze of morning. We took care of our business in the slop jar, then dressed and left the room, leaving our belongings there in the hope that no one would steal them since the door had no lock on it. If someone did intrude, perhaps they would steal the slop jar or tomcat instead.

As we marched past the counter, I nodded at the clerk. "Good morning, Sunshine, will you be emptying the slop jar for us?"

"Nope," he said. "You can carry it to the outhouse and dump it yourself."

"You're not very hospitable, Sunshine."

"Don't like your kind!"

"Why's that?" I wanted to know.

"You're Southern."

"So?"

"There's a southern fellow about town named Wilson. Named his son 'Wilkes Booth,' after the assassin of our beloved President Abraham Lincoln. That's not right, jackass."

"Don't blame me, Sunshine. During the war, I had a mule I named Abraham Lincoln."

He scowled, then held up his left hand. His middle finger was missing. "Lost it at Gettysburg to Rebel sons a bitches!"

"I lost a brother at Gettysburg. Seems you got off easier than John Adams Lomax."

Sunshine swallowed hard. "Your name Lomax, too?"

I nodded. "H.H. Lomax."

"You the same Lomax that took a dump in Wild Bill Hickok's hair while he was sleeping?"

I narrowed my eyes and tightened my lips, then nodded slowly.

"Pissed on it, too, and Hickok was too scared to do anything about it."

"My apologies, Mr. Lomax," Sunshine said. "I'll empty your slop jar while you're out."

"That's better," I scowled. "And I better not find anything missing from our room, or I'll hunt you down and show you some real southern hospitality."

His eyes widened as he nodded.

Wolfe and Dreban followed me outside, uncertain whether to laugh or not. "That true about you and Wild Bill?" Dreban asked.

I shrugged. "Who knows? I was drunk."

"Damn, Lomax," interjected Wolfe. "I don't want you drinking around me any."

"We can't afford to spend anything on liquor until we get provisioned up," I said.

"Even then," Dreban announced, "we don't want you drinking whiskey around us."

"Fellows, there's thousands of Indians where we are headed and you're worried about me drinking a bottle of whiskey? If I take to drinking, I promise you I won't scalp you."

"We're not worried about your scalping us, just using us for an outhouse."

"Gentlemen, you have my word your head and hair are safe from me, drunk or sober."

I'm not sure they trusted me as they started talking in Morse code as we walked, saying dot and dashes as they spelled out words I couldn't make out.

"You fellows don't believe me," I said.

They both smiled. "Just practicing our telegrapher skills," Dreban said. "We never know when we'll need them."

We turned into the J.W. Raymonds & Co. store, which boasted mining supplies. We had enough money to purchase shovels, miner's pickaxes, long-legged gum boots, washing pans, tarps, stakes, rope, a portable sluice box, slickers, gloves, a coffee pot, skillet, a stew pan, butcher knife, grindstone and a tent. We had everything delivered to the stable and then went to secure provisions at a general mercantile, buying ten pounds of coffee, two pounds of sugar, twenty pounds of flour, a sack of dried beans and, upon my insistence, a bottle of whiskey.

"You're not planning on drinking that and scalping us while we sleep, are you?" Wolfe asked.

"No, sir. It's for celebrating when we strike the mother lode!"

Their grimaces turned to grins. We paid for the supplies and had them delivered to the stables as well. Next I guided them to a gun shop where they each bought a six-shooter and a Henry repeating carbine. We purchased three cartons of ammunition each for our revolvers and carbines. When we left the gun shop, we returned to the hotel where the clerk greeted me.

"Mr. Lomax, the slop jar has been cleaned. I went ahead and added sheets and a blanket to your mattress," he announced. "Is there anything else you need?"

"Thanks, Sunshine. I guess the last thing I need before I leave is a haircut. Any place around where I can find one?"

Dreban and Wolfe looked at one another and shrugged, then turned to me. "Why you need a haircut, Lomax? We're heading out into the wilderness, aren't we? No women folk to impress there."

"Fellows, when I go out into Indian country, I make it a practice to cut my hair as short as I can so I don't make an attractive target for some buck that thinks my scalp would look good hanging from his belt."

My partners looked at one another, then shook their heads. "We could probably use haircuts, too," Dreban answered.

"Now, Sunshine, any barbers?"

"Two, Mr. Lomax. There's Chris Heli, he's German."

"He a friend of the Iron Chancellor?" I asked.

The clerk shrugged. "And there's, W.H. Coner, he's—"

"—American?" I interrupted.

"Yeah," Sunshine answered. "You might say that." He gave us directions to Coner's shop down the street.

After we dropped our carbines and ammunition off in our room, we headed for the barber shop. When we stepped inside, we discovered that Coner was not only an American, but also a black American. Having just roomed the past several months with the smartest man I ever met, a Negro at that, I stepped right up to the chair and seated myself.

"Good day, gentlemen," he said, "welcome to Coner's Tonsorial Parlor. I'm W.H. Coner, owner and proprietor and the best barber not only in Bismarck, but also these United States."

"Cut it close," I said. "I'm headed out tomorrow to Sioux country and I don't want them envying my hair."

"You're a man of rare intelligence, Mr.—" Coner said as he strapped the barber cloth around my neck.

"Lomax," I said. "H.H. Lomax."

Coner gasped. "Oh, Lordy," he said. "You wouldn't be the Lomax that shaved Wild Bill Hickok's head and sold his hair to a wig maker, would you? If you are, you are a legend in tonsorial circles."

"Nope," I said, pointing to Dreban. "He's the one that did that. He's my brother."

Dreban gasped, then me when Coner announced that Dreban's haircut was on the house!

Chapter Sixteen

With fresh haircuts and shaves, we slept well that night except for the tomcat that prowled our room, guarding against rats and occasionally arching its back and rubbing against the soles of our feet, purring his satisfaction. We slept past sunrise as it was pointless to arise earlier since we didn't have any lamp or candle to see with, and we thought burning the place down would create too much light and too much trouble. We made water in the slop jar and left it adjacent to the mattress, then packed up our meager belongings. My carpetbag carried my whorehouse suit and shirt, my shoulder harness and five-shot pistol along with a carton of ammunition plus a change of drawers, an extra pair of socks and the coat I had bought in Waco. I thought about discarding the whorehouse suit, but reconsidered, figuring once I was rich I would need some fancy clothes to match my newfound wealth. My pocket pistol lacked enough punch and range to scare the Sioux, but you couldn't have too many weapons in Indian country. Too, the peashooter was powerful enough at close range to blow your brains out as that was always a preferred alternative to letting the Indians capture and torture you to death.

As we were finishing our packing, I glanced over at the mattress and saw the tomcat peeing on it. I jumped his direction and kicked at him, but my boot caught the slop jar, which bounced on the mattress, overturned and dumped its contents across the bedding.

"Damn," I said.

The tomcat scampered to the corner of the room and just stared at me like I'd made a bigger mess than he had.

"Glad we're not staying another night," Dreban said.

With that we picked up our belongings and marched out of the room, down the hall and past the desk where Sunshine was rubbing his eyes.

"Good morning, Mr. Lomax," he said. "I hope you had a nice night's rest."

"He did," Wolfe answered for me, "but he had a little accident on the mattress."

"He didn't mean anything by it," Dreban added. "He's just not housebroke."

I scowled at my partners as we marched past the desk toward the door.

"Good luck in the Black Hills, Mr. Lomax. You might want to watch out, as I hear Wild Bill's there. I've even heard tell that Buffalo Bill's headed that way. I hope you find gold first."

"I will," I said. "Hickok's too drunk, and Cody's too lazy to do mining work."

"Damn, Lomax," said Wolfe. "Quit lying about men you've never met. It's bad luck."

I laughed as we reached the door. "If you'd spent more time getting out rather than sticking your nose in a *Scientific American*, you might've met some legends yourself. I've never seen a dime novel about a scientist."

We emerged into the brisk morning air and crossed the street to Ostland's where we checked that all our provisions and equipment had been delivered, then saddled our mounts. That was the easy part. Next we had to load our three mules. That was when I realized we lacked the pack saddles necessary for a mule to carry a heavy load of freight. My tenderfoot partners hadn't realized that oversight, as it was not the type of thing *Scientific American* was likely to write about. Fortunately, the proprietor had a few pack saddles for sale. Unfortunately, they were overpriced, further depleting our money reserves. That would become a moot point, however, once we found gold, assuming we could carry all our nuggets out of the Black Hills by mule. I was beginning to have my doubts as I watched Dreban and Wolfe fumble with the pack saddles. They were as confused as a temperance unionist in a brewery.

"No, no," I explained as I grabbed a pack saddle from Dreban and twisted it around. "You had it on backwards, start with a saddle blanket first." Then it dawned on us all we needed saddle blankets. The smiling proprietor obliged us with three overpriced pads, our grubstake diminishing even more. Then I resumed my lesson, mounting the pack saddle on the first mule, careful to rest the weight on the animal's ribs, rather than its spine. Then I had Wolfe and Dreban stack provisions and equipment on the contraption as I started a lash cinch with a rope under the mule's stomach and proceeded to complete a diamond hitch, which secured the load at six different points on the pack saddle. After that mule was done, we moved to the second. Wolfe and Dreban understood the basics of placing the pack saddle, but seemed befuddled by the diamond hitch, something I learned during my freighting days. We finally crowned off the last mule with the portable sluice box and two canvas bags I didn't recognize.

"What are those?" I asked, as my partners wedged them among our supplies and tools.

"Some *Scientific Americans*," Wolfe answered, "something we can read on the trail."

"We'll find a use for them," Dreban added.

I had an idea where they could stuff them, but then I remembered we could use them to wipe rather than stuff. "Excellent idea," I said.

"I'm glad you're seeing the value in scientific literature, Lomax," said Wolfe.

"They're smoother than a corncob or prairie grass," I answered.

My partners scratched their heads as I finished the diamond hitch on the third mule, our sluice box riding like a throne atop the last mule. By the time I had finished my third lesson on tying a diamond hitch, I realized the intricacies of securing our equipment were beyond their more scientific minds. I understood then that I'd be tying every knot each morning or we'd spend our time on the trail picking up our supplies and equipment. By the time we emerged from Ostland's, it was almost noon so we decided to spend two bits apiece at an eatery. We found a place for lunch, tied our animals outside and entered to enjoy our last regular cooked meal for weeks.

After lunch, we headed south along the upper bank of the Missouri River. The river, I would learn, had more twists and curves than a politician's logic so I never knew whether to call it the eastern or northern bank. Same with the lower bank as some called it the western and others the southern side. As I had had trail experience, I took command of our partnership, taking it easy the first afternoon, allowing the mules to become accustomed to their loads. I named them Shadrach, Meshach and Abednego for some characters I remembered from my momma's Bible readings. As I recalled, Shadrach, Meshach and Abednego stood up to all the challenges they faced, including a fiery pit. I called them Shad, Mesh and Ab for short. We made it five miles to Whiskey Point, a motley collection of saloons for drinking, gambling dens for betting, cribs for fleshing and a single dirty eatery for less important cravings. We might have gone farther, but the last ferry of the day had already crossed the river to Fort Abraham Lincoln, so we waited the night.

Cursing our luck at missing the ferry, we decided to have a drink at the saloon that looked the least dangerous. The Bloody Bucket, it was called. Even in the late afternoon sun, the place was dingy, lit only by candles, which were little compensation for the lack of windows. It didn't make sense to me, neither did the grizzled proprietor, who must've been a Civil War veteran because he was missing his left forearm. "Claude Armstrong, owner and proprietor of the Bloody Bucket at your service, gentlemen," he announced when we entered. I figured he'd been more aptly named Armgone, but didn't mention it, Yankees generally being touchy about losing appendages to Confederate fire. "Any of you three needing work?" he asked.

"Just a drink," Wolfe responded.

"Damnation and tarnation," he said, as if he didn't appreciate our business.

"Can't find help anywhere. Everybody's heading to the Black Hills."

I nodded. "Good help must be hard to find."

"I'm past good help. I'd take poor help if I could get. Seems everybody's heading to the gold fields. I suppose that's where you three are headed, am I right?"

We all nodded.

"Then what'll you boys have?"

"Whiskey," I said.

"Just not too much for, Lomax," Wolfe said, pointing to me.

Armstrong froze. "You wouldn't be the Lomax hombre that tied firecrackers in Wild Bill Hickok's hair, then lit them and watched him dance, would you?"

"That's me, but it wasn't firecrackers. It was dynamite," I said, figuring if Dreban could get a free haircut out of a rumor, I might get a free drink.

"Damn," Armstrong said, "I don't know that I want your kind around here."

"You said you'd take poor help."

"Indeed I did, yes sir," Armstrong said, "but taking bad customers is another thing. It can give the place a bad reputation."

I looked around at a place that was empty of customers except us, had no windows, a dirt floor, a bar made from unfinished pine planks and a half dozen tables with chairs that didn't match. The only sunlight in the building came from the cracks between the logs and the only amenity other than the liquor cached behind the bar on a table was a jar of pickles on the counter.

"If you don't serve Lomax, you don't serve us," Wolfe said.

Armstrong knew he was as licked as if he had been challenged to a game of patty cake. "A whiskey apiece it is." He poured us a drink in three dingy jiggers and set them on the bar. We helped ourselves to a pickle for our supper, then settled up with him. Armstrong lightened up some after we paid him, then jabbered about his army service at Shiloh and Stone's River, where he had lost his arm. By the time we finished our whiskey and our pickles, we were about as good a pals as you can be with a fellow you've known for half an hour. He agreed to let us stay the night in a shed with our animals, even offering to let us stay in one of his back rooms. We declined, preferring to sleep with our stock and supplies to safeguard them against any thieving Whiskey Point riff-raff. Come morning we saddled our horses and packed the mules, me tying the diamond hitches. Come ferry time, we were waiting at the landing as the rickety transport loaded us and a dozen other passengers and animals headed for Fort Abraham Lincoln. After a short ride, we emerged on the lower bank of the Missouri and stepped off the ferry for our mining adventure.

We headed southwest toward the Black Hills and we were barely a mile from the fort before I encountered the biggest surprise of my new prospecting career—rattlesnakes. Seemed you couldn't take three or four steps before you'd see one to the left or to the right or straight up ahead. There were long ones, short ones, fat ones, skinny ones. I'd never seen so many rattlesnakes, save in Texas, where most of the rattlers were two-legged and had high opinions of themselves. Every night when we camped, we had made sure we were on good ground, away from ledges and dens where the rattling reptiles might hide. We took rope and beat the ground around us to send any hiding rattlers slithering away. Only after we had cleared a perimeter of thirty or more feet did we unload, tend to our mounts, cook our supper and throw our bedrolls. The days began to run together as we moved toward the Black Hills. We followed the general route outlined in the *Bismarck Weekly Tribune.* I was always wary of Indians, but my tenderfoot partners said the odds of us encountering Sioux or Cheyenne or any other tribe in the vastness of the territory were slim. To my knowledge, no tenderfoot had ever killed an Indian, though the opposite could not be said. After several days on the trail, they complained that I was too skittish. On occasion, they talked to each other in dots and dashes, Morse coding their messages so I wouldn't understand if they were calling me a jackass. So we traveled, day after day. Twelve miles to Oak Springs, eleven to Fire Heart Creek, then ten to Sandy Creek and seven to Timber Creek. From there, it was twelve to Three Butte Creek, twelve more to Cannonball River, thirteen to the South Fork of the Cannonball, then eleven to Hidden Wood Creek, which we were able to find in spite of its name, eight to Grand River and seven more to Slim Butte Creek, the halfway point.

We rested there an extra day and then resumed our journey, going fifteen miles to Slim Butte itself, ten to the North Fork of the Moro River, then ten more to the river's South Fork and fifteen miles up the South Fork. From there it was twelve miles to Dead Horse Creek, fifteen to the South Fork of the Cheyenne, twelve to Oak Creek and then fifteen more to the Black Hills. The final few days we were able to see the Black Hills on the horizon. They looked dark and ominous.

When Dreban and Wolfe weren't Morse coding, we talked about our past as we rode. Though I believed everything they said, they seemed skeptical of my stories, like riding with Jesse James on his first bank robbery, surviving the Indian attack at Adobe Walls the year before, helping Buffalo Bill shoot his namesake quarry and killing the meanest guerilla partisan in northwest Arkansas during the Civil War. I avoided one subject, though.

"What about Wild Bill Hickok?" Dreban asked.

"Yeah," Wolf echoed. "What about him?"

"It's a sore subject," I responded, "even if it happened seven or eight years ago."

Dreban scoffed. "Sounds like to me you've struck gravel in the mother lode of tall tales you've been spinning for us."

"Nobody gets around that much," Wolfe said.

"You tenderfeet'd be surprised how much you can do when you don't have your nose buried in a *Scientific American* and your finger glued to a telegraph key," I answered, then changed the subject when I saw a big rattlesnake slithering along off the side of the trail. "If we'd been prospecting for rattlers, we'd be rich by now."

"Assuming we weren't dead from a bite," Wolfe replied.

"I'd suck the poison out of your bite," Dreban offered.

"Indians can kill you, too," I offered. "It's harder to suck an arrow out." I was tempted to shoot the large rattler, but if we'd shot at every snake we'd passed since leaving Bismarck, we'd've run out of ammunition days ago. I saved my bullets for Indians or claim jumpers.

Dreban laughed. "We're three weeks from Bismarck and haven't seen a single Indian."

"That don't mean they ain't seen us," I replied.

The laugh died on Dreban's lips. He hadn't given that possibility much thought.

"The Black Hills is sacred Indian land," I said. "Some say it's haunted by their spirits."

"I don't believe in ghost stories," Wolfe said.

"Maybe so, maybe not," I offered, "but just because you ain't read about it in *Scientific American* don't mean it ain't so."

While we hadn't spotted any Indians, as we got closer to the Black Hills, we began to see distant prospectors headed for the gold that we believed was rightfully ours. From what we saw, prospectors outnumbered Indians, but some of them were just as likely to kill you. So, in addition to the Indians and rattlesnakes, we generally avoided other prospectors, just to be safe. Most were likely honest men, but a few were bound to be thieving murderers.

Our second day in the hills, we came upon a broad grassy valley with a narrow stream running down the middle. In the distance I spotted, a camp with a half dozen wagons circled around a red-and-white tent as gaudy as one you'd find at a circus. Seven other smaller canvas tents were scattered among the wagons. In front of the big tent stood a makeshift flagpole with a limp American flag hanging from the top. Close to a hundred horses grazed in the distance under the watch of guards. This outfit was better equipped than ours, for certain.

I reined up and waited for Dreban and Wolfe to join me. They eyed the outfit suspiciously. "What do you think?" Wolfe asked. "Is it an Army camp? Will soldiers force us to leave?"

"Is it a merchant trying to sell over-priced goods?" Dreban inquired.

"Boys," I said. "Let's go down and visit for a spell. There's only one man I know that would travel the Black Hills with an outfit like that."

"Who is it?" Dreban asked.

"I'm not saying," I replied.

"Why not?" Wolfe asked.

"Because you wouldn't believe me if I told you." I nudged my horse and decided to trick the boys. "Just shut up when we get into camp. Don't say a damn thing and, for God's sake, don't make any sudden moves or somebody'll have to suck a bullet out of your gut."

I looked back over my shoulder. Their faces were as grim as an undertaker's at a pauper's funeral. Damn, they were gullible, scared for no reason and completely oblivious to real danger.

As we approached, a few men emerged from the tents or from behind wagons, staring at us and our three pack mules. My suspicions were proven correct when a tall, lanky man dressed in fringed buckskin stepped out of the gaudy tent and eyed us. His flowing brown hair hung down to his shoulders and framed his face with its matching mustache and goatee. Only one man traveled out west with such an ostentatious outfit, and that man was William F. Cody, who occasionally led buffalo hunting expeditions for government officials, foreign dignitaries and American businessmen and millionaires who wanted a Methodist sprinkling of life in the West rather than a full Baptist immersion in the frontier.

Approaching the camp, I began to grin and Cody stepped toward us, shading his eyes with his hand as he tried to identify us.

"Oh, my God," asked Dreban, "is that Wild Bill Hickok?"

"If it is," Wolfe whispered, "we're dead."

"Yeah," Dreban said. "We'll tell him we just took up with Lomax this morning."

"Hush, you two," I commanded, deciding to scare them more. "You want to get us killed? Anyway his hair's grown out, and he was so drunk he won't remember."

"I hope you're right," said Dreban.

"Now shut up, unless you want Bill to fill you with lead. I'll do the talking."

Both of them gulped audibly as we came within carbine range, then fell behind me when we were within reach of sidearm fire. Slowly, they dropped behind me a couple horse lengths.

I decided I'd give them a little more to worry about. "If he starts shooting," I instructed, "each of you jump off your horse, shoot your mount in the brain, then use his carcass as a breastwork to return their fire. That'll probably give you a few more minutes of life before they finish you off and leave you for the buzzards." I glanced over my shoulder. Both looked as nervous as a yearling at steering time. My partners had swallowed a whole bottle of my Gullibility Tonic. "Remember," I cautioned, "no sudden moves or you may wake up dead in the morning."

Drawing up my horse twenty paces in front of Cody, I watched as he lowered his hand from his eyes. A grin broke open between his mustache and beard. He strode toward me.

"Well, I'll be damned," Cody said. "If my sight doesn't deceive me, it's Leadeye Lomax, the worst buffalo shooter on the plains."

"Your eyes are as sharp as ever, Bill," I said as I dismounted.

"How the hell you been?"

"Making money and making do," he answered. "Much as I hate to admit it, I owe my good fortune to you. If you hadn't nicknamed me Buffalo Bill, I'd probably still be scouting for low wages rather than getting paid for leading expeditions for wealthy men and even performing my exploits on stage for paying customers."

"Maybe I need a cut of your take if I'm the cause of your good fortune."

Cody laughed, then walked up, grabbed my hand and shook it vigorously before grasping me in a bear hug.

"You don't need a cut, Lomax. I returned the favor by knighting you Leadeye Lomax."

"The name's yet to catch on but I'll give you a quarter interest in the proceeds in exchange for a quarter share of the profits from your name," I offered.

"No deal, but I'll introduce you to folks that can make your name as famous as mine."

When I escaped Cody's bear hug, I turned around and motioned for Wolfe and Dreban to dismount. The fear had drained from their faces, though I hoped it hadn't reached the seat of their britches. Dreban and Wolfe stepped beside me, very careful with their movement.

"Fellows," I said, "I'd like you to meet William F. Cody, better known as Buffalo Bill."

With a dramatic gesture he must have learned from theater work, he yanked off his hat and bowed like a performer after a standing ovation. That was Cody. He craved attention and acclaim as well as the women that always seemed to be with him when his wife wasn't.

As he straightened up and replaced his hat, I said, "Bill, these are my partners, Douglas Wolfe and Brian Dreban. They're telegraphers."

Cody stepped to them, grabbed their hands and shook them vigorously. "You boys won't find many telegraph wires in these parts, smoke signals more likely."

"You're *the* Buffalo Bill?" Dreban stammered.

"Absolutely, friend. I can't afford to hire an imposter."

"And you know, Lomax?" Wolfe wanted to know.

"Known him for years," Cody replied. "We've hunted together, fought Indians together, eaten from the same pot of beans and even shared the same woman on occasion."

"We didn't believe him," Dreban said.

Cody slapped me on the shoulder. "I've never known a man to

tell more truths than Leadeye Lomax. Of course, if he's in a bind, he might stretch the facts a little."

I grinned. "These boys only believe things that are printed in *Scientific American*."

"Well, friends, have you ever read *Buffalo Bill, King of the Bordermen* published by Ned Buntline? Now that'll give you an education about life in the West."

Dreban and Wolfe shook their heads.

"Any of it true?" I asked.

Cody grinned. "The first two words of the title." He slapped me on the back. "You've got to remember that Buntline is a former newspaperman so he's never let the facts get in the way of a good story or healthy sales." With that, Cody put his arm around my shoulder and started toward his tent. "I've got some gentlemen I'd like to introduce you to. Maybe they can make you a dime novel hero. It's free money, if they use your name."

"What are you doing out here anyway, Cody?"

"We told the newspapers it was a buffalo hunting expedition, but like everyone else, we thought we'd see if gold was as easy to find as the press reported. Like most newspaper accounts, it was overdrawn. To be honest, there's more truth in dime novels than newspapers these days."

I glanced over my shoulder and saw Dreban and Wolfe leading our mounts and mules toward Cody's stock. Cody pointed at my partners.

"Why'd you take up with a couple tenderfeet, Lomax? This is dangerous country for men that don't know what they're doing."

"I figured my savvy and their scientific smarts would make us all rich."

"Or dead," Cody said.

We entered the tent and I spotted a handful of well-dressed men, sitting around a table playing poker. By their tailored attire, I knew they were industrialists or railroad men, who had paid well to accompany Cody on his "buffalo-hunting" expedition.

"Before I introduce you to the boys," Cody said. "I've got a question for you."

"Shoot," I said.

"What did you do to Hickok? Whatever it was, he's still furious about it and threatening to get even! Only problem, he's not talking about it."

"And neither am I!"

Chapter Seventeen

We stayed two nights with Buffalo Bill and his party, most of whom were bigger tenderfeet than Dreban and Wolfe, monied men more attuned to Broadway than the broad axe, self-importance rather than self-reliance and spending rather than earning money. The only calluses on their palms came from shaking the hands of working men. When Cody first took me into his tent to introduce me to a quartet of rich businessmen, not a one got up from his seat at the poker table to shake my hand. Cody introduced me to the well-to-do northeasterners, who even as they sat at the poker table looked down their noses at me, as if I was a nobody rather than Cody's equal. Then the thought struck me that I might have been Cody's equal, but I had nowhere near the status of Buffalo Bill, even if his status was a creation of the nickname I had given him. Cody's stature had grown with all the dime novel lies that followed. I needed a dime novel name, and I was in luck as the last magnate Cody introduced could've made that possible.

"Lomax," Cody said, "I'd like you to meet Mr. Adams of the House of Beadle and Adams."

Right off I was confused. First, Cody never called anyone mister. Second, the only houses I was familiar with were those of ill-repute like my previous employer. I couldn't believe a respectable man would promote himself as the baron of brothels, the prince of prostitution. Maybe Mr. Adams—Cody never did tell me his first name—was to whorehouses what Vanderbilt was to railroads and railroading and what Carnegie was to steel and stealing. I figured I could go fetch my carpetbag, put on my whorehouse suit and have a job and a buddy for life, once I explained my past success. My job possibilities collapsed when Cody continued.

"This is my long-time friend Leadeye Lomax," Cody informed him, then turned to me as I shook hands with what I thought must be the titan of titties. "Mr. Adams is a partner in one of the most successful publishing houses in America. The House of Beadle and Adams prints thousands of dime novels each month."

Adams' hand was soft, but his gaze was hard. He held my hand longer than was necessary as he evaluated me. Meanwhile, I studied his bushy brown sideburns, dark eyes and thin lips. Releasing my hand, he acknowledged me. "Leadeye, is it? That your given name?"

"Given to me by Cody."

"His publishing house made me famous," Cody jumped in, "and when you're famous, you're apt to have more opportunities to make a fortune. Whoever thought I'd be acting on stage? Mr. Adams, you might want to consider Leadeye Lomax for a series of dime novels. He's had as many adventures as I have, I suspect. Tell him Leadeye."

I saw a fortune in my future, the road no longer paved with gold but rather papered with pages from a Beadle and Adams dime novel about me, Leadeye Lomax. I laid it on thick, but truthful. "I've ridden with Jesse James, driven cattle from Texas to Abilene, fought Indians at Adobe Walls, protected soiled doves in Texas, and—"

"Lomax, Lomax, where have I heard that name?" Adams asked, scratching his sideburns like he had the mange. "Oh, yeah! Wasn't there a Lomax that braided Wild Bill Hickok's hair to a bedpost one night when he was so drunk that he almost scalped himself when he got up the next morning?"

"That's what I've heard tell," I admitted, figuring it would enhance my reputation as a colorful dime novel hero.

"That's too bad, Leadeye," Adams announced. "We can't make a dime novel character out of someone who has humiliated an established dime novel hero like Wild Bill, whose very name sells thousands of books a month."

So much for my career as a literary hero. Mr. Adams looked back down at the card table and resumed his poker game. He never said another word to me, which was fine, as I had decided there was more honor in whorehouses than publishing houses.

After seeing my literary career collapse barely moments after he had suggested it, Cody shooed me outside where we could visit without offending our betters from the northeast.

"Your day will come," Cody said, waving Wolfe and Dreban over for the conversation.

They joined us, but I could tell they still couldn't believe that me and Cody—or should I say Buffalo Bill?—were friends. They just listened as Buffalo Bill carried on about his life since I had last seen him years before.

"After Buntline had success with *King of the Bordermen*, he wrote more dime novels about Buffalo Bill and decided to stage a play with me and some of the other sons of the prairie. So, Texas Jack Omohundro and I teamed up almost three years ago now and debuted *The Scouts of the Plains* on stage in Chicago and toured the northeast. The next year, we invited Hickok to join us. He didn't take too well to the stage, Hickok didn't, saying he still had some scores to settle out west. He mentioned your name as one of them, Leadeye. I'd watch out, if I was you, as he's supposed to be in these parts. He wouldn't say what you did, but he was plenty angry."

Wolfe and Dreban gulped.

I shrugged. "It was years ago. And, it was a matter between friends."

"Former friends. Hickok ain't forgot it, Leadeye."

"You've been playing too many theatricals, Cody, making this into a melodrama."

"Maybe so," Cody shrugged, "but I wouldn't want to be you around Hickok."

"Hickok don't scare me," I said, "so let's hear more about your stage acting."

Cody obliged us, extolling the advantages of the theatre, including the applause, the recognition, and the money, not to mention the young women that usually waited at the stage's back door after performances.

I couldn't resist. "How's the wife? Irma Louise, wasn't it?" I asked.

Cody shook his head. "She's fine, Leadeye. Thanks for reminding me. Your charm must be the reason Hickok wants to shoot you. But what would you expect from Hickok when he gives up the easy life of the stage for the hard life on the frontier. You know, Leadeye, the frontier's dying, so I'm gonna make my living on the stage, recreating frontier adventures."

I scoffed. "Cody, you're too big for the stage. A man with your reputation should be outdoors where the whole world can see you." I threw my arms back and pointed to the mountains and the sky. "You can't capture the West on a tiny stage lit by gas lamps with props for animals. You need spectacle and authenticity to recreate the West."

Cody stopped and stared at me, a subtle smile sliding across his face like that of a thief stealing goods right from under a proprietor's nose. "Leadeye," he said, "I'll return a favor for you one day and put in a good word for you with Hickok the next time I see him. Does that seem like a fair trade?"

I shrugged. "I guess so. I'm not sure what we're trading, but if you throw in food and provisions for today and tomorrow, we'll call it a deal."

He agreed. The rest of that day and the following one, Cody treated us like royalty, though not as good as he took care of his rich friends. We feasted on canned goods, including oysters, while our horses and mules grazed on nice grass, drank fresh water from the steam and enjoyed a day-and-a-half of rest while we soaked up Cody's hospitality.

The second morning we slept a little later than we normally would on the trail, but got up in time for a breakfast of fried saltpork and biscuits with apricot preserves, washed down with good strong coffee that made a man feel he could whip the world if he needed to. As we saddled up our mounts, Cody came over to visit.

"You boys be careful. A small party like yours can get in big trouble," he warned.

"Indians?" Dreban asked.

Cody nodded. "Them and the riff-raff that always follows easy money. There's been some murders over claims and some killings over nothing other than meanness."

"We'll be on our toes," I said.

"I know *you* will, Leadeye, because you're a survivor. It's your partners I'm worried about."

Dreban and Wolfe looked at one another and swallowed hard, finally realizing the dangers were real for tenderfeet like them, not just a figment of my imagination. They walked to the mules to secure the pack saddles and stack our goods. I tied a pack with the diamond hitch that was beyond their grasp. Cody handled the second load for me and I did the third. When Shad, Mesh and Ab were burdened, my partners and I each tied one to our saddle rigging, mounted up and said our goodbyes.

"We appreciate your hospitality," I offered.

"And thank you for your idea," Cody said. "Wish Mr. Adams was inclined to publish dime novels about you."

"It's probably best," I replied. "If my books pushed yours out of the limelight, you'd be as mad at me as Hickok is."

As Cody laughed, I leaned over and shook his hand, then turned our animals deeper into the Black Hills. I glanced over my shoulder and waved a final time. Cody waved back. I wasn't sure what idea Cody was talking about, and I wouldn't know until the next time I saw him some seventeen years later. It didn't bother me at the time, though it would later when I ran into Cody in Chicago.

After we left Cody, we rode deeper into the Black Hills, uncertain of our destination. Others were hunting gold, too. We'd run into five or six outfits a day, all close-mouthed and suspicious. If silence was indeed golden, everyone we ran into was rich because they wouldn't tell us a damn thing, barely greeting us before patting their sidearms or Winchesters and letting us know we'd be safer moving on. Wherever we found gravel, we'd put on our gum wading boots and step into the stream and pan for gold. My father, who had learned to pan during an unsuccessful expedition to California in '49, had taught me how to do it in the stream behind our cabin in Arkansas. I showed Dreban and Wolfe how to scoop gravel into the pan and tip it, then agitate the pan, allowing the heavier gold flakes and, if you were lucky, nuggets to sink to the bottom while the lighter matter spilled over the side. The work was brutal on the knees for all the squatting and hard on hands for all the time in the frigid water. We were either unlucky or poor prospectors because we turned up nary a flake in our dozens of stops.

What we did pick up was a couple roughs that tended to follow us wherever we went. Invariably, they'd be anywhere from a hundred yards to a quarter mile behind us, always staring our way but never panning for gold. They rode mangy horses and led a pack mule that, the best I could tell from a distance, carried no mining implements. Dreban and Wolfe seemed oblivious to them, but I kept an eye on them, at least for the first week. After that, they seemed to be no more of a threat than the jays and woodpeckers that watched us from the trees.

After the prairie land we had traversed to reach the Black Hills, the terrain seemed like a Dakota Territory Garden of Eden with tall pine and spruce on the mountains and lush grass in the valleys, traversed by streams that drew deer, antelope and an occasional buffalo along with prairie dogs, squirrels and foxes. And like the Garden of Eden, serpents abounded, though not as many as we had encountered on the prairie yet enough to make you watch your every step. In places the mountains had gentle, slopping sides while in others they were scattered with boulders, broken by crevices or sheathed in the debris from landslides.

In one of these rougher stretches of land where I was making my own trail through the ridges, I spotted something that looked unusual—a flat sandstone rock that had been wedged between two other rocks. I lifted my hand for Dreban and Wolfe to stop behind me.

"What is it?" Dreban asked.

"No sudden moves," I answered, pulling their legs again. They froze like statues. Ever since Cody had confirmed my worries about Indians and other threats in the Black Hills, they took my word, even when they didn't need to. I pointed to the rock. "It may be a sign."

I walked over some rocks to get to the one that had caught my eye. As I squatted down to look at it, I saw a couple leather thongs extruding from beneath it. I yanked on the thongs, but they were so weathered, they broke in my fingers. Curious, I grabbed the rock and began to wiggle it free. When I finally pulled it out, two things caught my attention. First, a leather pouch had lain hidden beneath the stone for a long time. Second, someone had scratched a message on the stone. Dropping the rock by my boot, I picked up the pouch and unknotted the leather thong which held it shut, the ancient leather again crumbling in my hand. I wedged my finger into the pouch and forced it open, then dumped the contents into my palm. I couldn't believe it, but I had struck gold. I counted nine nuggets the size of my little fingertip or bigger.

"Boys," I said, closing my fingers around the nuggets. "We've found gold."

Dreban and Wolfe jumped off their horses and noisily scampered to me. I heard the buzz of a rattlesnake. I jumped up and backed away until I spotted the snake about six feet away. He was a big one, but he stopped rattling and slithered beneath a rock.

"I told you no sudden moves," I chastised them, as if I'd known the snake was there all along. "You're gonna get us killed yet."

They were so mesmerized by the mention of gold that they barely heard what I said. I turned my fist over and unfolded my fingers so they could see the gold in my palm. Their eyes widened. "Boys, we've found our first gold." I dumped the nuggets into Wolfe's hand, then picked up the sandstone slab that had originally caught my eye. I brushed the dirt and residue from its face and read the message to myself. I whistled.

"What is it?" Dreban asked. "Directions to more gold?"

"Only if the golden streets of Paradise count," I replied

"What?" Wolfe said, offering the nuggets to Dreban.

I read the inscription aloud. "Came to these hills in 1833, seven of us De Lacompt—Ezra Kind—G.W. Wood—T. Brown—R. Kent—Wm. King—Indian Crow—all dead but me, Ezra Kind, killed by Indians beyond the high hill, got our gold June 1834."

Dreban whistled, though I wasn't sure if it was from the message or the gold he fingered.

"Look," Wolfe said, pointing to the back of the rock. "There's more."

I turned the rock over and brushed away enough of the dirt to make out the rest of the message, then started reading aloud. "Got all the gold we could carry, our ponies all got by the Indians. I have lost my gun and nothing to eat, and Indians hunting me."

Dreban whistled. "Sounds desperate."

"What you gonna do with the rock?" Wolfe asked.

"Put it back where I found it. We can't help them forty years after the fact."

I squatted and shoved the sandstone slab back in place when another voice entered the conversation.

"Howdy, neighbors!"

I froze, cursing myself that I had let someone slip up on us. Twisting around slowly, I saw the two riders that had been shadowing us. They held the reins to our horses. Both wore twin sidearms and cradled Henry carbines in the crook of their arms. Their long black hair and shaggy beards made them look like the illegitimate offspring of the ugliest momma black bear in all of creation. Best I could tell with them mounted, they were about the size of Dreban and Wolfe, but they looked like they had been dressed in the poor house, their clothes about as shaggy as I'd ever seen on white men, their shirts threadbare and stained, their pants ripped in places and worn thin at the knees. The rags they wore helped disguise their overall ugliness. One had a gouch ear and the other had a crooked nose, their most pleasing and distinguishing physical features. If ugly had been brains, those boys could've spoken Greek and read Latin.

I arose slowly my hand sliding to my holster and lifting the leather catch from the hammer of my pistol just in case. With my left hand, I patted the knife in my scabbard.

"You neighbors having any luck prospecting?" asked Gouch Ear.

I prayed Dreban and Wolfe would remain silent, but God must not've heard my plea.

"Just a few nuggets," Dreban said before I could stop him.

"Is that so, neighbor?" asked Gouch Ear.

I stepped between Dreban and our new friends so I could do the talking.

"We wish," I said. "Fact is, we ain't as much panned a flake of gold. If we had, we'd've stayed at the location and kept working. You fellows don't seem to be doing much digging or panning or anything."

"That's a fact, neighbor," said Gouch Ear. "We've found easier ways to make money. We file mining claims for neighbors like you."

"That's big of you," I said. "What do you charge?"

"Depends on the claim and the prospectors," he continued.

"You have a calling card you could leave us, in case we needed your services?"

"Fresh out," Gouch Ear said, "but we'll find you when you need us."

"Obliged!"

"We just rode up to introduce ourselves and to give you neighbors a warning," he continued.

"What's that?" I asked.

He and Crook Nose held up the reins to our mount. "You might not want to leave your horses unattended. We've been seeing an Indian skulking around. Where there's one, there's always more."

"Obliged again," I said. "I'll have my partners take the reins." I motioned for Dreban and Wolfe to head down to our animals. I didn't care to take my gaze off of our new friends in case they tried something funny. I trusted them as much as I did a rattlesnake without a rattle.

Dreban slipped the nuggets into his pockets as he moved toward our mounts. Our new friends sat on their horses like vultures awaiting their next meal or maybe, in their case, a new suit of clothes. Those flimsy rags wouldn't provide much warmth come winter. As the two scavengers watched Dreban and Wolfe pick their way down the rocks, I noticed Gouch Ear and Crook Nose sliding their free hands down toward the revolvers at their sides. I slipped my revolver out of my holster and prepared to plug them if they tried anything.

When they looked my way and realized I was holding my pistol, their hands relaxed and retreated away from their sidearms. All this occurred without Dreban and Wolfe realizing the silent drama that had just transpired. As my partners reached the pair, the twin uglies tossed the reins of our horses to them.

"Thanks," offered Wolfe.

Gouch Ear tipped his hat. "Just being neighborly, neighbors. You fellows remember to watch out for that Indian that's been skulking around. You never know what a thieving redskin might do if he gets the chance."

"We'll stay on the lookout for *any* kind of trouble," I replied.

Both Gouch Ear and Crook Nose nodded, then turned their

mounts around and started back down the mountainside. I was tempted to shoot them in the back because I knew they would do the same for us if they had a chance. Even if we didn't have much gold, our mounts, mules and supplies would've brought a pretty penny out here in prospecting country.

"Nice they gave us the warning about the Indian," Wolfe offered.

"They were just sizing us up, looking over what we had and deciding whether it was worth the risk to take us on one day," I explained.

"So, the stalking Indian was a ruse?" Dreban asked.

"Probably," I replied, "but you never know."

Dreban patted his pocket where he had dropped the nuggets. "Least we can say we found some gold."

"It's dead man's gold," I replied. "That's bad luck."

"You're too superstitious," Wolfe chided.

"Could be," I admitted, "but it's just a feeling I got. It don't help having those two buzzards following us around as they have for the last week." I re-holstered my pistol and hooked the leather over the hammer. I bent down, retrieved the empty pouch and tossed it to Dreban. "Put the nuggets in there and give them back to me."

"Why do you get to keep them?" Dreban wanted to know.

"Because I know not to open my mouth whenever I find gold. You ain't figured that out yet. When the time's right, you'll both get your share. I counted nine nuggets, three apiece."

Dreban pulled the nuggets from his pocket and dropped them one by one into the pouch so Wolfe and I could both count them. He offered me the pouch.

I stepped toward the horses, taking the pouch and slipping it in my pants pocket. After that, we mounted up and warily continued the search for our fortune. I feared I was going to wear my neck out, looking back over my shoulders for Gouch Ear and Crook Nose. Occasionally, I saw them in the distance, but they seemed to be falling behind but never out of sight.

With them on our tails we moved deeper into the Black Hills, ever on the lookout for trouble and terrain that might be hiding our fortune in gold. As we rode, my anxiety grew. Something wasn't right! I'd glance from side to side and then over my shoulder, checking for the problem I could never identify. Nothing worked as we rode deeper into stands of pines and spruce.

"You sure are jumpy," Wolfe observed.

"Something ain't right, I can sense it," I said, then noticed the ears on my horse flick forward. He'd heard something. I scanned to the left, to the right and ahead of me. Nothing!

Maybe my mind was playing tricks on me, so much so that once I thought I saw a ghostly figure hiding in the woods. I did a double take, but said nothing to Dreban and Wolfe. I didn't want them to think I was crazy. I rubbed my eyes with my free hand, certain I had seen a half naked man, moving among the timber. I could've sworn this specter had a yellow zigzag painted down the left side of his face. Was I going crazy?

"You look a little pale," Dreban observed.

"A mite nervous, I suppose. I don't like those two buzzards trailing us."

"Maybe it's your nerves from carrying all *our* gold," Wolfe said.

I shrugged. "You'll get *your* gold, fellows, when the time's right."

We made camp that night among the trees. After we unsaddled our horses, my partners unpacked the mules while I searched for enough firewood to cook supper. I took two armloads back to our camp and started the fire. Then I retreated to look for some more. I had another armful when I saw the specter again.

It was an Indian!

He stood between two trees scowling at me, almost taunting me with his arrogance. I dropped my firewood and grabbed for my pistol. Before I could cock it, the Indian disappeared.

"What's the matter?" Dreban called from camp.

"Saw something."

"What was it?"

"An Indian."

"No," said Wolfe. "You're pulling our legs again. We've gotten wise to your pranks, Lomax."

I re-holstered my pistol and picked up my firewood, then marched to camp. We fixed supper and were throwing our bedrolls when I looked up past the campfire and saw the Indian, peeking around a tree.

I tossed the bedding down, grabbed my pistol and jumped past the fire and ran to the woods. Again he was gone.

"You see another ghost?" Dreban asked.

"I don't know what I've seen."

When we finally climbed into our bedrolls, I was tired, but couldn't sleep for worry about the Indian. The two buzzards had been right that we were being followed. I tried to convince Dreban and Wolfe that Indians were out there and watching us. As I began to hear the heavy breath of their sleep, I saw him standing just at the edge of the fire's illumination.

I jumped up. "There he is," I screamed.

Wolfe and Dreban bolted up in their bedrolls.

"There," I pointed "standing on the other side of the fire."

My partners twisted around, but saw nothing. They just shook their heads and crawled back down in their bedrolls.

Now I had two problems. The first was the Indian always lurking just out of our reach.

The second was that my partners now thought I really was crazy.

Chapter Eighteen

For the next three days, I was more nervous than a felon on the witness stand. I know I saw my Indian ghost several times, either afoot or astride a white horse with war markings on its flank, but Wolfe and Dreban never spotted him as we worked our way deeper into the hills, finally finding a place where a gravelly stream ran between a thick stand of pine on one side and a rough mountain splotched with boulders and cut by narrow ravines on the other. The stream provided cold water and the banks were lush with thick, sweet grass which made for good stock grazing. We set up camp and started panning for gold, uncovering enough flakes that we set up our small sluice box for the first time and began shoveling gravel in search of more gold.

While my partners kept both their eyes on the sluicing, I kept one on the surrounding terrain, hoping to spot the Indian apparition and either shoot him or make certain my colleagues saw him so I could redeem my sanity. Mid-afternoon I caught a glimpse of him out of the corner of my eye, hidden in the shadows among the trees. I kept working. "No sudden moves," I told Wolfe and Dreban. "Now just keep working, but he's watching us."

"Who? Your imaginary friend?" Dreban asked.

"I see him," I whispered under my breath as I slapped the water in the sluice box.

"You've been spooky ever since we found that inscribed rock," Wolfe said.

"I call it the tombstone," Dreban added.

"We won't get any tombstones if this Indian catches us flat-footed," I said. "It may be forty years before someone runs across our skeletons. But I still see him, fifty yards away."

"Well, what do you want to do?" Wolfe asked.

"I'm gonna count to three, then both of you spin around to spot him."

"You told us no sudden moves," Dreban said.

"I'll make an exception for this. One … two …three."

They whirled about instantly. The phantom dove to the ground and disappeared. Dreban and Wolfe shook their heads.

"Don't see a damn thing," Wolfe said.

"Me neither," Dreban added.

"He was there, I swear."

"I've got a question for you, Lomax," Dreban said. "Are you trying to scare us off so you can get the gold?"

"I ain't that kind," I said.

"Could be a visual mirage," Wolfe interjected. "I read a story about that a while ago in *Scientific American*. It could be that."

Dreban shrugged. "Or it could be that Lomax is imagining things. Maybe he's turned lunatic from all this time sleeping under the moon, that and the thin air."

Wolfe and Dreban, bless their hearts, wanted to come up with any explanation that they could to rationally explain my visions. They came up with all sorts of possibilities except the only legitimate one: I was actually seeing an Indian. They started talking even more to each other in Morse code, discussing my sanity, I suppose. As sunset approached, we carried our sluice box back to camp and started supper. Back down the stream a quarter of a mile or so, I saw the campfire that I took to be that of Gouch Ear and Crook Nose, who just couldn't seem to find their own trail. I looked around for my Indian tormentor, but didn't spot him until after we built our fire. Then I glimpsed him, but said nothing as I didn't want to contribute to the growing case for my lunacy. Two more times I spotted him, coming ever closer to camp. He never made a sound, nor lingered in a single spot. I felt he was watching me all the time, even when I couldn't see him.

As the ghost stalked us, Dreban and Wolfe discussed what they wanted to do next. I wanted to find that damn Indian, scalp him and prove to my partners that I wasn't crazy.

"What do you think, Lomax, about moving on upstream to find the source of the flakes?"

"Do what you want, but I intend to find our stalker and kill him before he kills us."

"So you're breaking the partnership up, is that it?" Dreban asked.

"You fellows think I'm crazy so what's the point in staying together?"

"I suppose you'll take the pouch of gold," Wolfe said.

Nodding, I let him know I would. "I'll be returning with your gold. Besides, you'll keep my mule and my share of all the equipment and provisions until I return. I'm just taking my horse, canteen and weapons."

Dreban and Wolfe talked the proposition over in Morse code. By then I'd about had enough of the future and its language of dots and dashes. I was trying to keep the Indian specter from dashing our brains out and dotting his scalping knife with drops of our blood.

"Okay, Lomax," Wolfe said. "We've agreed to let you go while we continue on upstream. If you're not back by sundown, we'll consider the partnership dissolved. If that happens, we take over your mule and your share of things."

I shrugged. "If that's the way you want it, but you boys need to be wary of Gouch Ear and Crook Nose. If they realize it's the two of you alone, they might try something."

"We're big enough boys to take care of ourselves," Dreban said.

I wasn't so sure about that, but I couldn't convince them otherwise. We ate our supper and retired to our bedrolls. Wolfe and Dreban each pulled a copy of *Scientific American* from one of their bags and read by the firelight. I just watched for the Indian, seeing him once, maybe twice, but by then I was so confused I didn't know what I was seeing.

Come morning we got up and went to work, saddling our mounts and packing the mules, me doing the diamond hitches. We didn't talk much as I guess we were suspicious of the others' motives. As Dreban was loading Shad, the mule balked, throwing its load atop a couple pieces of extra firewood and tripping Dreban.

"Dammit," said, Dreban as he pushed himself up from the ground and kicked at one of the logs. In the process, he knocked the heel off of his right boot. The heel went flying under Shad, who brayed and kicked at the air with his hind legs. Dreban shoved the mule back enough to pick up his heel. Yanking off his boot, he tried fitting the heel back on and grabbed the piece of firewood that had caused the trouble to begin with and pounded the heel back in place. We all knew the heel would not stay, but neither Wolfe nor I said anything for fear Dreban might pound us with the log instead. Silently, we finished packing up. The morning had started badly, except for one thing—I caught a glimpse of my Indian friend downstream. I knew what direction I would head when we parted company. I went to my carpetbag and pulled out my pocket pistol rig. I slipped the harness over my shoulders and shoved the pocket pistol into the holster. I took the carton of ammunition and put it in my saddlebag. "Good luck, boys."

Dreban and Wolfe marched over and offered me their hands. "Thanks for everything," Dreban said. Wolfe nodded his agreement.

I shook their hands. "I'll see you by sundown."

"We hope so," Dreban said.

"You will," I replied. "I saw him a few minutes ago."

They just shook their heads. "How come you see him and we never do?" Wolfe asked.

"I've had more experience in the wilderness than you boys," I said. "Remember, I'm not the one who tried to start a cattle herd with two heifers."

They laughed and nodded. "See you before sunset, partner," said Dreban.

I mounted up and turned my mount downstream, trying to screen my movement in the trees, not so much to hide from the Indian as to make sure Gouch Ear and Crook Nose didn't realize I was abandoning my friends for a few hours to kill a ghost. Once I had eased past their camp, I began to stalk the ghost. This specter left tracks of an unshod horse. Occasionally, I glimpsed the ghost, who seemed to relish this cat-and-mouse hunt. Every time I thought I had lost him, he made an appearance and I changed my course to find him. I wondered if he was leading me away to distract me so other warriors could attack Dreban and Wolfe—or me. Maybe I was crazy after all, heading out to prove that this ghost of an Indian actually existed.

I concentrated so hard on finding him that I lost track of time. The ghost led me toward a rugged mountain, splotched with boulders, studded with small stands of trees and veined with gullies and rivulets traversing the mountainside. I swallowed hard, realizing that the ghost had led me to a perfect spot for an ambush. Halfway up the mountain, I saw his horse tied to a tree. He had made no effort to hide it. That was his way of letting me know the chase was ending and the fight was about to begin.

I'd survived Adobe Walls where hundreds of Comanche and Kiowa had attacked. With so many Indians and so much danger coming from all directions in the Texas Panhandle, I didn't have time to get frightened. I just reacted. Now, I had plenty of time to think. I admit it, I was plenty scared. I drew up my mount, slid out of the saddle and tied the reins tightly to a waist-high branch of a dead scrub pine. I patted my bay on the shoulder as he leaned his head down to nibble on grass at the base of the tree. I probably should've given him more slack, but I was just thinking about the ghost somewhere up the mountain and didn't. Instead I untied my canteen and draped the strap over my shoulder, then pulled my carbine from the saddle scabbard and checked the load. I took a deep breath, then glanced at the sun. It was mid-afternoon. If I didn't kill the Indian quick and ride fast back to Wolfe and Dreban, our partnership would be dissolved. Maybe I could win their grace and resume our partnership, if I returned with the Indian's scalp.

I began the climb, wondering if this was a one-way trip to eternity. I crouched, darting from one hiding place to the next, a tree, a boulder, a fold in the mountainside, whatever would screen me from him, even though I didn't know where he was. I had just seen his horse. For all I knew, he was on the opposite side of every place I hid. Since he was certainly watching me, I didn't have to be quiet. Maybe if I made enough noise, I could flush him out.

"Hello, Indian," I yelled. "I got a haircut not long ago. My scalp isn't going to look that good hanging from your belt."

Silence.

"I got nothing against you," I continued, "except that you broke up my partnership, making my friends think I was crazy."

Perhaps I was crazy, yelling up the mountain at an unseen threat. I looked around the edge of the rock that covered me to see if I could spot him. I didn't. He was waiting for a kill shot, I was certain. Quickly, I peeked over the rock that sheltered me to see if I might spot him. I didn't. Nor did I spy a better hiding place in front of me. About fifteen yards to my right were a pair of boulders resting against each other in front of a half dozen tall pine trees. From there I could angle toward additional cover that surpassed that immediately to my front.

I darted to the two boulders, the canteen beating against me as I ran. I made it to the rocks, then caught my breath and peeked around both boulders. Nothing.

"Where are you?" I yelled. "I just want to shoot you before you shoot me."

More silence.

The only way I could find his location would be to expose myself and risk getting shot. I didn't like that idea, but I'd heard of an old Indian fighter using a stick to raise his hat above a rock enough to draw fire from a hostile. I didn't think my quarry was that dumb, but I didn't have anything to lose. Removing my hat, I slipped it over the barrel of my carbine and lifted it until just the crown was visible over the rock. It hadn't been there but a few seconds when I heard a swish-thud as the carbine vibrated in my hand. I yanked my carbine down. It was hatless. I looked around behind me and saw my hat pinned to a tree. The angle of the arrow told me the location of my enemy up the mountain.

I jumped up and fired two shots that general direction and charged up the mountain toward more cover in his direction.

I saw a flash of movement. It was him.

I fired and dodged.

An arrow ricocheted off a boulder by my shoulder. I jumped up and fired as I spotted the ghost running to a new den of rocks. He jumped. I fired.

I feared I had fired behind him, but I heard a savage scream that pierced the air and seemed to echo all around loud enough to startle my horse at the base of the mountain. I glanced quickly at my bay, and saw him rear up and fight the reins and the tree branch, which broke off. My horse trotted away. Now I had two problems—killing my tormentor and catching my horse.

The ghost kept screaming and crying. I must've hit him good, maybe in the jinglebobs, the way he kept shrieking. Or, maybe he was just decoying me, waiting for me to get close enough to plant one or more of his arrows in me. I pondered whether to take my time and slip up on him or charge him as fast as I could and finish him off. The more he cried, the farther I feared my horse would run away. Being afoot in this country was just as deadly as having an Indian tracking you.

I pulled some cartridges from my belt and re-loaded my carbine, then took a deep breath and darted to the circle of rocks where I had last seen the Indian. As I got closer, I dove to the ground and rolled over so I could see and shoot him if he popped up over the rocks. That's when I heard the buzzing over his moaning. I shivered at the sound and inspected the ground around me. Nothing. I sighed then stood up and inched up the boulder until I could see my enemy.

Never had I felt sorrier for a man that was trying to kill me than this Indian. He was propped against the boulder behind him, swatting his bow at the biggest rattlesnake I'd ever seen. The Indian was bleeding on the leg from puncture marks.

I didn't care for Indians, but I hated rattlesnakes almost as much as Texans. I didn't know which one to kill first, then I took aim and shot the rattlesnake, once, twice, three times. The reptile writhed in the dirt, contorting and twisting in its death throes. I figured if I'd've stretched it out, it would've been at least seven feet, maybe eight, and as thick around as a good piece of firewood. On top of that, I'd never seen a rattle as big, maybe eighteen or twenty segments with a button.

The only thing bigger than the rattle was the ghost Indian's eyes as I turned my carbine toward him. But it wasn't just me. I heard some more buzzing and glanced back at the dead snake. I spotted a gap in the ledge where a couple other rattlesnakes were slithering out. I pulled my carbine around toward the gap and fired a couple shots, sending the snakes back inside where I'm sure they awaited instructions from Satan. I stood up on the top of the rock and hopped from one to another until I was at the Indian's head. I should've shot him, but I felt sorry for him. I reached over the rocks and offered him my hand.

He nodded, but held up his hand like he wanted me to pause. He pulled a knife from his scabbard and crawled to the big snake to cut the rattle off his tail. Then he crawled back toward me. He grabbed his bow and tossed it over my head, then did the same thing with his quiver of arrows. I put my carbine down, took his hand and pulled him up and out of the snake den.

When he realized I wasn't going to kill him, he started trying to rub the rattle on the puncture wounds. I guess it was some primitive cure the Indians had used over the years. I shook my head.

"No," I said, "we need to suck the poison out."

He didn't understand. Even though I had a knife on my scabbard, I held my hand for him to give me his knife. He did so, skeptically. I put it under my arm, dropped to my knees and untied the leather thong that kept the bottom of my holster secure to my leg, then yanked the strap free and tied it around his leg, just below the knee.

The ghost that had been trailing me was now human, a Sioux, I reckoned. He still looked at me like he was unsure of my intentions. I took his knife and cut an x over each puncture wound. He grimaced, but never let out a sound. I dropped the knife down beyond his reach, then bent over and sucked out the wound. I would draw on the flesh, then spit out blood and poison. I sucked as hard as I could until I could draw no more blood or poison. Next I unplugged my canteen, took a sip to rinse out my mouth, then spat the water atop the puddle of blood and poison. I poured some of the water over the puncture wounds to wash them off, then offered the warrior a sip. He drank it readily. Then gave the canteen back to me.

After I corked the canteen, I untied the makeshift tourniquet and shoved my palms against the four puncture wounds, putting all the pressure I could on the wound to keep him from losing too much blood before the wound clotted. Occasionally, I would lift my palms to check on the flow of blood. After ten minutes, the bleeding stopped enough for me to release my grip.

I stood up and used some of the canteen water to wash the blood off my hands. I wasn't sure he could walk very far so I felt I owed it to him to drag him away from the snake den. I helped him up, and he used me as support to hop fifty feet away. As I propped him up against another rock, he lifted up his hand and offered me the huge snake's rattle.

"You keep it," I said. "It might bring you good luck, be strong medicine."

He kept pushing it toward me, but I shook my head. I retreated to where I had left his bow, quiver and knife. I picked them all up and carried them to him. I pulled an arrow out of the quiver.

"Let me have this," I said, figuring this arrow plus the one that had nailed my hat to the tree would be enough to prove to my partners that I hadn't been crazy after all.

The Sioux nodded, then lifted his right hand in front of his neck, palm out and with the two first two fingers straight and the other two bent. He raised his hand until the tips of his first two fingers were at the level of his scalp.

I replicated the sign as best I could and watched as he then unfolded all the fingers of his right hand and held it palm inward by his right ear. Twice he moved his hand past the front and back of his face.

Again I repeated the gesture. He nodded and smiled.

I smiled, too, thinking it odd I'd saved the life of a man who's name I didn't know. "I'm H.H. Lomax," I announced. "I'll call you Snakebit. Why I saved you is beside me, since you shot at me and planned to kill me, but it just seemed the right thing to do. Goodbye, Snakebit. I hope you recover and leave me alone."

Not knowing what I had said, much less how to reply, Snakebit just stared at me with his black eyes.

I turned around and walked away, wondering with each step if Snakebit might shoot me in the back with an arrow. He didn't and I made it safely to my hat. I yanked the arrow from the tree, slid my hat off the shaft and placed it back on my head. Surely the two arrows would convince Dreban and Wolfe that I had not been crazy or hallucinating.

I glanced up at the sky, knowing that our partnership would be over in an hour as the sun was beginning its final descent, but I hoped my partners would take me back, especially after I returned with the pouch of gold nuggets. I planned to ride hard the next day to catch up with them, but my bay had other ideas. I couldn't catch him. Every time I'd get within ten feet, the bay would shake his head and the broken branch still tied to the reins would bump his legs, the horse would dart away, terrified by the limb thumping his legs. I didn't catch him that night and it wasn't until noon the next day that I was finally able to reach him and only then after the dead branch had snagged between a log and a rock. When I finally caught the reins and untied the broken limb, the animal's forelegs were so bruised and bloodied from the beating that I had to go slow, riding him some and leading him at other times.

I finally reached the stream where my Indian hunt had begun and turned upstream to search for my partners. I didn't see any sign of Gouch Ear and Crook Nose, which was a good thing. About noon of the fourth day, I reached Dreban's and Wolfe's last campsite or what was left of it.

And, of them!

The campsite had been ransacked, *Scientific Americans* were strewn everywhere; the sluice box had been smashed to pieces; one of the mules was dead with an arrow in its side; the tools were scattered all over the place; my carpetbag was thrown aside. And then there were the two bodies, both with their heads cut off and nowhere to be found. I supposed their scalps were hanging from some warrior's horse and their skulls were decorating some Sioux lodge. I recognized them by their clothes and by the missing heel on Dreban's right boot. Odd thing was, Dreban had his boots on the wrong feet. The way I figured it, Indians attacked early in the morning. In his haste, Dreban had put his boots on the wrong feet. The bodies were mutilated so that I couldn't bear to look at them. I blamed myself for their deaths. If I had never left them in pursuit of the Indian ghost, I might have been there to help fight off their attackers.

Their dreams of striking it rich had left them dead and cost me two of the best friends I'd had since leaving home. There wouldn't be any telegraph in their futures unless someone was able to string a copper wire to the Pearly Gates. I kicked every *Scientific American* that I saw as I looked for one of our shovels. I finally found one in the stream where the attackers had thrown it. I began to dig a grave, my sweat mingling with my tears. It took me some three hours because I wanted it deep enough that animals wouldn't dig up the bodies and mutilate them further. Since their heads were missing, I excavated a shorter grave.

When the hole was done, I dragged their bodies to the pit and laid them in as gently as I could. I picked up what other pieces of them I could find scattered around camp, then tossed those atop the two carcasses. I looked for a blanket or something to cover them with, but the attackers had made off with their bedrolls and the provisions. Then I spied all the *Scientific Americans* scattered around the camp. I collected them and opened the magazines up and dropped them over their bodies, trying to cover as much of their remains as possible. Now they would have some reading material for their journey to eternity. Then I remembered they were headless so they probably wouldn't be reading much of anything. When I had covered as much of their mutilated bodies as I could with the magazines, I began to shovel dirt atop them. It hit me that I had made a promise to them that I would return with the pouch of gold nuggets we had found from our unlucky predecessors forty years earlier. I dug into my pocket, pulled out the pouch and dropped it in the grave atop them.

"There's your gold, boys. My share, too. You'll have a little spending money when you get to Paradise," I said, as I finished covering the grave. When it was mounded over, I offered a prayer. "Dear God, take care of the best prospecting partners a fellow ever had. Amen."

I hadn't had much to eat the last few days, but I wasn't hungry after what I'd seen. I scrounged through the mess that had been Dreban's and Wolfe's last camp and found a piece of the sluice that would serve as a tombstone. I carved their names and "my partners" in the wood and shoved it into the ground where their heads would've been if they still had them.

I retrieved my carpetbag with my whorehouse suit still intact and picked up a few other small things that might come in handy on the trail, then moved downstream to camp the night. I built a small fire and dug through my carpetbag and found the bottle of whiskey we had bought in Bismarck to celebrate the day we found our fortune. I wasn't planning to celebrate now, but rather to forget what I had seen and buried. I tossed down my bedroll, used my saddle for a pillow, climbed under the blanket and nursed that bottle until I drew nothing but air. The liquor made it worse. I couldn't forget. I kept dreaming that I could see Dreban and Wolfe getting attacked by Indians. Hard as I rode I could never reach them in time to save them in my nightmare. I tossed and turned, but the night terror only worsened. Someone grabbed my hair to scalp me. I recognized the face.

It was Snakebit!

He had come back to kill me!

Snakebit lifted my head and slipped a leather thong over it and around my neck to strangle me. I fought against him, but nothing seemed to work. I was in his control. As I fought, I heard a rattle. Damn snakes! Now they would consume my corpse once Snakebit killed me. Everybody and everything was against me, except the whiskey. I could no longer tell what was real and what was not. The past few days had been horrible.

None of it made sense, especially when I awoke!

I was still trembling from the ghastly dream, shaking my head to clear the pain and the grisly nightmare. I had a terrible hangover! Most horrifying of all, around my neck I now wore a leather necklace with a serpent's rattle—eighteen segments and a button—tied to the end.

Chapter Nineteen

It took awhile to recover from the hangover, but I couldn't get past losing Wolfe and Dreban, nor could I figure out why Snakebit had followed me and given me the horrendous necklace. Maybe it was his way of thanking me. I loathed snakes and was repulsed by the rattle, even more so when I tucked it inside my shirt and felt it cold against my chest. Despite that revulsion, I kept the necklace, as if to prove I had actually encountered the Indian, though the people I most wanted to prove it to were dead and buried.

Slowly, I got up that morning, salvaged what else I could from camp and shoved it in my carpetbag. I saddled up my horse and tied the carpetbag over my bedroll. Next, I walked over to the stream and filled my canteen. After tying my water to the tack, I stepped over to the grave.

"Sorry to leave you boys," I said, taking off my hat. "I guess I protected you from the wrong Indians. I should've stayed here and fought it out with you. Maybe then we'd've found our fortunes." I wiggled my finger through the hole in my hat. "See, this is where Snakebit shot at me." I guess it was foolish talking to them because their ears were somewhere else with their heads. Realizing both that they couldn't hear my feeble explanation and that all the words in the world wouldn't bring them back, I turned for my bay. Mounting without looking back, I started my horse toward Bismarck.

Along the way, I ran into other prospectors covering some of the same ground me and my partners had traversed. An optimistic lot, they still believed a pot of gold rested at the end of their rainbow. At the end of my rainbow was nothing but a lonely grave for two.

"Giving up, are you?" one grizzly prospector asked me.

I shrugged. "Indians got my partners."

The prospector scratched his scraggly beard. "Some say Crazy Horse is roaming these hills, killing small parties. Could be him or other bands of Sioux or Cheyenne stalking us."

"Only Indian I saw was Snakebit."

"Ain't heard of him," the prospector said.

"I reckon few have."

"Good luck on your trip to wherever you're going. With one less prospector around, that means more gold for me," he said.

"Enjoy your gold and the winter," I replied, then nudged my horse toward Bismarck, hoping to avoid any more Indians. I retraced our route as best I could, though it took me almost a month to get back to the safety of Bismarck.

By the time I reached my destination, November had arrived and winter was breathing across the prairie. I was broke and had little to my name other than my horse, tack and carpetbag. I figured I could sell my horse and buy a train ticket back south to visit my home in Arkansas. By then, I'd've even settled for Texas, just to get away from the terrible memories of Dakota Territory. Problem was, people weren't buying horses this close to winter because they'd have to feed them during the cold months. Some folks just turned their extra horses loose during the winter, expecting them to feed and fend for themselves and hoping to find them when warm weather returned in the spring. So, I had a worthless horse and nothing else of value to sell, other than my weapons and I'd need them for certain. My only option was to find work, but nobody in Bismarck would hire me after I introduced myself. It seems that Sunshine, the clerk at the Miner's Hotel, had told everyone that not only had I dumped a sack of cow manure on Wild Bill Hickok's head while we were both in a drunken stupor, I had also peed on the mattress when we checked out of the hotel back in the summer.

My only option was to find a saloon with a poker game so I could win enough money to get the hell out of such an inhospitable place as Bismarck. However, the unfriendly folks of Bismarck made that impossible, outlawing gambling in their saloons, it being uncivilized. The nearest gambling tables were out at Whiskey Point. So, I trekked the five miles there and returned to the Bloody Bucket, the best of the motley collection of saloons, gambling dens and cribs that catered to the cravings of the soldiers across the river at Fort Abraham Lincoln. I walked inside the dingy, windowless saloon and saw one unconscious trooper collapsed on a table, an empty bottle at his side, and a woman sitting in a corner doing hand-sewing.

Standing behind the bar was the one-and-a-half-armed proprietor, Claude Armstrong, who looked up and squinted at me. "Don't I know you?"

"Me and my partners passed through a few months back."

"Headed to the Black Hills to make your fortune?"

I nodded.

"What happened to your partners?"

"Indians."

He grimaced. "Sorry to hear that."

"I was looking for a gambling table to make some money."

"You won't find any for six weeks or more, not until the payroll arrives and the soldiers get paid. Things get tight as winter approaches."

My luck was getting worse by the second. "You interested in buying a horse?"

Armstrong shook his head. "Costs too much to feed him during the winter. I only keep one horse during the snowy months."

"You still looking for help?"

"Could be if the right man came along. Remind me of your name."

"Lomax," I said. "H.H. Lomax."

Armstrong cocked his head. "You the same Lomax that pissed on the mattress at the Miner's Hotel?"

I shook my head. "A cat did it, not me."

"That's not what the clerk said."

"Look, I've tended bar at the best whorehouse in Texas."

"There's more to it than working the bar," Armstrong said. "You gotta keep the firewood stocked, empty spittoons, break up fights and prevent any thievery. Frankly, you don't look like you would cater to the high class clientele we serve."

Armstrong's definition of high class and mine were different from the look of things. "You want class," I said. "I can show you class. You got a room I can change in?"

The proprietor pointed to a door at the end of the bar. "There's a room back there you can use."

I scampered out the front door to my mount and untied my carpetbag. Returning inside to the back, I saw two rooms, each with a bed. The first had a woman's belongings in them, and I assumed this was the seamstress's room. The second room had a bed squeezed in among kegs of beer and cases of whiskey as well as boxes of cigars. I shut the door, threw the carpetbag on the bed, unlatched it and dug out my whorehouse suit. I quickly changed and marched back out to the bar.

The seamstress whistled when I made my entry, and Armstrong nodded his approval.

"These are my bartending duds. They'll enhance the reputation of your refined establishment."

Armstrong crossed his stub and his good arm over his chest, then nodded. "You've got the job, on the condition you don't piss on any mattress of mine or into any beer or whiskey barrel, jug, bottle or glass."

"Agreed!"

"You're hired, Lomax. Now let me introduce you to Daisy. She waits tables and takes an occasional soldier to her bed."

Daisy looked up from her sewing with a shy smile. "Pleased to meet you, Lomax," she said, her words syrupy with southern inflection.

I took off my hat. "The pleasure is mine, Miss—"

"Daisy will suffice."

"You're not named for any mythological goddesses are you?"

"No, sir. I'm a country girl from the mountains of North Carolina."

"I'm from the hills of Arkansas, Cane Hill, Arkansas."

She smiled. "It's nice to meet a southerner up here. There are so few of us, or at least very few that will admit they're one of us."

Armstrong interrupted our discussion. "Okay, Lomax, time to get to work. I'll pay you five dollars a month. You can use the storage room for your quarters. You'll chop firewood when we need it. You can keep your mount in the stable behind here as long as you provide the fodder for him and keep him and my horse watered when he's there. You'll clean spittoons and do whatever else I tell you."

"Sounds like a lot of chores for five dollars a month."

"Four dollars a month if you pee on my mattress."

"Understood." We shook hands and sealed the arrangement.

"Unpack your belongings and take care of your horse, then we'll start to work."

As I retreated out the door, Daisy offered to help.

"There's not that much," I replied. "I travel light." I got my bedroll, canteen and carbine in the first trip, then decided to bring in my saddle and tack on the second trip. I felt my meager belongings were safer in the back room with all the whiskey than in the stable. When I went out to tend my horse, I learned my decision was right. The stable was little more than logs planted in the ground with a puncheon roof. It was cramped with room for three horses maximum and one was already there.

When I returned inside, Armstrong started me emptying four

spittoons and polishing them until they were shiny enough for the President of the United States to spit in. If he wasn't available, I was sure plenty of soldiers from across the river were willing to handle the task for him. As I was putting the final shine on the spittoons, I sat with Daisy, who kept busy with her sewing.

I learned she had developed a liking for men in blue during the War Between the States. Being from western North Carolina, she had sympathized with the Yankees, so much so that she helped Union escapees from Confederate prisons traverse the mountains to safety in eastern Tennessee when it was occupied by Federal troops. After the war ended, she left home like me to escape those who still carried war grudges. A couple years later, she met and married a Union infantryman who was assigned to Fort Abraham Lincoln. As the summer ended, he died from some disease, leaving her a widow in the Dakotas. Like me, she was working to earn money to leave. She would bed soldiers in blue to increase her nest egg. She had no qualms about fornicating, having been raised on a farm and watching farm animals mate.

As she explained it to me one day, "Horses do it, cows do it, even chickens do it, so why shouldn't people do it when they got the urge?"

I couldn't answer because I'd never thought of it that way. My opinion was shaped by my momma's teaching and her Bible readings about fornication and similar evils. Now I had not avoided such sins since I left home, though my conscience did bother me about it from time to time, which made it acceptable in my mind.

Daisy didn't have the same outlook because the Bible had not been a part of her upbringing. So, whenever she bedded a soldier—and she only took Army men to her mattress, not other fellows like me—she enjoyed it.

As we got acquainted, Daisy explained to me the hierarchy at the saloon and at Whiskey Point. Mingling infantry and cavalry was not a good off-duty mix so the Bloody Bucket was one of three saloons designated for infantry. Two others were assigned to the cavalry. However, the designations were reversed for officers so the Bloody Bucket served infantrymen and cavalry officers. Saloons that served cavalrymen also catered to infantry officers. That way, everyone could drink without worrying about offending their higher ups. Daisy worked at the Bloody Bucket because Armstrong's clientele were foot soldiers like her late husband.

"What are you sewing?" I asked her as I sat down the last spittoon.

"Lace on a kerchief," she replied. "A lady can never have too many fine kerchiefs because her life is too often filled with tears. Do you ever cry?"

I looked around to make sure Armstrong wasn't near. "I did a month or so ago."

"Lose your girl?"

"No, it was my partners. We'd gone to the Black Hills in search of gold. I was away from camp one day when Indians attacked and killed them."

"Scalp them?"

Grimacing, I shrugged. "It's sort of hard to know. The savages cut their heads off so I don't know if they left the hair on or not."

"It's grim business fighting Indians," she replied.

"We went looking for gold," I said, "not Indians."

"Indians," cried the soldier, who awoke from his stupor at the next table. He jumped up from his chair and staggered to the door. "Indians," he screamed as he charged outside to fight his demons. I hoped he didn't run into Snakebit. After all, the soldier was one of our customers.

Armstrong walked over and shook his head. "Lomax, I hope you don't scare all of our customers away like that."

"No, sir, I won't. In fact, by the time I'm through you'll have more business than you'll know what to do with."

"I doubt it," Armstrong said. "You don't look that smart."

So began my tenure at the Bloody Bucket. I cleaned the place and tended bar when we were busy, but mostly I chopped wood to build up our log pile for the approaching winter. No matter how much firewood I secured, it was never enough. As the chill of winter began to set in, I realized I would probably freeze to death feeding the appetite of the voracious stove which kept the saloon warm. For all the difficulties with firewood, I found time to read the *Bismarck Weekly Tribune* to keep up on the news and did a lot of visiting with Daisy during the slow hours. For such a dingy dump, the Bloody Bucket drew an interesting clientele, more than just soldiers and officers. Some city folk came out to gamble after the soldiers got paid and others visited to do their drinking away from the prying eyes of wives or Bismarck busybodies.

Mark Kellogg was the most frequent visitor. A reporter for the *Bismarck Weekly Tribune*, Kellogg came by at least once a week to see if he could pick up any news on happenings at the fort, especially on George Armstrong Custer and the Seventh Cavalry. Additionally,

Kellogg wrote stories for other newspapers under the nom de plume of "Frontier." He was a serious looking fellow with dark eyes, thin lips and bushy sideburns that reached all the way down to his jaws. He told me he got his start in newspapers by learning to operate a telegraph, a valuable tool for someone to disseminate lies far beyond shouting range. He'd worked for a couple telegraph companies before taking up the newspaper trade and trying to support his two daughters after his wife died a couple years after the war. Kellogg mentioned wanting to scout the Black Hills, maybe find some gold to support his girls. After I told him the story of Wolfe and Dreban, he decided he could wait until the Indians had been removed. After I got to know him a little bit, I tried to sell him on the idea of writing dime novels about that great frontier hero Leadeye Lomax, but he always refused me.

"Dime novels are for fools," he said. "I want to do quality work and hitch my wagon to a rising star, like General Custer. He's going places and I want to be there to write about it."

"How about a dime novel on Custer and Leadeye?" I offered, perfectly willing to share my fame and royalties with the general. Of course, that was before I ever met the boy general.

"I'll not lower the standards of the newspaper profession to write tripe like dime novels," Kellogg countered. "There's some talk in Democrat circles that General Custer might be a good one to run for president one day as he's got connections in Washington and New York City. In fact, I believe he's in Washington now. Not sure when he'll be back. Sometimes I learn those things, visiting all the fine establishments at Whiskey Point." He took a sip from the mug of beer Daisy had placed before him.

"The Bloody Bucket is definitely the finest drinking establishment out here, and we do appreciate your patronage, Mr. Kellogg, but have you ever considered the possibilities of Leadeye Lomax running for president?"

He spit his beer halfway across the room.

"I suspect not," I said, answering my own question.

From that day on, Kellogg always called me "Mr. President."

The Bloody Bucket drew more than just a low-class clientele like foot soldiers and newspaper reporters, it also attracted college men like Frederic Gerard, who worked as an interpreter for the Army. He had spent four years studying at Xavier before giving it up for the frontier and the fur trade with the American Fur Company. During the War Between the States, he and seventeen other men held off an attack by some 600 Yankton warriors until he was rescued, at least that's what he told me. Gerard was one of my favorites and I got to know him fairly well. When he wasn't interpreting, he had a little farm he maintained, raising chickens and selling eggs to soldiers whenever he had a chance. Sometimes, he'd barter eggs with my boss in exchange for some liquid refreshment or other amenities Armstrong offered. When Armstrong got eggs, he would boil them, then turn them over to Daisy, who would make deviled eggs, which Armstrong sold to his customers for triple what the uncooked egg would have brought.

"You barter when you can," Armstrong instructed me. "Sometimes you can make more money that way."

I took his lesson to heart and looked for ways to exchange some of our whiskey or beer for goods we needed like firewood. Ultimately, my bartering got me in trouble with the military and led to a most unfortunate experience—my introduction to George Armstrong Custer.

Some visitors to the Bloody Bucket arrived on business, not choice, such as Dr. Henry R. Porter and the famous Missouri River steamboat captain Grant Marsh. Porter had graduated from the Georgetown University School of Medicine about three years before I met him. He kept an office in Bismarck and occasionally accompanied the cavalry on various expeditions into Indian country. I got to know him on occasional Bloody Bucket visits to patch up a soldier wounded in a saloon altercation or revive another from a drunken stupor.

Marsh had been piloting steamboats on the Missouri since 1862 and up the Yellowstone River for the past two years. It was said he could float a steamer on a teardrop. He visited the saloon occasionally before the river froze over, seeking crewmen who had lost their way in the Bloody Bucket. When I first met him, he was captain and pilot of the *Far West*, a stern-wheeler known for her speed and shallow draft, allowing her to grasshopper over the Missouri's numerous sandbars. The stern-wheeler was owned by the Coulson Packet Line, which contracted with the army to supply various expeditions against the hostiles.

"It'll be a good year for Coulson and me," Marsh explained on his first visit to reclaim an inebriated crewman, "thanks to the Army contract. We'll make a fine profit in 1876."

"My dealings with the army haven't always been good," I said, harkening back to my time in Arkansas during the War Between the States.

I offered him one of Daisy's deviled eggs for free, figuring to let bygones be bygones, but he declined.

"In business, it's wiser to decline a first offer," Marsh informed me.

"Even a free offer?"

"No matter what it is, even free," Marsh explained.

I scratched my head. "An egg in the hand is worth two in the hen."

Marsh shook his head. "That's advice I got from Mark Twain, though he was known as Samuel Clemens then, when we learned the steamboat trade together on the Mississippi."

"I can't say I've ever heard of either gentleman."

"Clemens is a writer. Twain is his penname."

"A man writing under an alias must be on the run from the law," I observed.

"You remind me of Twain with your cynical outlook."

"How about a couple deviled eggs on the house?" I offered, figuring he would refuse.

"Don't mind if I do." He smiled. "Always refuse the first offer, even if it's free because a better offer will come along." Marsh gobbled down the deviled eggs and gave his compliments to Daisy, who sat nearby doing her hand-sewing. He helped his drunk crewman to his feet, then departed, returning to the Bloody Bucket occasionally after that, either to retrieve a wayward crew member or see if I would offer him any more deviled eggs for free. I didn't.

Among the Fort Abraham Lincoln officers that visited the Bloody Bucket, none was more frequent nor more embittered than Captain Frederick Benteen, who was the commanding officer of Seventh Cavalry's Company H. Benteen had lost an infant son that winter and came to drink away the loss. His son's death was only one of his many grievances against life. Most of his complaints involved his commanding officer, George Armstrong Custer. The first time I encountered Benteen, he threw a book on the table and demanded a full bottle of whiskey.

"Reading Twain, are you?" I asked, trying to make conversation with him.

"Hell, no," he spat out. "I'm reading the greatest liar of all time." He held up the book for me to read the cover—*My Life on the Prairie*—by George Armstrong Custer. "There's a typographical error in the title. It should be *My LIES on the Prairie* because it's nothing but bald-faced fabrications." He slammed the book on the table. "Bring me my whiskey, dammit!"

Perhaps he should have been reading Twain, if Custer's book angered him so. I retreated to the bar and returned with a glass and a bottle of whiskey, which he paid for. He uncorked the full bottle and took a full swig, then motioned for me to sit down.

Things not being busy, I obliged.

"Best friend I ever had in the army, Major Joel Elliott, died because of Custer," Benteen said, then proceeded to tell me about the Battle of Washita eight years previous when Custer attacked a village of Southern Cheyenne camped on the Washita River in Indian Territory. After ransacking the village, Custer had abandoned Major Elliott and some seventeen other soldiers who had pursued an escaping band of Indians only to be surprised and slaughtered by a larger party of warriors riding to the village's rescue.

"Custer never even tried to aid Joel and his men, just turned tail and ran!" Benteen held up the book. "This is a pack of lies to justify his abandonment of the major and his men." He took a deep drag on the bottle. "Two weeks later we returned and found Joel and his men a few miles away, frozen solid. They were riddle with arrows. As if that wasn't enough, they were mutilated so bad that you could barely recognize a one of them. Joel deserved better."

I decided Benteen ought to read more Twain and less Custer. Over the following weeks, I learned from Benteen so much about the sordid side of army life, including the jealousies, pettiness and outright crookedness of the military, that I could not understand how the Union had defeated the Confederate Army. During that time, I learned to let Benteen drink in peace when he wanted and to provide him company when he needed to get matters off his chest.

Benteen was in one of his leave-me-alone moods, the first time a fellow appeared that would be a regular visitor to the Bloody Bucket over the coming weeks. He walked in dressed like a gambler in a long broadcoat, a white shirt, a string-tie and a black flat-brimmed hat. He headed straight for me. I figured he'd want to set up a gambling table in the saloon, but apparently he had purer motivations.

He marched straight up to me and pointed his long boney finger at my nose. "You have the mark of Cain upon you."

I couldn't help but be flattered that a man could tell by looking at me where I was from. "Yes, sir, I'm from Cane Hill, Arkansas, proudly," I said. "How could you tell?"

"You misunderstand," he said. "The mark is not about your birthplace, but your destination. You have the mark of Cain, the firstborn of Adam and Eve and the murderer of his brother Abel. Because of his sin, Cain was forever marked as a wanderer and a fugitive from peace. So, too, are you."

"Who the hell are you?" I asked.

"Truett Byars," he answered.

"What the hell are you?"

"A theologian."

"A theo what?"

"A preacher," he said.

Oh, God, I thought.

Chapter Twenty

As cold as it got outside after the first of the year, I decided a little fire and brimstone might help heat the Bloody Bucket, so I came to accept the Reverend Truett Byars' presence in the saloon. By then, the weather had grown so cold that the river froze over and Claude Armstrong had come to trust me enough that he let me run the saloon by myself while he stayed in a warm hotel room over in Bismarck. He even agreed to let me trade merchandise—whiskey and beer—for firewood so I could keep an eye on the place around the clock. Mostly, it was me and Daisy by ourselves in the saloon during the day and a few soldiers who deserted the fort in the evening for a drink or two. Business was better on Friday evenings and Saturdays and Sundays when more soldiers got passes to come across the river to sin, as the reverend would say. Come Sunday morning, Byars was there to preach to the wayward military sinners who were passed out, hung over or nostalgic about home and family.

To my disappointment, Byars didn't preach much fire and brimstone. Rather than try to scare the hell out of us, he opted to reason with us about the advantages of a virtuous and Godly life. I feared I had sinned so much in life in my more than a quarter of a century on earth, that I had very little chance of ever redeeming myself, particularly with snow piling up outside, the thermometer falling below zero most days, and the howling winds from Canada whistling through the gaps in the walls. Cold as it was, a little of hell's warmth might have felt good. In fact, I'd have even settled for time back in Texas, I was so cold.

The only things that saved me from freezing completely were the *Bismarck Tribune* and a deal I'd worked out with soldiers for firewood. I advised the infantry that frequented the place that I would offer a free drink for every six pieces of firewood a soldier brought to the Bloody Bucket. I settled on six because I thought that was the amount a soldier could carry in his arms when he crossed the frozen river. It had to be firewood, though, not kindling or twigs. After word got out of my offer, I never had to worry about chopping any more firewood.

Now, I didn't ask where the firewood came from, I just took it for granted that the soldiers got it by honest means. It never dawned on me that the government hired contractors to chop wood and deliver it to the fort until one day a wagon pulled up behind the Bloody Bucket and began to unload two cords of wood by the stable.

Hearing the commotion, I stepped out back to check on the noise. "What's going on here?" I asked the teamster and his helper as they began to stack firewood up against the stable. I couldn't see much of the teamster because he was dressed in heavy coat, gloves, fur winter cap with earflaps and a muffler that covered his face, save for his eyes.

"Who are you?" the teamster asked.

"I'm H.H. Lomax. I run the Bloody Bucket. Now what's going on?"

"Just following orders," the teamster answered. "Was told to deliver this load of firewood over here so soldiers wouldn't have to tote it across the river. Some feared the extra weight might cause them to break through the ice. The army can afford to lose a little firewood, but not any soldiers."

"Who ordered this?" I wanted to know.

"Just one of the soldiers. They all look alike to me."

As my stack of firewood grew, I realized I'd run out of liquor before the spring thaw would allow Armstrong to replenish his supply. "I don't know. This don't seem normal."

Shrugging, the teamster replied, "You're the genius, not me."

"How do you figure that?" I asked.

"You're the one that got a job staying inside during the winter, while I'm freezing my ass off every day chopping and delivering wood. You must be smart, even if you don't look it."

"I got enough brains to get by."

"What I don't understand is why Armstrong hired you, brains or not, after you peed on the mattress at the Miner's Hotel. It true you also peed on Wild Bill's hair while he slept?"

"No truth in either of those stories."

"Too many accounts of both for there not to be a grain of truth in them."

"There's not a drop of truth in either of them," I replied.

The teamster shook his head and returned to unloading and stacking my wood. "Just the same," he said, "I won't be drinking in your establishment."

I turned to go to the stove inside. "By the way, enjoy your time in the cold while I settle into the warmth of the saloon."

The teamster grumbled, but went about his work. I figured my troubles were over, but in reality they were just beginning.

Inside the reverend and Daisy awaited me, wanting to know what was going on. When I explained, Byars shook his head. "Nothing good'll come of this," he said.

I disagreed. "We'll be warm for the winter."

"But at what cost?" Byars asked. "Earthly wrongs multiply our earthly woes."

I picked the latest copy of the *Bismarck Tribune*, which also helped us get through that winter. First, it provided entertainment when we had no customers. Second, it kept us up on the news, especially involving Custer. Third, it helped us start fires if the logs ever burned down in the stove after a long winter's night. And finally, it provided chinking we could put between the logs to help block out the whistling winds.

Every day we read or re-read the paper until the next one came, then tore the previous paper in strips, soaked the strips in a water-and-flour paste, then pushed the strips in cracks between the logs to block the gusts that found their way inside.

All the time, Byars worked on our salvation, suggesting I find honest work that didn't contribute to the downfall of man and encouraging Daisy to quit sleeping with men until she remarried.

"I'm a widow," she said. "Not much else I can do to make ends meet, certainly not until spring. Don't want to do laundry, not in weather like this. Don't have many options."

"How about this?" I offered, looking up from the newspaper. "Says here, 'Nude Women: A Rather Strange but Honest Way of Making a Living.' Apparently at the Pennsylvania Academy of Fine Arts ladies appear nude before young men for drawing lessons." I looked up from the news story. Daisy was amused, though Byars looked as stern as the father of an unwed mother. "Let me continue. It says 'These nude, live figures only appear before the life classes of the academy for sketching. The ladies who follow this strange mode of procuring a living are in every instance respectable.'"

"What do you say about that, Reverend?" asked Daisy.

Without answering, Byars picked up his big Bible and thumbed through it. I thought he was stalling for time, but he came to the end of the book and read. "This is from Revelations 'though mayest be clothed and that the shame of thy nakedness do not appear."

I wasn't sure exactly what that meant and knew I was in a losing battle with a theologian, but I answered back. "Wasn't Adam and Eve naked?"

"Yes, but they learned otherwise after eating of the fruit of knowledge when tempted by the serpent Satan."

"Was the serpent a rattlesnake, Reverend, like this one?" I reached beneath my coat, sweater and shirt and pulled out the rattle on the end of the leather thong Snakebit had presented me. "Maybe I killed Satan!"

"The Good Book does not say, but why do you keep that filthy thing close to your heart?"

"To let Satan know I can deal with his kind," I answered. "After all, you're the one that said I was cursed with the mark of Cain. Didn't Cain come from Adam and Eve's nakedness?"

Daisy snickered. "Reverend, Lomax may tie you in religious knots before he's done with you. Just tell me, would it be better for me to whore or appear naked for men to sketch me."

Now, Byars grinned. "Maybe you're right, Daisy."

Daisy smiled at me, then Byars. "You are both good men at heart, though Lomax often goes about it the wrong way."

That was one of many discussions we had over the *Bismarck Tribune* that winter, during the slack time when Daisy did her hand-sewing, Byars worked on making us religious and I kept the saloon running. From the papers, we learned when Custer was at the fort and when he was in Washington. He had made some accusations against the Indian agencies and their crookedness and had implicated President Grant's brother in the shenanigans. I wasn't a military genius, but I considered it unwise to anger the commander-in-chief. The more I learned about the U.S. Army through local gossip and *Tribune* accounts, the more confused I got. It seemed the soldiers hated the officers, the officers hated each other and everyone hated Custer. I came to believe one reason the officers looked the other way when soldiers visited the Bloody Bucket was to give them enough freedom to temporarily escape the yoke of army life so they wouldn't mutiny.

Of course, Byars was there on Sunday mornings to preach and shame them into being better and more Godly soldiers, who loved their fellow man, including the red man. Byars had come north from Texas out of a genuine concern for the Indians. He spoke of treaties broken by the government and the white man, of the Black Hills being promised to the Indians forever and of the dignity of all human beings. I thought that odd, coming from a Texan, a breed barely human to begin with and certainly not dignified. He attacked the greed of the white man and his covetousness of the land of others. Byars opposed the intrusion into the Black Hills by prospectors, calling it an abomination what the white man was doing to the sacred Indian lands.

Byars admitted he had come to Dakota Territory after learning of the army's plan to conduct a winter campaign against the Sioux and Cheyenne when they least expected it. However, army infighting, bureaucratic incompetence, logistical deficiencies and the weather realities—it got cold and snowed in Dakota Territory—led to the postponement of the offensive until the summer of 1876. Since he couldn't minister to the Indians that winter, he decided to work on the soldiers, giving a sermon every Sunday morning in the Bloody Bucket.

"Why don't you preach in town?" I asked him one day. "There's sober people there that would listen to you."

"This is where the sin is and this is where God wants me," he replied.

I figured the Bloody Bucket was where God wanted me since that was where I was, even if I was a purveyor of sinfulness in Byars' eyes. I forgot most of his sermons except the one on the Bible's greatest miracles. Byars proclaimed the greatest miracles to be Jesus feeding the multitudes, raising Lazarus from the dead and walking on water, not to mention the resurrection itself. That's when some of the enlisted men, their minds muddled by a night of drinking offered their own theological interpretations.

"What about when Jesus turned the water to wine?" asked one semi-sober infantryman.

"I'll drink to that," said another, who took a swig from the dry mug he had emptied earlier. "I need a miracle," he cried, then lifted his empty mug in the air.

"The greatest miracle," interjected another, "was Moses parting the Red Sea."

"Not if it was as shallow as the Missouri," answered the water-to-wine soldier.

"Theee greates' mira-cull of dem alls," slurred the drunkest soldier in the Bloody Bucket, "was whens Moseses tieds 'is ass to's a treeee an' marched forty miles. Moseses hads a limber butt to stretch 'is ass that far."

"He tied his donkey, not his butt," corrected Water-to-Wine.

"Twas 'is ass, not 'is donkey," cried the inebriated theologian.

"Not so," cried Water-to-Wine.

"Twasn't 'is donkey, buts 'is ass," cried the drunken Biblical scholar, who stood up, shoved his chair down and lunged at the soldier with a different scriptural interpretation.

Water-to-Wine dodged a blow, then connected with a right to the nose of the Moses expert. A dozen more soldiers entered the theological argument, swinging their fists and elbows at differing religious interpretations. They were too drunk or hung over to do much damage, but I grabbed chairs and glasses and moved them out of the way to minimize the breakage. When I could grab a table, I pulled it to the wall so it wouldn't get smashed. Shortly, all the soldiers were piled on top of one another on the floor, swinging lethargically at each other.

I saw one soldier fumbling to draw his revolver. I dashed to him, yanking my pistol from my shoulder holster and sticking it in the soldier's ear, suggesting he leave his pistol where it was. He wasn't too drunk to understand that even Leadeye Lomax wouldn't miss at that range. If I had to shoot him, I wondered if I'd be arrested and tried for murder or for damaging government property. I never learned the answer to that dilemma as the soldier slowly shoved his pistol into its holster. I backed him toward the door, opened it and sent him out into the cold. I shoved my pistol back into my shoulder holster as I closed the door and turned to face the riot.

Byars and Daisy waded into the throng, pulling the combatants from one another and shoving them aside. It wasn't much of a brawl, more of a religious discussion with raised fists rather than raised voices making the theological points. Once we had them separated and they had forgotten what Biblical issue had started the melee, I turned to Byars. "I'm no theologian, Reverend, but something tells me you're not doing it right when your preaching leads to a brawl."

Byars shook his head and laughed. "It's the liquor, Lomax. Nobody thinks straight when they're drinking the devil's brew."

"You're looking at it the wrong way, Reverend," I responded. "They devil's brew is keeping us warm this winter, what with bartering whiskey and beer for firewood."

"Nobody in the end, Lomax, benefits from a pact with the devil," he said, then helped one of the soldiers to his feet.

That brawl, which was minor compared to some saloon scraps I'd seen, was the worst we had all winter. Except for a few bumps and bruises on our customers, damage was limited to a broken whiskey bottle, which fortunately had been empty at the time of its demise. Byars never again asked a question of the troops during a Bloody Bucket sermon.

During the slow times, the three of us sat around the table nearest the stove to read and discuss the news in the *Bismarck Tribune*. Daisy would read aloud the weekly installment of Harriet Beecher Stowe's serialized novel, *We and Our Neighbors or the Record of an Unfashionable Street*. Byars would sometimes read his Bible aloud, trying to save me and Daisy, who always had her hand-sewing to keep her busy. The reverend's persistence began to take effect on Daisy, who professed one afternoon that she would no longer call her cooking specialty "deviled" eggs, but would henceforth refer to them as "salad" eggs.

As the frigid winter wore on, I found myself admiring Daisy. In spite of what she did on occasion, she had a soft almost innocent look about her. She might not have been as striking as Medusa's girls, but there was an inner beauty that made up for it. When Byars would leave for the night and no one else was around, we would just sit and talk while she did her hand-sewing, usually adding lace trim to handkerchiefs or to the sleeves and collars of her blouses. Sometimes, she would just sew little designs on a plain handkerchief, adding a little beauty to an otherwise drab piece of cloth. She seldom complained about anything except when her hands would get too cold to sew. On occasion, I would hold her hands, just to help warm them, or at least that was what I told myself. I had to admit, I relished the touch of her long, elegant fingers. She would smile and we would just sit there, not saying anything, just enjoying the closeness. Now I never tried to kiss her as I didn't want her to think I thought of her as anything but a decent woman. Too, I didn't own a Yankee uniform.

Sometimes she would talk about her late husband and what a fine man he was, especially for a soldier. She recalled a Valentine's Day when they were courting and he had offered her a bag of licorice, not realizing she despised the flavor. She said she about gagged eating the candy in front of him, but she smiled as best she could. When he learned that she detested licorice but had eaten it anyway, he had proposed to her. I wasn't that familiar with the idea of Valentine's Day, but as she talked about it as a special day for sweethearts, I thought about getting her something special for a gift as that day approached in February. We were holding hands one day when it came to me. When Byars and I were alone, I asked him on his next trip to Bismarck to purchase for me a pair of women's gloves. I wanted a pair that would keep her hands warm, but not so thick that she couldn't sew.

A couple days later, Byars returned with a pair of white cotton gloves, which he slipped to me when Daisy stepped to her room. I paid Byars two dollars and told him I planned to give them to Daisy for Valentine's Day.

"That's thoughtful," Byars said. "Maybe I should get her something, too. We could have a celebration, the three of us. Valentine's this year falls on a Monday, our slowest day."

I nodded, but wasn't sure I wanted the reverend intruding on my plans with Daisy, but he had secured the gloves for me and treated me fine. "That's a good idea, Reverend," I said with what enthusiasm I could muster.

"Great, Lomax. We'll have a grand time."

"Just promise me one thing, Reverend."

"What?"

"No sermons."

He nodded. "No sermons, Lomax, I promise."

That night after Byars departed, all the customers had left and Daisy had retired to her room, I found her sewing box and slipped out her scissors. I knew Daisy was frugal and that if she had bought the gloves or accepted them as a gift, she would never do what needed to be done to ease her sewing. Carefully, I snipped the tips off the thumbs and forefingers on the both gloves so she could hold a needle or cloth with the fingertips of her first two fingers and keep the rest fully covered for warmth. I hoped she would find that mutilation thoughtful. Having nothing pretty to wrap the gloves in, I tore a sheet from the previous week's *Tribune* and laid the gloves in the center, then folded the paper over them, borrowing a couple pins from Daisy's sewing box to secure the ends. Then I hid the gift under the bar until Valentine's Day.

When that Monday arrived, Byars rode in from town, bringing a burlap bag with him. He pulled out a gift the size of a cigar box wrapped in red tinsel with a silver hair clip pinned atop it. Then he carefully extracted a wicker basket from the sack and placed it gingerly on the table. First, he lifted the flap on the basket and pulled out a small box, which he opened for both Daisy and me to see six brown eggs.

"I thought you might make some salad eggs for us, Daisy. We would enjoy that."

She smiled. "I'll start boiling water."

"Not just yet," Byars said, as he pulled from the basket a package wrapped with brown paper and twine. He untied the knot and showed us some ham slices he had bought from a Bismarck butcher. "We can fry it on the stove to have with our salad eggs."

"That's wonderful, Reverend," said Daisy.

"I'm not done," Byars said.

Next he pulled out a round tin the size of a plate and removed the lid to reveal a small stack cake with vanilla icing.

Daisy clapped. "This will be a wonderful Valentine's Day."

On the one hand, I was excited to see the food as it was better fare than we normally ate, but on the other hand, Byars' spread and tinsel-wrapped present made my simple gift look paltry by comparison.

Once I got past my jealousy, we had a fine time. Daisy boiled the eggs then sliced them and removed the cooked yolks, which she mixed with oil and chopped onions and pickles before returning the yellow to the boiled whites. Then she fried the ham in a skillet atop our stove and when it was ready, we sat down. Byars offered a blessing over our meal, thanking God for bringing us together and using us to do His will in an uncertain world.

"Did you know," asked Byars, "that the correct name for today is Saint Valentine's Day, and it started out as a Christian day of feast honoring Valentinus, one of the early saints?"

Daisy and I shook our heads.

"The Romans martyred Valentinus for ministering to Christians and marrying soldiers forbidden by the emperor to wed. While he was imprisoned, he healed his jailer's daughter, writing her a farewell letter, which he signed 'Your Valentine.'"

"That's a lovely story," Daisy said.

"How do you know so much, Reverend?" I asked.

"Schooling and reading," he answered.

"My schooling tells me it's time to eat," I said. We dug into the meal, relishing every bite, both Byars and me trying to outdo each other in complimenting her eggs. I figured my words were topping Byars' until I made a simple mistake. "Best deviled eggs I ever ate!"

"Salad eggs," she corrected.

"Salad eggs," I repeated.

After eating the ham and salad eggs, we split half of the cake among us and relished the sugary sweetness of the icing. Once we finished the cake, Byars pushed his gift toward Daisy.

"How sweet," she said.

"Just a minute," I interjected, jumping up and running to the bar. "I've got one too, just not as fancy." I returned with my limp gift wrapped in newspaper and placed it before Daisy.

"And you're sweet, too, Lomax," she said as she removed the pins and unfolded the newsprint, revealing the gloves. "How thoughtful. Gloves to keep my hands warm." She smiled, but her grin disappeared when she saw the missing tips.

"It's so you can still use your sewing fingers and keep your hands warm," I explained. "I hope you like it better than licorice."

She smiled. "You're so thoughtful, Lomax. I'll use them for certain." She turned to the reverend's gift. She removed the silver comb and slid it in her hair. "This is so thoughtful, Reverend." Carefully, she then unwrapped the colored tinsel so she could save it. She exposed a big cigar box, then opened it and removed a Bible. "Thank you, Reverend. When I am not sewing, I will have something to read."

"You're welcome, Daisy. A gift for the body and a gift for the soul."

"Thank you, both," she said, standing up and coming to me. She kissed me hard on the cheek and then turned to Byars, doing the same to him.

I couldn't remember feeling more pleased in Dakota Territory than when she pressed her lips against my cheek, though I'd felt more so had she not given Byars the same thank you.

We spent the afternoon talking and visiting, finishing off the cake for supper before Byars left to return to his room in the city. I had to respect his courage in riding the five miles back and forth to Bismarck in some of the worst weather imaginable. I had to admire my luck in being alone with Daisy because I planned to share my feelings with her and maybe see if we might court and one day marry. Unfortunately, a trooper came over from the fort and wanted to lay with Daisy. When she agreed, it dampened my ardor for the evening. I decided I would talk with her the next day and let her know my feelings.

I never got the chance, though, because the next day was when the soldiers came to arrest me.

Chapter Twenty-One

I arose the next morning as usual, pulling off layers of blankets and rattling my necklace for good luck, then dressing in my fancy suit, my shoulder holster, pistol and coat. I entered the saloon, added firewood to the potbellied stove and fanned the flames. I wanted to ask Daisy about the possibility of matrimony before the reverend arrived, but I was too nervous when she came out of her room. She joined me by the fire, but I didn't know how to bring up the subject, especially since she had spent part of her night with a soldier.

"Look," she said, holding up her hands. "I'm wearing my sewing gloves."

"Hope you didn't mind I cut the fingertips off," I said. "I wanted to give you something to sew with and I doubted you would cut them off yourself."

"That was so thoughtful of you."

I should've asked her then, but my courage kept failing me. We just stood there enjoying each other's company and the warmth. We had an apple apiece for breakfast, then went about our tasks, me toting a few bottles of whiskey from my room to replace the empty ones behind the bar. Daisy swept the floor where mud had been tracked in, then picked up her sewing box and began to embroider a handkerchief with her new gloves.

As I finally screwed up the courage and walked over to Daisy, the door flew open letting in the cold wind and Frederick Benteen. He was carrying six pieces of firewood.

"It true what they say about getting a free drink in exchange for firewood?" he asked.

I pointed to the woodbox. "Drop it there."

"Then give me a whiskey, Lomax."

As usual, Benteen complained about Custer and what a son of a bitch the general was.

"What brings you to the Bloody Bucket this morning?" I asked, as I retrieved a bottle and a jigger for the captain.

"Have to send a telegraph to Washington, a military matter for our esteemed commander," he sneered, then laughed. "If he keeps opening his mouth about corruption at the Indian Agency, he may wind up cashiered and out of the army. From what I read in the papers, the Republicans up there don't like what he's saying. An officer of the army should stay out of politics." He grabbed the bottle and glass from me.

"It true he wants to be president?" I asked.

"Wouldn't surprise me. He's got more ambition than sense. He's read so many glowing newspaper articles about himself that he thinks he won the War of the Rebellion, not General Grant. Rumor has it that Grant despises him. In fact nearly everybody hates him, save for General Sheridan. It makes me think a lot less of Phil Sheridan, I'll tell you that." Benteen took the first of many drinks, insisting that I join him and listen to his grievances. It was lunch time before he finished his complaints and the whiskey. Then he paid me for the bottle and left to deliver the urgent telegram for transmission to Washington.

For lunch Daisy and I split some canned tomatoes and hard bread. We talked some, but I couldn't bring myself to ask her if she'd thought about getting married again one day. I lacked the courage in spite of her warm smile and the knowledge that the reverend would arrive soon.

When the door opened about one o'clock, I wheeled around expecting to see Byars, but was shocked to see a dozen soldiers carrying revolvers, all pointed at me.

A captain strode up and poked his finger in my chest. "Are you Lomax, proprietor of the Bloody Bucket?"

"That's the son of a bitch," scowled one infantryman, who seemed vaguely familiar.

"I'm Lomax," I said.

"You're under arrest," the captain announced.

"What?" I cried. "I ain't done nothing wrong."

"You've been thieving government firewood," the captain answered.

"No such thing," I shouted back.

The officer shook his head. "You absconded with a wagon load of firewood. What's left is behind the saloon. We've a wagon coming over to reclaim that for the fort."

"I didn't steal it," I pleaded.

"If not, you knowingly received stolen federal property," he said. "Raise your hands."

Figuring my chances of surviving unharmed against a dozen armed soldiers, all with their guns pointed at my heart, were about as slim as a piece of chocolate candy remaining untouched in a room full of fat women, I lifted my arms.

"He's got a peashooter in a shoulder harness beneath his arm," cried the infantryman that had sassed me earlier.

I studied him and realized it was the soldier who had started to draw his pistol during Reverend Byars' sermon brawl. As I recalled, he was the one my eloquence had persuaded to re-holster his revolver and leave. Of course, the cold steel of my pocket pistol's barrel in his ear had helped, I'm sure. Now my friend approached me and stuck his revolver against my ear while another soldier shoved his hand inside my coat and extracted my five-shot revolver.

"What do you want me to do with it?" he asked the captain.

"Give it to the lady," I said, nodding toward Daisy. "She might be able to plug one of you bastards if you don't treat her well."

The captain shrugged, and the soldier gave her my pistol. "Let's go," ordered the captain.

My sermon pal removed the pistol from my ear and shoved it in my back. "You heard him," he growled, then pushed me.

"Can I get my hat and coat from my room?" I asked.

"No," grumbled the captain.

Daisy jumped up from her chair. "I'll get it." She raced away and back, offering me my hat and coat.

"Thanks." I smiled as best I could.

Daisy leaned over and kissed my cheek. "I'm sorry, Lomax. I'll be praying for you."

The theological expert with the gun in my back, shoved me forward. "You'll need more than prayer when General Custer finds out about this," he scowled.

I tugged my hat down and left the warmth of the saloon for the frigid chill of the February air and the even colder chill of army hospitality. This was my first forced march under military rule. I didn't like it. Fact was, I didn't like much about the Union Army, not having had a very good experience in Arkansas during the war. Further, these soldiers didn't even have the courtesy to come on horses so we could've ridden to the fort. Though the Missouri was frozen over, they felt the weight of horses might break through the ice so we walked the entire way.

"I'll get me a lawyer," I said.

"You do that," the captain said, "but it won't do you any good.

This is an army matter."

"I'm not in the army," I protested.

"Let's just say you're being volunteered for the army," he answered.

That's when I learned that military logic didn't always make sense. I would learn a lot more about military logic over the next four months.

We trudged down the slope toward the Missouri, then onto the river ice. A couple inches of snow allowed us to make our way across the river without sliding too much on the ice, though my sermon buddy did slip and bust his bottom. I would've laughed, but figured it was against military logic if not army regulations so I kept my snicker to myself. After we crossed the river, we marched up the slope toward Fort Abraham Lincoln and the guardhouse that would be my new home for weeks.

Fort Abraham Lincoln was divided into two posts—infantry and cavalry. I had the misfortune of being jailed on the cavalry post in the wooden guardhouse on the north side of the parade ground. The guardhouse was a solid wooden structure, tightly built to keep dangerous criminals like me from escaping. It was about thirty feet wide and seventy feet long, split in the middle by a sally port with solid planked double doors on either end of the sally port.

When we reached the door, the captain pulled his pistol from its scabbard and shoved it in my back, then dismissed all the troopers. When he was certain they were beyond the range of his voice, the captain growled. "Are you a damn Republican son of a bitch trying to embarrass my brother?"

I had no idea who my new friend was, much less his brother. "I don't know what you're talking about."

"Stealing government property from this fort to embarrass our commander while he's trying to clean up what's corrupt about the Indian Agency, that's what I'm talking about," the captain went on. "The only reason you weren't arrested before now was so I could get Company C on guardhouse duty. I'm company captain so they'll make sure you are well attended."

"I was doing fine taking care of myself before you came along. I didn't steal nothing."

"You stole a wagonload of firewood, you did," he replied.

"Some teamster or soldier delivered a load of wood to the Bloody Bucket."

"Name them, Lomax."

"I can't," I replied.

"Don't make any difference anyway," the captain replied. "You accepted property contracted and paid for by the United States Army. Same thing as if you'd stolen the firewood." He opened the sally port door, then shoved me inside.

"Who the hell, are you?" I asked.

"My name is Thomas Ward Custer, Captain Custer to you, and brother of George Armstrong Custer."

That's when I had the first inkling that bastards, like bananas, came in bunches. It turned out there were a bunch of cusses related to Custer at Fort Abraham Lincoln, including brothers, sisters, in-laws and cousins, not to mention his wife. Best I gathered, the boy general had to travel in a pack of relatives to have any friends at all. I'd about had enough of Tom Custer's arrogance, so I couldn't resist asking him a question. "How come your brother made general and you only made captain? You stupid or just dumb?"

Custer punched me in the nose. "I earned two Medals of Honor, so I acquitted myself well during the Rebellion."

I shook my head and wiped a trickle of blood from my nostrils. "Must be galling to have to take orders from your brother."

Custer extracted a skeleton key from his pocket and unlatched the door to the prisoner quarters. As he shoved me inside, a quartet of soldiers immediately jumped up from a table where they were playing cards. They saluted the captain stiffly. I stumbled toward the guards, but one of them caught me and kept me from scattering their poker game.

"As you were," Custer said to his soldiers.

"How many Medals of Honor do you boys have?" I asked.

"So, Captain's told you about his medals, has he?" one cavalryman said.

"He's got more than all of us combined," said another.

"And he doesn't let us forget it," said a third.

I thought their words had an edge to them, but Custer was apparently both dumb and stupid because his chest swelled like the president himself had just pinned the medals on him.

"Search him, boys," Custer commanded.

Between the four of them, they stripped me down to my long johns, checking every crease in my whorehouse suit. They removed my shoulder harness and tossed it aside, then one of them lifted the leather thong around my neck and exposed the rattle.

"Look at this, Captain," said my searcher. "You want this rattle for your collection? It's a big one."

Custer shook his head. "I don't want anything that'll remind me of this son of a bitch. In fact, leave it with him. Maybe he'll use the necklace to hang himself and save us from having to court martial or kill him ourselves."

The soldier gave me the necklace back.

"In fact," continued Custer, "give him the shoulder harness, too. Make him wear it under his shirt, though, so no one other officer will see it. I want him to have a couple options if he decides to hang himself like he needs to."

One of the soldiers picked up my shoulder harness. I put it on over my long johns, then put my shirt over it. I re-dressed in my whorehouse suit, which impressed my guards.

"Don't believe we've ever had a prisoner as well dressed as this one," said one.

"What's your name?" asked another.

"H.H. Lomax," replied Custer before I could answer.

"Damn," whistled a third one. "You the same Lomax that poured a can of paint on Wild Bill Hickok's head while he slept?"

"My reputation is vastly overstated," I said.

"Damn," the last guard said. "We've got a big shot here."

"Take care of him unless he tries to escape," ordered Custer. "In that case shoot him. Don't wing him, but plug him good and dead. Twenty dollars to any man that shoots him dead."

The soldiers all smiled. One of them nudged me. "Make a run for it."

"Now!" laughed another.

"Which cell do you want him in, Captain?" asked one of the men.

"The dead man's cell," Custer said.

The soldiers' faces turned gravely serious.

"You sure?"

"That's what I said, dammit. And remember, if he tries to escape, don't just shoot him, kill him, if it takes every bullet in the armory. When the shooting's done, I want him delivered to the dead house, not the infirmary."

"Yes, sir," the men said in unison, then saluted as Captain Custer exited the guard room.

When he was gone, the four soldiers sighed. "What the hell have you done, Lomax, to rile him so?" asked one.

I shrugged. "Apparently, I made his brother look bad."

All four of the men laughed, then introduced themselves.

"I'm Gus Finkle, August Finkle is how I enlisted," said the one with sergeant stripes on his blouse. Finkle stood just over six feet tall and was reputed to be the tallest enlisted man in the Seventh Cavalry. His eyes were gray, his hair black, his complexion brown and his disposition light, certainly in comparison to his captain. "Don't mind the captain," he said. "He's always grumbling about something. Thinks he's in charge of everything when his brother's away."

Peter Thompson introduced himself next. Born in Fifishire, Scotland, he spoke with a brogue and a lilt in his voice so it was sometimes higher pitched than you would expect from a man. I pegged him for twenty-two or so and five-feet, nine inches tall. His brown hair matched his eyes, which seemed to sparkle from behind his ruddy complexion.

"Sarge is right about the captain," Thompson said. "He sticks to his own kind."

"What kind is that, an ugly son of a bitch?"

Everyone laughed.

James Watson, like Thompson, was a private. Born in Hudson, New York, he had enlisted in the army in Cincinnati the previous September and had the shortest cavalry tenure of any of my guards. I estimated he stood five and a half feet tall. His brown hair was thick and his blue eyes looked the color of a pond on a cloudless day.

"You'll like the dead man's cell," he said.

"Not by the name of it," I replied.

"The last prisoner the captain assigned there escaped," Watson informed me.

I perked up, but Thompson interjected himself into the conversation. "Let's just say it may have been a contrivance."

Scratching my head, I wondered what a contrivance meant. "Did he get shot?"

"Nope," said Thompson, "but he was a Sioux chief. You're a white man. Won't be any incident report to fill out if you're shot. Getting where you can't shoot an Indian for all the paperwork you've gotta do."

"I'll go to my grave satisfied I didn't cause you gentlemen any extra paperwork."

They laughed, none harder than Jimmy Russell, the final of my four guards. I should have expected it because Russell was a Texan, born in Corpus Christi, he later told me. He disproved the belief that everything was bigger in Texas as he stood only five feet and five inches tall. He ran his fingers through his brown hair as he stared at me with his steel-gray eyes. I later learned his father had been an officer in the Confederacy, which set well with me, but I didn't know if it offset him being a Texan.

After the introductions, my guards put me in my cell and shut the plank door without barring it. A high slot in the door allowed some light to seep into my cell and gave them a chance to look in on me whenever they felt like it. The cell was small but tall with a high ceiling over me. Winter sunshine cascaded in through a glass window high on the outside wall, but iron bars eliminated that as an escape option. As I studied my new quarters, I took in the wood frame bed with a straw mattress, feather pillow and two blankets, a stool, a small table and two nearby pails, one half-filled with water for drinking and the other empty for me to fill whenever nature called. I told myself I need never to confuse the two pails.

I lay down on the mattress and stared at the rafters overhead, much too high for me to reach, much less hang myself from. I'm sure Thomas Ward Custer would be disappointed that I didn't follow his suggestion. Renegade Yankee soldiers had tried to hang me back during the difficulties in Arkansas, but I realized that day how much I enjoyed breathing. As best I could recall, this was the first time I'd ever been in a jail cell—while sober at least.

As I studied the room, I couldn't figure out how the Sioux chief had escaped. The floors looked solid, like the walls, and the window was too high to reach without putting the bed on end and using it as a ladder. Even then, there was still the bars to defeat. On top of that, the window was so small I would have to go out head first, likely breaking my neck landing on the frozen ground.

"Who was the chief that escaped?" I called out.

A muffled "What?" answered me, then the door swung open. Finkle stood there. "What do you need, Lomax?"

"I asked the name of the chief that escaped."

"Rain-in-the-Face," Finkle informed me. "He was convicted of killing a couple white men and sentenced to be hanged."

"You say he escaped?"

"Not before promising to kill Captain Custer. He hated the captain."

"I can't say I blame him, based on my one encounter with the pompous ass. Any idea how Rain-in-the-Face escaped?"

"There were some shenanigans," Finkle said, "at least in my mind. I think some higher ups thought it was less of a problem for him to escape than it was to hang him. They made it easy for him to escape."

I grinned. "Like leaving my cell un-barred."

Finkle laughed. "You don't look smart enough to escape, Lomax. Besides that, if you hate Captain Custer like the rest of us, you can't be all bad."

"Glad to know I'm among friends and even have a brother among the red man. Rain-in-the-Face must be a fine Sioux if he despises Custer."

"Some say there's no tougher warriors among the Sioux than Crazy Horse, Sitting Bull and Rain-in-the-Face."

"I'll keep that in mind when I escape."

Finkle just laughed. "Captain Custer's opinion of you is a high recommendation, so if you give us your word you won't try to escape, we'll eliminate some of the formalities and keep you under what we call loose guard."

"What's loose guard?"

"We leave your cell unlatched unless officers visit. You can play poker and visit with us as long as you slip back into your cell if you hear someone on the sally port."

"Sounds like free room and board—you do feed me, don't you?—compliments of the U.S. Cavalry," I responded.

"You eat what we eat."

I extended my hand and we shook.

That evening about dusk, we were joined by John Lewis, a cavalryman who brought us a kettle of stew from the cookhouse. Finkle informed Lewis who I was and then told me that Lewis was a native of Povey County, Pennsylvania, in his second cavalry enlistment. He stood about five feet, eight inches and had an easy gait when he walked. His hair was brown, his eyes gray and his handshake warm.

While Finkle acquainted me with Lewis, Russell, the little Texan, brought bowls from a cabinet and Watson got spoons. The six of us sat down at the table and started eating. The stew was tolerably good, made better by the fact it wasn't costing me a thing. The four guards explained my crimes against the cavalry to Lewis, who shook his head.

"Was it the Bloody Bucket?" Lewis asked.

I nodded.

"Where Captain Benteen would go to drink?"

"Yep," I answered.

"Captain Custer hates Benteen. All the Custers do, ever since the Battle on the Washita. The Custer bunch think he's making too big a deal about the loss of Elliott and his men, blaming Benteen for some unfavorable letter that appeared in print in various newspapers."

"Bottom line," said Watson, "is the Custers care more about their reputations than their men."

"It true you stole firewood from the fort?" Lewis asked.

"Nope. I'd swear that on my mother's Bible. I was just minding my own business one day and a wagon showed up behind the saloon. A teamster and a soldier started unloading two cords of wood. They were bundled up so I couldn't recognize them, but who's gonna refuse firewood in the winter in Dakota Territory? I didn't think nothing of it until today when Captain Custer and his men arrested me."

Thompson scratched his head. "General Custer's been having some trouble in Washington, making accusations of corruption against the administration. I'm not sure it's blood as much as newspaper ink that runs through his veins the way he likes to read his name in print."

"But what's that got to do with the firewood?" I asked.

"Depends," Thompson said, "on whether Custer was trying to get good press or prevent bad. Could be the Custers had it delivered so they could make an arrest and show how they didn't put up with thievery of government property. Or, maybe they didn't know about it and feared it would reflect badly on the general, who couldn't keep corruption out of the Seventh Cavalry while testifying about it in other departments."

"Either way, you're in heap of trouble."

"I know Mark Kellogg of the *Bismarck Tribune*. Maybe I could explain my side of things to him and settle it right now."

"Who you think Kellogg would believe, Lomax?" Russell asked. "You or an officer in the U.S. Cavalry? Corruption makes a story, not integrity."

"Yeah," echoed Thompson. "You know the most dangerous spot in all of the frontier, Lomax?"

"No." I shrugged.

"Any place between General Custer and a newspaper reporter."

"Then I'll get me an attorney and defend myself in court."

The men went silent, shaking their heads and looking from one to another.

"What is it?" I asked. "What's wrong?"

Finkle cocked his head and shrugged. "Well, let's just say General Custer doesn't always follow the formalities."

Russell lifted his empty spoon and waved it at his fellow soldiers. "We are all slaves to his cruelties and petty jealousies."

"I remember an Iowa cavalryman writing to a Des Moines newspaper," Thompson said, "complaining that the memory of Custer as his commander would be a stench in his nostril and the nostrils of his children's children to the remotest generation, or something like that."

"After the War of the Rebellion," said Lewis, "he sent men after four deserters with orders to shoot them. When the troops found the deserters, they surrounded and shot them without so much as a chance to explain themselves, much less to stand before a court martial. One of the four died and when the other three were carried to the fort for treatment, he wouldn't even let the doctors touch them."

"I fear," said Finkle, "that's why Captain Custer assigned you the dead man's cell because he knows what his brother will order whenever he gets back from Washington."

"He can't just shoot me," I insisted.

"You don't know General Custer," Finkle replied. "He's been court-martialed two or three times, gotten out of numerous scrapes against Confederates and Indians alike without a scratch. They call it Custer's Luck."

"Well, he's never come up against H.H. Lomax," I replied.

Their laughter rang in my ears for hours after dinner had ended and I had returned to my cell.

Chapter Twenty-Two

I spent the rest of February and all of March in the guardhouse under the care of Company C. The men of the company rotated through and I got to know nearly all of them, but Gus Finkle, Peter Thompson, James Watson, Jimmy Russell and John Lewis were my favorite. They gave me liberties the others didn't and shared out-of-town newspapers they received from time to time. When they were on duty, my door was never barred and the couple of times officers came to the guardhouse, I either heard them in time to get back in my cell or grabbed the broom and made out like I was sweeping the place.

About once a week, Reverend Truett Byars and Daisy would cross the frozen river and visit, bringing me the latest *Bismarck Tribune* to keep up with the news.

"It's not as much fun without you around," Daisy told me.

That made me feel that she maybe did like me, but Byars always accompanied her and I never had a chance to ask. Too, I feared the guards might overhear me.

"How's your relationship with The Lord?" Byars asked on one of his trips.

"I guess it's okay," I said. "He hasn't told me otherwise."

Byars shook his head. "You need to get right with God. Are they treating you okay?"

"It's tolerable from the soldiers, everyone except Captain Custer. He's as big a waste of hide and tallow as I have ever seen."

"Deliverance from Satan comes only through The Lord," he preached.

"I'm more worried about deliverance from the Custer brothers," I informed him as they were a more immediate threat to me than Satan.

At the end of every visit, Byars would pray for my deliverance from both earthly threats and eternal damnation. As he prayed the three of us would hold hands in my cell and I always thrilled at the touch of Daisy. Then they would leave me with my newspaper reading until the next week.

The *Tribune* reported on a planned summer campaign against the Sioux and Cheyenne. From the best I could put together, hundreds of Sioux and Cheyenne had abandoned the Indian Agency the previous fall to return to their nomadic way of life in the Black Hills and beyond. The government had set a deadline of the last day of January for them to return to their reservations. Those that failed to do so would be targeted by the army's summer campaign. The newspaper said the army planned to send troops west from Fort Abraham Lincoln, east from Fort Ellis in Montana Territory and north from Fort Fetterman in Wyoming Territory to trap the Indians. Now, I didn't know if any of the Sioux or Cheyenne subscribed to the *Tribune*, but if they did, it was all laid out for them, what they could expect when the weather warmed.

Though the campaign was inevitable, General Custer's status as commander of the Seventh Cavalry was not. It seems he had alienated President Grant and some of the civilians in the War Department and was spending more time in Washington, D.C., defending himself or testifying against others. Best I could determine from the newspapers, Custer had been back east in New York and Washington as far back as December and had remained there until late February when he started back for Fort Abraham Lincoln. Though the Northern Pacific had quit running regular trains to Bismarck because of the great snowpack, the railroad company put together a special train to deliver General Custer to his command. However, a blizzard struck Dakota Territory and left the general and his wife and their three hounds stranded for a week. I learned that from Captain Thomas Ward Custer himself on one of his visits to check on me.

He strode into the guardhouse one afternoon wearing so many coats I thought a grizzly bear had broken in. When he unwrapped his muffler and unbuttoned his coats, I realized it was a weasel instead of a grizzly. Fortunately, I was resting in my cell as my favorite guards were off that day when the captain arrived.

"What's the status of Lomax?" he asked.

"See for yourself," offered one of my guards, who unbarred the door and flung it open.

I was resting on my bed, reading a newspaper when he marched in. Glancing over the top of my newspaper, I stared into hate-filled eyes.

"Get up, soldier," he commanded.

"I ain't a soldier," I reminded him.

"Guards," he called out and two were instantly beside him. "Help Lomax to his feet."

The two soldiers stepped to the bed and grabbed me by the arms, yanking me to my feet, the newspaper falling to the floor.

Captain Custer shook his head. "I hoped he was losing weight, maybe starving to death."

The two guards didn't know what to say so they grabbed my arms tighter.

"Troopers," said Custer, "I'm taking a stage and driver to retrieve my brother from a snowbound train seventy miles from here. If in my absence Lomax hung himself or froze to death after escaping, I think all of us would feel a lot better."

"I wouldn't," I said.

"Your opinion don't count," he snapped, then nodded at the guards. "You can let him go. In fact, why don't you leave his cell unlatched and if he walks out just go ahead and shoot him for trying to escape. Don't just wing him, kill him."

The two guards looked at each other like Captain Custer was crazy.

"Enjoy your trip, Captain," I offered. "May your peter freeze off along the way and may Rain-in-the-Face find it and club you to death with it."

My best wishes annoyed him. "If you was a soldier, I'd have you shot for insubordination."

"I ain't and you can't," I taunted.

The captain scowled. "Put him on bread and water until I return," he ordered. "I can damn sure do that."

"Yes, Captain," my guards responded in unison.

With that, the weasel began to wrap himself up again. I wasn't sure whether to wish for him to freeze to death or not because I didn't want to be on bread-and-water rations for the duration of my stay. He stormed out of the guardhouse.

"Bastard," I called after he'd shut the door.

The two guards laughed.

"What'd you do to rub him the wrong way?" one asked.

"Just my natural charm," I offered.

They laughed again, then one of them picked up my newspaper and offered it back to me. "It would be nice if he froze on the way to rescue the general."

"Make that his return trip," the other one said, "so all of them Custers'll freeze, including his woman, the way he taunts us with her."

I didn't know what he meant, but I would learn in a couple months when I started out with the Custers on the journey that led to the Little Bighorn. But that was weeks into the future. For the time being, I was just hoping that the temperatures dropped even farther below zero and that General Custer and his brother turned into icicles on the return trip.

Reverend Byars braved the blizzard conditions and visited me the day after Tom Custer's departure, though I was disappointed that Daisy had stayed at the Bloody Bucket. I asked Byars if he would pray for me as I was uncertain of my standing with God.

"I shall be glad to pray for you, Lomax," he said, offering me the latest *Bismarck Tribune*, "but I have been praying greatly for you and your salvation every day of your imprisonment. What can I ask of God for you?"

"Ask him for the worst blizzard in the history of Dakota Territory. Might that be possible?"

"All things are possible with God, Lomax, but why such a strange request?"

"I want General Custer and his brother to freeze to death before they can return here."

Byars sputtered and spat like he had expected lemonade and had swallowed whiskey. "I'll pray no blasphemous thing. Why would you wish such? Have you even met the man?"

"No, but I've met his brother."

"The general is not his brother's keeper."

"No, but he is his commander, and they plan on killing me."

"Where have you gotten such notions, Lomax?"

"I've heard the soldiers talking."

"Gossip, Lomax, just pure gossip."

I shook my head and marched around my cell. "I didn't steal any army firewood. You were there. A wagon showed up. A soldier and a teamster unloaded it."

"Perhaps you should've informed the fort when it came, but you didn't because it saved you the work of chopping and hauling wood."

I nodded that the reverend had a point. "But you enjoyed the heat, too."

By Byars' delay, I knew I had a point not easy to refute, but he fell back on immorality as a defense. "Intoxicating drink always spawns trouble. Your offer of free liquor for firewood allowed Satan to trap you in his clutches."

"I'm not as worried about Satan as I am the Custers," I protested. "They plan to kill me."

Byars shook his head. "You are listening to too many rumor-mongers. I will not pray for another man's demise, but I shall pray for God to deliver you from both Satan and the Custers, but you must promise not to sin and not to do evil."

"Reverend," I said, "look around. It's hard to sin when I can't get out of my cell."

"Sin and evil," Byars responded, "are not just deeds, but thoughts. You should not think badly of others."

"Even when they want to kill me?"

"You must turn the other cheek as the Good Book says," Byars offered.

His religion was making me as nervous as a tongue-tied lawyer. I wasn't sure I had anyone on my side now, not if Byars had turned against me because that likely meant God was on Custer's side. Though the reverend said a prayer—a long one at that—on my behalf, I was too nervous to hear much other than "Amen."

"See, Lomax. You can pray for God's wisdom and blessing without praying against someone else."

"Thank you, Reverend. That will be a great consolation come my funeral."

"As I told you from the day I first saw you, Lomax, you have the mark of Cain upon you. You will wander as an outcast for most of your years upon this earth."

I looked around my cell. "I won't be wandering far."

Byars placed his arm upon my shoulder. "Place your faith in God. When you do, your wandering will end. Then you will come to His home where you shall not fear for your life. I will return next week to comfort you again."

I wasn't sure Byars had brought me much comfort, not when he refused to implore God to smite the Custer brothers. They way I looked at it, he would be doing them a favor. He'd be getting them out of the cold because I knew they would be headed for warmer climes once they departed this earth. In spite of our theological differences, I thanked the reverend and asked him one more favor.

"Say hello to Daisy, would you? Ask her to come next time."

Byars smiled. "Certainly, Lomax. She misses you." He turned and left.

Two days later I began to wonder about the effectiveness of Byars' prayers, when a commotion began on the sally port and my favorite guards jumped up from the table, yanked me away from our poker game and shoved me into the cell. One of them shut the door and clanked the iron bar in place behind me. I figured God had come to inspect the place and account for sins. I was wrong. This wasn't God; this visitor was bigger than God. It was General George Armstrong Custer himself. I couldn't see him, but I heard Sergeant Finkle call, "Attention for the general."

It was mid-March, likely the thirteenth because it was the unluckiest day of my life.

"At ease, men of Company C," answered a voice I recognized as Thomas Custer's.

"Where is the son of a bitch that's been defrauding the United States Army of firewood?" cried a grating voice. By the tone of his question, it was obvious the man had issued more orders than he had ever obeyed.

"We just returned," Thomas said, "and this is the first place the general insisted on coming. Now open up the cell."

Sergeant Finkle replied, "Yes, sir!"

I heard the bar being removed from the door. I positioned myself in front of the door, my legs spread, my fists knotted and planted in the side of my hips. I was going to show the general I didn't fear him like his army lackeys did. The door swung open and I stood face-to-face with George Armstrong Custer. He mirrored me, standing akimbo and glaring. I looked him over while he returned the favor. He stood about my height, five-foot-ten or so, with dirty yellow hair that reached below his shoulders. When he removed his fur cap, the long hair in back accentuated the receding hair line up front. I'd seen dogs with the mange that had better hair than Custer, but I'd never seen a dog with as ugly a mustache as his. His mustache, though, was downright cute, compared to his nose, which was red from snow burn. His eyes were clear blue and empty, so clear and empty that I figured if I looked in one ear I could see light out the other.

His nose made me snicker.

"What's so funny, soldier?"

"I ain't a soldier," I reminded him.

"That's right, you're a thief."

"I'm H.H. Lomax," I answered. "Who are you?"

He glared at me and took off his coat, tossing it to Watson, who caught it and shot him a look of disgust. I stared at Custer and his uniform. I was expecting to see stars on his shoulder. There were none.

"Perhaps you've read about me. I'm George Armstrong Custer, General Custer."

"You're no more than a major best I can tell from your insignia," I shot back.

"Lieutenant colonel, United States Army, brevet major general."

"What the hell's a brevet?"

"Honorary title for previous service," he explained.

"Hell," I replied, "I've got a reporter friend with the *Bismarck Tribune* that calls me 'Mr. President.' Does that make me a brevet president."

"I told you he was a son of a bitch," Thomas Custer interjected.

I figured the Custer brothers would have been experts on sons of bitches, having grown up with one another. At that moment, I regretted having given my cane gun to Earl Eaton, so I could've whacked them both in the jinglebobs and stymied the next generation of Custer sons of bitches.

"You're awfully cocky for a man that's in big trouble," Custer said.

"I ain't done nothing."

Custer sneered at me, then wiped the back of his hand across his lips and mustache. "Stealing government property is a serious charge."

"To my knowledge, I haven't been charged with anything, lieutenant," I challenged.

"It's general," he corrected me.

"Okay, colonel general," I said.

"Lieutenant colonel," he answered.

"You got so many ranks, I'm confused, lieutenant colonel general major."

Custer stomped the floor in frustration. "It's general."

I shook my head. "I'm a civilian and never been in the army. I want a lawyer."

"Army justice and civilian justice are two different things," Custer informed me, then turned to Finkle. "Sergeant, you and your men need to take him out and shoot him, right now."

The entire room went deathly silent except for my heart, which I could hear pounding like a bass drum.

"Maybe you shouldn't do that, Autie," said Thomas. "You remember all the hell you got for having the deserters shot on sight."

Finkle saluted Custer, then said, "Yes, sir, I'll carry out the execution once you provide me written orders as is my prerogative to request."

Custer scowled, then reached for the cell's plank door and slammed it shut. "Lock him up," he commanded. "We'll have to do this in other ways, ways that won't draw any attention to his death. I can't have him embarrassing me and the Seventh Cavalry when I've been fighting corruption and malfeasance with the Indian agencies and the sutler contracts."

"We'll figure out something," Thomas replied. "We can keep him in the guardhouse and cut off his rations."

Then everyone's voices went quiet. Someone barred my cell door and then all I could make out were hushed whispers that were even scarier because of their unheard but implied threats. Someone slammed the door into the guardroom and I assumed the Custers had exited to the sally port. I pressed my ear against the cell door. Though my guards were whispering, I couldn't make anything out. I retreated to my bed and lay there for about thirty minutes until Sergeant Finkle opened up the door.

"Supper'll be here shortly," he said. "Care to join us?"

"Sure."

Finkle shook his head. "Lomax, I gather the general doesn't care for you. Of course, none of us can converse with the general like you did."

Jimmy Russell, the little Texan, chimed in, "It was all we could do to keep from laughing. He was so mad, his ears turned redder than his nose."

"Yeah," added Pete Thompson. "Some of the Cheyenne call him 'Red Nose' because of his sun-burnt snout."

"We've all seen him mad before," James Watson advised me, "but never that mad."

I shrugged. "I just have a way with people."

Finkle grimaced. "Fact is, Lomax, they were talking about murdering you."

"You boys gonna let me escape like Rain-in-the-Face?"

All the soldiers looked at their sergeant.

Finkle shook his head. "Can't do that. If we did, he'd use it as an excuse to hunt you down. If you didn't freeze to death first, he'd just have others shoot you, say you were trying to resist capture. We'll do what we can, Lomax, because this ain't right, but I'm not sure there's much we can do without risking a firing squad."

"Yeah," said the diminutive Texan, "we like you, but we like ourselves better."

"Then I've got more friends than General Custer," I said proudly.

Watson nodded. "Only ones that like him are his kin, but there are a lot of them."

Then we heard some noise on the sally port and I jumped back into my cell, the door closing behind me for a moment, then opening back up by Finkle's hand. "It's only John Lewis with our supper."

I stepped back outside as the soldiers set the table to eat. I joined them as Lewis dipped out servings of potato soup into our bowls and the others recounted my introduction to General Custer. All five of them worried about my safety, but doubted they could do much to ensure it.

After supper, we washed our dishes in a bucket of cold water, then sat back down at the table and played some poker, betting imaginary fortunes and soaking up the heat from the fireplace at the end of the room. I was enjoying the cards and the conversation until Watson posed a question.

"How do you think the general could get rid of Lomax without raising any suspicions?"

They all dropped their cards and cogitated about the many ways I could be exterminated.

"Chain him to a tree until he froze to death, then remove the chains and say he escaped only to die from the cold," Russell offered.

"How about just burning down the guardhouse and roasting him inside?" Thompson asked. "Didn't the general's house burn down here a couple years ago?"

"Yeah," said Finkle, "but we'd just have to rebuild it. No, it needs to be something that would draw less attention to his death."

"How about poisoning his soup?" Lewis suggested. "The doctor could just say he died of old age."

"I ain't even thirty yet," I protested.

"Send him out on a wood-chopping detail, hack off his foot and let him bleed to death," Thompson suggested.

"No, no, that would be too messy," Watson countered. "I'd say just chop a hole in the river ice and shove him in to drown or freeze. Come the thaw and the spring rise, the body'd float downstream and nobody would ever be the wiser."

"Hell, fellows, can't anybody think of a way to save me?" I asked.

The room fell silent as my friends looked from one to another for what seemed like five minutes, then Finkle shrugged. "Nothing comes to mind," he offered. "Besides, it's more fun to plot your demise."

"For you, maybe," I said.

They all laughed, got up from the table and came to my side, patting me on the back.

"We like you better than General Custer," Thompson said, "but he outranks us."

"Maybe," said Russell, "you need to ask your reverend friend to pray for you."

"Did that days ago," I offered.

"Then it must not be working," Finkle said.

After the conversation, I felt like I didn't have a friend on earth, much less in heaven so I retired to my cell. I spent a lot of time thinking, wondering what I could do to extricate myself from my predicament. It didn't matter how many cavalry friends I had, none of them outranked a general or whatever the hell Custer's rank was. I couldn't go to sleep for a long time that night, worrying about my future or what little there was of it. I didn't feel like I'd done anything wrong. I don't know that I'd always done things right, but I refused to believe that I had done anything wrong in this case. Sure, I hadn't told those two fellows not to unload two cords of wood outside the back of the Bloody Bucket, but who other than a lunatic would've stopped that in the middle of a frigid winter? Then I realized that little guys like me always got stepped on by powerful men—or should I say sons of bitches?—like George Armstrong Custer. I had no answer, but knew I wouldn't become a bastard if I became rich and powerful. No, all I wanted to be was fat and lazy. When I finally went to sleep that night, I dozed fitfully.

I awoke the next morning in a cold sweat, shivering from fear more than the low temperatures. When my guards opened my door, I joined them for a breakfast of dry bread and mush. Before I took my first bite of either, I swapped my assigned portion with Russell.

"What the hell's wrong with you?" he asked.

"He thinks you may've poisoned his portion," Finkle answered.

They laughed uproariously, nudging each other with their elbows and making fun of my squeamishness. Every meal I shared with them after that, they passed around their plates or bowls until I was comfortable that my dish hadn't been poisoned.

On the third day after General Custer's visit, I learned the value of genuine prayer, not that I had been praying that much, but I knew Truett Byars surely had, him being a righteous and pious minister of Baptist persuasion.

Sergeant Finkle broke the news to me when he opened up my cell and invited me to join the others for breakfast.

"Lomax," he said, "you are the luckiest man alive."

"I don't feel like it," I responded.

He nodded. "You are because General Custer has been summoned back to Washington to testify before Congress about Indian Agency corruption."

"You mean it?"

"He'll be leaving in a matter of hours for Fargo where he'll take a train back east."

I smiled. Reverend Byars' prayers had surely worked, worked without claiming General Custer's life. I liked my original prayerful wishes better, but I couldn't complain about the reverend's results. Maybe I had been all worked up and worried for nothing. My anxiety evaporated so much that I wished the general a memorable eastbound train trip, one filled with derailments, bridge collapses, boiler explosions and head-on collisions.

Chapter Twenty-Three

The Reverend Byars came to visit a couple days later. I was glad to see him, but disappointed that Daisy had not accompanied him. When the guards let him into my cell, he cocked his head and smiled. I knew what he was thinking, but I cut him off before he spoke.

"I suppose you're going to lecture me on the power of righteous prayer and how God took General Custer away without taking his life," I started.

"First, I was going to tell you that Daisy says hello. She misses your good humor."

I was touched that Daisy still thought of me. "I miss her, too. You as well, for that matter, Reverend. But you were going to lecture me on praying for the right things, correct?"

Byars grimaced, then looked over his shoulder to see if anyone was outside the door. He pointed me to the bed. I retreated and sat down as he moved the stool from the table and plopped it down before me. He looked at the door, then at me, his face as serious as an overdue mortgage.

"You were right, Lomax."

"What are you talking about?"

"They *are* planning on killing you!"

My throat tightened.

"You've become a potential embarrassment to them and the general's political future."

I shrugged. "They hate me, I know, but I'm no threat to them. Surely not?"

"It's beyond you, Lomax. You're just a fly that's gotten caught up in national politics."

Byars wasn't making sense, or I was as confused as a lawyer at the Pearly Gates. "I ain't been involved in politics. Don't recall I ever voted in an election. Maybe I lean Democrat, but what native son of the South wouldn't after what the Republicans did to us after the war. Don't know that I lean anything, now that I've met Custer. Ain't he Democrat?"

One of the guards stopped by the door and peered in. "You boys sure are quiet today. You aren't conspiring or something, are you?"

Byars shook his head. "I'm talking to Lomax about his personal faith. It's something between me, him and God."

"Then carry on," said the soldier before moving on. "From what I hear, Lomax needs divine intervention, if he's gonna save himself."

I figured Byars had just told a little white lie and even though I wasn't sure how that would square with God, I was glad he did.

"I thought you were crazy, the stories you were telling me, but I owed it to you to ask around a little. A lot of people know about you at the fort, but nobody wants to talk about you. Everyone gets suspicious here or in town, if I bring up your name."

Shrugging, I asked, "Then did anyone talk?"

"One officer, one you might know named Frederick Benteen. You know him?"

"Yeah. He hates Custer."

"That would be true," Byars said. "He came to the Bloody Bucket last night. He started drinking, and we started talking. Your name came up. He said he wouldn't care to be in your boots right now because the general plans on assassinating you."

"But why? He barely knows me. Granted we didn't hit it off in our first meeting, but what did I do to him?"

"It's not what you did, but what you might do."

Throwing up my arms, I complained, "This is as confusing as some of your Bible talks."

The reverend leaned in closer to me. "Benteen says it began when you started bartering free drinks for firewood."

"So? How does that involve Custer?"

Holding up his hand and shaking his head, Byars said, "Be patient and I'll explain."

I took a deep breath. "Go on."

"Soldiers started stealing wood from the fort to get free drinks. That cost the fort sutler, a man named Robert Seip, business on liquor sales, vastly overpriced liquor I might add. Custer had already accused Seip of overcharging soldiers, paying kickbacks and fostering corruption. Both Custer and Seip hate each other, and Seip was looking for a way to get back at the general. You offered him that opportunity."

"I don't know him, never met him, wouldn't know him if I ran into him in the middle of the frozen Missouri River. I haven't taken a single penny from him unless he slipped into the Bloody Bucket and paid for a drink."

"You don't need to know him. He bribed a soldier and a woodchopper to deliver the load of army firewood to the Bloody Bucket."

"So? How does it all tie together?"

"Seip was setting things up so it looked like Custer was crooked and profiting from the theft of government firewood. It's politics."

"We can just explain it all, can't we?"

"When politics are involved, some people won't accept an explanation, even if it's true," Byars said. "You are a potential embarrassment to General Custer and his political ambitions. It's simpler to kill you, Lomax. The mere fact that you could be accused of government theft and might have to testify in court about kickbacks to the general could end Custer's career."

"I never gave him any money, never would with him being such a son of a bitch."

"It doesn't matter, Lomax, that's what I am trying to tell you, not when money and politics are involved."

"Dammit, Reverend, doesn't the truth matter?"

"Not in politics," he said. "It's not truth that counts but the perception of truth. You're a pawn in the war of shenanigans that are going on here and in Washington. You can read about it in the latest *Tribune*." He reached inside his coat and pulled out last week's edition.

I took it and shook my head, then pinched the bridge of my nose in frustration. I had never felt so helpless against enemies that I didn't even know. I had ridden with Jesse James on his first bank robbery, and now believed that was more honest an endeavor than politics, though apparently nowhere near as profitable.

"What can I do?" I asked, figuring the Reverend would suggest we pray again.

"I don't know, Lomax, I just don't know," he said, his words tinged with helplessness.

At that moment, I became genuinely worried. The reverend had always been confident and so sure of God and the power of prayer. Maybe the government was so corrupt that even God himself couldn't unravel the evil without getting his hands and reputation dirty.

I reached over and patted him on the shoulder. He grimaced and dropped his head. In that moment I actually felt sorrier for him than for myself. I'd been in tights and scrapes before and had somehow always lucked out. I could only hope—and pray, if it would make the reverend happy—that Custer's Luck would run out before mine.

"Would you like me to pray, Reverend?"

Byars lifted his head in surprise. "Sure, if you wish. That would fill my soul with joy."

I sighed, closed my eyes and bowed my head. "Almighty God, please smite the wicked and save the righteous. Amen." When I was done, I cracked my eyes open.

Byars was smiling. "Concise and to the point, Lomax."

"I didn't want to confuse God."

Byars stood up and patted me on the shoulder. "I must go, but I am thinking about you and praying for your deliverance. The web of wickedness entangles so many, even the righteous, that it is hard to see how all good can survive."

"Somehow, I've survived in spite of myself and in spite of the mark of Cain."

"My heart believes you will survive as wanderers do, but my mind sees no way out." He turned toward the open cell door.

I dropped the newspaper on the bed and accompanied him, patting him on the shoulder. "It'll be okay, Reverend. God hasn't put me in a mess yet that I haven't gotten out of."

"I hope you're right," he said.

Then I got bold. "Will you do me a favor?"

"Sure, Lomax, what is it?"

"Tell Daisy I send my love."

Byars smiled. "Why sure, Lomax. She'll like that, I'm certain. She's a loving woman."

Thoughts of Daisy helped soften the worry over my predicament. I had fallen into a bigger passel of trouble than I could ever remember. I wished Douglas Wolfe and Brian Dreban were still around so I could chew them out for hauling me to Dakota Territory in search of gold to begin with. The pursuit of easy money—or easy firewood for that matter—could result in a lot of trouble and misery, I learned. I scoured the latest *Tribune* for details on Custer's trip back east and what awaited him, but the paper was dated before he left. I read every word in the broadsheet, including all the advertisements, to keep from fretting about my future.

The next day I had an unexpected visitor. My favorite guards were off that day so I was locked in my cell, reading the *Tribune* a second time, when I recognized the voice of the author of so many of the paper's lies, Mark Kellogg.

"I'm here to see the prisoner H.H. Lomax," Kellogg announced.

"By what authority?" asked the head of the detail.

"By the authority of the First Amendment of the Constitution of these United States," Kellogg proclaimed.

"Huh?" replied the soldier.

"The same constitution you swore to uphold and defend," Kellogg continued.

"And you are?"

"Mark Kellogg, correspondent for the *Bismarck Tribune* and the renowned *New York Herald* and confidant of General George Armstrong Custer. Deny me my First Amendment right to visit the prisoner, and I'll report it to General Custer when he returns. Your name, trooper?"

The soldier hesitated.

"Your name?" Kellogg demanded.

"Okay, fellow," the soldier said. "You can see him as long as no names are given."

"Excellent," the reporter said. "Glad you understand rank."

Shortly, I heard the bar on the door being removed and watched as the door swung open. I arose from my bed as Kellogg entered.

"Close the door behind me," Kellogg ordered like he was either the guardhouse commander or a Custer. "I'll rap on the door when I am ready to leave."

I grinned.

"Good morning, Mr. President," he offered. "I see that you are being well cared for."

"What brings you here, Mark?"

"Rumors, I hope. There's some scurrilous gossip going around the fort and even in town that you've been stealing army property to line your pocket and to embarrass General Custer, though I never took you to be that smart nor that stupid. I hope it's not true."

I shrugged and motioned for him to sit on my stool while I reclined on the bed. "I'm not sure what truth is anymore, and I certainly don't have any faith in a newspaper correspondent to recognize it, even if it slapped him up beside the head."

"Such a callused perspective on such a noble profession as the newspaper business where we seek the truth as long, of course, as it suits our ambitions, Mr. President," Kellogg said as he sat on the stool.

"What is it you want to know, Mark?"

"Did you set out to embarrass General Custer or just to steal government property?"

"All I tried to do was stay warm for the winter. Nothing more."

"Then you did steal the army firewood, right?"

"No! A wagon load was delivered to the Bloody Bucket. I never requested it or knew it was coming. Apparently, I got caught up in fort politics, unbeknownst to me."

Kellogg pointed a finger at my nose. "Are you scheming with the sutler to humiliate General Custer and ruin his political destiny?"

"I'm only concerned with my destiny, which doesn't look real good from what I hear. Besides, I've never met the sutler. Are you interested in truth or not?"

Kellogg stared hard at me. "I'm interested in hitching my wagon to George Armstrong Custer, who's been fighting the corruption in the Indian Agency and the federal government. In a couple months, the Democratic National Convention is scheduled to open in St. Louis, June twenty-seventh to be exact. It'll be the first national convention west of the Mississippi River, an indication of the direction the future of this country is headed."

"Then I suppose all the thieves, robbers, rapists and murderers in St. Louis will have competition from the Democrats this June."

His lips tightened as he shook his head. "Always with the impertinent remark, Lomax. It's one reason you have so few friends. Let me warn you this: There's talk General Custer might be a dark horse nominee for president. His willingness to stand up to the corruption of this wicked administration has caught the eyes of a lot of committed reformers. General Custer could be a compromise choice for president."

"So what if he is?"

"I plan to ride his coattails to Washington and a job with a major newspaper. I intend to beat the drum for him all I can through the *Tribune* and the *New York Herald*." Then his eyes narrowed. "I'll not let anybody in Bismarck sully his reputation or ruin his—and my—chance to go to Washington. He's the type of man we need running this country."

I nodded because I knew Custer was just the type of man the nation needed, if we wanted to run the country into the ground. That's when I came to understand that ambition trumped truth and the quest for political power trumped decency. I had never wanted much more than all the money I could spend, but certainly not political power. I saw an ugly side of life in the newspaper correspondent or maybe it was just the hideous nature of journalism as the painted woman of politics. Either way, I felt events closing in around me. A general wanted me dead. A whole regiment of cavalry would follow his orders—and wishes—to see that I didn't survive the summer. A newspaper correspondent cared little for the truth—or my life—when it interfered with his ambitions. For an instant, I wished I was back in Texas. After all, Texans were too stupid to weave such an intricate web of deceit and corruption.

"I understand what you're saying."

"That's best for your future, Mr. President," Kellogg said, the sarcasm rising in his voice.

For the first time, I realized his moniker—Mr. President—for me was not a friendly nickname, but rather one of mockery. I was not his equal, but rather an inferior person with no chance to become the leader of the country or even rise to the low level of newspaper correspondent. I now knew that my side of the firewood issue did not matter to him. He cared nothing about finding the truth, only perpetuating his ambitions.

Kellogg arose and shook his head at me. "Who knows, Mr. President, if I play this right, I could be in a high government position, maybe even a cabinet post."

I decided I'd like to lock him in a cabinet or beat him with a fence post, but I didn't figure that would leave me in good standing with any future journalist that might want to write about Leadeye Lomax.

"Good luck," I said, knowing nothing else to say after so frank and fruitless a discussion.

"You need the luck more than me, Mr. President," he informed me, "because Custer's Luck trumps everything. If I stay close enough to him, it'll rub off on me."

From what I'd seen, Custer's luck was more like a contagion. Sure, Custer had survived against long odds, but those around him had not fared nearly as well.

Kellogg marched to my cell door and rapped his knuckles against it. "Guards, I am through visiting with your prisoner."

The door opened and Kellogg exited without another word.

I looked at the *Tribune* on the bed and considered ripping it to pieces, but then decided I should save it, either to read or to use more appropriately after an encounter with the slop bucket. It seemed like everything was stacked against me. As long as General Custer was away in Washington fighting corruption, I figured I was safe. Once he returned, however, the days ahead would be menacing as I was uncertain both of my friends and of my fate.

About the only times I ever felt at ease was when Reverend Byars visited or Finkle's crew worked as my guards. My faith in them, however, was challenged one evening when I saw Thompson put something in my stew. I couldn't believe the Scotsman was poisoning me. When we all sat at the table, I switched bowls with Jimmy Russell, the tiny Texan. Oblivious to the assassination attempt, he took a few bites, then grabbed his throat and began to gasp for breath. His eyes rolled upward, then he fell off his chair onto the floor.

"Ooops," said Finkle, "we should've let him know about the poison."

"We'll get it right next time," Thompson said.

I sat in stunned silence, not knowing what to say now that my last friends had turned against me. The silence lasted about thirty seconds, then Russell began to stir, moaning and flailing against the floor before jumping up with a huge grin on his face. The stony demeanor of the other guards cracked and they began to laugh uproariously.

Thompson slapped me on the back. "We had you going, Lomax."

"Not very funny," I said, my frown slowly twisting into a grin.

Russell sat back down and gobbled up his soup while everyone else took bites between the laughter. It was a pleasant moment, one that took my mind off my predicament. March turned to April and April neared its end. I just hoped my drama wasn't nearing its end. During those weeks, I studied the Seventh Cavalry as it began to assemble at Fort Abraham Lincoln. As I understood it, the planned summer expedition against the hostiles would be the first time all the regiment's companies had been together since shortly after the Civil War. The thing that surprised me most was that more than four out of ten soldiers weren't American. Almost a hundred came from Ireland, while three-quarters of that number came from Germany with their heavy accents and difficulty understanding or communicating English. Another two dozen or so were born in England. Then there were several from Canada, Scotland, Switzerland and Denmark as well as a handful from countries as remote as Italy, Russia and Australia.

The rest of the troopers were American born, the vast majority of them coming from Yankee states, like New York and Pennsylvania, where John Lewis was born, as well as Massachusetts, Ohio, Indiana and Illinois. In all, Finkle told me twenty-nine states were represented in the Seventh Cavalry. I asked him to check if any trooper hailed from Arkansas. He reported back that I was the only known Arkansas native within a hundred miles of Bismarck. That told me I was out of place, which I could have accepted had I been out of jail. To assure me I had some southern brethren around me, he informed me the Confederate states had supplied six men from Virginia, two each from Georgia, North Carolina, Louisiana and Tennessee and one each from South Carolina and Texas, Jimmy Russell being the sole representative from that state.

When I wasn't occupying myself with learning more about the Seventh Cavalry, I tried to keep up with Custer's drama in Washington. An effort had been made to impeach Secretary of War William Belknap, but he resigned before the politicians could kick him out of office. His resignation led to more questions about the how the army was run, especially the appointment of crooked sutlers like Seip at Fort Lincoln. Apparently, bribes, kickbacks and nepotism were rampant in the way Belknap had run the army posts. President Grant's son, brother and brother-in-law had been implicated by association if not by deed so the scandal reached all the way to the president.

Custer testified before a committee overseen by Congressman Hiester Clymer and pointed fingers everywhere there was a Republican and nowhere there was a Democratic. Just by the newspaper accounts, you would've thought Democrats were angels and Republicans were the devil incarnate. I discussed the newspaper accounts with Finkle and his men whenever they were on duty. The best we could tell, Custer had no solid proof of anything, just gossip.

Finkle summed up Custer's testimony. "The general has a great talent for believing gossip about his enemies and discounting facts about his family and friends."

"It's called lying," said Watson.

"I didn't know the general had any friends, just family," Russell added.

It was hard to determine who had the lowest opinion of Custer among the five. Since none of their lives were at stake like mine—or at least that was what I thought at the time—I had the lowest opinion of all.

"I hear he wants to be president," I said.

"That's what I've heard you say," Finkle answered. "I can't imagine that any man would vote for him for president. Hell, I'd vote for old Jefferson Davis before I'd vote for Custer. At least the outcome of the war knocked Jeff Davis down a notch or two. Nothing's ever changed Custer's opinion of himself."

We followed the drama from Washington for weeks, then came a report from one of the New York papers that Custer was being relieved of command of the Seventh Cavalry and would not be allowed to lead his regiment on the summer expedition against the hostiles. Maybe Reverend Byars was right after all that God did work in mysterious ways through prayer as long as you offered your need in a Godly way. Every night I had prayed that General Custer would get what he deserved. I left that up to God, and it seemed to be working, if the newspaper accounts were true. I began to think I might survive my unfortunate time in Dakota Territory after all. According to the newspaper accounts, more now doubted Custer's future than my own.

As April drew to a close, I grew more confident about my future. The prolonged cold had broken, and the Missouri River had thawed, though ice floes still floated down the river and past the fort, making it difficult and dangerous to cross the river between the fort and Whiskey Point. From what Finkle said, the summer expedition couldn't begin until the river was clear of ice since the army would need steamboats to run upstream to supply the excursion. Finkle said it would be the middle of May or later before the expedition could begin because of fickle Dakota Territory weather that brought blizzards as late as early June.

In the crush of events required to mount the summer expedition, I hoped that I might escape like Rain-in-the-Face. If I did, I would leave Dakota Territory for good and remove the stain of Custer from my memory forever. While the Seventh Cavalry was heading west to round up the hostiles, I would go east and then find my way south, maybe to Arkansas to see my family or even into Texas. All the sons of bitches in Texas combined couldn't be as detestable as Custer alone.

Then in early May came a decision from Washington that sealed my fate. Reverend Byars delivered the stunning news. He told me that a telegram had arrived in town to notify the fort that General Custer would be returning in a matter of days. Worse yet, Custer would lead the Seventh Cavalry against the hostiles.

"All that prayer wasted," I said. "I even tried to pray in a Godly way, Reverend, not that Custer would die, but that he would get what he deserved."

"God works in mysterious ways," Byars responded.

And, God's timing was impeccable. At that very moment, someone entered the guardhouse and marched to my open cell door. I looked up and saw Captain Thomas Custer.

"Hello, Lomax," Custer said, "you'll be going Indian hunting with us in a couple weeks. I just wanted to let you know so you could mull it over in your mind. Good day, Lomax. It will be one of your last."

Custer spun around and marched away.

Custer's words did not surprise me, but Reverend Byers' response did.

"Bastard!" he said softly.

Chapter Twenty-Four

The second week of May, General George Armstrong Custer arrived back at Fort Abraham Lincoln, in spite of my many prayers otherwise. Post activities accelerated as Custer resumed command of the Seventh Cavalry. As best I could put it together from the *Tribune* and overheard gossip from my guards, the Dakota column would leave Fort Abraham Lincoln under the command of Brigadier General Alfred H. Terry and head west with units of the Sixth, Seventeenth and Twentieth Infantry and Custer's entire Seventh Cavalry. A second column would head east from Montana Territory with the Seventh Infantry and Second Cavalry, all under the command of Colonel John Gibbon. A command under the charge of Brigadier General George Crook would drive north from Fort Fetterman in Wyoming with units of the Second and Third Cavalry and the Fourth Infantry. The goal was to entrap the Indians and force them back on the reservation or decimate them for their impertinence in not doing what they were told by the federal government.

Sergeant Finkle informed me that word had been passed down that I would accompany Custer's headquarters command when the Dakota column pulled out of Fort Lincoln.

"Odd thing about the orders," Finkle said, "was that they were committed verbally with instructions not to list your whereabouts in any written communications. Looks to me like they don't want any record of you on this expedition. They plan on killing you and leaving no trace of your trail or their part in your demise. You best be on your guard."

"I can take care of myself."

Finkle grinned. "Sure you don't want us to go ahead and poison you. It'd make it a lot simpler on the army and save you a lot of worry."

"Your thoughtfulness is touching."

We both laughed. Finkle went about his guardhouse duties, and I just waited in my cell. I took an inventory of my possessions, which weren't many. I had my whorehouse suit, shirt, socks and shoes plus my long johns, my empty shoulder holster and the necklace from Snakebit. I pulled the rattle from beneath my shirt and looked at it, then shook the leather thong.

"Damn," said Finkle, rushing to my cell. "Did I hear a rattlesnake?"

I held up the rattle. "No, just me, biding my time. This came from the biggest rattlesnake I ever saw until I met General Custer. I'll clip the general's rattle before I'm done."

"You against the whole Seventh Cavalry, Lomax?"

"Reverend Byars is praying for me. I figure God is on my side."

"God's had a lot of chances to get General Custer before now. The whole Confederacy couldn't clip his wings, so I don't give you any better chance, though I'm not a gambling man."

"Well, I've given up gambling and all sins until this expedition is over. I don't want God holding anything against me if it comes down to me and the general."

"I admire your religious devotion, Lomax."

"Yes, sir, you might say religion comes naturally to me when I need it."

Finkle laughed and went about his business while I thought about my chances of delaying my demise. My odds were slim.

The Friday after Custer returned to Fort Lincoln, Reverend Byars visited and assured me he was praying for my deliverance. He told me that the expedition would form up over the weekend and depart on Monday for the unknown. He pleaded with me to confess my belief in Jesus so he might baptize me before I departed. I didn't think a bath in the cold waters of the Missouri River would do me much good at the moment, so I put him off, figuring if by some miracle I returned, I would convert then.

"I hope to see you off when the expedition leaves," Byars told me. "I know God will provide you armor for the tribulations you will face. Daisy's even sewing you something to take along. She's a good woman, Lomax, and she thinks highly of you."

He prayed with me and then left. The coming Saturday and Sunday, the expedition formed up south of the garrison. I could near the noise of canvas-topped supply wagons rattling by, of braying donkeys complaining about the packs on their backs, of officers shouting orders, and of soldiers cursing their fate. Everyone was ready on Monday, everyone but God. He sent heavy showers that made life miserable for the animals and the men who had abandoned their barracks for canvas tents as they prepared to march against the hostiles. The rains delayed the departure until May seventeenth, a Wednesday.

At four in the morning, reveille sounded and I was roused from my cell by some new guards who told me to put on my clothes and go with them. I did as I was told, and they escorted me outside where I was assigned an army mule to ride. It was a cold and misty morning, and I wasn't dressed in anything other than my whorehouse suit. I complained about the cold and having no hat, but they told me to quit bitching and to get on my mule. I climbed into the saddle, then my three guards mounted and escorted me to the assembly area. I figured it was a waste of government money to assign me three guards, when none would've done, and I could've just ridden off into the mist without looking back. Of course, they'd probably have chased me down for stealing an army mule then. Seems like I couldn't win against the army.

I was directed toward the assembly ground where Custer and the Seventh Cavalry prepared to march out. I rode past a few cavalrymen that had guarded me, including Finkle, Thompson, Watson, Lewis and Russell.

"Give him hell, Lomax!" called the little Texan.

"Russell," cried Finkle, "remember our orders. Lomax is not to be acknowledged."

Chastened, Russell nodded. "Give him hell, man who doesn't exist!"

The nearby cavalrymen laughed, while my three guards looked at each other, not knowing what to think of my familiarity with some of the soldiers. My guards escorted me to the front of the assembling troops and toward General Custer, who was surrounded by a circle of officers and soldiers seeking instructions. Two scowling women sat sidesaddle nearby, watching the whole spectacle from their mounts.

Custer looked up and saw me, then grimaced and returned to issuing orders. I realized something was different about him. He was as cocky as ever, his nose was as sunburned as always and he was as big a son of a bitch as before, but something was missing. I studied him, then realized he had cut his long hair.

After most of those around him had scurried away to attend to last minute details, Custer rode my way, accompanied by his brother Tom, several other officers I didn't recognize, *Tribune* reporter Mark Kellogg and Dr. Henry Porter, the physician who occasionally came to the Bloody Bucket to patch up soldiers.

Approaching me, General Custer lifted his arm like he was halting a line of cavalrymen. "Guards," he said, "you are dismissed." My three keepers turned their mounts around and rode back to guardhouse. After they were out of hearing distance, Custer turned to his fellow officers.

"Gentlemen, this is H.H. Lomax," Custer announced. "He'll be riding with us, unofficially, of course. Don't ever let him out of gunshot range. He'll stay with headquarters command as he has been known to steal government firewood. In the event that something happens to him on our expedition, he is to be buried in an unmarked grave."

"I ain't scared of you, your men or even the hostiles," I lied.

Unaccustomed to back talk, Custer shot back, "You ought to be scared."

I shook my head. "I'm not the one that got my hair cut. You afraid of being scalped?"

Custer's eyes narrowed and he spat at the foot of my mule. "I knew you'd be riding with us, and I heard what you did to Wild Bill Hickok's long hair."

The others gasped and one lieutenant shook his head. "This is the Lomax that dumped a quart of molasses on Wild Bill's head? He don't look that brave."

"It was me," I admitted, tired of denying every rumor about me and Wild Bill.

"Wild Bill's in the Black Hills now, from what I hear," General Custer said. "We ought just to escort you to Deadwood and let Wild Bill finish you off."

Wild Bill and I had had our differences, but I didn't see any point in discussing them with these yahoos, so I changed the subject. I pointed to the two mounted women. "General, I didn't know you let whores ride with the cavalry."

Custer's faced reddened like his nose. "That's my wife and sister." Custer spat.

I sputtered. "Your wife is your sister? Never seen that before, not even in Arkansas!"

"His *sister is my* wife," huffed the lieutenant that had falsely accused me of soiling Wild Bill's hair with syrup.

"See, gentlemen," Custer continued, "Lomax is as contemptible a man as I've ever met. He doesn't know his place or his manners among the officers of the Seventh Cavalry."

Custer's lieutenant brother-in-law scowled at me as Tom Custer tapped his fingers on the butt of his cavalry revolver.

"Don't worry, Jim," said the general. "He'll get his due on this expedition." Custer turned to the doctor. "Henry, if he gets injured or wounded on our journey, you are not, I repeat not, to treat him."

Porter nodded, then rolled his eyes when the general looked away.

The impromptu meeting was my introduction to Custer's kin. I later learned the lieutenant was named James Calhoun, Custer's brother-in-law. Other strangers I came to know in the group were the general's younger brother, Boston Custer, who was working as a scout and forager, and Autie Reed, a nephew of the Custer brothers and a so-called herder on the expedition, though I never saw him herding any animals, save the Custer clan, of course. The quintet made up the Custer brood, as I called them, and they were my tormentors for the next thirty-nine days, everyone of them looking for a way to get me killed without being seen or blamed.

General Custer stared at me for a moment, the silence being so awkward that the others departed to handle their assignments. After they left Custer lifted his hand and pointed his index finger at my nose like he was about to threaten me.

Before he could speak, though, I heard a familiar voice behind me. "General Custer," called my preacher friend, "may I have a word with you? I am Reverend Truett Byars, and I am accompanied by Miss Daisy."

I yanked the reins on my mule and turned him around to see both Byars and Daisy approaching me on horseback. Unlike the proper Custer women, Daisy sat astride her horse. She wore a smile rather than a scowl and seemed glad to see me.

"What is it, Reverend?" Custer asked. "Can't you see I'm a busy man?"

"Yes, sir," he said. "But might I offer Mr. Lomax a humble gift?" He held up a haversack and unknotted the tie, extracting a book from it. "It's a Bible," he said. "I thought it might bring protection and comfort to Mr. Lomax on this expedition." Byars flipped through the pages so the general could see there was nothing hidden in the volume other than the word of God. Then he held the haversack by the bottom and turned it upside down so the general could see nothing else was inside.

Custer nodded. "I suspect Lomax will need as much protection as he can get."

"Thank you, General. You are most considerate, a man worthy of his noble reputation," Byars said.

I cocked my head, trying to keep from grinning as Byars fed Custer's vanity. Byars maneuvered his mount near my mule and offered me the haversack. I took it and lifted the strap over my arm and shoulder. The haversack felt heavy with the Bible inside, but the word of God was weighty, I had to admit.

"Might you grant a similar favor to Miss Daisy? She sewed the haversack for Mr. Lomax, but she also has a gift for him, a straw hat, something he will need on this journey."

Daisy lifted up a cheap hat for the general to see, then smiled at me again.

Custer nodded his permission.

Daisy maneuvered to the side of my mule opposite Custer, and lifted the hat toward me, moving her horse closer to my mule. I took the hat and plopped it on my head. Daisy leaned toward me, then backed away and looked at Custer.

"General," she started, "might I dismount and give Mr. Lomax a farewell kiss?"

Custer nodded. "Get on with it."

She dismounted and walked toward me. I leaned over to kiss her, but she held back.

"General, can Mr. Lomax dismount so I can give him a proper kiss?"

Again Custer nodded.

I slipped off the mule, which screened me from the general.

"Is Mr. Lomax under arrest?" Byars asked.

Custer sputtered and tried to explain as Daisy stepped to my side. I wrapped my arms around her and kissed her full on the lips, wondering if she would be the last white woman I ever smooched. She slipped her left arm around me, and fumbled for something with her right hand. Then I felt her slip something in my left coat pocket before enveloping me with her right arm and kissing me. As we kissed, Custer explained that I had volunteered to accompany his troops.

"That's enough, Lomax," Custer finally said.

I broke from Daisy's lips and patted my coat pocket, detecting the form of my five-shot peashooter that the army had left in the Bloody Bucket the day the soldiers arrested me.

"I hope you are pleased," Daisy said as she turned around to her mare.

"Most definitely," I said as I helped her into the saddle.

As Custer explained why I wasn't really under arrest in spite of my three months in the stockade, I leaned into my mule to screen my body from prying eyes and quickly switched the revolver from my coat pocket to the shoulder harness. I pulled myself back atop my mule.

"Thank you, General, for your courteous explanation of his situation," Byars said. "Should Mr. Lomax not return safely, I will press inquiries with the War Department."

"Nowhere could be safer," Custer said, "than with the Seventh Cavalry in coming days."

Byars turned to me. "Go forth, Lomax, forearmed with the holy word of God."

"I most certainly will," I replied. "Thank you both for seeing and for providing for me."

"Be gone, both of you," Custer instructed. "The Seventh Cavalry has business to attend."

Daisy waved and rode away. I hoped I would see her again one day to propose marriage.

Byars nodded. "Good luck, Lomax. The Lord be with you."

He turned about and quickly caught Daisy. It was good to be armed with the word of God. I patted the Bible in the haversack. It was even better to be armed with my peashooter. I refrained from shooting General Custer in the back as he rode away. My restraint in not shooting him was a courtesy I doubted he would extend me in the coming weeks.

As the troops finalized preparations, I rode to the front of the regiment, noting that Tom Custer was keeping an eye on me, tailing me so I would never be out of gunshot range. While I waited, the women and children of the troopers gathered on the perimeter, hoping to see their husbands and fathers off and praying they would return. Somberness permeated the mist that was gradually diminishing as the sun tried to break through the dwindling clouds.

About seven o'clock that morning, Custer gave the command and the regimental band, all astride white horses, started playing "Garry Owen," a jaunty song that failed to lift the spirits of the men, much less their women and children, even though I figured I was the only one headed for certain doom. With company banners and regimental colors flying, the Seventh Cavalry started toward the Little Bighorn. It was an impressive sight, Custer having previously colored, as the men called it, his companies so each unit rode horses of matched color. Company A rode brown bays; Companies B, I and M, light bays; Company C, light sorrels; Company D, blacks; Company E, grays;

Company F, light bays; Company G, mixed sorrels; Company H, blood and light bays; Company K, sorrels; and Company L, bays.

I fell in line with Dr. Porter, not saying much. I looked over my shoulder and saw the reverend and Daisy waving at me. When she saw I was staring her way, she blew me a kiss. Her affectionate gestures gave me hope for the future—if I survived the present!

"Don't worry, Lomax," Porter announced, "if you're injured. I'll take care of you just like any other patient."

"Thank you, doctor."

The procession passed the teepees and log huts of the Indian scouts, mostly Arikaras—or Rees as the troopers called them. Their women moaned or sang a plaintive song like Indian women had done for decades when their men went off to war. Then the caravan marched through the fort proper, traversing the cavalry parade ground where officer's wives and children watched. Custer ordered a halt on the parade ground so the officers could give a final farewell to their families. The officers scurried quickly about, then returned to their mounts. Custer ordered the band to play "The Girl I Left Behind." As the music carried across the parade ground, the line of cavalrymen started toward the hostiles.

Once we cleared the fort and started up an incline toward open prairie, I saw a most peculiar hallucination, something that I can only describe as a mirage. The strange combination of dwindling mist and emerging sunshine created a reflection in the sky so that it looked like the caravan was riding not only up the incline but also into the sky itself. It was an unsettling vision. I stared at the illusion, thinking myself crazy until Dr. Porter spoke.

"That's a bad omen."

"What?" I asked.

"The cavalrymen riding into the heavens," he said, pointing forward.

I nodded. "I see it, but was afraid to say anything for fear you might think I was crazy."

"We're not the crazy ones on this march," Porter said.

I'm sure others on the expedition were worried about their future as well. The difference was, I was the only one that had to worry about surviving both the hostiles and the cavalry.

As we topped the incline where the ghost cavalry rode on into the sky, I turned around in my saddle and looked at the spectacle lined out behind me. The caravan stretched almost two miles. Me and Custer along with his staff and his brood rode at the head of the line, followed by a company of his cavalry and two infantry companies assigned to pioneering duty, such as clearing the trail or making routes suitable for supply wagons to cross. Then came more infantry and cavalry units plus a platoon of three Gatling guns, followed by more than a hundred army wagons, pulled by teams of six mules and capable of hauling up to 5,000 pounds of supplies. Behind them came smaller civilian wagons pulled by two horses and carrying up to 2,000 pounds. Then followed the replacement horses and mules, which would carry the supplies once it became prudent to abandon the wagons. Mostly the wagons carried ammunition—a quarter of a million rounds I heard—and a limited amount of forage for the horses.

From what I understood, the steamboat *Far West* and Captain Marsh were to meet us upriver to re-supply forage for our horses, which couldn't live on prairie grass like Indian ponies. Somewhere in the line of soldiers rode General Alfred H. Terry, who was in overall command of the Dakota column, though you would never have known it by the way Custer strutted about in the vanguard, variously attending to his army duties and then his wife and sister. Once I saw him pointing at me. He informed them in a loud voice I could hear, "He's the son of a bitch that stole army firewood and tried to damage my reputation." The women's faces tightened as they glowered at me. I tipped my straw hat and their faces puckered like a year-old prune.

"The general doesn't care for you," Dr. Porter informed me.

"I'm not sure the general cares for anyone except himself," I replied.

Porter smiled. "Vanity can be a dangerous sickness."

"So can stupidity," I replied.

Porter laughed so loudly it drew Custer's icy gaze. A lesser man would've withered beneath Custer's glare and would've abandoned me, but Porter lifted his chin in defiance, letting the general know that he did not consider me an outcast.

"It's not right what they've done to you, Lomax," Porter said.

"Thank you, Doctor, but I've learned a lot from the experience."

"Like what?"

"What a son of a bitch General Bluster is."

Porter laughed even harder, drawing Custer's further disdain. I tipped my hat again, then tried to ignore Custer as best I could the rest of the day as we traversed the prairie and rolling hills on our way toward our destiny. We halted early in the afternoon on a flat grassy plain bordering the banks of the Heart River, which was fringed with cottonwood trees. The site was large enough to accommodate all the troops, animals and supply wagons with good grass and good water. The view across the rolling prairie was inspiring in its vastness if a man had the courage to look upward because he was better served looking at his feet since the plateau teemed with rattlesnakes.

"Have the men clear the field of rattlers," Custer ordered Thomas. "Don't collect any specimens, Tom, not on the trip out. You can grab as many as you like for pets on the return."

As Tom rode off, I clutched the rattle around my neck, hoping it would bring me good luck on this expedition or at least scare away any rattlesnakes that might be inclined to bite me. Soon soldiers were dismounting and lining up to march across the plateau, driving the snakes ahead of them, beating them with sticks, slicing them with sabers and occasionally shooting one with a revolver. After the snake drive, the soldiers began to set up camp. We had only gone a dozen or so miles since we left Fort Lincoln and still had six hours until dark, so it didn't make sense to me at first. Then Custer announced that he had brought along the paymaster to hand out pay for the last two months. It was considerate of him, I thought, to pay the men far from the Bloody Bucket and other places where they could've spent their money. Then it dawned on me that the paymaster and his men would be returning to the fort come morning, a convenient contrivance to make sure his wife and sister had a military escort back to their homes.

Mostly the soldiers grumbled that their pay did them little good in the wilderness and groused even more when a clerk from the fort's sutler set up a table next to the paymaster to collect what was owed the store before the balance was handed to the soldiers. Not only could they not spend their money, but they also didn't get all they thought they were due.

As I had no responsibilities to the army on this expedition other than to get killed, I kept my eye on Custer, hoping a rattlesnake might slip past the guards and bite him on the nose or other appendage so he would endure a slow and painful death. When Custer's personal camp had been set up apart from the troops, Tom Custer spotted me, walked over and grabbed me by the arm, then pulled me toward the soldier who had done all the work.

"Private Burkman," Tom called as we approached the fellow.

Rather than salute, Burkman ran his hands through his dark brown hair, then stood staring at me with his hazel eyes. He didn't say a thing. Fact was, Burkman didn't ever say much and when he spoke he said even less. I would learn his full name was John Burkman, and he was the general's "striker," a military term for personal slave, doing all the menial tasks beneath the dignity of the general. Rumored to have been born in Germany, Burkman spoke with a thick accent that I found hard to understand.

"Private, this is H.H. Lomax," Tom informed him. "He's an enemy of General Custer. Treat him accordingly. Shoot him, if he tries to leave."

I smiled and tipped my hat.

"Perxactly," answered Burkman, whatever the hell that meant, then went about his business, the most important part placing planks across two sawhorses in the general's tent. He dragged a mattress from the general's wagon and placed it atop the slats making a bed for the general and his wife. Apparently, his sister was not accorded such inviting accommodations, her husband being lesser in rank than the general.

That night after the meals had been finished and the soldiers had retired to their blankets on hard ground, Custer and his wife retired, though not to sleep. They rutted like animals, noisy animals at that, so much so that soldiers gathered sat up from their blankets and wished they had the general's privileges. I had worked months in a whorehouse and had never heard so much noise as I did that night. Three times during the proceedings over the next five hours, I heard the general shout out, "Hallelujah, John!" Each time the soldiers groaned with envy. If they'd been paid back at the fort, they could've bought female companionship. As it was, they had an itch in their britches that only they could scratch.

The next morning the soldiers awoke stiff and jealous from their night on the hard ground. Custer emerged from his tent with a smile as wide as if he had had a woman three times overnight. I never saw more surly frowns on men than that morning when Custer taunted his men by giving his wife a long kiss and sending her on her way. As the two women left with the paymaster, the men all cheered. Custer surely thought they were offering a gesture of respect for his wife. In reality, the soldiers signaled their relief that once the concubines were gone, the troops would not face another such hard night on the trail.

Chapter Twenty-Five

After the paymaster and the Custer women departed, we crossed the Heart River, the wagons struggling through the three-foot waters but aided by a gravel bottom. We lost three hours getting the expedition across the river. Since my responsibility consisted solely of waiting to be killed, I had a lot of spare time with the headquarters command. So, I began to consider how I might escape or survive. First, I draped my haversack over my right shoulder and under my left arm so people would think I was going for my Bible if I ever had to pull my peashooter. And, having nothing else to do, I frequently pulled the Good Book out and read a few chapters. That's when I realized something odd about the haversack—it was heavier than it should've been when empty. As I began to feel the four seams at the corners, I realized Daisy had sewn some kind stiffener in the seams. Fingering one of the seams, it dawned on me that she had hidden bullets in a loop of cloth in each corner of the haversack. Not only did she provide me with a loaded gun, she had also supplied me with extra ammunition. Granted, I'd almost have to be close enough to shake an Indian's or a general's hand to do any damage with my peashooter, but at least I could give them a bee sting or two before they dispatched me to the happy hunting ground or an unmarked grave.

Fact was, I didn't know how to go about saving myself. I figured I could slip into the general's tent when he was asleep and shoot him one night, but he had four stag hounds that stayed in his tent after his wife departed. Even if I got past the hounds, I'd still have his brother and the rest of his brood to deal with, not to mention his striker, who looked at the general like he was God incarnate. I was sure Burkman's opinion of Custer matched the general's view of himself. Then I thought I might win some allies if I shot Custer in the pecker. If I did, all the regular soldiers might protect me from his brood after all the misery he had caused his troops the first night on the trail. I knew they would rally to my aid if I dampened the general's ardor.

Once the last wagon crossed the river, Custer himself rode over beside me. "Let's go for a ride, Lomax."

"Why so you can shoot me, General Bluster?"

"Don't be ridiculous, Lomax."

I snickered that Custer didn't catch the mispronunciation of his name.

"I wouldn't shoot you with so many witnesses around. Once we encounter hostiles, that's when you'll need to worry. I can split up the troops to reduce the number of possible witnesses, then shoot you during a skirmish so everyone'll think the Indians did it. Or, I may even ride out of sight of the troops with you, shoot you and claim a Sioux or Cheyenne did it. Nobody'll question me."

"Reverend Byars might, once you return without me."

"Who'd believe a preacher, especially one that's up here to defend the savages when they stand in the way of this nation's destiny? And my destiny!"

"What's your destiny, General Bluster?"

"Lomax, it may be hard for you to comprehend this, you being an ignorant Southern boy, but I intend to be president, possibly as early as next year, if things go my way. President Grant's made a mess of things, and people are tired of Republican rule and corruption. The Democrats hold their convention in St. Louis next month. When I rout the hostiles, I'll be a national hero again once Mark Kellogg sends his dispatches to the papers. My bravery will propel me to the presidency! Now put up your Bible and mount up, Lomax. I want to demonstrate what I think of you."

I slid my Bible back in the haversack and patted the gun in my shoulder holster. It brought me comfort, if not protection. I climbed aboard my mule and turned him toward Custer's mount, then followed the general north while the expedition moved west. When we reached a small rise, we rode over it and just out of sight of the troops. At that point, Custer handed me his reins and dismounted. Then he began to unbutton his trousers, dropping them and squatting to attend to nature's most unpleasant task.

"This is what I think of you, Lomax," Custer said, his ruddy face reddening from the strain.

"General, I don't know how to tell you this, but you're losing your mind. Your brains are leaking on the grass." My observation failed to endear me to the general but it shut him up because he couldn't think of anything to say. I prayed for a rattlesnake to come up and bite him on his buttocks, but there wasn't a reptile that brave—or stupid—in the entire world. Besides, the snake might catch something from the general. Then I realized, I didn't need a rattlesnake to bite him just to have a little fun.

Carefully, I maneuvered my mule around so Custer's horse screened me from the general. Then I slipped the necklace out of my shirt and grabbed the rattle. Taking a deep breath, I shook the rattle as hard as I could. The buzz startled Custer's mount, which reared.

"Rattlesnake," I yelled.

The general leaped up from his squat, tried to run, but tripped on his pants and fell headlong into earth.

"Behind you, General," I cried.

Custer rolled away from the spot, then pushed himself up and grabbed for the scabbard at his side. He lifted the cover and yanked out his revolver. "Where is he?" he screamed.

"Between your legs," I cried, pointing at his feet. He stumbled backward, tripping again.

I slid the rattle back inside my shirt.

"Shoot him, shoot him," Custer screamed.

"I don't have a gun, General," I lied, then held up my haversack. "I can read him a Bible verse. Maybe that'll convert him."

"No, dammit!" he screamed. "Where is he?"

I pointed about five yards away. "He slithered into a hole over there. I think you're safe for now, General."

Custer stood back up and looked all around before he bent down and grabbed his trousers. As he did, I caught a brief glimpse of his equipment. It was obvious General Custer was not well-armed. In fact, it made me wonder what all the noise had been about the night before because I had seen roosters carrying bigger pistols.

Walking toward his nervous mount, he glared at me, never taking his eyes off mine until he stepped in the mess of his own making. Then he dragged his boots through the grass and kicked his feet to sling off the mud.

"Do you want me to share your tale of rattlesnake bravery with the newspaperman?"

"You'll say nothing about it, Lomax, and that's an order."

I shrugged. "I ain't a soldier. You may be able to shoot me, but you can't order me around."

He stormed over and grabbed the reins to his skittish mount. He leaped into the saddle and turned toward the men he did command. "Don't linger, Lomax, or I'll have them shoot you with one of the Gatling guns." He galloped off.

I stayed a moment, studying the dark clouds to the north. A storm was brewing. I turned around and started back to rejoin the cavalry. Throughout the whole episode, my mule had remained as calm as a dead man. More and more I decided that, other than Dr. Porter, my mule was the only living thing I could trust on the Dakota plains. I also had time to get to know my mule. It seems life generally provided me with more mules than horses, so I was at home riding on something less than a horse but better than a donkey. "My name is Lomax," I said by way of introduction. "You may be the only friend I have on this expedition."

I leaned over and patted him on the shoulder. He didn't offer me his name by way of introduction so I decided I would give him one. He needed a name of honor and dignity. I pondered a term that would do him and me proud, if not Custer. Then it struck me: CIA-HA. Pronounced see-ah-ha, the word, I decided, was Comanche for "Custer is a horse's ass!"

"Let's go, Ciaha," I said and nudged him in the flank with my heel. My mule moved with a bounce in his step and pride in his new name. I liked it, too. I'm sure the general would have liked it because he had lost too many brains on the backside of the hill to fully understand the translation.

I rode Ciaha over the rise and rejoined the cavalry command. Dr. Porter looked at me and shrugged when I reined Ciaha in beside him. "What happened to the general? He was madder than a barrel of wet wildcats."

"A rattlesnake slipped up on him while he was laying logs. His bravery is overrated based on what I saw."

"That's what worries me," Porter said. "I fear his bravery or his ambition might threaten us all before this expedition is over."

As the physician spoke, a cold breeze whipped by, sending shivers up my spin. I glanced to the north where the clouds had darkened further. Daggers of lightning stabbed the ground and distant thunder rumbled toward us, warning of the hazards to come. A little before two o'clock, Custer led the caravan atop a modest plateau with gentle slopes that rose about fifty feet above a modest creek that skirted the perimeter of the tabletop rise. Periodic rushes of cold wind warned of the coming storm. Pointing to the site where he wanted his headquarters established and his tent erected, Custer instructed Burkman to get whatever help he needed to set up his shelter before the approaching thunderstorm unleashed its fury and waters upon us.

Upon Custer's command, soldiers dismounted, most lining up to march across the plateau to kill or flush the rattlesnakes away. The brisk breeze and dropping temperatures had already driven most snakes back into their holes or dens. Burkman commandeered three dozen cavalrymen to help set up the general's tent quickly, once the general's wagon arrived with his equipment. Burkman pointed at me and then the wagon, apparently wanting me to help unload.

I shrugged and said, "Perxactly."

Burkman grinned and went about his business while I sat on Ciaha and watched the flurry of activity. Only after his tent was set up and the smaller tents for his brood erected did Custer allow his troopers to set up their own shelters. By then, though, occasional raindrops were falling from the sky as the roar of approaching rainfall grew nearer. Knowing I would not be granted shelter in the general's tent, I nudged Ciaha toward the Custer's equipment wagon. I jumped from the mule's back and tied the reins to a wagon wheel. The sky darkened until a bolt of lightning shattered the air. The rumbling thunder knocked the bottom out of the clouds, and rain poured from the sky,

Custer and his brood stood in their tents, looking out the door and laughing at their men as they scrambled to stay dry. I crawled under Custer's wagon for shelter from the downpour. The splattering rain struck me but never enough to soak me. Most of the soldiers were drenched before they could set up their tents. Poor Burkman had done all the work to get the general's camp and tent ready, and yet Custer left him on his own against the rain, never inviting him to share shelter with the general, his brother and his brother-in-law. I thought about inviting Burkman to join me under the wagon, but decided he was too dumb to come in out of the rain. Even so, reading the Good Book had tainted my soul with a drop of compassion.

"Burkman," I called, "you can shelter under the wagon or even in it."

He shrugged. "Work to do."

"Perxactly," I replied, figuring Burkman believed part of his job was to get wet. Maybe it saved him laundry and bathing time that he could devote to the general's comfort. He was as loyal as a puppy to Custer. Since I had the ground under the wagon all to myself, I began to work the bullets one-by-one out of the seams of my haversack, pocketing them so I would have them available when I needed them to defend myself. I extracted forty bullets from the bag. With the five in the revolver, I had a total of forty-five bullets. By my estimate, there were some seven hundred cavalrymen accompanying Custer, not to mention hundreds more infantry. By my arithmetic, I figured I'd have to knock out about fifteen cavalrymen per shot to fend off the Seventh Cavalry and then I'd just have to outrun the infantry. Even if I did that, Sioux and Cheyenne would be waiting to scalp me or chop off my head like they did to Wolfe and Dreban, God rest their souls. I didn't like my chances, though I hoped they were better than Custer's shot at becoming president.

Maybe I could save myself—and the country—if I figured out a way to eliminate the general before he got his certain victory over the hostiles. I knew I would be lucky to keep my little peashooter hidden and that I could not hide one of the army weapons. If I couldn't get a weapon, perhaps I could at least get some cavalry ammunition to create havoc without wasting any of my own bullets. That's when I decided to visit the boys of Company C.

After about forty-five minutes, the rain broke and soldiers began to emerge from their shelters, shaking like dogs after a bath as most had gotten saturated anyway. When the sun broke through the clouds, Custer and his brood emerged from the dry comfort of their tents. In the hot, sticky air, steam rose from the ground where the Custer clan walked, making it look like they were emissaries from hell.

Just as I crawled out from under the wagon, the *Bismarck Tribune* reporter walked up and greeted me. "Good afternoon, Mr. President," Kellogg said.

Before I could answer, Custer strode over. "Not yet, Mark. After your telegraph dispatches inform the nation of my great victory against the hostiles, then I think you'll be able to use that title for me any time you want."

"It's a sobriquet I have given Lomax."

I wasn't sure what a sobriquet was, but I'd always been sober around Kellogg so he had no reason to challenge me on my drinking.

"Jackass is a sobriquet more suited to Lomax," Custer said, then spun around and left.

"He doesn't like you," Kellogg said.

"He must think I'm running against him as a Republican."

"Could be," Kellogg said.

"Why would you want to tie your reputation to a jackass like him?"

"Ambition," he said. "He's going places and he can take me places with him."

"Going to hell, as best I can tell. I wouldn't want to share in that ride."

Kellogg laughed. "Even there he'll make a splash. Now I best go and make sure he's not mad at me for my acquaintance with you."

"Good luck," I offered. "Ask him if he's had any encounters with rattlesnakes lately."

As Kellogg ambled on to stroke Custer's vanity, I untied Ciaha and led him back toward the forage wagons to feed him. When he had had his fill, I led him down to the stream to water. There a couple dozen soldiers had made fishing poles from branches and were trying to catch a few fish for supper. After Ciaha had quenched his thirst in the stream, I led him back up the plateau and wandered among the camp, searching for Company C. When I came across their tents, I looked for Sergeant Gus Finkle and Privates John Lewis, Jimmy Russell, Pete Thompson and James Watson. Finkle spotted me before I saw any of them.

"Lomax," he waved, "over here."

I looked to my right and saw the men, squatted around a little fire they had built to warm up and dry out their uniforms. The little blaze was creating more smoke than heat. I walked their direction, then shook hands with each of them as I reached their fire.

"You come over for another bowl of poison?" the little Texan asked. Everyone laughed.

"I'm surprised you're still alive," Finkle said.

"The general says he won't kill me until we get in Indian country. Wants to make it look like the Sioux or Cheyenne did it."

"He actually told you that?" Watson asked.

"Oh, yeah." I nodded. "He thinks he's going to be president."

"Of what?" Thompson wanted to know.

"The United States," I said.

All of them laughed again.

"Told me so himself," I added.

"Seems you and the general are getting to be great friends if he's confiding his aspirations in you," Finkle observed.

"I don't have any friends in headquarters."

"Not even Major Reno? I understand he hates Custer," Watson said.

I decided I needed to get to know Major Reno. "Only friend I can trust is Ciaha."

"Never heard of him," Russell said.

I pointed to my army mule. "That's Ciaha."

"Then you're hard up for friends," Finkle noted.

"Odd name for a mule," Russell observed.

"It's Comanche for 'Custer is a horse's ass.'"

All the soldiers laughed.

"Spell it," demanded Thompson.

"C-I-A-H-A."

"Pronounce it for us slowly, like Comanche would," Russell said.

"See-ah-ha," I replied.

The soldiers looked at each other and began to chant, "Ciaha! Ciaha! Ciaha! Ciaha!"

Finally stopping, they all chuckled and slapped me on the back, then stroked my mule's neck for good luck. Ciaha enjoyed the attention, especially on a full belly.

"It may not be safe for us to be seen near you, Lomax, if word gets out you are fluent in Comanche," Finkle said.

"Yeah," said Russell, "especially if Custer finds out. He'll have another reason to kill you."

"What are you going to do, Lomax?" Thompson asked.

"Survive!" I said as convincingly as I could. "Somehow," I added, less confidently. I could tell by their facial expressions they were skeptical about my survival.

"I wish there was something we could do to help," Watson added.

Licking my lips, I nodded. "Perhaps there is, if you would each give me a cartridge."

Their grins all evaporated. They looked around to make sure nobody else was paying attention to our conversation. When they talked again, they barely spoke above a whisper.

"We can't do that, Lomax," Finkle said. "We can't let you shoot the general. They could hang us for that."

"I don't have a gun, fellows."

"Look around, Lomax," Finkle said. "There's plenty of guns you could steal when no one was looking."

"One bullet from each of you is all I'm asking," I pleaded. "Five bullets in all."

"No, Lomax, we can't do it," Finkle responded.

His decision was followed by an awkward silence as my friends looked at the ground and toed the wet grass with their boots. "Ciaha," I said softly.

"Ciaha," Finkle echoed me.

I turned toward my mule, ready to mount up and return to the general's camp when I felt a hand on my shoulder.

"Awww hell, Lomax" said the little Texan. "I'll give you five bullets of my own. With your luck, you'll miss the horse's ass anyway."

My estimation of Texans went up a tad, not because of Russell's assessment of my aim as much as for his generosity. I now ranked Texans just ahead of politicians and lawyers and way ahead of generals. "Thanks, Jimmy."

Discretely Jimmy pulled five cartridges from the loops on his gun belt and handed them to me like he was shaking my hand. When we released hands, I closed my palm around the bullets, but one fell to the ground.

"See," Russell said, "I told you he couldn't aim straight."

I laughed. "That's why the buffalo hunters always called me Leadeye since I wasted so much ammunition."

"Remember, Lomax," Finkle chided, "to always save the last bullet for yourself."

"Not sure I can," I replied as I squatted to pick up the bullet I had dropped. "These cartridges are army property and I want to return them personally to General Custer, maybe stop his presidential bid and save the nation."

The fellows laughed again. "I don't know what's funnier," Thompson said. "Custer as president or you saving the nation. It's a sorry state of affairs if either of those come to pass."

Standing back up, I slipped the bullets in my pocket and climbed aboard Ciaha. "Fellows, if I don't see you again, it's been a pleasure doing time in the guardhouse with you. And, Jimmy, thanks for the gift."

As I turned my mule toward Custer's camp, I heard my friends chanting, "Ciaha! Ciaha!." I twisted around in my saddle and saw other soldiers gathering around them. When they all laughed, I assumed my pals had explained the word's meaning. Soon, the whole company was chanting my Comanche word. I felt as proud as if I had compiled a dictionary, and I suspected the Comanche people would've made me a blood brother for such a valuable contribution to their language. I was feeling pretty good until I rode up to my camp.

General Custer was waiting, his hands on his hips. "Where the hell have you been?"

"Feeding and watering Ciaha," I explained.

"Ciaha?"

I pointed to my mount. "My mule."

"What kind of name is that?"

"Comanche," I said.

"Don't leave again without letting Burkman know where you're going, or I'll have you shot."

"What difference does it make since you are going to shoot me anyway?"

"It makes me sleep better knowing you are safe, for now at least."

That night while Custer and his brood dined on roast beef, mashed potatoes, raw onions in vinegar and warm biscuits, Burkman and I gnawed on a square of hardtack apiece. We might have become friends if we hadn't had opposite opinions about Custer, and if Burkman would have said something more than "perxactly" during a conversation. I figured we might slip in after the officers had eaten and grab some of the leftovers to enhance the bland taste of hardtack, but the general fed the leftovers to his four stag hounds—Tuck, Swift, Lady and Kaiser.

As we were bedding down, I took my bedroll under the wagon to give me a little cover and lay there trying to go to sleep. I thought I ought to wait until the general dozed off and try to slip past the hounds, then put my peashooter in his ear and pull the trigger. The problem was, Custer didn't require as much sleep as the rest of us, and I could never stay awake longer than he could. Some nights he would write articles for the magazines, visit with Mark Kellogg about his plans, write out orders for the next day or retire to bed and read. Some nights when he blew out his lantern early, he stayed awake, occasionally calling out "Hallelujah, John!" apparently when he was thinking about his wife.

That night after the thunderstorm most of us in camp were already asleep when he went to bed. He slid into bed and realized something had crawled in before him. It wasn't his wife or a squaw. He screamed and leaped out of bed, then fired two shots. I hoped he had shot himself, but I was disappointed when he jumped out of the tent and I saw him in the glow of the dying fire. He was terrified. Burkman was the first to reach him.

"What happened, perxactly?"

Lieutenant Calhoun and Custer's nephew ran to him. Tom Custer, though, never left his bedroll. He lay there laughing. "Did a rattlesnake crawl into your bed?" he asked.

"Tom Custer," the general said, "I'll get even with you for this."

"He was dead before you shot him, Autie."

"I should've known your hand was in this as you're the only fellow I know that doesn't mind handling those vile things." Custer retreated to his tent, came out with the headless snake and tossed it toward Tom. "Get up and let the sentries know we just killed a rattler and there's nothing else to worry about."

Tom grumbled, but arose and did as he was ordered. That was the first of several practical jokes the Custer brood played on each other, things like replacing the sugar with salt in the sugar bowl when the general went to sweeten his coffee. He spat the result halfway across the territory. The practical jokes were endless among the Custer brood. They were like schoolboys away from their mother for the first time. They relished the jokes but just as much the recounting of them the next morning around the breakfast fire. That gave me an idea of how I just might knock off Custer so one of his brood might take the fall.

I was feeling pretty good the next morning when I got up, ate another square of hardtack and readied Ciaha for the day's ride, a very difficult ride as it turned out because the ground was saturated. Wagon wheels sank into the earth, horses and mules carried another five pounds of mud on their hooves when they tried to walk and the skies hung like a wet threat above us. We crossed the little creek by our campground okay but the next tributary we came to was fifty feet wide and impassable so rather than camp and wait, Custer had us backtrack and move to the southwest rather than westward.

It was a long tedious day, the only bright spot came when Company C came riding past on their light sorrels. I was near Custer when they approached and someone cried out "Ciaha!" and then the entire company took up the chant, doffing their hats as they passed their commanding officer.

"Ciaha! Ciaha! Ciaha! Ciaha!" they cried out.

"Tom," said Custer, "Find out what the hell your company is chanting and report back to me by this afternoon."

Tom saluted and said, "Yes, sir!"

I gulped.

Chapter Twenty-Six

Travel was slow the next few days because of the wet ground and periodic rains that kept the earth marshy between our feet. Rattlesnakes were still a problem, three or four cavalrymen a day being thrown by horses spooked by rattlesnakes as we rode. The general sent out his scouts to pick up the trail of the hostiles, but they never found anything that pointed us toward the Sioux and Cheyenne. Likewise, Tom Custer could not pry from anyone in his company what Ciaha meant. Not only that, my friends in Company C apparently began to spread the word to other companies about the true definition of the Comanche word. Soldiers I didn't even know began to use the word and wave at me and my mule every time they saw me.

What was most fun about the mysterious word was that it drove the general crazy because he didn't know its meaning. Further, the soldiers seemed to relish keeping the secret and sharing the inside joke as it gave them something to laugh about during their difficult trek across muddy trails, on cold nights, over bad food and with idiots for leaders. I just kept my mule plodding along with the others, often times pulling out my Bible and reading it to break the monotony of accompanying Custer and his brood. I looked for divine inspiration to provide me a way to kill Custer before he killed me. My constant prayer was that Custer get what he deserved, and that I wasn't harmed in the process.

I was riding my mule and reading my Bible three days after Ciaha had entered the vocabulary of the Seventh Cavalry when the general rode up beside me. "Lomax," he said, "let's go for another ride."

"You gonna take another dump?" I asked.

"I never reveal my strategy to the enemy."

"So I'm the enemy."

Custer nodded. "The only thing that would make you a worse piece of scum was if you were a Republican, Lomax."

"Well, general, you won't be getting my vote for president."

"You won't be around to vote by then, Lomax."

"Well, General, if the weather stays wet and travel is as slow as it has been from the start, you won't be able to find and whip the hostiles in time for your newspaper toady to get a dispatch back to civilization and that convention of lunatics known as Democrats."

"You're not as dumb as you look, Lomax. Now let's ride."

I closed my Bible and slipped it in my haversack, then followed Custer. As was his habit, he led me from the troops and over a small hill out of sight of the others. There Custer handed me his reins and dismounted, beginning to unbutton his britches to attend to his dirty business. Before dropping his britches, he looked up at me. "What's Ciaha mean?"

"It's what I call my mule."

"Why is it every trooper in the Seventh Cavalry knows your mule's name?"

I shrugged. "Ciaha's just naturally likable."

He pushed down his britches.

I reached inside my shirt and slowly extracted the serpent's rattle.

"Something tells me you're behind the mischief with that word."

Custer squatted down and began his business.

"General," I said, "you're losing your mind again."

He scowled.

I wanted to plant a seed of fear in his mind. "If you're bit by a rattlesnake, General, you're on your own because I won't be sucking the poison out of your bottom."

"There won't be a need for that, Lomax. I inspected the ground well before I dismounted."

That's when I shook the snake rattle as hard as I could.

Custer bolted upright.

"Rattlesnake," I yelled.

Grabbing for his britches, Custer stumbled away, screaming for deliverance from Satan's emissary. He tripped but managed to stay on his feet, then spun around about five yards away and looked back to the nest he had started. "Something's not right here."

"The rattler must be stalking you, General," I offered. "He's a sneaky one. Must've already crawled in another hole. That's the only logical explanation."

"Dammit, Lomax, you're behind this."

I smiled. "I do what I can, but the way I see it, I've saved you from two awkward rattlesnake bites."

Custer yanked up his britches and reached toward his holster, lifting the cover and grabbing the butt of his army pistol. He might have shot me right there, but he paused at the sound of a horse nickering. We both looked around and saw four Ree scouts and the interpreter Fred Gerard watching barely forty feet away.

The general grumbled, but released the butt of his pistol and closed the flap on his holster. "I figure you're behind the rattlesnakes and this strange Ciaha word. I will get to the bottom of this, Lomax. It's just one more reason I'll enjoy killing you when the day comes." He finished buttoning up his britches, strode over and yanked the reins from my hand. He was so mad, he didn't notice the rattle dangling from my other hand. He climbed onto his horse and galloped away, never acknowledging Gerard or the Rees.

I dropped my necklace, not bothering to tuck it back inside my shirt, then took my reins in both hands and turned Ciaha toward the interpreter and his Arikara scouts. All were grinning widely when I drew up in front of them.

"You see it all?" I asked.

Gerard nodded. "Never saw the general move so fast. The Rees enjoyed it. They've decided to call you 'Man Who Rattles Like Snake.'"

"Tell them I am honored."

Gerard conveyed my message through words and hand signs. The Rees nodded.

"Now, Lomax," said Gerard, "tell me what Ciaha means."

"It's my mule's name."

"Yeah, maybe so, but I heard it means something else."

I shrugged. "You know any Comanche?"

"Not enough to translate."

Needing all the friends I could get since I already had in Custer the biggest enemy in Dakota Territory, I decided to explain. "Ciaha is Comanche for Custer is a horse's ass."

Gerard cackled and quickly explained the joke to the Arikaras. They all laughed and spoke gibberish to Gerard, who translated for me. "They say you are a funny man."

With that, we started back together toward the line of soldiers, animals, wagons and Gatling guns heading west toward the anticipated rendezvous with the hostiles.

"Rumor has it Custer doesn't care for you and plans to kill you, Lomax."

"He thinks I'm a threat to his ambition to be president."

"You're kidding," Gerard answered. "Him, president? I don't believe that."

I shrugged. "He's involved in politics up to his neck. Says the Democrat convention in St. Louis next month might turn to him as a candidate, especially after he whips the hostiles."

"Him, president?" Gerard *still* couldn't believe it.

"I'm just telling you what he said. He believes I've threatened his ambitions if word gets out that firewood was being stolen from his fort. He thinks I'm responsible for the theft."

Gerard laughed. "From what I've heard and observed, most of the soldiers can't stand him so they've enjoyed taking up your cry, especially the way he treats them. Never any consideration for their needs or comfort."

"I've been praying he gets what he deserves."

"Praying? I never took you for much of a religious man, Lomax."

"Sometimes we all get in over our head. I don't see any way out of my predicament without God's intervention. Hell, I've got the whole Seventh Cavalry after me, if he so orders."

"After you've introduced Ciaha into their lexicon, I don't think I could find a one that would shoot you."

"I'm not worried about them, just him," I replied. "And what's leprechauns got to do with it, anyway?"

Gerard let out a long sigh. "There's been a lot of bad omens around this expedition," he said. "Some of us are nervous. Custer is hot-headed. He attacks without reconnoitering. Could spell trouble for us all, Lomax."

As we neared the line of soldiers, Ciaha and I veered away from Gerard to re-join Custer's crew. I wondered about scouting and interpreting as a profession when I got out of this mess. How hard could it be? You come across a trail. You advise the general, there's the trail. You come across a campfire. You let the general know your quarry camped and ate here. Talk about an easy job. As for interpreting, you just made up what you didn't understand.

Dr. Porter was grinning when I rejoined the others in the command party. "The general was infuriated again. What do you do to anger him, Lomax?"

Shrugging, I reined Ciaha in beside Porter's horse. "I stand guard against rattlesnakes while he attends his business."

"You must be doing a poor job as mad as he comes back."

"He ain't been bit yet, has he?"

"No, sir."

"Let's say the general got bit by a snake, would you treat him? I wouldn't."

Porter shook his head. "Sure I would, Lomax. I'd owe it to the profession, having taken the Hippocratic oath."

"No hypocritic oath could make me treat a fellow that plans to kill me."

Porter laughed. "Maybe in your case it would be the hypocritic oath. You remember when the general told me not to treat you if you got hurt."

I nodded. "And you told me you'd do it anyway."

"Just following the Hippocratic oath, Lomax. You'd do the same thing as a doctor. You owe it to humanity."

Shrugging, I answered, "I'm not sure General Custer has any humanity in him. I suspect it's all ambition and greed."

"That's surprising coming from someone who reads the Bible as much as you."

"Like your hypocritic oath, Doctor, I don't understand a lot of the Bible. Reading it gives me something to kill the time until Custer kills me."

Porter laughed. "You're imagining things, I'm sure, Lomax."

"Just promise me one thing, Doctor."

"I've already told you I will treat you if you are hurt."

"If I'm dead, I won't need treatment, Doctor. What I will need is a grave marker and I want you to promise you'll see that the inscription reads: KILLED BY THE BIGGEST SON OF A BITCH IN THE UNITED STATES. Will you do that for me?"

"Sure, but one piece of advice. With your imagination, you should write dime novels."

Porter nudged his horse ahead and left me alone and worrying that a decent man like Dr. Porter didn't really believe Custer was stalking me. I rode alone a mile or so before an officer approached me on horseback. I had seen him around the command party a lot, but he never lingered as he was not a part of Custer's brood or inner circle.

"Are you Lomax?"

I nodded. He reined his horse in beside Ciaha.

"I'm Marcus Reno, Major Reno," he announced. "I noticed you and General Custer don't get along too well."

"He plans to kill me, General."

"Major," he corrected. "I don't insist on my brevet rank like the lieutenant colonel."

"Rank aside, he plans to kill me."

"Son, he may kill us all before this expedition is done. He'd charge hell with a bucket of coal oil to put out the fire, that's how confident the guy is. But that bastard aside, is it true you gave your mule a Comanche name?"

I hesitated to answer, uncertain if Reno could be trusted.

Reno didn't wait for an answer. "I'm just seeking a translation for a Comanche word, Lomax. That's all."

"I know a little Comanche," I admitted.

"The word is Ciaha."

I studied Reno a moment and decided I wasn't in any more danger if he was a Custer ally than I was now. Besides that, I might gain a friend if he and Custer were enemies. I took a deep breath. "I named my mule Ciaha. It's Comanche for Custer is a horse's ass."

Reno laughed. "Smart people those Comanche. Most of the regiment, nearly all the troopers and some of the officers are laughing at your mule's name. What's fun is nobody'll tell the Custer clique what it means, nobody."

"Maybe it'll drive them crazy," I offered.

"Crazier," Reno responded. "They were insane before you came along, the general, his brother, the whole bunch of them. You need to watch out for them."

"I'm doing my best to."

"On paper, I'm second in command of the Seventh," Reno said, "though paper don't amount to much with his clique. If there's something I can do to help, let me know."

"Thank you, Major," I said.

"I best be going or he'll get suspicious if he sees us riding together."

"Nice to meet you," I answered. "If you see the general, you might ask him if it's true a rattlesnake is stalking him every time he attends his business."

Reno nodded. "By the way, are you the Lomax that splattered acid in Wild Bill's hair?"

"That's the rumor," I replied.

"No wonder the boy general chopped off his thinning hair," Reno said, then rode away.

Come supper I had another square of hardtack plus a slice of cornbread I took off a platter meant for the general and his buddies. Then I sat on the perimeter just beyond the glow of the campfire and watched, wondering how I could extricate myself from my predicament with my peashooter and ammo, plus the five cavalry cartridges that the little Texan had given me. Every night Custer and his brood would spend half an hour or so around the campfire, discussing the day's events, laughing at the practical jokes they'd played or conspiring about the misery they would inflict on the troops the next day.

Custer always sat with his back to his tent. Then I came up with a plan to shoot him. I'd start helping Burkman with chores around the camp, especially the fire. Then I'd plant my five bullets in the fire pointed in his direction and hope the bullets would explode and plug the son of a bitch in the head. Rather than being pleased I was offering to help, Burkman was suspicious of my motives, apparently believing I wanted to harm his hero. To the contrary, I just wanted to kill Custer.

After a few nights Burkman let me build a fire without watching over me like a mother hen. I gathered some rocks and made a circle, careful to slant the rocks so I could plant the five bullets between them to explode toward the tent. I built a fire and waited. About the time they were finishing up their supper, I slipped to the fire under the guise of adding wood to the flames and squatted down, reaching as close the flames as I could without getting burnt and dropping the bullets into place.

I moved away as the others gathered, waiting for the general to take his accustomed place. I prayed that the bullets would await Custer's arrival. My prayer was answered when he took a seat, but then I feared they would never go off. I decided my plan had failed when the first bullet exploded.

Ka-blam!

Custer's eyes widened and he flung himself on the ground. I'd never seen him move so fast with his pants up. Sure the first bullet had missed, but with him on the ground one of the next four might strike him. Everyone else fell to the ground, clawing for cover.

Ka-blam! Ka-blam! went the next two cartridges.

Nobody moved.

Ka-blam!

Custer lay still. Maybe he was wounded. I thought I heard him moaning for a moment. Then I realized he was giggling. Apparently my bullet had struck his funny bone.

He got to his hands and knees, then pushed himself up on his knees eyeing the fire and the others on the ground around him. Then, he started laughing, uproariously.

Ka-blam! went the final bullet.

Not a single shot had drawn blood, only laughter as the others began to chuckle.

Custer climbed up and dusted off his uniform, still laughing. "Okay," he said, "which one of you threw cartridges in the fire? Who pulled the prank? Was it you, Tom? What about you, Calhoun?" He eyed them all.

Burkman lifted himself up from the ground, crossed his arms over his chest and nodded in my direction. "Lomax fault," he said.

"He's no friend of ours so he wouldn't joke with us," Custer replied.

"Unless he was trying to kill us," Tom interjected.

"Perxactly," answered Burkman.

Custer stared hard at me and shook his head. "Lomax is too dumb to think of something like that." He stared at his brood, then laughed again. "Which one of you did it?"

They all looked blankly at one another, though Burkman kept mumbling "Lomax fault."

I swore that was the last time I would help Burkman build a campfire, if he was no more appreciative than that. After the campfire incident, the days began to run together. They were cold and wet, with misty mornings, mushy trails and slow progress. Every day of delay reduced Custer's chances of subduing and humiliating the hostiles in time for Kellogg to alert the papers to sway the Democratic convention to nominate him for president. The soldiers shot one sick mule, causing me to pray I wouldn't get a disease or catch a cold and give Custer an excuse to have me executed. Other mule teams were playing out from the strain of dragging heavy wagons across rain-softened prairie. At least one team was too weak to go on. They were left on the trail to fend for themselves. A pair of soldiers got sick, one shot himself in the heel while mounting his horse. We passed landmarks named Twin Buttes, Wolf's Den Butte, Dog Teeth Butte, Cherry Ridge, Rainy Butte and Rattlesnake Den Butte. I was tempted to volunteer to escort General Custer to Rattlesnake Den Butte in case he needed to heed nature's call, but he had abandoned me as his potty pal after his second encounter with my serpent rattle. I hoped before long a landmark might be named in the general's honor, something like Custer Grave Butte or Crazy General Ridge. On the first day of clear evening skies, the general ordered a concert by the regimental band. I could never tell if the music lifted men's spirits or just made them more homesick. Most clear evenings after that and before we got into serious Indian country, Custer would command the band to play.

During the march, Custer would ride off on whims, sometimes

to scout ahead and other times to stalk an elk or let his hounds chase jackrabbits. Every time he rode out of sight, I wished that to be the last time I ever laid eyes on him. However, he always rode back. I wished one day he would just ride back dead. Two weeks into the expedition, not a soldier one had laid eyes on an Indian or even sign of an Indian. One morning we all awoke to see acres of primroses that had opened up overnight. I never remember seeing more flowers anywhere and the sweet fragrance overwhelmed the nose. A few days after that, one of the soldiers was bitten on the hand by a rattlesnake as they became more numerous and more active. Between the blooming flowers and the more vengeful rattlesnakes, I figured spring had arrived to stay, but I was wrong.

The last night of May we set up camp as sinister clouds moved in from the north, dropping temperatures quickly and uncomfortably. A strong rain hit first, then pelting sleet and finally snow before darkness enveloped the camp. Fortunately, the soldiers had had time to set up their tents and nearly everyone but me managed to stay out of the weather. Without a tent or anyone willing to share one with me, I slept under the general's baggage wagon. When I awoke at reveille after a frigid and restless night's sleep, I saw the camp blanketed in a couple inches of snow. I had seen snow before but never in the month of *June*. None of us had any winter gear so the chill was biting with little we could do about it. We spent the day in camp, clustered in our tents or around campfires that gave off more smoke than heat. Based on all the bad weather we'd had in the two weeks since leaving Fort Abraham Lincoln, I came to believe that God agreed with me—General Custer did not deserve to be president of the United States.

The extra day's rest in camp would've been better if it hadn't been so cold and if it hadn't given the general more time to wander about camp to harass and threaten officers and soldiers. It seems there had been a burr under the general's saddle ever since I had named my mule Ciaha and most of the troopers had taken up that cry. It annoyed Custer greatly because he suspected me for assaulting his dignity. Now I didn't think it should be such a worry since I had done nothing more than state the truth. Further, I knew if it was put to a vote of the Seventh Cavalry I would win by an overwhelming majority. After all, CIAHA!

I knew trouble was brewing when Custer returned to his tent accompanied by the interpreter Fred Gerard. While the general conversed with his brood in his tent, I sidled over to Gerard. "Trouble?" I asked.

Gerard kicked at the snow. "Weather's slowing everything down. On top of that, the Ree scouts are getting scared, saying the bad weather is another bad omen."

"Custer's the bad omen," I replied.

"He don't like you, Lomax. Says you're out to embarrass him."

Shrugging, I stared at Gerard. He was nervous. "I'm just trying to survive."

Gerard grimaced. "I fear you may be the first to go."

"As in leave or as in die?"

"Die," he said, just as Custer marched out of his tent with his brood. They trampled through the snow toward me, Tom at the general's right and his brother-in-law Calhoun at his left. I'd seen happier faces at funerals and I wondered if I was standing at my own wake.

"Lomax," charged Custer, "you're a lying son of a bitch."

"Which lie are you talking about, General?"

"Your mule's name. Ciaha, that's what I'm talking about."

At that point, Gerard left me and tramped three strides through the snow to Custer's side. He crossed his arms and glared at me. I wished Ciaha was nearby so I could jump on him and try to escape, but I doubted the mule was fast enough to outrun their bullets.

"It's a Comanche word," I responded.

"How do you know Comanche?" Custer demanded.

"I fought Comanche and Kiowa at Adobe Walls awhile back. Me and fewer than twenty others fended off some seven hundred attacking warriors for several days. I picked up enough Comanche there and buffalo hunting to know a few words."

"A walking Comanche dictionary, are you?" he answered.

"Enough to get by."

"Well, explain this. I've talked to a few soldiers that have said you told them Ciaha was Comanche for Custer is a horse's ass. Now, tell me, Lomax, is that true?"

I swallowed hard. "I don't know where they came up with that, General."

"Then you better explain what it means because I've got an interpreter here to confirm whatever you say."

Gerard's eyes narrowed. He shook his head to affirm his responsibility.

"I can't believe you would accuse me of such impertinence, General. Not after I saved you from two rattlesnake attacks."

Custer spat at my feet. "Is that why the Rees call you Man Who Rattles Like Snake?"

"I don't know about that, General, as none of them have talked to me."

"Quit stalling, Lomax. What does Ciaha mean?" Custer demanded.

I let out a slow breath, trying to give myself time to think what I was going to need to survive. I realized I would need a little courage and a lot of luck to survive the explanation. Then it struck me—courage!

"I'm waiting, Lomax."

"Ciaha," I said slowly, all the time gauging Gerard, "is Comanche for courage. Ciaha means courage."

Custer turned to Gerard.

My fate rested on Gerard's interpretation.

Chapter Twenty-Seven

General George Armstrong Custer stamped his boots impatiently in the snow, splattering some of it my direction as if he was kicking dirt over my grave. Perhaps he was.

Gerard stood there, scowling and shaking his head at me. His gestures told Custer my fate and the general smiled at me, confident he had trapped me in a snare of my own making.

I licked my cold, dry lips.

"I'm no authority on the Comanche language, though there are some similarities in most Indian languages," Gerard began. "Most Indians lack a language capable of describing such a complex concept as courage."

Custer clapped his gloved hands and shouted, "Hallelujah, John!"

I feared this was my last day on earth, until I saw a subtle sign from Gerard. He offered me hope with a wink so slight I doubted I had actually seen it. Gerard rubbed his chin. "Indians understand bravery because that is how reputations are made in a warrior culture."

His smile melting away, Custer turned his glare from me to Gerard.

"From what I know of Comanche or the general languages of the Southern Plains Indians," Gerard continued, "I would interpret Ciaha to mean 'brave as a bear.'"

As Custer's smile died, mine began to bloom. Gerard must have agreed that Custer certainly was a horse's ass.

"So," Gerard concluded, "while Ciaha might not describe the word courage in the mind of the Comanche, it does denote bravery. As interpreters, we have to make judgments regarding differences in the concepts between the white man and the red man. I would say that Lomax's definition of Ciaha as courage would certainly be appropriate, if not entirely accurate in the eyes of the Comanche."

Custer looked angrily at me and then back at Gerard. For a moment, I thought he wanted to kill Gerard more than he wanted to shoot me, but he quickly returned to his senses and pointed a gloved finger at me. "I'll get you yet, Lomax."

"Be careful," Gerard interjected. "Lomax is not as dumb as he looks."

I appreciated Gerard's support, I thought.

Custer spun around and marched back toward his tent, stomping his boots in the snow. His brood trailed behind, walking gingerly for fear Custer might turn his anger on one of them.

Gerard grinned at me, then shook his head. "You owe me one, Lomax." Then he scratched his chin and shook his head. "No, maybe not. This story'll perk up the soldiers, even the Ree scouts. Everybody enjoys a joke at the general's expense, pompous ass that he is. You and Ciaha are about the only things the troops have to enjoy on this expedition. Bad signs, bad weather and bad leadership are pointing to disaster, and we've yet to see a single Indian."

"I'm honored to bring hope to the soldiers."

"Not hope, Lomax, but humor, which may be more important before all of this is over."

I offered Gerard my hand. He shook it warmly and offered a bit of advice. "Don't come up with more Comanche words. I might not be able to pull your butt out of the fire next time."

I agreed and Gerard went back to the Ree scouts. In no time Gerard's story got around to the troops, and Ciaha had become the motto of the fighting men of the Seventh Cavalry. Any trooper that knew me and many that didn't greeted me with the word and a laugh. Sometimes whole companies would shout it out when they passed the general. He would salute smartly, and then they would snicker after they rode by.

By the time the snow quit on June second, about six inches had fallen. The frigid cold, though, continued the next day when we resumed our march, Custer fretting that lost time and delayed victories would cost him the nomination. We traveled at a snail's pace in the soft earth across some of the worst terrain we had encountered since leaving Bismarck. Even so, Custer forced us twenty-five miles, the longest distance and day of our journey up until then. Cavalry horses and mules tired out, as did men having to help push wagons when they mired down in the muck left by the melting snow. The labored breaths of men and animals exited their nostrils in puffs of white vapor. I couldn't believe this was June. Custer never noticed the toll on animals, much less on the men. He had two horses—Vic and Dandy—which he alternated so each had time to rest. His horses never tired out. The rest of the cavalry had only one bone-tired horse apiece to ride. Nor did Custer ever get down and help with problems along the trail. Instead, he yelled at men to push harder against a stuck wagon or to hurry up instead of slowing to catch their breath. That is why the soldiers had taken so well to Ciaha as a motto.

A couple days after Gerard had confirmed my definition of Ciaha, I happened to be riding near enough to Custer to hear him talk to his brother. "Tom," he said, "the regiment has taken to Ciaha. The Comanche word has boosted their morale. I love to see the smiles on their face when they understand the challenge ahead and the courage it will take to whip the hostiles."

Tom shrugged. "I'm not sure all of them interpret it the way of the Comanche."

"No, matter. The correct interpretation is what matters," Custer responded. "If I am nominated by the Democrats, Ciaha might make a fine campaign slogan."

I coughed to hide my laughter. Custer and his brother turned to scowl at me, then nudged their horses and rode out of hearing range. I didn't know if Ciaha would make a good campaign slogan, but I knew it would be the most accurate one in the sordid history of American politics. On top of that, the more problems the weather and Custer's own incompetence threw in our way, the more I came to believe God was a Republican.

After the snowfall, the days began to run together and I could no longer keep track of one from another. The snow went away. The general did not. Nor did our problems evaporate. Beaver Creek, swollen by melting snows, became a problem to cross. Where we had water we didn't have good grass. Where we had grass, we didn't have good water. Where we had General Custer, which was everywhere, we didn't have good sense. While our problems multiplied, the nation's challenges diminished because each delay decreased the likelihood Custer would have any news to report before the Democratic National Convention.

In spite of the delays, each day brought us closer to the hostiles, even if we didn't know where to find them. About a week after we left our snow camp, Custer sent Major Reno, six companies of the Seventh Cavalry and a Gatling gun west to scout for Sitting Bull's camp between the Powder and Tongue rivers. I suppose General Alfred H. Terry, who was in overall command of the Dakota column, was the one ordering Major Reno on his jaunt, but I rode with Custer and he always tried to make it seem like he was issuing the orders that counted or succeeded, though never the orders that ended in failure or disaster. The rest of the Dakota column kept marching toward the designated spot on the Yellowstone River where we were to rejoin Reno's men and rendezvous with the steamboat *Far West*, which Captain Grant Marsh was piloting up the Missouri River tributaries to re-supply us.

By the time we reached the river site on June twentieth, General Custer was flustered and mad. The Democratic convention would be kicking off in St. Louis's Merchant's Exchange building in a week and he was days from the telegraph line that would deliver the news of his impending victory. As we approached the rendezvous, we topped a hill, and I saw the most surprising site of the entire trip—the *Far West* moored on the bank of the Yellowstone. The steamboat seemed so out-of-place. We had ridden days across all configurations of land, most of it waterless, or crossed tiny creeks that might widen with flood waters but were generally small. And now, to spot a huge steamboat in the middle of the prairie spewing smoke out of its stacks seemed unbelievable. That was the first of many bizarre events awaiting me in coming days.

When Custer saw Reno's troops camped by the steamboat, he galloped off for information about the major's expedition. Shortly, he was galloping back with news that Reno had spotted Indian sign to the west. He was anxious to start in that direction immediately, but General Terry evidently reined him in by insisting that he rest his troops the night and then attend a war conference the next evening aboard the *Far West*. At least that was what I could pick up in the snatches of conversation I overheard between the general and his brother. He was furious about the delay. Even though he didn't have orders to pursue the hostiles, Custer was issuing commands to his men so they would be ready to move out as fast as possible when he received the go ahead. Custer announced plans to leave behind the trio of Gatling guns and all the wagons as they would only slow the foray down. Supplies were to be packed on mules so his command didn't have to bother with broken wheels and axles or stuck wagons. If mules petered out, soldiers could shoot and eat them to reduce the rations the column would have to carry. He ordered his men to leave their sabers behind to reduce the rattling noise of soldiers on the move. Custer was thinking of everything he could do to hasten the departure and ensure surprise of the hostiles. I was thinking of everything I could do to survive. And, I'm sure Ciaha was thinking how glad he was not to be a pack mule.

With the *Far West* moored on the Yellowstone at the mouth of Rosebud Creek, we set up camp beside Reno's companies. Custer designated a spot within a stone's throw of the *Far West* for his camp location and gave his striker Burkman two instructions. "See that my quarters are set up here and don't let Lomax wander off," he ordered. "We're in Indian country now. I wouldn't want him to wander away and get killed by hostiles out of my sight."

"You prefer to do it yourself, is that right, General Bluster?" I asked.

"I always want a task done right, even if I have to do it myself," Custer replied.

Just then, the *Tribune* reporter Mark Kellogg walked up. "Good afternoon, General."

Custer spun around. "Not if we don't find those hostiles and rout them soon enough for you to telegraph St. Louis the news." With that, Custer stormed off to issue more orders.

Kellogg turned to me. "Well, Mr. President, how are you getting along?"

"Better than the general."

"That's what I'm gathering. I came here to talk with him about his plans for my final dispatch before we strike the hostiles. Once we leave here, who knows how long before he'll send mail back to Fort Lincoln and Bismarck."

Kellogg and I visited while Burkman sat up the camp according to the general's specifications. Kellogg then borrowed a chair and a camp table and sat down to write his dispatch. I sat down in the shade of the general's wagon and pulled out my Bible, reading a lot that I didn't understand, but knowing I'd need some help from the Great Republican in the Sky. I hoped Reverend Truett Byars and Daisy were still praying for me back in Bismarck.

Waiting to be killed is an easy assignment. You just sit around and worry. Other than read my Bible, I made sure Ciaha was well fed, well watered and well rested. On occasion, I tried to work my way out of Burkman's sight so I could double check the load of the peashooter in my shoulder harness, but Burkman eyed me like I was intent on killing his boss. Once I confirmed my bullet count, I figured I'd need to reserve one for Custer and one for myself if we encountered hostiles. I didn't want to lose my head like Dreban and Wolfe, even if I was dead, but I realized I wouldn't have much say in the matter. If worse came to worst, I just hoped I outlived Custer so he wouldn't have the satisfaction of seeing me die. If we both died, I decided we wouldn't be crossing paths because I was sure he was headed for that Democrat convention in hell, and I hoped I was going to join that Great Republican in the Sky. After all, I'd been reading a lot of the Bible since leaving Fort Abraham Lincoln.

While I was tending Ciaha or reading my Bible or trying to slip out from under Burkman's gaze, word got out that the sutler from Fort Lincoln had brought a load of goods along on the *Far West*, should the soldiers care to spend any of the money they'd been paid the first day on the trail. The sutler and his helpers set up a couple temporary tables near the gangplank to the *Far West* and waited. The soldiers lingered, too, hoping for permission to do business with the sutler. He had the usual tobacco, playing cards, kerchiefs, socks and medicinal cures for all ailments a trooper might encounter on the trail. He also had several stacks of straw hats and enough whiskey to float the *Far West* all the way to Bismarck. Next to the whiskey, the straw hats were the most popular item because the weather had been so unpredictable since the snowfall. Some days were scorching hot and others were bone-chilling cold because of great northern winds that delivered and shared the chill with us.

When the troopers received permission to visit the sutler, they walked up by company to attend their business. After Company C completed transactions with the sutler, I spoke with Finkle, Watson, Lewis, Thompson and Russell, who looked half goofy in his new straw hat.

"You're a legend, Lomax," said Finkle. "Ciaha!"

"Ciaha!" the other four cried.

"Comanche for courage my ass," Thompson said.

"Where do you come up with all that crap, Lomax?" Watson wanted to know.

"You damn sure ain't a genius," said Russell.

"But at least I ain't a worthless Texan, Jimmy," I replied.

He yanked off his new straw hat and swatted me with it.

"Men," yelled Tom Custer from near the river bank, "get back to your tents."

"That's our company commander," Finkle said. "We gotta go." The five scurried away while Tom glared at me.

I held up my Bible. "You should read it. It tells how to treat your fellow man."

"We already know how to treat you, Lomax, for embarrassing my brother. Even the Bible and God himself won't save you. One of us just has a few days to live, Lomax."

As it turned out, Tom was right.

I went back to reading the Good Book under Burkman's watchful eye as afternoon faded away into twilight and then night. General Terry transferred his command headquarters to the *Far West* and its more comfortable accommodations. General Custer scurried about, visiting the teamsters at the supply train to confirm his instructions for when the march began, then visiting the Arikara scouts camped on the perimeter of the army tents to let them know his expectations when they began to hunt the hostiles. He called a gathering of his officers that night. They came in ones and twos to his tent. Some were sober, others questionable. I saw Major Reno and Captain Benteen as they approached the camp. Reno ignored me, but Benteen laughed.

"Ciaha, Lomax!" Benteen cried, much too loudly for my comfort.

When he grabbed my hand and shook it vigorously, I realized he was trying to annoy the Custers.

"Keep up the good work, Lomax. Ciaha!"

The Custer brothers glared at Benteen. They hated him as much as he hated them for abandoning Major Elliott at the Battle of Washita. From the whiff of Benteen's breath, I realized more than enlisted men had found whiskey that night. After listening to Custer bitch about the delay in starting the Indian hunt, I missed most of the rest of the discussion when the interpreter Fred Gerard came by from the Arikara encampment.

"What brings you this way?" I asked. "Need another definition of an Indian word?"

He whispered, "Ciaha is now the most used word not in the Comanche language."

"Glad to be of assistance, Fred."

"I came by to let you know you were right."

"About what?"

"General Custer. He gave gifts and talked to the scouts tonight, telling them about his visit to Washington."

"That all?"

"No," Gerard continued. "He said after this next victory, even if it was only against six Indian lodges, that he would become the Great Father, president of these United States. He promised if they helped him hunt and defeat the hostiles, he would always look after the Arikaras and consider them his children, providing them with rations and blankets and tobacco forever."

"Ciaha!" I said.

"Ciaha!" Gerard repeated, then pointed at Burkman, who was edging within earshot.

"The general has him clinging to me like a tick to a dog," I said. "The general's afraid I'll slip away without giving him the chance to kill me."

"Nothing against you, Lomax," Gerard offered, "but when the shooting starts, I hope I'm nowhere around you."

"Ciaha!" I said.

He patted me on the back. "Ciaha!" he answered, then disappeared into the night.

Once Gerard walked out of sight, Burkman turned around and went about his business. The conversation among the officers continued for a long time, but I grabbed my blanket and tossed it under the wagon, my accustomed place for rest. I fretted much of the night away, unable to sleep on account of my worries and the carousing of the soldiers who'd bought whiskey. I thought about making something of myself, finding an occupation where I could make my family proud and asking Daisy to marry me. She wasn't perfect and neither was I, but we were both decent people at heart. I figured if I got out of this, I'd write a letter home to momma and pa or maybe send them a telegram so they'd think I must be doing better than I was if I could afford to send them a telegram. I just wished Wolfe and Dreban were still around to send it for me. In the darkness I pulled my five-shot revolver from under my shirt and confirmed it had a full load. Then I counted the bullets in my pocket. I had forty. I'd have to keep count.

I finally got to sleep late but awoke early as reveille came well before dawn. Custer pranced around issuing more orders, instructing officers to have their troops take fifteen days of rations and to carry on them twenty-four rounds of ammunition for pistols and a hundred rounds for their carbines. Most of the soldiers moved slowly as they dealt with the hangovers that followed the carousing and what revelry they could do without women around.

After our regular rations for lunch, Custer and the other high-ranking officers assembled on the deck of the *Far West* before joining General Terry to discuss their plans for teaching Sitting Bull and his warriors a lesson. Custer permitted his troops to visit the sutler again so the men of the Seventh Cavalry bought out the remaining whiskey the trader had brought from Bismarck. As darkness enveloped the camp, I could hear the noise of troops enjoying their liquor as well as the occasional arguments among the officers meeting on board the *Far West*. They were uncertain where the Indians camped and how many they would find.

For the second night in a row, I had plenty of time to think and I actually began to empathize with the Indians. I remember Truett Byars talking about how the government had not lived up to its promise of protecting their sacred lands from settlers and prospectors like me, Dreban and Wolfe, all trying to make a buck at their expense. It reminded me of bad memories of the War Between the States, when blue-coated soldiers had invaded our home in Cane Hill, Arkansas. They'd killed two of my brothers, stolen everything they could carry, tried to hang me and made our lives miserable when all we wanted to do was lead our lives as we saw fit without them anywhere around. Of course, the damn Yankees hadn't allowed that for us, and wouldn't allow it for the Sioux and Cheyenne. I'd've had more sympathy for the Indians, though, if they hadn't butchered my friends in the Black Hills. Perhaps the attacking warriors saw Wolfe and Dreban as no better than we Arkansawyers had viewed the carpetbaggers after the war.

Tribune reporter Kellogg, who was still working on his final dispatch, came to Custer's tent to wait on the general. The officers' meeting ran long and the weather turned ugly again, as storm clouds from the north brought with them a hailstorm that pounded the camp. I jumped up from under the wagon and ran to where I had staked Ciaha. I yanked him toward the wagon and pressed him up against its wooden sides to give him some protection from the hailstones. The hail was followed by a torrential downpour that soaked us all, save for the major officers who stayed on the *Far West*, enjoying the protection of its wooden decks. When the storm passed, I re-staked Ciaha and returned to my now damp blanket and slept as best I could.

Reveille again came early, and the chill of the night was softened by cups of coffee. The men of the Seventh Cavalry scurried about, offloading ammunition from the *Far West* to carry on their person and more to be loaded onto the pack mules. The men were also instructed to carry twelve pounds of oats for feed for their horses. From the farriers, the cavalrymen grabbed two spare horseshoes, one for the foreleg and one for the hind leg. I'd heard horseshoes brought luck, but they didn't to most of these men. Fact was, many of them had but four days to live.

So they could travel light and fast, Custer ordered his men to leave their tents behind. A lot more of them would've survived, if they'd left the general himself behind, but that was not the way the army worked. While his men had to dress in their regular summer uniforms, Custer dressed like he was going to a whore's funeral with a wide-collared campaign shirt, a gaudy red kerchief around his neck, a wide-brimmed felt hat, fringed leather jacket and fringed leather gloves. Ciaha was all I could think.

The biggest trouble came with the pack train. These army mules were accustomed to wearing a harness, not a pack saddle and they weren't interested in learning on the fly. They balked and kicked and brayed and stamped their anger. On top of that, there weren't enough teamsters to manage all the mules so they drafted troopers to help. The soldiers didn't know how to tie a diamond hitch worth a damn. Even if they'd wanted to learn, most of them were wearing grim-faced hangovers. They would've saved time if they'd just invited Sitting Bull, Crazy Horse and all their warrior friends to steal their ammunition and supplies because the hostiles wound up with a lot of it as it fell off mules and was abandoned along the trail over the next four days. It brought me comfort knowing that things were going so poorly that word of Custer's impending victory might not reach civilization until the Democratic National Convention of 1888.

As I watched the circus General Custer's political ambition had caused, *Tribune* reporter Mark Kellogg rode up on his army mule, waving several sheets of writing paper at me. "I've got a question for you, Lomax. I'll let you read my dispatch, if you'll answer my question."

"You're assuming I want to read it. I'm not as big a fan of General Bluster as you are."

He pressed the papers into my hand. "Hurry and read it as I must deliver it to the *Far West* where couriers will take it back to Bismarck."

I humored him like I was reading it, but I merely scanned it. Two things caught my eye. First, he wrote that Major Reno had disobeyed orders and erred in his scouting trip. Maybe so or maybe not, but either way I knew Custer was behind the attack on Reno. The second thing was the odd lines, "By the time this reaches you we would have met and fought the red devils, with what result remains to be seen. I go with Custer and will be at the death." To my way of thinking, he left out the two words that would've explained Custer's true motivation for this expedition. If Custer had edited it, I suspect he would've submitted it as "...will be at the death of Lomax."

"Fine story," I lied. "I'm sure General Bluster will approve. What's your question?"

"What's Ciaha mean, Lomax?"

"It's Comanche for courage. If you don't believe me, ask Fred Gerard."

Kellogg looked at me skeptically. "You sure there's no other meaning."

"I'm as sure as the facts in your story."

"Very well, then," he said. "Good luck to you on this hunt."

He trotted off to deliver his dispatch to the steamboat where someone would courier it back to Bismarck and the world.

After Kellogg rode off, Burkman motioned for me to mount up and go join Custer at the head of the line, forming his twelve companies in a column of four troopers abreast. I rode up to the general, who was talking to three other mounted officers. One was General Terry, but I didn't recognize the other two. One of them, a colonel by his uniform, cautioned Custer. "Now Armstrong, don't be greedy, but wait for us so we can share in the fun."

"No, I will not," Custer replied, but I was never sure if he was saying he wouldn't be greedy or he wouldn't share in the fun.

As he reined his horse around, Custer saw me. He scowled. As he passed me, I pulled Ciaha in beside him.

"Did you send for me, General Bluster?"

He grinned. "You'll have the honor of riding with me at the head of the column because your time is growing short." He signaled his buglers and they started playing "Garry Owen." I looked behind me and saw almost 700 officers, cavalrymen, scouts and civilians in line with Mark Kellogg pushing his mule to get to the head of the column. As each company passed General Terry and the other two officers, they saluted and were answered in kind. It was a remarkable sight until you saw the pack mules bringing up the rear. They were bucking and fighting and flinging their loads. Soldiers walked beside the mules, holding packs on the mules' backs as they began to shift or the ropes loosened. The caravan made it by the general without any embarrassing spills, but it was obvious the mules would have to be re-packed not far down the trail.

It was an awkward beginning for a march that would end in Bluster's Last Stand.

Chapter Twenty-Eight

Once the parade had passed General Terry, the Arikara scouts and interpreters moved to the head of the column and the Seventh Cavalry marched up the Rosebud toward the rivers named Bighorn and Little Bighorn. No one was exactly certain where the Sioux and Cheyenne were, but they had to be somewhere and Custer was intent on finding them first so he could rout them and claim all the glory for himself before the Wyoming and Montana columns joined him. With the Democratic National Convention starting in five days, Custer knew the door was closing on his chance of becoming the Great Father, at least in this election year.

We had not ridden but thirty minutes before officers from the pack train galloped up and advised Custer that a halt was necessary to fix the loads on most of the mules. The general ranted about the men's incompetence and the need to move with haste. Using the wisdom that comes from army logic, Custer appointed Lieutenant Edward G. Mathey of Company M to oversee the pack train so that each individual company was responsible for its pack mules. The company with the fewest spills each day would lead the next day's march. The company with the most spills would bring up the rear and breathe all the dust the march kicked up.

As Mathey turned about to return to the pack train, I heard him mutter "Ciaha" as he passed. We waited while the mules were reloaded, then resumed our march, but the troubles persisted and Custer halted the advance about four o'clock that afternoon. We'd've made better time if we'd loaded our supplies on tortoises. I felt sorriest for Lieutenant Mathey, who wore his horse out riding from one pack spill to the next to note which company was at fault and keep a running tabulation. Away from General Terry, Custer had no one to blame but himself for the poor progress. I began to think all the mules were Republicans, even if they did have donkey ancestry in them. But all the mules together didn't make as big a jackass as the furious Custer did that first day. I thought about quoting him some Bible verses or perhaps just going ahead and shooting him. Based on the surly mood of the troops that afternoon, I thought I had a fifty-fifty chance of being made commander of the Seventh if I did plug him.

About sundown the general called all the officers together at his bivouac for a meeting to express his displeasure with the day's progress and to outline his plans for the next day. He and Captain Benteen got into an argument after Custer questioned the loyalty of some of his subordinates. I couldn't hear all the details because the striker Burkman kept making noise as he hovered nearby to make sure I didn't escape or hear too much. Custer ordered that trumpet calls stop, now that we were nearing the hostiles. Instead of buglers, the horse pickets would awaken the troops each morning at three o'clock and preparations would ensue for a five o'clock departure. He emphasized the importance of the companies staying close enough together to support each other and especially for the pack train not to fall too far behind. Custer estimated that the Seventh Cavalry would face a thousand to fifteen hundred hostiles before the campaign was done.

Toward the end of the meeting his bluster had drained away into despondency, him even asking officers for their opinions on the battle ahead and inviting them to offer advice at any time. I heard that some of the surviving officers later said he was depressed because he had foreseen his own demise. I felt otherwise. That night was the first time he truly realized that his chance at both a quick victory and the Democratic nomination had collapsed in a heap like the load from a pack mule poorly loaded. When Custer dismissed the meeting, several officers departed, singing a song together. That wasn't the only singing that night as some of the Arikaras began to sing a haunting death chant. Even the Indians knew we were headed for disaster. Everyone seemed to realize it but the general. I pitched my blanket that night beneath the stars instead of under Custer's baggage wagon as it had been left behind at the Yellowstone.

I slept well until Burkman came by and kicked me. "Get up," he growled.

"Perxactly," I replied. "And good morning to you, private."

"Perxactly," he echoed.

I pushed myself to my hands and knees, folded up my blanket and then arose, walking over to Ciaha, where I had staked him. I fed and watered, then saddled my mule. Next I walked over to the fire where Burkman was frying some bacon between other chores. When the bacon was about done and he wasn't looking, I forked a couple pieces out of the grease and gobbled them down, even if they did scorch my tongue. I didn't figure I'd get much more to eat beyond a square of hardtack, if Burkman had his way. Then I poured myself a cup of coffee, enjoying it and Burkman's scowl while I drank.

The best I could figure, it was a Friday, June twenty-third, right at three weeks since the snowstorm. Even in the early morning hours, this promised to be a hot day. There would be no snow and no rain to arrest the dust that our caravan kicked up. Lieutenant Mathey strode up that morning to deliver his report on the pack train and its many failures. Approaching the general, who was stretching his arms and yawning, Mathey saluted smartly.

"Please report, Lieutenant," Custer commanded. "Three companies had the same number of problems overnight, sir. Company H, Company—"

Custer held up his hand to interrupt the report. "Lieutenant, have all three companies follow the pack train. As Company H is Captain Benteen's, put him in charge of the detail. Report again to me in the morning."

"Yes, sir," Mathey said, then departed.

It didn't pay to argue with Custer as Benteen had done. Ciaha!

At five o'clock we mounted and started for Rosebud Creek, Custer in the lead with two sergeants on either side, one carrying the regimental flag and the other carrying his headquarters flag. I overheard a couple officers grousing that Custer at his lieutenant colonel rank was no longer entitled by army regulation to post a headquarters flag. I didn't figure he was entitled to shoot me by regulation, but no meaningless army rules would stop him from doing that.

With Custer in the lead, nine companies followed him as we crossed Rosebud Creek. Then came the pack train and the three slackard companies under Benteen's charge. The mules, especially those burdened with the heavy ammunition crates, balked at stepping into the uncertain waters of the Rosebud. The waters were maybe waist high and slow moving, but the mules didn't know that and they fought their handlers all the way across the creek. It took ninety or more minutes to get the mules and supplies across.

While the banks of the Rosebud were gentle slopes lined with pink roses in bloom, the land beyond the Rosebud turned rugged and broken, plenty of places for hostiles to lurk and observe. Everyone was on edge, me more so when Custer sent word he wanted my company. I nudged Ciaha ahead and joined him.

"Don't stray far from me from now until we find the hostiles. I want to make sure you don't get hurt," he informed me.

"Ciaha," I replied.

"Courage is a commodity you will certainly need in the coming hours," he replied.

The terrain slowed us down, especially since the route that Custer chose forced us to cross the Rosebud three or four more times, each occasion delaying us further because of the hassle in getting the pack mules across the water.

Then the interpreters began to ride up and advise Custer that the scouts had seen sign of Indians but no hostiles themselves. The signs included the remains of solitary campfires, horse droppings, the shaft of a broken arrow and little things like that. By early afternoon, the advance companies had cleared the roughest ground and reached rolling prairie and shallow hills, though the pack train still trailed far behind. Impatient to find Indians, Custer decided to lead his nine companies ahead without delay and leave the three trailing companies to make do as best they could. He issued orders accordingly and sent couriers to deliver the message.

"You're making a mistake, General Bluster," I informed him. "You need to keep your ammunition nearby."

"Shut up, Lomax, and watch for Indians."

"Yes, sir, General Bluster."

Funny thing about it was I don't know how many times I'd called him General Bluster since I had had the unfortunate opportunity of making his acquaintance. Not once in all that time did he correct me. Maybe his hearing was as bad as his judgment. Or, maybe he had been too close to too many cannons during the War Between the States, and their explosions had damaged his ears. Or, maybe he was just so vain that as long as you called him general he didn't pay attention to what followed.

About three miles past the point where Custer left the pack train on its own, we came to the remains of a vast Indian camp. I was neither a scout nor an experienced soldier, but I was smart enough to know that this meant trouble. There were hostiles ahead, hundreds if not thousands. Odd thing about the camp was the dozens of brush shelters the Indians had made by tying the ends of neighboring brush together at the top to form a primitive shelter from the elements. Nobody could quite figure it out, except Custer. He decided the hostiles built the brush shelters for their dogs. Since he was the general, everyone agreed. I learned later that the Indians called these places "wickiups" and their occupants had not been dogs but unmarried warriors without teepees of their own. One officer reported counting the remains of more than four hundred campfires at the location.

Custer was excited that we were nearing the Indians and, I suppose in his mind, that he was nearing the Democratic nomination for president when the convention began. The rest of us were just worried we were edging closer to our deaths.

Still, we moved on, the country turning rugged again with outcroppings of sandstone and rocky terrain. Some of the sandstone rocks were scratched and carved with strange symbols. I feared they were warnings left by the Indians for trespassers, but I'm sure Custer thought the etchings were the work of hostile dogs after spending a night in a wickiup. Before sundown we passed two more abandoned Indian camps, each larger than the previous one. When we left the final camp, we crossed an Indian trail that was a quarter of a mile wide. I wasn't an expert tracker but I wasn't stupid either. It took a lot of dogs and horses pulling travois to scratch out a trail that wide. The farther we went and the more sign we discovered, the more fearful all of us got, all of us except General Custer. He was as excited as kitten with three balls of twine. "Hallelujah, John!" I heard him mutter three or four times.

Periodically, Fred Gerard would ride up to Custer to report on his latest discoveries. If he had a chance, he'd ride over and say a few words to me. I pointed at an inscription in one of the sandstone outcroppings.

"It's a warning," he nodded. "It means death awaits. I've never seen the Rees so frightened. They're a superstitious lot, but this beats all. Everything's a bad omen since we left the *Far West*, if not since we departed Fort Lincoln."

I pointed to Custer. "He's the worst omen of all."

Gerard removed his hat and wiped the sweat from his brow. He sighed, then snugged his hat on his head. "There may be four of five thousand hostiles ahead. The general doesn't understand what he's facing. He won't have time to kill you, Lomax, once the shooting starts."

"I figure he'll go for me first, regardless of the hostiles. Ciaha!"

"Ciaha!" Gerard said as he rode back to rejoin the scouts.

We marched a couple more hours, Custer finally calling a halt about five o'clock on a broad sage plain bordering the Rosebud. We'd started the morning crossing the Rosebud and still hadn't gotten shed of it by afternoon, but at least it would provide water for ourselves and our animals. As we made camp, I'd never seen such a sober group of men, and it wasn't because no liquor was available to share.

These men were terrified of what lay ahead, especially with General Bluster in the lead. About two hours later, the pack train caught up.

The Seventh Cavalry was all together that night when the attack came, not from Indians but from mosquitoes. They swarmed up from the river and assailed us and the animals mercilessly. Their perpetual buzzing and our slapping ourselves at each bite kept most of us awake that night. The insect assault made me wish for another sudden snowstorm to drive the pests away. Though night was hot, I covered my head with my blanket in spite of the heat. My head sweated profusely but I preferred that to letting the mosquitoes feed on my flesh.

The next morning's routine was the same as the day before, except that we were glad to move and abandon the plague of mosquitoes. We started the day's march at five o'clock in the morning after Captain Benteen had complained to Custer that the pack train was vulnerable to disaster if the other companies rode too far ahead to provide support in case of attack. Custer promised it wouldn't happen again, then proceeded to outdistance the pack train the rest of the day. We had marched an hour or so before Indian scouts approached and through sign language let Custer know fresh signs and a large camp was about ten miles ahead. Custer smiled. He likely realized if he missed the Democratic nomination this year, he would be a cinch for 1880.

The general issued orders that he and two companies would ride a half-mile to a mile ahead of the main body to check out the report. The main body of troops would be close enough to help either Custer's two companies or the pack train as it fell behind. Once he finished his military matters, the general rode over to me.

"Ride with me, Lomax," he instructed.

"Ciaha!" I said.

"Courage," he replied.

We rode forward together, him probably thinking about his glorious future and me wondering if he would risk shooting me in front of two companies of witnesses. We moved ahead at a fast walk so as not to put too much distance between us and the following troops. When we came to the abandoned camp, we found Fred Gerard and several of his Arikara scouts waiting. I studied the campgrounds and swallowed hard. It was the biggest yet and in the center of it all stood the poles of a great lodge the hostiles had built.

Custer rode over to Gerard. I followed. Before Custer could speak, Gerard asked a question that stunned me.

"General, is it true you plan on shooting Lomax?"

Custer cut a glance from Gerard to me and back.

"Preposterous," Custer spat out. "If you were a soldier, I'd have you court-martialed and shot for such impertinence."

"Shot like Lomax," Gerard persisted.

"No, no, no, Gerard," Custer sputtered.

"I may need Lomax's interpretation skills before all this is over, and I plan on keeping an eye on Lomax whenever I'm around."

"You do that, Gerard. Now tell me what we've found."

I felt a little better knowing that I had a friend other than Ciaha accompanying the Seventh Cavalry.

Gerard explained that the Arikaras had determined the Indians had held a Sun Dance at this spot and made medicine, preparing for battle and drawing representations in the sand of how the conflict would end. Gerard motioned for us to follow and he rode about twenty yards away, pointing out drawings in the sand and three stones painted red.

"Those rocks are a sign that the Great Sprit has assured them of a victory over the white man," Gerard said.

"Mere superstition," Custer replied.

As we spoke, soldiers from the two accompanying units and the Indian scouts began to wander among the debris of the abandoned camp.

Custer pointed to the lodge poles where five Indian scouts examined the wooden skeleton. "What was that?"

"The great lodge where they held the Sun Dance," Gerard said. "They believe the dance will bring them great power and victory over the white man and his army."

Suddenly, the five scouts started wailing and stomping their feet as one pulled free a small branch that had been tied to one of the poles. They screamed and wailed. Custer stared at them, then back at Gerard, who motioned them to come over. As they approached, the two sergeants carrying the Seventh's guidon and Custer's headquarters flag rode up.

The scouts gave Gerard the branch and he offered it to Custer. Dangling from the end was a scalp. "It's from a white man," Gerard said, "and it appears to be fresh."

Custer took the branch and examined the grisly trophy. As he did, a sharp gust of wind struck us all, the scalp waving in the breeze and Custer's guidon snapping in the sudden draft and breaking the tie that attached it to the pole. The flag fluttered to the ground as the embarrassed sergeant jumped from his horse to reattach it to the standard. The five Indian scouts wailed again, then spoke to Gerard, who turned to Custer.

"They say it's a bad omen, General, the latest of many."

"Mere superstition," he replied. "If the sergeant had paid attention to my banner and secured it properly to begin with, this would never have happened. It's not an omen, but incompetence."

The offending sergeant's face turned red with humiliation. The general had made himself another enemy!

Rather than linger around the camp with all of its depressing implications, Custer ordered the men to move forward and on we marched. Less than an hour later he ordered a stop for men to rest their horses and eat a square of hardtack. We stayed there two or three hours before we resumed the march and entered a wide valley. I had this notion I was being watched, like the time in the Black Hills when Snakebit was tracking me. Maybe Custer didn't believe in superstitions, but I couldn't discount them so handily. My skin crawled with worry. I didn't have ambitions to become president. On this day, my only ambition was to survive.

We kept moving and finally stopped for the night about eight o'clock before it got too dark to see. I estimated we had traveled almost thirty miles since five o'clock in the morning and we were all exhausted, even more so the men with the pack train, which reached us two hours after dark. They had to unload their mules while the rest of us just dropped to the ground and tried to rest, not even taking time to drive rattlesnakes away from our bivouac. Too tired to build fires for supper and too hungry to sleep, we managed the best we could, while Custer and his officers met briefly to discuss plans for tomorrow. They estimated we were within twenty miles of the hostiles, and we should be ready for anything the next day. Most of us, collapsed on our blankets and went to sleep. Fortunately, we camped far enough from water that mosquitoes were no longer an impediment to our sleep. Unfortunately, Custer was.

Shortly after most of the soldiers, save for Benteen's companies still tending the pack mules, had gone to sleep, I was still awake trying to determine how I would survive the next day when I heard a rider approach the general.

"It's Lieutenant Varnum, General," he announced himself. "I've got word from the Crow scouts."

Up until then, I'd thought the Seventh Cavalry used only Arikara scouts, but apparently they had Crow scouts as well and the Crows were mortal enemies of the Sioux. Varnum explained that the Crows wanted the soldiers to take a night march to the Crow's Nest, a high butte that in the early morning light offered a view for miles down the Little Bighorn Valley. If the Sioux and Cheyenne were anywhere in the valley, they would be spotted and the troops would be in position to surprise and rout them. Custer decided their plan was brilliant and sent Varnum to accompany those scouts to the Crow's Nest so they would be there come morning. He then had Burkman pass word along for the officers of the Seventh to gather at his bivouac. The meeting was short and to the point. The Seventh Cavalry was breaking camp and heading toward the valley of the Little Bighorn. There were to be no fires, no unnecessary noise and no delay in preparing to move.

Less than two hours after most of us had fallen in our blankets, we were up and preparing to ride on. The men of the pack train had barely had a break at all as they had to start reloading the pack animals. As I saddled Ciaha, I thought about escaping in the dark, but feared I might run into some Indians. I preferred my chances with Custer rather than alone on the prairie. The soldiers were too tired to waste energy grumbling and cursing so they just did what they were ordered. We marched out an hour or so before midnight.

I was flattered that Custer insisted I ride up front with him. I figured he might just haul off and shoot me in the dark, but I guess he was torn between that and being president. By my way of calculating, the new day we rode into was Sunday, June twenty-fifth, two days before the Democratic National Convention opened. I had no idea how long political conventions lasted, but I knew he thought he still had time to whip the hostiles, send Kellogg's dispatch back to civilization and accept the nomination for president. Custer also sent word for Kellogg to ride with us so he could report upon the general's military brilliance and personal valor. So off we rode into the darkness, most of us fighting against the sleep we so desperately needed versus the fear we felt if we were separated from the others and captured by the Indians. I'd seen what they had done to Wolfe and Dreban. I preferred a different outcome.

We rode and rode and rode, stumbling along in the dark, trying to stay together, trying to stay alert and trying to catch what rest we could without endangering ourselves and others. I have to say this about Custer, he had great endurance and didn't seem to be bothered by no rest.

As dawn approached, we stopped beside a grove of trees that

gave us cover. Most of us fell off of our mounts and dropped to the grassy earth to catch whatever sleep we could. I tied Ciaha's reins around my wrist and lay down. I quickly fell into a deep trance, but not for long before Burkman kicked me in the shin.

"General says ride," he advised me.

I rubbed my eyes. "Perxactly," I replied, stood up and untied the reins from my wrist. I took a drink of water from my canteen and checked that my peashooter still nested in my shoulder harness. I knew I would need it before the day was over. I mounted Ciaha and rode over to the general and several other mounted men, including Tom Custer, a few Indian scouts, Fred Gerard and other officers and couriers. As long as Gerard was along, I felt safe. Together we trotted toward the promontory called Crow's Nest. Hours had passed since dawn when the light was clearest, but we still arrived before ten in the morning and climbed up the slopes of the promontory. Several Crow scouts and Lieutenant Varnum greeted us.

"It's them, General," Varnum announced. "A huge camp." He pointed down the valley.

Custer giggled with delight, then looked the direction of Varnum's finger. He looked, silently for a moment, then lifted his hand over his eyes and stared again. "I don't see anything."

I focused on the distance and couldn't make out much, except for a writhing kind of movement that reminded me of maggots on a carcass. Gerard stepped up and offered me his field glasses. I took them and stared, gradually focusing the lenses. The movement I had picked up with my bare eyes was a horse herd, moving about and grazing in the early morning. There were hundreds of horses and beyond them I thought I could make out the tops of teepees, though I could not be certain for the soft haze that hovered over the valley. Gerard took the field glasses from me and offered them to Custer.

Custer lifted them glasses to his eyes. He studied the distance, then returned the field glasses to Gerard. "I can't make out anything for certain," he announced.

I was beginning to think Custer was not only deaf, but also blind.

"The haze of their camp fires has clouded the view," Varnum said. "Trust me, they are there. Not only that, they are there in the biggest numbers I've ever seen."

Custer scoffed. "I need proof."

Varnum responded, "We saw two of their sentries riding our direction at dawn. They are there, believe me."

"I only believe what I can see with certainty," Custer replied.

"But several of us have seen them, they are there," Varnum protested.

"Even if they are, we won't attack until tomorrow morning when we can surprise them like we did at the Washita," Custer replied, his voice rising.

I couldn't help myself. "Ciaha!" I exclaimed.

Custer looked at me. "Courage, absolutely," he said.

Everyone laughed except the general and his brothr Tom.

We left Crow's Nest all knowing that the general was wrong.

What we didn't know was that he was *dead* wrong.

Chapter Twenty-Nine

Descending from the Crow's Nest, we could see to the east the line of cavalrymen riding toward us, the mule train already lagging behind the main body. Most worrisome, the horses and mules were kicking up a cloud of dust that promised only to worsen as the hot morning air turned into a scorching afternoon. The dust would certainly reveal our approach.

"What the hell are they doing?" Custer said to Gerard when he realized his men were advancing. "I told them to wait."

Gerard shrugged. "You gave them orders to march."

Custer slapped his thigh, "I countermanded that order."

"I don't remember such a command," Gerard responded.

Custer shook his head. "I know what I ordered," he shouted, then kicked his mount in the flank and galloped to head off the command.

The general was not only losing his hearing and his sight but also his mind.

Gerard steered his mount toward me and Ciaha. Shaking his head, he mumbled, "It's going to be a long day."

"And a hot one," I added.

By the time we reached the vanguard of troops, Custer had already issued an officer's call and stood lambasting his subordinates for following his orders instead of his intentions. Gerard and I rode up and dismounted on the perimeter of Custer's circle. He had barely finished chewing out his men, when a junior officer arrived with a bad report. One of the mules during the night march had lost part of its load, including a box of ammunition. When the soldiers backtracked this morning, they found two Indians had beaten them to the missing box. Seeing the soldiers, the two hostiles had bolted up on their ponies and scampered away.

At that point even a man who was losing his hearing, his seeing and his memory could not deny that his expedition had been discovered. "Now we can't wait until morning to attack," Custer said. "We've got to find them before they find us." With that, he issued a flurry of orders. All soldiers were to carry a hundred or more carbine rounds with them; each company was to assign six men to stay with and protect the pack train as it advanced; and the Arikaras were to ride to the hostiles' encampment and stampede their horse herd.

Gerard just shook his head. "He doesn't know what he's getting into. He needs to reconnoiter, so he knows what we're facing."

At that point Burkman galloped up to the general and asked to accompany Custer into battle. "No, Private," Custer said. "You're tired. I want you with the pack train so you can rest and keep my hounds. You'll arrive in time to share in the glory."

Burkman pleaded to go with Custer, but the general waved him away, then looked around, pointing at me. "Lomax is riding at my side so that I can see he's taken care of." Burkman scowled at me with simmering, disgusted eyes.

"Perxactly," I said.

Burkman spat at my boots and rode away as I examined the troops. Exhausted cavalrymen, their eyes listless, sat silently in their saddles with heads down and shoulders slumped, their faces and uniforms powdered with trail dust, their brows streaked with sweat. The men's mounts, too, were fatigued. It had been a day or more since the horses had watered well, so they were thirsty and exhausted. On a day as hot as this, they would need endurance.

The sun was approaching noon when the officers reported back to the general that all was ready. He lifted his arm and gave the command that would send many of his men to eternity and himself to hell by nightfall. "Forward," he cried, then turned to me. "Stay with me, Lomax."

"Good luck, Gerard," I offered as I passed him.

Before long we crossed the divide between the Rosebud basin and that of the Little Bighorn. In the distance I could make out a hazy blue cloud that I took to be smoke from the campfires of a thousand hostile lodges. I judged it to be fifteen to twenty miles away. We crossed the grassy western slopes of the divide, then struck some rougher land and some dry ravines, where the horses struggled down and then up the slopes without benefit of water at the bottom. The farther we rode the hotter and thirstier we all became.

"It'll be a glorious day," Custer said to me apparently. "Tomorrow the Democratic National Convention begins. I am certain my future is in politics."

I figured his future was in hell, then realized politics and hell were likely one and the same, there not being a decent person in either. I kept my opinion to myself, though.

"I once thought myself a Democrat," I said.

"What happened?" Custer wanted to know.

"I met you," I replied.

Custer glared at me. "You'd make a good Republican with all your experience stealing army firewood." If we'd kept on discussing politics the tragedy that followed that afternoon might have been avoided, but I'd concluded that Custer was more interested in killing me at that moment than he was in becoming president. He licked his lips and nodded. "You'll not see sunset today," Custer then informed me.

"There are men here that know your plans for me, General Bluster. You'll not get away with it."

"Who'll they believe, some unknown vagabond or the most famous general in the land? On top of that, who'll even care about a nobody like you, Lomax?"

I reached for my peashooter, thinking for a moment I might just go ahead and shoot the son of a bitch right then, but thought better of it. Instead I patted the Bible in my haversack.

Custer laughed. "The Good Book can't save you now. Fact is, even God couldn't save you today, Lomax, because there'll come a time when it's just you and me with nobody around. Then I'll enforce military justice."

I figured it impossible for him and me to be alone on this day, not with so many troopers, teamsters, interpreters and Indian scouts around. Shortly, Custer called a halt to the march and ordered his officers to join him. All of them showed up except one.

"Where's Reno?" Custer asked.

"Must not've gotten word," Custer's adjutant replied.

"Then take a message and tell him to take command of Companies A, G and M and position them on our left wing," Custer ordered.

I'm sure Custer wanted to give the impression to the other officers that he was devising tactics for the attack. I knew better. He was splitting up his forces so he would have the opportunity to shoot me without witnesses. At that moment, I offered the first military observation of my life. "General Bluster, you shouldn't be dividing your forces in the face of a hostile enemy of unknown number."

Captain Benteen and some of the other officers snickered as this was the first time I'd ever called him "General Bluster" in the presence of others. The Custer brood, however, grumbled their hatred, even more so when Benteen spoke.

"He's got a point, General," Benteen said.

Custer turned his anger from me to Benteen. "I'll not tolerate insubordination from an officer of lesser rank."

"Lomax is not an officer," Benteen reminded him.

"And you won't be one for long, Benteen, if I bring charges for a court martial against you," Custer announced.

Benteen backed down.

Custer turned to his adjutant. "Now deliver that message to Major Reno." He looked back at Benteen. "Now, Captain," Custer began, stroking his chin and looking off in the distance, "I want you to take Companies D, H and K and head southwest to those bluffs in the distance. Do you see them?"

"Yes, sir," Benteen replied.

"Examine that region and let us know if you see sign of the hostiles' camp," Custer commanded.

"Hadn't we better keep the regiment together like Lomax says, General? If the hostiles are as many as reports say, we'll need every man we have, even Lomax there."

"You have your orders, Captain."

"Yes, sir. Anything else?" Benteen asked.

Custer shook his head.

Benteen saluted, then turned about to pull his companies from the line and head toward the bluffs, which I made out to be five or six miles away. Between Reno's and Benteen's commands as well as the main body and the pack train, Custer had divided his forces into four battalions, his being the largest, of course, with six companies.

As Benteen's battalion did a left oblique and marched away, Reno pulled his three companies from the caravan and led them across a small ravine that fed into the Little Bighorn. Reno's thirsty horses stopped to get water from the small stream, but remained only until their riders spurred them onward.

What concerned me was that we had picked up a wide Indian trail and Benteen was riding away from it and Reno was paralleling it while Custer was intent on following it with only half of his men. His hatred of me was interfering with military prudence. I hadn't graduated from West Point, but I wasn't stupid either. I knew this was not going to end well for the Seventh Cavalry or, worst of all, for me.

Once his officers had ridden back to their posts, Custer nudged his horse toward me. "Don't think I'm so stupid, Lomax, not to understand you calling me 'General Bluster' throughout this expedition. I let it pass as long as you just said it between us, but I'll not have you insult me in front of my officers."

Maybe he wasn't as deaf as I thought, though there was no doubt he was definitely stupider than I originally believed.

As we started forward, Custer's and Reno's columns ran parallel and even, but as we rode Reno's units fell behind ours until Reno and his leading company were even with the final company of Custer's battalion. Shortly after that, Custer pushed his companies ahead at a trot. I suspect he would have preferred to ride faster and harder, but he knew my mule could never keep up so he kept the pace manageable for Ciaha. Further, if Custer lost sight of me now, he might not see me again until all the shooting was done.

After a mile or two at that pace, several of the horses began to slow to a walk, totally exhausted, some stumbling ahead, some just stopping and balking against the commands of their riders. Ahead of us rode the Indian scouts with Fred Gerard returning periodically to report Ree findings to the general. A couple times Custer rode out with Gerard before sending the interpreter on and returning to me. Custer's eyes widened with wild excitement. Behind him, his men watched with tired eyes. Some began to unbutton their shirts to deal with the stifling heat. Some removed their hats and fanned their faces. Some lifted canteens to their parched mouths and tried to suck water from the containers, but little remained and certainly not enough to quench the day's thirst. The troopers were exhausted and thirsty and famished and their lives now rested with a man whose reason was as empty as their canteens.

As we advanced, Custer seemed invigorated by the prospect of battle, even more so when some of the Arikara scouts ahead discovered a single teepee. Shouting and whistling, they charged ahead and rode their ponies in a circle around it, slapping at it with their quirts, then jumping from their horses and slicing at it with their knives until the fabric was shredded. Suddenly the scouts backed away, and their excitement evaporated. Then we saw why. The teepee shielded a scaffold holding the blanket-wrapped body of a dead warrior.

As Custer and I neared the teepee, the superstitious scouts backed away. Custer stood in his stirrups and looked over his shoulder toward Reno at the lead of his command. With a wave of his arm, Custer signaled for Reno to come forward with his troops. I hoped the general was coming to his senses to reassemble his soldiers for what lay ahead. It was about two o'clock.

Custer dismounted and led his horse to the teepee. I could see the deceased's buffalo robe, his bow and arrows, his moccasin and his pipe plus his personal effects hanging from the scaffold. Custer emerged with the pipe for a souvenir, then flung it on the ground when he looked skyward. He pointed ahead to a shroud of dust rising to the heavens like the earth was giving up its very soul.

Without orders, Gerard and a lieutenant spurred their horses toward the crest of a ridge some fifty yards beyond the tepee. Gerard reined his horse around and bolted back toward Custer.

"It's the edge of their camp about two miles ahead," he called to Custer. "Forty or more warriors stand between us and the camp."

"The dust? What about the dust? Are they escaping?" Custer shouted.

"Can't say," Gerard answered. "There's a bend in the river and I couldn't see much past the timber beyond that."

"We can't let them escape," Custer said. "Ride with the scouts and attack the village."

Gerard passed on Custer's instructions, but the Arikaras and Crow scouts did not move.

"Ride," Custer shouted, but the Indians remained motionless. He looked at Gerard.

Gerard queried them and two responded, then he translated it for Custer. "Their job was to find the village, not lead the attack. They will go but they will not lead."

Enraged, Custer shook his fist at the scouts. "Tell them that any man not brave enough to charge will be relieved of his weapons and be called a woman."

Gerard translated and then gave their response. "General, they say you, too, are a woman if you will not lead the charge like a great chief."

"Then have them move aside."

Gerard conveyed Custer's instructions and the scouts backed their horses away.

Custer then told an orderly to carry word for Reno and his three companies to attack the village. As Reno organized his three companies to charge the encampment, Custer turned to his Gerard. "You ride with Reno's men as I don't want the coward scouts riding with my soldiers."

Gerard looked at me, shaking his head. Both he and I knew Custer intended to separate us so the interpreter wouldn't see Custer shoot me. "Good luck," he said.

I nodded. "Ciaha!"

"Ciaha!" He laughed back, then turned his horse and rode toward Reno. The Arikara and Crow scouts joined him, shouting what

I took to be curses at Custer. Moments later, Reno started his men toward the ridge that screened the village from us and toward the battle and the fate that awaited them.

From what I overheard of Custer's instructions for Reno, the general made no mention of what he intended to do. It didn't make sense to me that he hadn't shared his plans with his fellow officers for a coordinated effort. Then I realized that all his plans centered around killing me first for embarrassing him and the Seventh Cavalry. After he attended to that deed, he would devote his military genius to the hostiles.

Minutes later various officers and troopers galloped up to Custer with reports. The general listened, then sent them away. Each time, he turned and made sure I hadn't escaped. I wasn't going anywhere, not with hundreds of hostiles around. After what seemed like an eternity, we heard gunfire. Reno had struck the village.

Custer moved his companies forward, me at his side. We followed Reno's trail just over the ridge then veered away. "You're making a mistake by abandoning Major Reno!"

"Not as big a mistake as you made stealing firewood from the United States Army," Custer replied as he waved for his soldiers to follow him.

I kept Ciaha at an easy pace, hoping Custer would gallop ahead of me in his excitement, but he stayed at my side, so fixed was he on shooting me when the fighting started. The best I could figure, Custer hoped that Reno's attack would distract the warriors so that he could slip around the village, make a flank attack, kill me in the process, then earn an impressive victory that would carry him to the presidency.

We rode two miles toward a series of bluffs to the north where more Indians had been spotted. Even at the modest pace, the soldiers on tired horses dropped out of the formation. As we advanced the entire line began to fall apart, some men staying with Custer, some getting confused and riding away from the bluffs toward the river, likely because their horses smelled water and could not be stopped. I'd never seen so much confusion. At one point I saw the *Tribune* Reporter Mark Kellogg fall from his mule, then scramble up and remount.

Custer rode wide-eyed and confident, certain that he would triumph in battle and in politics, but we had yet to fire a shot while the distant gunfire confirmed Reno and his men were heavily engaged. Finally, Custer led his men up the slopes that overlooked the river valley in hopes of spotting the hostiles and more of their village. He directed the troops away from the river so that they could reassemble without being spotted by the Indians, at least that was what I thought initially.

"Keep the troops here," Custer ordered his subordinates. "I'll scout by the river and determine our plan of attack." Then he looked at me. "Come along, Lomax."

I hesitated.

"Now!" he screamed.

I turned Ciaha in beside Vic and the madman who rode him, working my mule to Custer's right side so I would have a better chance of pulling my peashooter from my shoulder harness without being observed.

Custer issued his final orders. "Do not let a man near the edge of the ridge. I don't want to risk the hostiles spotting us."

This was it. Custer planned to descend the ridge and then shoot me while he was out of sight of his soldiers. Then all he had to do was blame my death on an Indian sniper. He was clever. It didn't matter that some of his men under Reno were probably being massacred back down the river or that he had no idea about the fate of Benteen and his troops. All he was concerned about was my fate and his reputation, the hell with his men.

As we rode toward the ridge, I looked back over my shoulder a few times, hoping some of the soldiers disobeyed the general's orders, but they were too tired and, I suspect, to scared to defy his command. By this time, I wasn't scared as much as mad. As we reached the top of the ridge, Custer looked over his shoulder to make sure no soldiers had followed. As he did, I slipped my hand under my coat and shirt and pulled the pocket revolver from its harness. I let my right hand slide down my side. I coughed to hide the sound of me cocking the pistol.

We descended the slope toward the brush along the river. On the other side of the river, beyond a stand of trees, I could see the tops of teepees, but mostly I watched Custer, waiting for him to pull his gun. Once he reached for his weapon, I'd shoot him. He stared straight ahead, paying more attention to the river than to me. I couldn't understand why he was taking so long to make his move, then I glanced to the river and saw an Indian maiden, standing in the shallows bathing, her tawny skin glistening with the water, her bosom heaving with each breath. She was a comely woman, no doubt, and her nakedness had extended my life. Perhaps she even saved me because he was so fixated on her, he forgot about me until we drew within thirty yards of her. At that moment she spotted us and ran naked back toward the village to sound the alert.

When she disappeared behind some trees, Custer remembered the business at hand. He turned to me. "Well, Lomax, it's time you got what you deserved for trying to kill my political future. It wouldn't surprise me if the Republicans and President Grant himself had put you up to it, just to humiliate me."

"I'm entitled to a trial, General Bluster."

"There you go, mocking my name again," Custer said. "You'll get all the trial you deserve right here." He looked back up the slope to make sure none of his soldiers were spying.

I kept my gaze on him, raising my pistol into my lap so I could plug him quickly when he moved for his gun.

As Custer stared at me, his face warped with an odd smile. "It's time to render a verdict in the case of the United States Army versus H.H. Lomax!" He lifted his hand toward his gun.

As I was about to shoot him in the gut to get his attention, I heard a cry from downriver.

"General, General Custer," yelled a voice.

Custer glanced from me downstream and back again. "Damnation!" he grumbled.

Downstream I saw two cavalrymen, one riding a fatigued horse and the other holding onto its tail to pull himself along. As they came closer, I stared in disbelief at two of my former guards, James Watson atop the mount and Peter Thompson, hanging onto the horse's tail.

They approached us and saluted Custer.

"What are you men doing here?" Custer demanded.

"My horse collapsed," Thompson said.

"Mine can barely walk," Watson added.

"There's warriors all along the creek. We've been hiding out, trying to get back to Company C."

"You'll not catch up. Head back toward Reno's battalion and support them."

"Yes, sir," they answered, "once we catch our breath."

"One more thing," Custer said. "I am ordering you not to report seeing Lomax with me."

"We won't," Thompson said, "as long as you don't shoot him. If you do, we'll report you up the chain of command."

"That is insubordination," Custer said.

"No, it's what's decent and right, not that the army'd know anything about decency and righteousness," Watson said.

Custer grumbled something incoherently, then looked at me. "Lomax stays with me."

"Maybe so, but if you shoot him before you ride up that slope and rejoin your troops we'll make sure the world knows about it," Thompson replied.

"Very well, men," Custer said. "Carry out your orders, and I'll see Lomax over the hill."

Both cavalrymen nodded.

"Good luck, Lomax," said Thompson.

"Thanks, boys," I replied. "Ciaha!"

They laughed, then echoed me in unison. "Ciaha!"

"Come on, Lomax," said Custer, turning his sorrel about. "Let's ride."

I saluted Thompson and Watson, then returned up the hill with Custer, who kept glancing over his shoulder to see if the two were still watching us. They were. When we reached the top of the slope, I waved my arm at them, forgetting I still held my revolver.

"Where'd you get that?" Custer demanded.

"Burkman gave it to me," I lied. "Said for me make sure you didn't get hurt, even if you wouldn't let him ride along."

"Good old Burkman," Custer said. "Always looking out for me."

"Yeah, good old Burkman," I answered. "He never thought I might use it to shoot you."

When we rejoined Custer's companies, everything was confusion, officers shouting over Indian sightings or arguing over tactics. Some, I think, were surprised to see me return alive.

The general ordered the troops to swing back in the direction we had come, staying close to the river for a ways, then veering more toward the direction where we had left Reno. Time and events began to run together in my mind, especially after we saw warriors gathering on our perimeter, assembling to attack. Custer finally realized our predicament. He shouted for an orderly and instructed his adjutant to send a message for Benteen to come quick and bring the ammunition. The orderly galloped away as best as his exhausted horse would carry him. He was the last trooper to escape the ring of hostiles now encircling us.

All around me soldiers began to pull their carbines and check their loads. The exhaustion in the cavalrymen's eyes had been replaced with fear. I looked at the gun in my hand and realized it was trembling uncontrollably. I had not been this scared at Adobe Walls.

At least we had some walls there between us and our attackers. Here we had nothing to stop a bullet or an arrow. Arrows began to sprinkle from the sky upon us. A hailstorm of arrows and bullets would follow. Custer forgot me for a moment, deciding to attack our attackers.

"Men," he cried out, "today we ride for glory."

Most men were more interested in riding for their lives than for glory, but never Custer. He wanted fame and immortality more than anything else. The rest of us were petrified at the enemy before us. We knew we would not live to see the sun set on this day.

"Today will demand courage from each of us," Custer shouted. "The Comanche have a word for it—Ciaha!"

"Ciaha!" the soldiers shouted together.

And then, they charged to their deaths, yelling Ciaha!

Chapter Thirty

It seemed like forever, but it was over in an hour or less. We rode from the rise through a gentle, barren valley toward another rise where Sioux and Cheyenne warriors converged on us from all sides, screaming like demons, shooting their bullets and their arrows at us. I stayed with Custer, deciding the soldiers would try to protect their commander, even if he didn't deserve it. Terrified, Ciaha ran hard for an exhausted mule, inspired perhaps that Custer and so many soldiers had shouted his name as they rushed ahead.

Some soldiers fell behind as we raced up the rise toward a distant hill. The charge bled soldiers one by one as we bolted up the rise. Some were shot from their horses, others fell beneath their exhausted mounts as they collapsed from exertion. I saw one terrified horse race through a line of Indians, several of whom gave chase. I saw what must've been thousands of Indians, though I didn't stop to count, but held my fire as my little gun would do little damage at long range. Angry screams of the Indians mixed with the terrified cries of the soldiers. The acrid smell of spent gunpowder mingled with the choking dust kicked up by our horses. Every breath hurt the lungs.

The distance between us and the hostiles narrowed as they closed in. I could kill as many Indians as my bullets would allow, but there were just so many of them, a few on horseback but most afoot. Like angry ants, they poured out of the ground, no end to them, all intent on killing every one of us. I glanced ahead and saw about eighty men riding toward the summit. Behind me I saw dozens dead plus many wounded still fighting for their lives. I knew I would soon be among the dead. I felt the Bible flopping in the haversack at my side and thought about tossing it away to reduce Ciaha's load. Then I saw an arrow thud into my side. Though I heard the clump of the arrow and saw it sticking out of my side, I felt no pain. Then I realized the Bible had stopped the arrow short of my flesh.

As the hostiles closed in behind me, I leaned forward and slapped Ciaha on the neck with my revolver. When I tried to sit up, something dug into the back of my neck. I couldn't rise. I feared I'd been grazed across the back of the neck and paralyzed. I shook my neck and realized that the leather thong of the rattler necklace had snagged on the saddle. I freed it and sat up, the rattle bouncing against my chest as I rode.

"Ciaha!" I screamed and looked for the son of a bitch that had gotten me in this bind.

At first I didn't see him as I was encircled by the Indians in an ever tightening ring of fear and death. The attackers drew closer. Before long they would be close enough for me to shoot with my peashooter. Then up toward the summit of the hill, I saw Custer leaping from his horse as it fell to the ground. Other soldiers jumped from their horses around him. Some of the soldiers shot their horses to make barricades. Other horses bolted before their riders could stop them. I may have been the last white man to reach the hilltop astride my mount. I jumped from Ciaha and yanked on the reins, trying to tug him to the ground. He fought me for a moment, then a bullet grazed his neck, splattering blood on my face as my mule fell to the ground. He whinnied and thrashed on the ground. When I looked up, I saw Custer arising, not a dozen yards away. His eyes were wide and blank as he fired at the attackers. Then he saw me. Life and anger flooded back into his eyes.

"Lomax, you bastard," he screamed, "you're the cause of this." He waved his pistol and fired at me.

Missed.

I lifted my peashooter and shot back at him, but my hand was shaking so that I'd more likely hit the moon than him. I missed and pulled the trigger a second time.

He stuck his tongue out at me when I missed, then fired back at me.

Missed.

I was too terrified to take aim, so I tried to judge the sway of my hand and pull the trigger at that instant when my pistol barrel passed over him. I missed again.

He kept firing at me but by then he was out of ammunition. I jumped toward him, figuring I wouldn't miss if I stuck the gun barrel in his ear and pulled the trigger, but a soldier fell in my path and I tripped over him. Miraculously, I hung onto my gun and raised on my knees firing at him a fourth time. He stumbled and ducked my bullet.

Realizing his pistol was empty, he opened his revolver, dumped the hulls from the cylinder and started yanking bullets from his gun belt and shoving them in. We were ten yards apart and I knew I had to make this bullet count. I fell to the ground to steady my shaking arm and fired.

I don't know how, but I missed a fifth time.

I rolled over on my back and shoved my hand into my britches pocket and grabbed a handful of bullets. As I yanked my hand out of my pocket, I flung the bullets across the battlefield. Spotting two on the ground nearby, I grabbed them. As I did, I looked up and saw Custer standing over me, grinning as he took aim for a spot I figured was right between my eyes.

I heard a scream as an Indian galloped toward us. Custer looked up and shot at the intruder in our personal vendetta. The Indian fell. Custer looked back down at me.

I rolled over as quickly as I could, just in time to hear the explosion of Custer's gun into the ground where my head had been. I jumped to my feet and scurried back to Ciaha's thrashing form, dumping the hulls from my peashooter and sliding my two remaining bullets into the cylinder. I locked it in placed and turned to find Custer.

The son of a bitch was walking toward me, his aim seemingly steady.

I fired again and somehow missed.

Custer howled with delight and invincibility.

Knowing I had one bullet left, I had a decision to make. Should I try to shoot him again or should I kill myself and save the Indians the joy of capturing and torturing me.

Custer took another step toward me.

I got on my knees and lifted my gun.

He lifted his.

I put the barrel of my gun at my temple and said a quick prayer that Custer would get what he deserved, though it galled me I would not be the one to send him to hell. I hesitated to squeeze the trigger and in that instant a piercing pain exploded in my shoulder. By reflex, my arm flew forward as I pulled the trigger. Over the smoking barrel of my pistol, I saw Custer standing there bewildered, first staring at me, then at hole in his chest, then back at me. He took another step toward me, then collapsed at my knees, never to rise again.

I don't know if I killed him or not, but I liked to think I saved the nation by guaranteeing he would never be president. On top of that, I'd lost a brother at Gettysburg where he had fought so I had also avenged the death of John Adams Lomax.

But at that moment, I was running out of time to think about anything other than survival, which was looking grim. I tried to retrieve another bullet from my pocket so I could kill myself. The pain from my shoulder wound was small compared to the terror that I would be captured and tortured. Death seemed a more pleasant opportunity.

"Ciaha!" I cried. "Ciaha!"

I heard one soldier scream "Ciaha!" and more gunshots, but even through the dust I knew that I was one of only a handful still alive. Though I was losing blood and neither seeing nor thinking straight, I knew my time was up. By then, the Indian warriors had started walking among the surviving soldiers, killing them close at hand. Slipping up behind me, one warrior clubbed me on the side of the head. My brain exploded with white light and I tumbled forward, dazed and aching.

I didn't know if I was alive or dead, conscious or not. The noise added to my confusion. If I was dead, I was sure disappointed because it hurt like hell, the pain in my shoulder and in my head. Then I felt a bolt of fire pierce the back of my thigh. I tried to look at what had caused the excruciating pain, but all I saw was white light. I tried to roll over on my back, but rivers of molten lead seemed to shoot through my thigh and hip.

Gradually, the noise faded, save for the shouts of the victorious warriors and the occasional gunshot of a hostile that had found a surviving soldier. Then I heard these sickening thuds like a watermelons being dropped. I raised my head just enough to see warriors walking around, scalping their victims and then smashing their heads with clubs. I figured a smashed skull was better than no head at all so I had at least come out ahead, so to speak, of Dreban and Wolfe.

Closer the warriors came, making certain every white man in their path was dead. The instrument of my death was approaching on moccasined feet. I felt a strong hand grab my wounded shoulder and turn me on my back. I screamed at the ache in my shoulder and the even greater pain in my thigh where I now realized I had been pierced by an arrow. When I landed on my back, the ground pushed the arrow all the way through my thigh. I screamed, both from agony and terror.

My blurry eyes saw the profile of a hulking Indian over me. With one hand, he reached down and grabbed for my collar to pull me up. His other hand held a club, which he raised above his head. My collar slipped from his grip and he grabbed instead the leather thong of the rattlesnake necklace.

Gradually, my eyes began to focus.

The leather of the necklace band slid through his hand until his fingers reached the rattle.

As my eyes focused, I was blinded by the fire of the sun.

Then my captor moved enough that his head blocked out the glare. He shook the rattle on the end of the leather thong. Then he dropped the hand with the club and gently lowered my head to the ground.

At that moment, his face came into full focus. A yellow zigzag crisscrossed his left cheek. I had seen this face and marking before. This was the Indian I had saved from the rattlesnake bite. This was Snakebit!

I thought I might have a chance to survive until he pulled a knife from his scabbard. I feared he was about to scalp me, but he yanked the necklace taut, then cut the leather. He stood up, his legs straddling my torso. He waved the necklace over his head, screaming "Yiiiiaaahaa!"

"Ciaha!" I managed.

He tied the rattle to his wrist, then bent down and picked me up. I ached from my injuries and groaned with his every step. All around me I saw warriors scalping, stripping and mutilating the bodies of the dead. I knew my fate would be worse, that I would be taken to camp and tortured for entertainment.

Reaching his horse, Snakebit threw me over the animal's back, then pulled a water bag from his mount, uncorked it and held it to my lips so I could wet my parched mouth and dry throat. I drank voraciously until he pulled the container away and took a drink himself, then re-tied the bag to his horse. He climbed atop his horse behind me, took the reins and directed his pony through the chaos of the fight's aftermath.

Indians ran up beside Snakebit, shouting at him. I suspect they wanted him to kill me right then, but he just kept riding, gradually walking his pony through the debris of dead men and horses. One warrior ran up and wiped my face with a bloody scalp, but Snakebit kicked him away and nudged his pony into a trot. The farther we rode, the fewer bodies we encountered, though dead cavalrymen were strewn out for a mile or more. I tried not to look at the bodies as we passed as I knew too many of them, but sometimes I couldn't help it. By then, though, the dead soldiers were too mutilated to recognize. The last body I remember passing was that of Mark Kellogg and his mule. Kellogg had written his last dispatch for the *Bismarck Tribune*, and he was there at the death, just as he had written. He apparently had been one of the first killed, his mule falling behind all the other mounts and leaving him alone and defenseless.

Beyond Kellogg's body, Snakebit began to sing. I hoped it was a song of victory, rather than a hymn before he dispatched me to the eternal. As I considered my fate, I prayed for deliverance and I offered thanks that Custer had gotten what he deserved, perhaps at my own hand. The question in my mind was what God thought I deserved. I thought of my life and how little I had made of it, nothing that would make my folks proud. I'd been a vagabond, never setting down roots and trying to become a respectable citizen. Riding on Snakebit's pony toward an unknown fate, I decided that if I survived this, I'd become a better person. I would return to Bismarck and I'd ask Daisy to marry me first thing. Then I'd go to Reverend Truett Byars and have him baptize me in the Missouri River, even if it did endanger all the fish downstream. I intended to make something of myself, if I lived through this journey with Snakebit.

As we rode, the pain in my shoulder, thigh and head dulled into a persistent throb. Then I realized I was making plans for a future when I might not survive the day, not with multiple wounds and me at the mercy of a Sioux warrior. We kept riding what seemed like miles and miles, but I was balanced on the ridge between consciousness and delirium, so I was never certain what was real and what was imagined. Eventually, I heard the sound of gunfire. The noise grew louder until I realized I was among the shooters. I opened my eyes and saw dozens of warriors hiding in the grass and shooting toward the distance.

Snakebit created a commotion when he directed his horse among the fighters. They shouted at him, maybe even cursing him for not killing the captive white man. Snakebit yelled at them and they stopped both screaming and firing. Although the Indians had quit shooting, I could hear the whiz and thud of incoming cavalry bullets. I twisted my head around and opened my eyes, trying to focus on the distance. Through blurry eyes, I made out blue-shirted soldiers firing toward us. It had to be Reno's men or Benteen's soldiers, if he had returned. As the Indians held their fire, Snakebit rode past them and held up his arm over his head, shaking the rattle he had tied to his wrist. Gunfire still answered him and I heard the hiss of bullets flying nearby. Snakebit lowered his hand and grabbed me by the collar and yanked me up where the soldiers could see me. I shook my arm to let them know I was alive. The firing from the soldiers stopped. Apparently, Snakebit had initiated a ceasefire. Perhaps my prayers had been answered. I might survive after all.

Snakebit dismounted and took the reins of his pony and led us toward the den of soldiers. He waved his hand over his head, the rattle buzzing like the snake it had been lifted from. Then he pointed at me and motioned for someone to join him. I could make out the heads of several soldiers peeking over their earthworks, questioning what Snakebit was up to. He shouted something in the language of the Sioux and with a wave of his arm invited a soldier to approach. When no one came, he tied the reins around his wrist and approached me. Gently, he pulled me off and stood me on my feet. Dizzy and weak, I wobbled and nearly collapsed until he grabbed me and put his arm around me. He yelled something again and I saw a man in civilian attire stand up and start walking toward me.

Snakebit advanced cautiously, holding me and leading his horse. Fighting to remain conscious, I took one labored step after another, trying to make it to the safety of the surrounded soldiers. The solitary approaching figure moved slowly, cautiously at first, then began to run toward us. Snakebit stopped and waited for him to reach us.

My rescuer approched me, grabbing me under the arms. "Lomax," he said, "are you okay?"

I recognized the voice of Fred Gerard, the Arikara interpreter. "Better than the rest."

"You look like hell," he said. "Arrows sticking out of you, bloody shoulder and face."

Gerard bent down and slid his shoulder under my good arm and then wrapped his arm around my back, taking the load from Snakebit. Gerard then said something to the warrior, who answered and stepped around in front of me. Snakebit lifted my chin, until I stared in his eyes. He spoke in Sioux, then released my chin and moved to his pony.

Gerard then guided me toward the soldiers. "Do you know who that was?"

"I always called him Snakebit," I said, grimacing with each step.

"That, my friend, was Crazy Horse!"

"The Crazy Horse?"

"That's the one, the fiercest warrior among all the Sioux. He announced that you had saved him and now he had saved you. If you meet again, it will be as enemies."

About halfway between where Crazy Horse stood and the soldiers had entrenched themselves, a soldier got up and raced toward us. He came up grabbed my right arm and lifted it over his shoulder to help Gerard get me the rest of the way back to the others. When he spoke, I recognized him as Peter Thompson, who along with James Watson had saved me from Custer down by the river.

"Custer didn't kill you after all," Thompson said, "but it sure looks like the Indians tried."

"God and Satan's tail saved me," I offered.

"You mean, Crazy Horse, don't you?" Gerard said.

"That was Crazy Horse?" Thompson gasped.

"That's what Gerard says. I just called him Snakebit. It's a long story, boys."

We finally made it to the perimeter where the soldiers lay with their guns pointed toward the Indians. When I looked back, Crazy Horse was still standing there beside his pony.

As I twisted around to wave, Snakebit turned and walked back toward the other warriors.

"That's Crazy Horse," Thompson announced as we passed the line.

A couple soldiers lifted their carbines and fired.

"No," I screamed. "He came under a truce."

"Stop firing," Gerard echoed. "I'll shoot the next man that fires."

No other soldier fired. I twisted about so see if Snakebit had been hit. He just kept walking, his back to us, oblivious to the gunfire. When he disappeared in the distance, the shooting resumed.

"What about the others?" Thompson asked.

"They're dead, all massacred from what I saw."

I don't think Gerard and Thompson believed me as they steered me to Dr. Porter's field hospital in the middle of the defensive perimeter. Porter approached, instructing my two crutches to put me down on the ground once he laid out a blanket for me. Porter grabbed a spare bedroll and unfurled it, tossing it at my feet. Gently, Thompson and Gerard lowered me down.

Porter knelt over me, checking the knot on my head, my bloody face, my shoulder and then my thigh. He smiled. "I think you'll be okay, Lomax. See, I told you I'd treat you."

"It don't matter," I replied. "Custer's dead. I killed him."

Porter glanced up at Thompson and Gerard. "He's delirious," he said, then called for an assistant to bring drinking water.

"We don't have much," replied one of his helpers.

As I lay there, Porter pulled a scalpel from his medicine bag and sliced open my right pants leg from the hem past the embedded arrow. Then he put the scalpel aside, grabbed the arrow at my thigh, then snapped the shaft, handing me the piece with the iron point. He lifted my knee and yanked the shaft's feathered end out of my thigh. I grimaced and realized the firing had picked up. We remained under siege. The doctor stepped away and returned with a medicinal bottle. He pressed the mouth of the bottle to the wound. What felt like hot lava drained into the gash. I screamed, then passed out.

It was dark when I came to. My throat was parched and my stomach growled from hunger. I started to reach for my leg with my right hand, but my arm was bound in a sling. I explored my wounded right leg with my left hand and felt a bandage over the tender, throbbing wound. A bandage had been wrapped around my head as well. Occasional gunshots shattered the calm, though I was never certain if the threats were real or imagined by jumpy sentries who fired at ghosts. Down the bluff and across the river, I could hear the shouts of the Sioux and Cheyenne as they danced and celebrated their victory to the ponderous beat of their drums, rejoicing in their triumph and likely planning to annihilate the rest of us come morning. Their joy was dampened only by the occasional wails of squaws who had lost men in battle.

"Water," I called out, but my voice was raspy and barely above a whisper.

Someone I didn't recognize came over and patted me on the forehead. "None left. We're all thirsty. Wounded will get water first when we get some." Then the stranger moved on.

Thirst was driving me crazy so I tried to listen to the sound of the hushed voices around me. The best I could put together, Major Reno and his men had attacked the Indian village, only to be repulsed and driven back across the river into the bluffs were I now recovered. Benteen and his men had arrived with the pack train in time to save Reno's command and set up a defensive perimeter. Together Reno's and Benteen's companies were able to hold off the attack. Porter had set up his hospital in the center of the ring, hiding his charges on the ground behind dead mules and horses to give a little protection. Thanks to the pack train, the survivors of the Seventh Cavalry had adequate food and ammunition for a long stand. The problem was water. We had none. Everyone else was suffering from thirst like me.

Occasionally, I thought I heard Benteen and Reno arguing, but I could not be sure. Sometime during the night Benteen strode to the hospital, looking for me. Finding me, he squatted down.

"Water," I said.

"We have none. Maybe we can get some later, Lomax."

I groaned.

"You're the last one to see Custer. He's abandoned us just like he did Captain Elliott back at the Washita."

I shook my head. "He's dead. I killed him."

Benteen scoffed. "That son of a bitch is too lucky and ornery to be killed by someone as dumb as you. You're delirious."

"Maybe so," I said, "but I'm alive and he ain't. They were all massacred."

His hatred ran so deep for Custer that he couldn't believe the general had died and gone to hell, much less that a man of my talents had put him in the grave. It was more accident than plan, the fatal shot, I admit but I was due a little credit for the service I had done for the nation.

"I hear Crazy Horse himself delivered you to us. How'd you come to be so lucky that a savage would save you and let all the others die, if it's as you say?"

Benteen would never have believed my long story about Snakebit. "We went to college together," I replied.

"You're hallucinating, Lomax," he said, standing up and retreating back to his command post, considering my information worthless.

After that I fell in and out of consciousness until dawn, when I awoke to the touch of a cool hand against my forehead. I opened my eyes and saw the doctor. "Morning, Lomax," he said calmly. "I was just checking you. I can't tell for certain, hot as it's been, but I don't think you have a fever. That's good."

"Water," I said.

He grimaced. "We don't have any and Major Reno won't let us open any of the supplies that might provide some relief, like the canned peaches and other goods. He seems to be more delusional than you. But stay tough. I think Captain Benteen is going to order a charge to the river for water. You're gonna survive." He moved from me to the next patient, shortly before the Indians resumed their attack.

Later that morning, several soldiers volunteered to run to the river for water. With a squad of men driving the Indians from the ravine leading down to the river, a dozen or more cavalrymen scampered down the bluffs carrying all the canteens they could. They returned with water, just enough to keep us all from going crazy from thirst but not enough to eliminate the craving all together. Consequently, several soldiers made unauthorized attempts to bring back more water, a couple dying in the process. Years after the fact, I learned that several of the survivors, including Peter Thompson, had earned Congressional Medal of Honors for their bravery in retrieving water for us. So, Thompson had saved my life twice at the Little Bighorn.

It was another hot, dry day, the only relief from the sun coming from solitary clouds passing overhead and giving us blessed but brief shade. As the soldiers exchanged gunfire with the Indians throughout the day, I wondered if I had survived the assault on Custer's hill just to die with the others on Reno's hill. By late afternoon, the gunfire tapered off and our lookouts noticed a dust cloud and then smoke from the direction of the hostiles' encampment. Some brave soldiers worked their way to the edge of the bluff to spy on the Indians, who had fired the grass to screen their departure. Excited, the soldiers returned to our perimeter and announced the Indians were leaving. More went to look and came back reporting an Indian caravan stretching two miles or more with six or seven thousand warriors and their families plus many more horses. It had been one of the largest gatherings of hostile Indians in the history of the frontier.

Finally, Reno let the camp open some of the stores from the pack train and we had a good, filling meal and plenty of water as men led mules down to the river to fill kegs for our use. Gradually, with our thirsts quenched, our bellies full and our wounds recovering, we felt we might survive after all. We had a restful night's sleep and awoke the next morning filled with a decent breakfast and with hope that we would survive after all.

Then we saw a distant dust cloud to the north. We looked at one another and grimaced. The warriors were returning with reinforcements for the kill!

Chapter Thirty-One

Everyone panicked, dreading another siege. Officers ordered some soldiers to set up defensive perimeters again and distribute ammunition, then commanded others to fetch water in whatever they could from the river so we would have an adequate supply for another standoff. Being among the wounded, I propped myself up on my good elbow and watched. The morning strangled us with a stifling heat, and a horrid stench permeated the air from the corpses of soldiers and decaying horses and mules. Everyone was skittish and scared. If the Sioux and Cheyenne didn't kill us, then the heat and the stench would. We waited and listened. Then we heard a noise that gave us hope.

A distant bugle call reached us.

"Hurrah," yelled the men.

Captain Benteen doused our optimism when he yelled, "Stay on alert, men! It may be the hostiles playing a trick on us."

Damn wet blanket, Benteen was! We waited and waited some more.

I sat up and looked around the makeshift entrenchment. Beyond the hospital circle, the surviving cavalry horses and mule were staked or penned in a rope corral in the shallow basin with the wounded. Beyond us and the stock, soldiers scooped out holes with knives, tin plates and their fingers when nothing else was available and then hid behind a makeshift breastwork of discarded saddles, packs, empty ammunition crates, dead mounts, and sacks of beans, corn and oats.

As I inspected our improvised fortress, Dr. Porter knelt at my side. "You better?"

I nodded. "Still a little lightheaded."

"That's not unusual from the loss of blood," he said, as he began to check my leg and bandages. "We must remove the dead animals or the putrid air will lead to infection."

I waited for him to unbandage all my wounds. "How am I doing?"

"It depends," Porter answered. "If you're talking about your wounds, I think everything is fine. If you're talking about the army, I don't know." He washed my thigh wound with water and covered it with two layers of lint, then a piece of oil cloth he tied with a kerchief.

"What do you mean?"

"When you arrived, I thought you were hallucinating about killing Custer. If Custer is dead, you are a potential embarrassment to the cavalry if they have to explain any debacle. First of all, you shouldn't have even been on this expedition. It was rumored Custer planned to kill you. Second, if you saw what you say you did, they may want to dispatch you just like Custer did to prevent further embarrassment."

"I said what I saw, Doctor."

"Then you best not say anything more about it, especially if this is the army approaching."

"So the truth doesn't count for anything?"

"Not in this army, not in these political times."

I nodded as Porter rewrapped my bandaged arm. "Thanks, Doc."

He patted me on my good shoulder and moved on to his next patient. I looked around and guessed I was one of some fifty wounded men, surrounded by the same number of dead horses and mules.

It seemed like forever before lookouts shouted that Custer was approaching, not the Indians, and we were saved. I knew better, but didn't say anything, heeding Porter's warning. When the lookouts realized the horses were mixed rather than uniform by company, they understood this was not Custer after all. It turned out to be the Montana Column under Colonel Gibbon and accompanied by General Terry.

As the column neared, the men began to cheer, though their exuberance was tempered by the mystery over what had happened to Custer and his men. I could have told them, but I kept quiet. The smiles on Benteen's and Reno's faces wilted as they greeted the approaching commanders. Gibbon and Terry rode stone-faced, the clench of their jaws and the narrowness of their eyes confirming what I already knew.

"Custer and his men are dead and mutilated," Gibbon announced for all to hear.

Soldiers gasped and looked at one another skeptically. No one could believe the son of a bitch was truly dead, even if he deserved it. Worse, though, were all the other soldiers—their friends—who had died with him. Some men sobbed, others cursed and some just stood with blank looks on their faces.

With the arrival of Gibbon's column, the focus changed to what had happened to Custer's troops and to preparing to move the wounded back to Fort Abraham Lincoln. Parties went to Custer hill to identify the dead and collect their belongings, while others stayed with us to bury our own dead, to move rotting animals away from the wounded and to build litters so that the wounded could start the long journey back to civilization. Everyone was anxious to leave this horrible place and get away from the stench of death and the thousands of green flies that had descended upon on us like a plague, adding to our misery.

At one point during the afternoon, Captain Benteen came to my blanket. "You were right, all along. The bastard is dead."

"I don't know what you're talking about, Captain," I responded.

"When the Indian brought you in, you said you'd killed Custer. Why else would the warrior not have killed you?"

"I must've been delirious, Captain."

Benteen shook his head at me. "You're hiding something, Lomax. That's for certain."

"A man can't be expected to think straight when he's got a knot on his head, a bullet in his shoulder and an arrow in his leg. I was hallucinating."

As Benteen turned to march away, I knew he didn't believe me. Shortly after Benteen departed, Fred Gerard came by.

"You doing okay?" he asked.

I nodded.

"It's true then that you were the last white man to see Custer alive."

"I must have been hallucinating," I said.

Grinning, he stroked his chin. "It's wise to deny everything from now on, Lomax. The army'll try to point blame somewhere. You don't want to be in the middle of that pissing match."

"You're not the first to tell me that."

"It's wise to listen," he said, then went about his business.

Toward dusk the soldiers that had ridden to Custer hill returned, all grim and sullen as they grappled with what they had seen. They would go back the next day to bury the remaining dead. Word was soon passed that Custer had a bullet wound in the chest and one in the head, but was otherwise un-mutilated. Other than him, nearly everyone else had been scalped and disfigured in ways beyond description. Names of the known dead slowly spread around camp.

Peter Thompson and James Watson, my friends from Company

C, came by to tell me the news. I knew it was bad by the dark expressions on their faces.

"Jimmy Russell's dead," Thompson said.

I grimaced. The little Texan was the one who gave me bullets to assassinate Custer when no one else would. I liked him, even if he was a Texan.

"John Lewis, too," Watson added.

I liked him, too, the Pennsylvania boy.

"As for Sergeant Finkle, we're not certain," Thompson said. "Some found a body with a head smashed in. Some said it was Finkle, some not."

"I saw the body," Watson interjected, "and I think they're wrong, but I couldn't study it long. It was too sickening."

"Thanks for letting me know. Russell, Lewis and Finkle were fine, decent men," I said.

Thompson nodded. "If we'd made bets before we left Fort Lincoln, I'd've wagered you'd be the one to die on this expedition, what with all your charm and all your enemies. Is it true Crazy Horse saved you because you shot Custer? That's the rumor going around."

"You can't believe everything you hear, fellows."

"I knew it was true," Watson said to Thompson.

"I didn't say it was true," I pleaded.

"You didn't deny it, either," Thompson added.

"You fellows are going to get me in trouble, so quit guessing what happened to Custer."

Watson smiled. "We're not guessing because we know you can weasel out of anything."

Grimacing, I feigned pain as I didn't want to say something that might dig me a deeper hole. "I gotta rest," I said, "so these wounds don't drag me down."

"If George Armstrong Custer couldn't bring you down," Thompson said, "a few scratches like that won't either."

With so many rumors about me circulating, I was not surprised that evening when I was visited by Captain Benteen, Major Reno, Colonel Gibbon and General Terry. They walked up and Benteen introduced me to the two commanders as Dr. Porter stood behind them listening

"We've got some questions for you," Gibbon said.

"You appear to be the last white man to see Custer alive," Terry added.

I shrugged.

"Why is it you are on this expedition, when you aren't listed on the civilian payroll?" Terry continued.

"You need to ask General Custer."

"He's dead," Gibbon responded. "Why did you accompany the expedition?"

"General Custer wanted to kill me."

"Now why," Terry wanted to know, "would Custer try to kill a nobody like you?"

"He thought I stood in the way of him becoming president."

Gibbon and Terry looked at each other, shaking their heads.

"Is it true you killed Custer?" Gibbon asked. "Is that why Crazy Horse saved you?"

"You'll have to ask Crazy Horse about that."

"Lomax, isn't it?" said Terry.

I nodded.

"Well, Lomax, Crazy Horse is not here, but you are," Terry continued. "Now tell me about Custer."

"He got killed because he split up his troops so fewer would be around to witness him shooting me. When he ran into the hostiles, he wasn't prepared."

"Some say you bragged about shooting Custer when you reached here," Gibbon said.

"I was delirious."

"I think you're hallucinating right now," Gibbon said.

"This is getting us nowhere," Terry added.

"If General Bluster hadn't been out to get me, none of this would've happened, Generals. You can believe it or not, but that's the truth. He had a vendetta against me."

"Why?" Gibbon wanted to know.

"I guess because I told him I'd turned Republican."

The officers shook their heads.

"Keep him under guard until we can get this sorted out," Terry said.

"Ciaha," I said.

Porter stepped up to Gibbon and Terry. "Generals," he said, "Lomax is a patient of mine. I request that you leave him under my watch. He sustained three wounds in the fight with the hostiles and needs care without additional stress."

Terry looked at Gibbon, then nodded. "Very well." They turned around and left.

"Thanks, Doc," I offered.

"Don't answer any more questions, Lomax. We just need to get you out of here and away from the army."

"Why do you care, Doc?"

"You were dragged into something not of your own making. The truth won't matter to the army, not now, not with a disaster like this to explain." Porter shook his head and walked away to tend to others.

As the day ended, I realized the Democratic National Convention must be in session in St. Louis. I didn't know who they would nominate, but I knew one man they wouldn't. I fell asleep proud of my contribution to American history, even if I couldn't talk about it.

We spent another full day on the field of battle while some soldiers prepared for the return to Bismarck and others went to bury the remaining dead on Custer Hill, a task made more complicated by the lack of shovels and picks. It was late afternoon when the burial party returned. They had found two survivors, a horse named "Comanche" that had been ridden by the commander of Company I and a mule. I didn't think a thing of it until Dr. Porter approached.

"We're leaving this evening, Lomax. Do you think you can ride?"

"Maybe," I answered. "I'm still stiff and sore."

"It might be easier on you than riding a litter. Too, the mule they brought back from the battlefield may be yours."

I sat up, my head swimming from the sudden movement, then gradually returning to normal. I hoped it was true.

"Stay here," Porter instructed, "and I'll see if I can have him brought over."

Barely had he spoken than Pete Thompson sauntered up, leading a mule.

"Look who we found, Lomax. Your buddy, Ciaha! The best named mule in the United States Army," Thompson yelled.

Porter smiled. "See if you can mount him."

Gingerly, I stood up and balanced, then took an awkward step toward Ciaha. My saddle was still astride his back. About the only thing different was an ugly red scab of a scar across his neck where a bullet had creased his spine during the fight and left him temporarily paralyzed. That wound had saved his life.

I hobbled over to him, rubbing his neck, then trying to mount. I was still weak, but I managed to haul myself aboard in spite of the pain in my leg and shoulder. It was almost as hard to dismount as it had been to get on him to begin with. I stumbled back to my blanket and collapsed on the ground, exhausted from the exertion. I wasn't sure if I could manage it or not until I saw a couple soldiers place a wounded trooper on a litter mounted between two mules. One brayed and bucked, then dumped the injured fellow on the ground. I decided I would take my chances atop Ciaha.

Thompson offered me a drink from a water pail, then laughed. "I've never seen a guy so poorly dressed."

I looked at what was left of my whorehouse suit. My shirt was bloody and torn. My pants were shredded beneath the arrow hole. My jacket on the ground beside the blanket was stained and ripped in several places. I realized I still wore my shoulder harness. Without my pistol, which was somewhere up on Custer hill, it was useless. I shucked the shoulder harness as Thompson left to return to his assigned duties.

A while later Porter came around and helped me atop Ciaha, rolling up my blanket and handing it to me, then my coat. "You may need these if it cools down."

About eight o'clock that evening, we started the caravan on the first leg of the trip back to Fort Lincoln. As I understood it, we were to follow the Little Bighorn to its confluence with the Bighorn where the *Far West* awaited to transport the wounded to civilization. I was still frail from my wounds and wobbled like a drunk in the saddle, but the litter mules kept balking and dumping their injured on the ground. Without enough mules to go around, some injured were carried on hand litters by other soldiers, who tired out and had to stop and change the litter bearers too often for anyone's comfort. Between the mule and hand-carried litters, progress was so slow that the caravan stopped after a couple hours and the soldiers fashioned Indian-style travois to drag on the ground. The wounded moaned or wept from the jolting ride over a night trail. It was a tedious journey over two days and nights across rugged terrain. Sometime late in the night of the final day we topped an outcropping and could see below the *Far West*, moored on the east bank of the Bighorn River. The river bank was illuminated by dozens of pine torches the crew had lit to make sure we could find the steamboat in the dark as General Terry had sent word that the wounded would be coming.

The final obstacle between us and the comfort of the steamboat was the rugged slope down to the river. Though some insisted on immediately starting the animals down the slope with the wounded, Porter balked, complaining that the animals were too tired to descend the rugged slope in the dark. The officers finally agreed and sent soldiers down the slope to bring back some of the torches to light the way. Then we began the slow final descent toward the *Far West*. Ciaha never stumbled and carried me safely to the banks of the Bighorn River.

With the advance word of the injured, Captain Grant Marsh had put his men to work cutting grass and piling it a foot deep on the main deck, then covering it with tarps so the men would have soft places to lie. I was ignored, not being a cavalryman, and feared I would be left behind as they finished loading the other wounded. They even led the wounded horse Comanche up the gangplank to a stall they had built for him at the stern near the paddlewheel.

I rode Ciaha up to the gangplank as well but was stopped before I could maneuver him onto the deck.

"What the hell do you think you're doing?" asked a deck hand.

"My mule survived the battle just like Comanche," I said.

The deckhand shook his head. "Only word I got was to let one horse on."

Some of the wounded saw what was happening and began to chant. "Ciaha! Ciaha! Ciaha!" they cried with their raspy voices.

"What's this?" the deckhand asked.

Dr. Porter approached. "Ciaha is the mule's name. You might say he is a mascot of the Seventh Cavalry. Let him aboard."

The deckhand relented and several of the wounded men cheered. I pulled my blanket and coat from Ciaha, dismounted and let the deckhand lead the mule to the back of the boat. I lay down on the tarp and waited. Shortly after noon that day, Captain Grant Marsh ordered the lines pulled in and we started on the 700-mile river journey back to Bismarck.

As the *Far West* pulled away from the shore, I realized how lucky I was to be alive. I vowed I'd do something to become a better man, settle down and do decent work, not whorehouse or saloon work, something a man could be proud to tell his children about. I'd start by marrying Daisy and taking her somewhere decent and warm, where winters weren't so overwhelming and Indians weren't so many. I decided I'd let the Reverend Truett Byars baptize me in the muddy waters of the Missouri and maybe give me some direction in life. Granted, I didn't have it in me to be a preacher because my mind couldn't unwrap the mysteries of religion or philosophy, but I vowed to try something decent.

As the *Far West* paddled back east, I thought about how little I'd accomplished after heading west from Arkansas after the War Between the States. I'd left behind LouAnne Burke, my first sweetheart, for fear she might get hurt by men carrying a grudge against me after the war. I felt bad that I'd never as much as written her a letter, but then I hadn't managed to write more than one or two letters to my momma and pa since the war. I'd ridden with Jesse James a spell, worked on an cattle drive to Abilene and hunted buffalo, but I hadn't accomplished much other than just survive. As the landscape passed by, I figured I'd change for the better. That's what I thought, though that's not how it turned out.

The *Far West* made good time or as good as possible in a fast flowing river no deeper than a man's little finger. We had to stop on occasion to chop and load wood to feed the three boilers and two engines that powered the 190-foot vessel. Each day my pain diminished and my endurance grew. To strengthen my wounded leg, I marched back and forth from one side of the steamboat to the other. It took but a dozen steps as the vessel was barely thirty-three feet wide.

Dr. Porter checked on me regularly and made sure I got grub to eat. He remained a friend throughout the expedition and worried more about my fate than I did. I figured if I could survive both Adobe Walls and the Little Bighorn, I could outlast any army bureaucrat that tried to bring charges against me for killing Custer. I'd just plead self-defense and run like hell as soon as I could get away. The farther we got from the Little Bighorn, the farther I got from the officers that might try to scapegoat me. Colonel Gibbon and General Terry had stayed with the expedition to try to run down the marauding Indians. It would take months for them to herd all the Sioux and Cheyenne back to the reservation. The army was not nearly as efficient as Captain Marsh and the *Far West* as he made a record run of 710 miles in just fifty-four hours, traveling day and night and doing so without a mishap. The only miracle greater than that return trip to Fort Abraham Lincoln was my survival from the carnage on Custer hill.

As we neared Bismarck, Captain Marsh draped the boat's derrick and jack staff in black and lowered the flag to half mast. As we turned the final bend in the Missouri River that night and spotted Bismarck up ahead, Marsh alerted the town and fort with long blasts of his steam whistle. At eleven o'clock the night of July fifth, we tied up at the Bismarck dock. I figured we would stop at the fort to unload the wounded first, but officers had to reach the telegraph office to report the massacre to their superiors in St. Paul and Chicago. Barely had we tied up and the officers had bolted for the telegraph office than a crowd of curious onlookers gathered, including Clement Lounsberry, editor of the *Bismarck Tribune*. He came on board to interview witnesses. He strode up to me, introduced himself and asked my name. Before I could answer, Dr. Porter joined us.

"Clement," he said, "I've got some bad news for you. Mark Kellogg died with some 250 others."

The editor grimaced and lowered his head. "That could've been me," he mumbled, "but my wife got sick and I sent him in my place." He sighed and shook his head, then looked at me. "What did you see?"

Porter put his hand on my shoulder and addressed Lounsberry. "He didn't see anything. Let me take care of him, Clement, and then I'll tell you what I know. You might see if any of the survivors want to talk." Porter yanked me by my sore arm and pulled me away from the editor, who went to pester others.

"This is your chance, Lomax," Porter said. "I'll escort you off before we move to the fort. You can stay in my office, rest up, clean up and then get out of town before the army knows you've disappeared."

As he spoke, a couple soldiers came from the stern of the boat leading Comanche toward the gangplank. "Make way for the sole survivor of General Custer's battle with Sitting Bull and the Sioux," cried one of the handlers.

"Ciaha," I said, grabbing my coat and blanket. "I can't leave him."

"Fine," answered Porter. He escorted me to the back of the boat. Ciaha perked up when he saw me. I put a halter over his head while Porter threw my saddle on his back and secured it. We marched back down the deck of the *Far West*, then down the gangplank through the murmuring crowd.

"Did the mule survive, too?" somebody yelled.

"Nope," cried Porter. "He had nothing to do with the battle."

The crowd turned their attention back to Comanche and let us pass without further bother.

Porter gave me instructions how to get to his office, then told me he would go to the fort to unload and treat the wounded and that it might be a few days before he could return. But I was to stay low and out of sight to avoid any complications, if the army missed me. Then he turned around and went back to the *Far West*.

Rather than go to his place, I decided I would head out to Whiskey Point and the Bloody Bucket, see if I could propose to Daisy that night, even if I looked like hell. I figured if I was going to let Reverend Byars baptize me, I would use the occasion for a bath as well. The ride seemed to take forever, though it was only a brief thirty minutes. I thought about how I would ask Daisy to marry me, but I couldn't find the right words for something so special.

When I reached the Bloody Bucket, I tied my mule outside and strode in. A half-dozen patrons, including a single soldier, were drinking. As I walked in, Claude Armstrong looked up from the bar and did a double take. "Well, I'll be damned, if it isn't H.H. Lomax." He studied me. "By the look of your clothes, you've been tending bar in a rougher place than this."

"Where's Daisy?" I asked.

"She's moved to the Cosmopolitan Hotel in Bismarck, Room Twenty. Doesn't work here anymore."

"Moved on to a better clientele," I said.

"You might say that," Armstrong replied. "I sold your horse as I couldn't afford to feed him, but your tack is out in the shed and your valise is in the back room. I can't afford to hire you back, business really dropped after your arrest and after the Seventh Cavalry rode out."

"No matter, Armstrong. I'm planning on getting married and doing decent work."

"Good luck, Lomax. You never struck me as the decent type."

I raced to the back room, got my valise and returned to Ciaha. I led him around the back, swapping the cavalry saddle and bridle for my own. I returned to Bismarck where the streets were filled with people sharing the news of Custer's demise.

As I rode toward Porter's office, one man grabbed my bad leg and yanked at it, sending a lightning bolt of pain up my spine. "Did you hear about Custer? He's dead!"

"That's what I hear," I said. "Such a shame. Ciaha!"

Chapter Thirty-Two

I found a bed in a back room of the doctor's office and went to sleep. I slept well past noon, then arose and glimpsed myself in the mirror. I looked like hell, hair shaggy, whiskers verging on a beard, patches of dirt and dried blood on my head. My shirt was filthy, my pants dirty with one leg shredded. If I had proposed to Daisy the previous night, I wouldn't have blamed her for turning me down. I picked up my valise from the floor, plopped it on the bed and opened it up, half expecting everything of value to have been stolen in my absence. My riding clothes were there, my gun belt and revolver, my boots at the bottom, a couple pairs of socks, some long johns and, most surprisingly, a roll of bills from my pay both from Miss Medusa's and the Bloody Bucket. I was missing my hat and that was about all. I repacked my valise and headed out the door, going to Coner's Tonsorial Parlor, where Douglas Wolfe, Brian Dreban and I had gone for a trim before heading to the Black Hills.

I walked in carrying my valise. "Welcome, sir. I'm W.H. Coner, the best barber not only in Bismarck, but also these United States. You look like you could use my services."

"I want the works, Coner. Hot bath, shave, haircut, shampoo and some of your best tonic to give me a fresh smell."

"That's fifty-cents for the bath, seventy-five if you want hot water. Then fifteen cents for a shave, thirty-five for the shampooing and thirty-five more for the haircut."

"I want a hot bath and all the rest," I answered.

"No offense, sir, but you don't look like you can afford it. It comes to a dollar sixty."

I sat my valise on the barber chair, opened it up and showed him my roll of money. "There's enough there to cover it and for me to give you a tip to boot."

"Yes, sir," he answered. "I'll start heating the water now if you want to follow me."

I carried my valise in the back room. He pulled a curtain behind us and put some water on a potbellied stove that he had let burn down. He picked up some chunks of firewood from the floor, opened the door and shoved the wood in. He grabbed a newspaper and began to fan the embers so the flame would take to the wood. I stripped down, handing him my coat. "Shove it in the stove," I said. "These clothes are beyond saving." He fed my coat into the mouth of the stove. As I continued to undress, I handed him my shirt, my pants and my union suit until I stood there dressed like the day I was born.

Coner eyed me closely, taking in the bandaged shoulder and leg. "You ain't running from the law, are you? Looks like you've had a run-in with somebody."

"Got in a scrape with some Indians, that's all. It's nothing to do with the law."

He offered me the newspaper. "It's this week's *Tribune*," he said. "Came out yesterday before the horrible news arrived."

"What news?"

"You didn't hear about Custer and his cavalry? They were massacred by Sitting Bull and Crazy Horse at a place called Little Bighorn. I can't believe you haven't heard."

"No," I answered, "I just got back in town last night late. I saw the commotion but was too tired to inquire."

"It's horrible, it is. I guess I gave him the last haircut he ever had, a few days before he rode out against the hostiles. He wanted it cut shorter because he said he was riding with a skunk that had been known to pull pranks on fellows with long hair. Course, his hair was thinning all around and looking a little scraggly. I did the best I could with what he had."

"Don't suppose he was cutting it to keep the Indians from scalping him, do you?"

"Oh, no," Coner answered. "He was figuring on whipping the hostiles and then running for president of the United States."

"I guess the Sioux and Cheyenne must've been Republicans."

Coner laughed.

I climbed into the tub and leaned against the cold side. I lifted my head and realized the general himself was staring at me from a photograph tacked to the wall.

"Where'd you get that?" I asked, pointing at the general's likeness.

"The *Tribune* gave away chromographs of General Custer for a year's subscription. Didn't know where to put it so I settled for above the tub to inspire customers."

"I guess it'd scare away intruders and rodents in the night," I said. "Mind if I read your paper, even if it doesn't have all the Custer news?"

"Certainly, I subscribe for myself as well as my customers."

Coner gave me the paper, and I held it up so I didn't have to look at the son of a bitch on the wall. I learned on page one that local resident Joseph C. Dodge had been killed by Indians in the Black Hills a few weeks earlier. I sighed, wondering if he had lost his head like Dreban and Wolfe. Then I read on page two that Samuel Tilden, not George Armstrong Custer, had been nominated by the Democrats for president. I lowered my paper until I could see the chromograph and stuck my tongue out at the general. Shortly, Coner poured a pail of warm water into the tub. As he heated additional water, I enjoyed the bath even more. He offered me a slab of lye soap and I began to wash away layers of dirt. If only it could've washed away the memory of Custer and the awful sights I saw during the massacre, I would've felt better.

Between a couple customers, Coner came in and shampooed me in the tub, then gave me fresh towels. I dried off, dressed in my clothes from the valise and stepped out front to take the barber's chair. Coner started to work on me with the scissors.

"Give me a haircut that'll last a while and shave all the whiskers off as well."

I watched in the mirror as my grizzled appearance disappeared beneath his scissors, the lather and his razor. As he clipped away at hair and whiskers, he stared at me and nodded. "I've seen you somewhere before, haven't I?"

"Last summer me and my partners came in before we to the Black Hills."

Coner nodded. "Oh, yeah, you're the brother of the Lomax fellow that shaved Wild Bill Hickok's head and sold his hair to a wigmaker. How's your brother?"

"Dead. The Sioux gave him a haircut all the way down to the shoulders."

"I guess nothing good comes to folks who mess with Wild Bill. Fact is, I hear he's in Deadwood now. Sure it wasn't Wild Bill that scalped your brother?"

"I'm sure."

"Well, my condolences for your loss."

When he was done, he slapped enough tonic on me to float the *Far West*. I paid him two dollars and walked out of Coner's Tonsorial

Parlor smelling as fragrant as a flower shop. I felt like newly minted money, even if it was counterfeit, as I marched back to Porter's place. I exchanged my valise for the haversack and Bible. I took a big breath, nodded my approval at the new me in the mirror and marched outside and down the street to the Cosmopolitan Hotel.

If I remembered correctly, she was staying in room twenty. I marched past the desk and the inattentive clerk, finding her room at the end of the hall. Taking another big breath, I knocked on the door and stood there grinning with expectation, hoping she wasn't with a customer. I knew my life was about to change.

The door cracked open and I saw an eye inspecting me. Then the door flung open and Daisy stood there as pretty as a ribbon on a puppy. Her hand flew to her mouth and then she started crying. "Lomax," she cried, "you survived. When I heard the horrible news last night, I just knew you were dead." Stepping to me, she flung her arms around me and kissed me hard on the cheek. "Come in," she said, "and tell me everything."

I stepped inside and held up the haversack she had sewn for me. "I'd never made it without this, not to mention the revolver you slipped me."

"Oh, I am so happy," she said. "Truett will be thrilled. You know he's prayed for you every day." She pointed to a chair, where a man's trousers lay across the seat and a shirt was hanging over the back. "Let me move this so you can sit down and tell me everything."

She draped the pants over the edge of the bed and placed the shirt atop it, then she sat on the mattress, her smile as sincere as I had hoped. "Oh, Lomax, our prayers have been answered, Truett's and mine, and he'll be so pleased when he returns."

"I need to thank him, too. On top of that, I've near decided to let him baptize me."

"That's wonderful, Lomax," she squealed.

Her voice was as sincere as a child's laugh and her eyes were as soft as a summer cloud. I knew I would enjoy spending the rest of my life with her. "There's something I'd like to say," I began, nervous that I'd muddle the words and frighten her away.

"Oh, Lomax, these last few days have been just wonderful with so many blessings falling into my life. You returning and our marriage."

It was like she was reading my mind and knew what to say so I wouldn't have to worry about my words.

"The only thing that's made me as happy as your return, Lomax, is marrying Truett. We were hitched on July Fourth. I only wish you could've been here. I'd've let you give me away." She held up her left hand and showed me a wedding band. "Isn't it beautiful?"

I nodded. "It is beautiful, just like you," I said.

"Who'd thought I'd wind up a minister's wife, Lomax? Not me, not a working girl like me. And Truett's starting a church here. We'll live in a little parsonage when it's completed."

Struggling to hide my disappointment, "I thought you'd make a good wife, so much so that I'd've asked you if Truett hadn't beaten me to it."

Daisy jumped up from the bed and rushed to hug me. "You're so sweet, Lomax. What was it you wanted to ask me?"

I stammered and looked at my feet, lifting the haversack as if I could hide behind it. My gaze fell on the rip from the arrow. I offered her the haversack. "This and the Bible stopped an arrow at the fight with the hostiles. Do you think you could sew it up?"

She took it from me. "Why sure, Lomax, I'd be glad to." She pulled out the Bible and offered it to me. "You'll need to take this."

"No, keep it until I return. Show your husband the pages the arrow damaged. Tell him it reached all the way to Psalms."

"Give me a day, Lomax, and I'll have it for you. Come by at noon day after tomorrow and I'll have it sewn up. Then Truett and I will take you to lunch."

"Sure, Mrs. Byars," I said. "That will be grand." I stood up and walked to her side, kissing her on the cheek. "You will make a wonderful preacher's wife."

"And Truett will look forward to baptizing you," she replied as she saw me to the door. "We can talk about that at lunch."

I smiled, took her hand and kissed it. I turned and walked down the hall as quickly as I could, praying I'd not run into the Reverend Truett Byars. God answered my prayers, and I made it to the street. I never returned for my haversack, my Bible or my baptism.

I strode to the nearest saloon, purchased two bottles of whiskey and ate a couple boiled eggs on the bar for patrons. Then I walked back to the doctor's office, where I realized I'd left Ciaha tied to a post without feeding and watering him properly. Ciaha was hungry and sullen when I untied him. He snapped at my hand, causing me to drop and break one of the liquor bottles. "You're right," I said. "I shouldn't have ignored you for a woman." I took him to the livery stable and paid to have him combed down, watered and fed for two days.

When that was done, I returned to Dr. Porter's office and retired to the back room, where I pulled off my boots, threw myself on the mattress, uncorked the remaining whiskey bottle and drank myself into oblivion. I awoke the next morning with a throbbing head and a mouth as dry as a millionaire's tears. I didn't know what I would do now that my marriage was over before it began. I considered going to Deadwood and confronting Wild Bill about starting all those vile rumors. He might kill me as a result, but I no longer cared in my drunken depression. Then it might be that I should just head back to Arkansas, see the folks, see if LouAnne Burke was still available and just marry her. Of course, I didn't know if the folks back home even cared to see me. But the more I thought about it, I figured they would at least like to know that I hadn't died at the Little Bighorn. What didn't strike my whiskey-addled mind at the moment was that they didn't know I'd ever ridden with the Seventh Cavalry to begin with.

After my head was clear enough to think and my gait steady enough to walk, I put on my boots and headed to the telegraph office. I stopped at a mercantile to buy me a hat so I could tug it low over my eyes and perhaps keep from seeing Reverend Byars or prevent him from recognizing me. All the talk was about the massacre of Custer and his men, as people passed along or embellished the same information over and over again. From what I heard in the mercantile, the telegraph office had been sending information continuously over the wire since the *Far West* had first brought the news to town. I wasn't sure I could even get a telegram back to Arkansas, but I went to the office to try.

A dozen men loitered outside, awaiting any new information. I moved past them and marched into the anteroom, where three other men were leaning against the counter, whispering to each other. The tippety-taptap of the telegraph echoed through the small office.

"I need to send a telegram," I said and the three men moved from the counter. I stepped up as two clerks wearing green shades came to assist.

My jaw dropped!

I was seeing ghosts.

I rubbed my eyes.

The ghosts still stood there reflecting my astonishment.

It was Brian Dreban and Douglas Wolfe.

Perhaps the drinking had warped my brain so that I couldn't think straight.

I crawled over the counter and jumped down, then went to Dreban. I grabbed him by the jaw and tried to yank his head off his shoulders. It didn't budge. I moved to Wolfe and grabbed him by the ears, tugging on his head. It stayed secure.

"I thought you were dead," I cried out.

"We thought you'd abandoned us," Dreban said.

"Figured you'd skipped out with our gold," Wolfe added.

I was bewildered. It didn't make sense.

"We don't have time to talk now, Lomax," said Dreban.

"There's a lot of news coming out of Bismarck with the Custer disaster. We were sent here to relieve the local telegraphers," Wolf informed me.

"Come back at six o'clock and we have an hour for supper so we can get caught up," Dreban said.

"Believe me, I'll be back," I informed them.

Stunned at the discovery, I left and went back to the doctor's office. Porter was there when I walked in.

"Almost didn't recognize you, Lomax, with clean clothes and a scalping," he said. "You smell good, too."

"I'd planned on getting married," I offered.

"It's sort of sudden. What happened?"

"It didn't work out. Unlucky, I guess."

"No, Lomax," Porter said. "I'd say your were the luckiest man in the country because you were with Custer, weren't you?"

"Yep," I said. "I saw him die."

"Ciaha!" Porter responded.

"Funny thing, Doc, that's what a lot of men were crying that day as they rode to their deaths."

"It's a shame, Lomax."

"He'll become a martyr in spite of his vanity leading to the death of so many others. For your own good, Lomax, you need to ride out of here and never mention this again."

"I'm heading out in the morning, once I have supper tonight with a pair of old friends. How are things at the hospital?"

"I've got help now. Most that haven't already died will live. They'll have stories to tell their grandchildren. Odd, isn't it, that you, the guy that knows the most about it, won't be able to tell the story or even be believed if you do."

"I've told my share of stories over the years so I'm accustomed to not being believed."

Porter nodded, then told me to take off my shirt and pants so he could inspect my wounds. He looked first at my head, which was still bruised on the side, but the knot was gone. Then he probed my shoulder, nodding that the bullet wound was closing well and shouldn't present any more problem, other than a little pain. Finally, he checked my leg and said he was satisfied.

"Just watch your wounds. If they redden or fester with pus, find a doctor quick. I've got to get back to the post infirmary now that I got what I came for. Go ahead and stay here the night. Good luck, Lomax. I hope you find whatever it is you are looking for."

"That's the problem, Doc. I'm never quite sure."

We shook hands, and I watched Porter walk out the door.

I paced the floor until it was near six o'clock and then headed back to the telegraph office, where Dreban and Wolfe emerged. They walked up and hugged me.

"There's a lot of explaining to do," Wolfe said.

Dreban pointed toward a side street, and we headed to another of those out-of-the-way cheap eateries they had found. "And don't tell us about some Indian stalking us," Dreban said.

"It's true, fellows. It's true. And you know who the Indian was?"

"Pocahontas," said Dreban.

"Sitting Bull," chimed Wolfe.

"No, Crazy Horse!"

Dreban and Wolfe just rolled their eyes at each other as we reached the eatery and went inside. It was another dark, cramped place, but the fried steak and potatoes were good. And as always, cheap.

I began to explain to Dreban and Wolfe how we had been shadowed by Crazy Horse, who was reputed to be in the Black Hills killing prospectors while we were there. I told them how I had given chase and finally trapped him after he had been bitten by the huge rattlesnake. Rather than kill him, I sucked out the poison, and he showed me his gratitude by giving me the rattler necklace.

"I didn't know who he was so I called him Snakebit."

"Sure," Dreban said.

"You fellows don't have a lot of faith in your partner."

"Former partner," said Wolfe.

Then I explained how I returned to catch up with them and found them dead and headless in their last camp. I told them how I spent a half a day digging their graves, then burying them and their *Scientific Americans* along with the pouch of gold nuggets we found.

They looked at each other and shrugged, uncertain whether or not to believe me.

"Okay, now I want to know how you kept your heads."

Dreban started by saying they were perturbed that I had run out on them with the gold.

"I was going to bring back Snakebit's scalp and prove to you I wasn't crazy," I explained.

"You should've told us you weren't crazy," Wolfe insisted.

"You wouldn't have believed me, if I had."

"Probably not," Dreban admitted.

Then Wolfe told how the evening after I left they had stopped to unpack the mules and set up camp when the two road agents—Gouch Ear and Crook Nose—returned and robbed them, stripping them of their boots, their guns and all their clothes save for their union suits and their socks. After that the two robbers threatened to kill them if they didn't run out of sight immediately.

"It must've been Sioux that caught up with them," I offered.

Both shrugged.

"I guess we were lucky they robbed us and set us adrift or the Sioux might have killed us," Wolfe acknowledged.

Then they wanted to know how I came to learn Snakebit was actually Crazy Horse.

"If you haven't believed me before, you won't believe this," I started, then explained how I had made enemies with Custer, who had me arrested and forced me to accompany him on the campaign so he could kill me and become president.

"You've been drinking some, Lomax," Dreban said. "I can smell it on your clothes."

I thought it was tonic water, but didn't argue.

"Seems more like he's been drinking a lot," Wolfe added.

"It gets better," I said and then explained how Custer had split up his forces so there wouldn't be witnesses around when he shot me. That decision led to the massacre, I explained.

Dreban huffed. "But that doesn't explain Crazy Horse, Lomax. It's just another one of your fanciful stories."

"Yeah," Wolfe said. "We've been hearing the telegraph and reading the dispatches. Nothing like your story has come through."

I explained how I had wound up with Custer at the end and how we had been shooting at each other as the Indians closed in. I told them I had decided I didn't want to get captured and have the Indians cut off my head like they had theirs. I explained that I had put the pistol to my head to kill myself, when I was shot in the shoulder and my reflexes yanked the pistol from my temple and fired into Custer's chest.

"Lomax," scoffed Dreban, "just tell us how you met Crazy Horse."

"Please," echoed Wolfe.

I outlined how an Indian grabbed me around the neck to bash my brains in when his hand slid over the necklace. Snakebit hesitated to kill me when he realized it was the necklace he had given me after I sucked the poison out and saved him.

"So," I continued, "Snakebit picked me up, threw me over his horse and carried me to Major Reno's battalion. There one of the interpreters, Fred Gerard, told me that Snakebit was Crazy Horse."

"Why'd Snakebit or Crazy Horse give a damn about you?" Dreban asked.

"I had saved him and he owed me the same courtesy. Snakebit damn sure had more honor than General Custer," I concluded.

"Do you still have the necklace?" Dreban asked.

"No, Crazy Horse took it after he dropped me off with Reno's men."

"Figures," Wolfe said. "You ought to write some of these tales down, Lomax. You've got the making of a dime novelist."

"Yeah," Dreban added, "Leadeye Lomax, wasn't it?"

"Well, fellows, that's the God-honest truth, whether you believe it or not. Now tell me how you got back to Bismarck."

"We spent about five days heading out of the Black Hills and finally encountered a party returning to Bismarck at about the same place we ran into Buffalo Bill and his expedition on the way in," Dreban said.

"You didn't believe me about Buffalo Bill until I introduced you. So why won't you believe this?"

Neither would answer that question before Wolfe picked up their story and said they were broke and made a deal with the railroad to work the next eight months as telegraphers before heading back to Texas. When the word of the massacre reached St. Paul, where they had been assigned, they were sent on a train to help the single telegrapher in Bismarck.

We finished our updates and our conversation, paid up and started back to the telegraph office so they could resume their shift.

"Come September when the heat's on the wane in Texas, we're heading back there," Wolfe said.

Dreban nodded. "There's a new mechanical and agricultural college opening there and we figure to teach science there. You want to return with us?"

"Yeah, we'd take you in spite of your tall tales," Wolfe said.

"I'd take up preaching before I took up teaching. Besides, I haven't taken a liking to Texas and most Texans."

"Where you going then?" Dreban asked.

"Deadwood," I said. "I hear Wild Bill's there. We've got some things to settle."

"I hear he's a dangerous man," Wolfe said.

"Yeah, Lomax, why's he got it in for you?" Dreban asked. "What did you do his hair?"

"Nothing except help him get rid of lice," I answered.

"Seems a decent thing to do," Dreban acknowledged.

"He didn't appreciate that I told someone about it, said I was trying to make him look filthy and unclean, which was bad for his reputation and royalties as a growing dime novel hero."

"I can see the title of your first dime novel: *The Hair-Raising Adventures of Leadeye Lomax versus Wild Bill Hickok,"* Dreban said.

Both fellows laughed as did I. We said our goodbyes, offered our best wishes at the telegraph office and went our separate directions. I never saw them again, though I heard they did well at the college before they split up and Wolfe went to work for a more prestigious university in Austin.

As for me, the next morning I mounted Ciaha to leave Bismarck, my last stop being the post office where I received a letter from Waco. Miss Medusa had written, telling me that all of the girls sent their love and their thanks as Bull Bonner had been sent to prison for twenty years for his savage attack on Nathan Quirt, who survived but barely. As Quirt recovered, the bridge company brought charges of fraud and theft against him so he was facing prison time as well. Quirt's wife took the children and left him and Waco, headed for parts unknown. Medusa and Minerva had yet to reconcile, but Earl Eaton was well, sending his regards. Medusa said Mr. Eaton had only one regret in life and it was that he and I were no longer roommates. I smiled and shoved the letter in my pocket.

Then I turned Ciaha toward Deadwood. If Wild Bill was really there, it was time for me to settle things with him, though that is a story for another day.

Chapter Thirty-Three

After I concluded my affairs in Deadwood, I didn't return to the region for years as there were too many bad memories of the horrors I had encountered. Too, I carried a secret about the Little Bighorn that I could never share without being accused of being the biggest liar ever to set foot in a western saloon. There was an inquiry into the massacre a couple years later in Chicago. From what I could tell from the newspapers, it was mostly finger-pointing between those that thought Custer could do no wrong and those that thought he could do no right.

Even a decade or so after I sent him to hell, I couldn't escape him. He'd be on posters in virtually every saloon I entered, thanks to Anheuser-Busch. I'd run into stories in newspapers or occasionally old-timers that claimed to have been there. They weren't. I was. They were lying. I wasn't. Even friends like Dreban and Wolfe wouldn't believe my story and maybe they had every right not to, but I never really lied unless it was necessary to get me out of a bind.

In early July of 1893, I came into some money and got the urge to attend the World's Columbian Exposition in Chicago. I heard that the exposition had some amazing electrified buildings, spectacular displays and something called a Ferris wheel that I just had to see for myself. It was the first time I'd been back in Chicago since I passed through in 1875 on the train to Bismarck and the Black Hills with Dreban and Wolfe. The city had muscled up since I had seen it before with tall buildings that touched the heavens and roads that carried trolleys and trains and all kinds of conveyances. I spent some time seeing the city sights, including the Palmer House, where the Custer inquiry was conducted.

Although I arrived with enough money for a stay in a decent hotel, though certainly not one as fine as the Palmer House, I had a run of bad luck with some city-slickers who cheated me out of much of the cash I had when I got off the train at the terminal. I guess I just looked too country not to attract swindlers like cash draws politicians. By the time I got to the exposition grounds themselves, I didn't have money for admission, much less for the Ferris wheel, a cheap hotel room or train fare back west. I stood there at the exposition gates looking in, not knowing where to turn. When I looked around, though, I saw something across the street that brought a smile to my face. Gaudy banners announced "Buffalo Bill's Wild West and Congress of Rough Riders of the World," and I knew I could rely on my old friend to give me a job and help me out of a bind.

I crossed the street and arrived about thirty minutes after the three o'clock matinee performance began. An evening performance was scheduled at eight-thirty. The ticket seller was a snidely little fellow that reminded me of the Waco bridge toll collector Nathan Quirt.

"I'm here to see Buffalo Bill," I announced.

"Isn't everybody?" he shot back.

"No, I don't mean to see him perform but to meet with him. I'm an old friend."

"Sir, if we let all his old friends in to visit, we wouldn't make any money, would we?"

"I don't intend to see the show, just him."

"Fifty cents, sir, or move on."

I suppose I could've afforded the fifty cents, but since I had lost so much money trying to identify which cup a pea was under, I was reluctant to give away any for a show I wasn't going to see. I bided my time, reading the banners that promised a show rain or shine with gates opening two hours before the performances. The covered grandstands featured 18,000 seats and were advertised as the coolest place when the sun shines and dry as a parlor when it rains. Buffalo Bill's banners promised genuine Russian Cossacks, authentic Arabs from the desert and good old American Indians, including Sioux, Comanche, Pawnee and Blackfeet. He promoted American cowboys, Mexican vaqueros, Rio Grande caballeros and Mexican ruralies as well as bucking horses, wild steers and buffalo galore. If that wasn't enough, he promoted his show as seen by the royalty and aristocrats of Europe. I had to admit I was impressed, but Cody had always been a great promoter, especially a self-promoter.

As I killed time, waiting for the matinee to end so I could slip inside the fence through one of the exits as people departed, I saw a new banner that caught my eye. It read: "Beginning in August Reenactment of The Battle of Little Bighorn." The advertisement said Sioux warriors who had fought in the battle would ride again. The ad named them as Plenty Horses, Painted Horse and Rocky Bear. It seemed I just couldn't escape Custer no matter how hard I tried.

After I read all the posters, I walked up and down the street, turning down the midway, which shared with the Wild West show the side of the street opposite the exposition. I marched down to the Ferris wheel, which towered 260 feet above the ground. I stood in amazement as people paid a quarter each to climb on board and ride a circle in the air, each cab stopping at the top to give a spectacular view of the midway, the exposition grounds and Chicago. When I heard a cascade of fake gunfire from the Wild West show, I rushed back to the exit gates and tried to stay out of view of the ticket sellers so I could slip in when the exiting crowd peaked. The grandstand convulsed with applause and cheers and I heard the band play the rousing finale as the performers took their bows, culminating with the appearance of Buffalo Bill himself. Then the people started coming out, a trickle at first, then a flood, all smiles and talk. When the crowd was at its thickest, I fought my way upstream and inside the fence, working my way around the grandstand to the livestock pens, tents and wagons needed for a production this size.

I was dressed in my usual attire, certainly enough to look country but not gaudy enough to be a performer. As the performers began to relax with each other or have a smoke, I asked where I might find Cody. Most of them ignored me, taking me for an autograph seeker or some indigent seeking a job, which I guess I was. Had I been young and female and curvaceous, everyone would've known to send me to him because Cody always kept a bell mare around camp to entertain him. Finally, a petite woman in a gaudy beribboned outfit took pity on me and pointed to a wagon. "He's meeting with our manager over there. Be careful, he's in a bad mood. He ripped his britches while mounting up for the attack on the settler's cabin." I thanked the woman and went on my way, not realizing I had just met Annie Oakley.

I opened up the door and marched inside like I was in charge. Cody was towering over a desk where his manager sat. They seemed to be discussing gate receipts. Buffalo Bill had gained weight and his flowing hair and beard had faded to a snowy white. I snickered at the rip in the seat of his pants.

"Get out of here," barked Cody without even looking up.

His manager eyed me suspiciously, and I saw his hand drop from the desktop to a side drawer. I figured he has fingering a gun in case I tried to rob them of the day's gate.

"I'm here to see Cody," I announced. "I'm H.H. Lomax, better known to Buffalo Bill as Leadeye Lomax—"

"The worst shot to ever aim at a buffalo," Cody said, then looked up without smiling or offering to shake my proffered hand.

"You know him?" the manager asked.

"From way back," he said, then eyed me closely. "I've dreaded this day because I always knew you would show up, wanting a cut of things."

"What are you talking about, Cody?"

"First, what do you want?"

"A job," I answered.

"We don't have any. Is that all?" Cody replied.

"That's all!"

"You sure you're not angling for a cut?" the showman wanted to know.

"What are you talking about, Cody?"

"You remember that fall in 1875 it was, when you and your prospecting partners ran into me and my hunting caravan?"

"Yeah, so what? All I remember is you promised to return a favor one day."

"You recall the suggestion you made to me? Your words stuck with me and it's the reason I'm here now."

I shrugged. "What are you talking about?"

"You told me the stage was too small for me, that I needed a platform as big as the outdoors."

"So?" I was still confused.

"That led to this."

"To what, Cody?"

"My Wild West show, Lomax. I got to thinking about your comments and came up with this outdoor extravaganza. Your idea made me a rich man, Lomax. I've toured the world because of you."

"Congratulations, then. You got a job?"

"You don't want a cut of my profits?"

"Hell, no! I don't remember what we talked about. It doesn't matter. I'd've never thought of putting together a show like this. Now, do you have a job for me?"

"No, nothing available, Lomax. Sorry, but it's been good to see you." He resumed counting his money.

I got to thinking, maybe I did deserve a little better consideration than Cody was giving to me for such a fine idea.

"Maybe I am due a share of your profits. It might hurt business if I went to the newspapers and said I'd come here broke just seeking a job and you wouldn't even pay me to feed the livestock or shovel manure, even though I'm the one that gave you the idea for this."

The manager looked at me, then at Cody. "We don't need that type of publicity, Bill."

I crossed my arms over my chest as Cody tugged on his beard. He may have been a great promoter, but he was never a great poker player. He was afraid to call my bluff.

"All of our cowboy slots are filled," Cody replied.

"What about B.J.?" asked the manager. "Broke a leg in a fall and won't be able to ride for six months or more, long after we're done here."

Cody grinned. "That's an idea. In fact, I like that idea. Lomax is not as good a shot as B.J., but why not?"

"There's just one condition," the manager said.

"What's that?" I asked.

"You sign a contract for the job and relinquish any and all claims current and future against Buffalo Bill's Wild West for appropriation of your original idea."

"Draw up the papers and I'll sign."

"Perfect," said the manager. "You'll start with tomorrow afternoon's performance. We don't have time to get you in tonight's show." He looked at Cody. "Another thing, when we change the finale next month from the attack on the settler's cabin to the Battle of the Little Bighorn, we can use another soldier."

Cody nodded. "You think you can die, Lomax?"

"Been close enough to death a time or two so I can manage."

"Okay, then, we're done," Cody said. "Wait outside and I'll have my manager take you to costume to get your outfit ready for tomorrow."

I stepped outside the wagon and waited while they counted their receipts. They both exited with broad smiles, the manager carrying a clipboard and a fountain pen. I thought they were happy to have me on board, but they had snookered me. Cody's man gave me the clipboard and I skimmed the one-page contract and signed on the line. At that moment, I was officially a member of Buffalo Bill's Wild West show.

When they took me to costume, they directed me to the women's outfits.

"What gives?" I asked. That's when I learned that B.J. stood for Barbara Jane, one of their female riders.

The next day I debuted with the Congress of Rough Riders wearing a riding skirt, a frilly blouse, a wig, a pink Stetson and rouge on my cheeks. I guess Buffalo Bill had the last laugh, though fortunately for me, Cody never asked me to be his bell mare. Annie Oakley always opened the show with her trick shooting, then I rode as B.J. in the third act and that was my only job until August when they changed the finale. In the attack on the settler's cabin, Buffalo Bill always rode in to save the day and drive the marauding Indians out of the arena. With the Little Bighorn finale, he rode in to chase the Indians away but too late to save General Bluster. It had about as much relation to the events of that day as I had to Queen Victoria, who Cody often reminded his performers was a great fan of his. Rumor was the queen liked Annie Oakley more.

Sometime in September after I exited the arena as B.J. and rode to pen my horse, I saw a tall man approaching the corral. There was a vaguely familiar look about him, but I couldn't place it. He had a set of field glasses hanging around his neck.

"Ma'am," he said. "Could I ask you a question?"

"You just did," I said, elevating my voice to see if he was going to ask me out.

"You've got an uncanny resemblance to a man I once knew, a man that died at the Little Bighorn. Your voice sounds like him, too."

"What was his name?"

"H.H. Lomax. Would you be any kin?"

I was stunned. This man knew me, but I couldn't place him. I lifted my hat and yanked off my wig.

"Well, I'll be damned. It's H.H. Lomax himself. What did they do to you, castrate you?"

"Close to it," I said in my natural voice.

"Ciaha!" he shouted.

Then his face became familiar. It was Sergeant Gus Finkle. I climbed over the fence, dropping my hat and wig in the process and shook his hand vigorously. "I thought you were killed at the massacre."

"I thought the same about you, from what I could learn from the newspapers. You're the first person I've met since the battle who was there."

I bent down and picked up my hat and wig, holding the hairpiece up for Finkle. "Custer's scalp!" We both laughed, then grimaced at the events a decade and a half ago. I guess you know Russell and Lewis died that afternoon."

He nodded. "I saw their names in the papers, but never saw Thompson's and Watson's names so I never knew for certain what happened to them."

"A chance encounter with them saved my life," I said. "Their horses gave out and when Custer rode with me out of sight of the others to shoot me, they called out to him."

"I guess Custer's Luck rubbed off on you that day, Lomax."

"On both of us, Gus. Listen, I need to go change for the finale. Hang around and we'll visit between the performances."

Finkle nodded. "I'll be here after the show."

I went to my quarters and changed, then rode my horse into the arena with Custer for the finale. I died. Custer died. Buffalo Bill arrived too late. The crowd showered applause on us. Buffalo Bill took a bow on his horse. The performers bet whether he would split his pants again. The crowd left the grandstands. All of us dead soldiers and Indians came back to life and went to the mess tent.

Finkle was waiting for me by the corral. I told him how I had been saved by Crazy Horse, omitting only the part that I had actually shot Custer.

In return, Finkle explained that his horse had run wild, dashing through the line of warriors and straight through the Indian camp. The warriors hadn't given chase, apparently assuming warriors in the village would kill him. He rode his horse until it died, then worked his way west, finding a trapper who kept him in his small cabin for a few days. The trapper gave him a horse and he rode west to Montana. By then he was more scared of the army than Indians for fear the military bureaucrats might think he had deserted and court martial him. Too, he didn't want folks to think him a coward. He had wound up in Washington state and had taken to farming and living a life far removed from that day on Custer hill.

Something he could not explain had pulled him from Washington to the Columbian Exposition. He said he didn't know why, but that he had been burdened with the secret he could share with no one. Finkle said he felt better getting the burden off his chest, but he pleaded with me not to reveal it to anyone else or ever mention his name.

I took him to the mess tent and found the interpreter that worked with the Indians and asked if we might visit with Plenty Horses, Painted Horse and Rocky Bear about the real Battle of the Little Bighorn. I explained that my friend Finkle had a cousin at the Little Bighorn, but his body had never been found. He wanted to know if any white men with Custer escaped.

The interpreter explained the question and the three Sioux began to talk and gesticulate, each holding up three fingers.

"There were three that got away from the hill where Custer died," the interpreter explained. "The first rode a wild horse that raced through the village and escaped in the direction of the setting sun."

Finkle looked at me and nodded.

"The second," continued the interpreter, "galloped east on a wild horse and five young warriors gave chase, but they ran out of bullets and arrows and were about to turn around and go club the dying soldiers back on the hill when the escaping soldier pulled his revolver and shot himself in the head."

I shrugged. "First, I'd heard of that," I told Finkle.

The interpreter waved his arm and shook his head as the three, then went on. "All three are mad about the third one. Crazy Horse saved him from the battle, then carried and released him to the soldiers dug in like prairie dogs at the other end of the battleground. They don't know why Crazy Horse would do that as he hated the white man."

I couldn't resist. "Ask them if it might be that the third white man was a great warrior, who had fought with bravery and honor."

The interpreter conveyed my question and all three laughed. They answered him. He laughed and spoke to me. "No, they say that that white man was so scared he couldn't hold his pistol steady. He should have been dressed as a woman."

Finkle grinned at me, then pulled three silver dollars out of his pocket for the Indian trio. Finkle and I spent the rest of the time in the mess tent eating and reliving our times together at Fort Abraham Lincoln and on the trail toward disaster. We were lucky and uncertain why we had survived and why so many others had died. We both held anger for Custer, yet were relieved to know we weren't the only one carrying a secret about that awful day. Finkle and I shook hands after dinner and never saw each other again. He went back to Washington, and I never mentioned his revelation to anyone until I sat down to write this story. After he left, I changed back into my B.J. outfit for the evening performance and then back into the cavalry outfit for the finale.

I rode with Buffalo Bill's Wild West show off and on over the next several years and I don't know how many times I refought the Battle of Little Bighorn, dying each time only to come back to life after the final applause. In every battle, from the actual confrontation on the hills above the Little Bighorn to the staged reenactments all over the country, one thing remained the same, whether I lived or died: I always shot at General Custer.

—The End-—

Author Bio

Preston Lewis is the author of more than two dozen historical, western and children's novels. A former president of Western Writers of America, Lewis has received Spur Awards from the organization for best western novel and best nonfiction article.

Now retired, Lewis began his professional career working for four Texas newspapers before moving into higher education communications and marketing at Texas Tech University and Angelo State University. He holds a B.A. in journalism from Baylor University and an M.A. in journalism from Ohio State University, where he was a Kiplinger Fellow. He subsequently earned a second M.A., this one in history, from Angelo State.

A native West Texan, Lewis lives in San Angelo with his wife, Harriet, with whom he shares a son and daughter and five grandchildren. For hobbies, he enjoys historical research, landscape photography and visits to historic sites of the Old West and the Civil War.

Printed in the USA
CPSIA information can be obtained
at www.ICGtesting.com
LVHW052135010823
754069LV00013B/1089